MAKIN'
WAVES

G. Bradley Davis

TELEMACHUS PRESS

Cover art and design by Bayley Ramos

Publishing services by Telemachus Press, LLC
7652 Sawmill Road
Suite 304
Dublin, Ohio 43016
http://www.telemachuspress.com

Visit the author website: www.GBradleyDavis.com

ISBN: 978-1-965121-12-2 (eBook)
ISBN: 978-1-965121-13-9 (Paperback)

Version 2024.12.22

"I can imagine no more rewarding a career. And any man who may be asked in this century what he did to make his life worthwhile, I think can respond with a good deal of pride and satisfaction: 'I served in the United States Navy.'"

—President John F. Kennedy

For our noble men and women in uniform, past, present, and future.

MAKIN'
WAVES

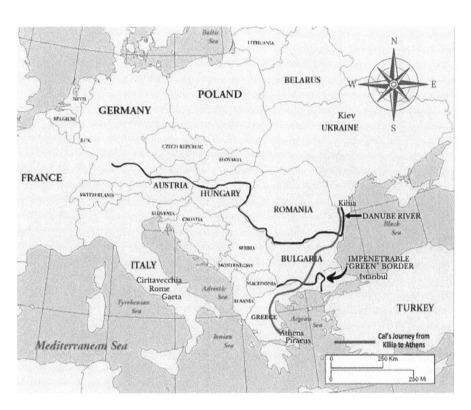

Cal's Journey

CHAPTER ONE

T he dot on the horizon looked more like a mosquito than a helicopter as it was still nearly nine miles from the ship. The sun's reflection off the water glittered in such a way it reminded me of how the sun would dance off freshly fallen snow back home in Pennsylvania. But this was the Black Sea, not Pennsylvania, and the serenity of an early morning winter day was about to turn into a blizzard of misfortune for me and the crew.

"You could hear that cook scream all the way down to the bilge. What exactly happened? Do you know the guy?" Dakota said as he looked at the helicopter through the "Big Eyes", a large mounted telescope.

"His name is Aquino. He's Filipino," I responded. "He's a cook. Only been on the ship a couple of months. Johnson told me the guy reached into the automatic potato peeler and lost three fingers. Nasty!"

"Well, he bled like a stuffed pig," Dakota said.

I turned and looked at Dakota with both a smile and frown. "Stuck."

"What?"

"The expression is, he bled like a stuck pig, not a stuffed pig, Numbnuts."

"Wouldn't a pig that's stuffed bleed more than a skinny pig?"

"I'm not going to argue the point," I said.

Our conversation about the sailor's accident continued while neither of us looked away from the helicopter.

"I wonder where they are going to take him," asked Dakota. "The *Saratoga* has a hospital onboard, don't they?"

"Yeah, but I doubt they can reattach fingers. They'll probably take him to the naval hospital in Naples," I said while trying to shield the sun with my hand.

Turning toward the bridge, Dakota said, "Hey, those civilians who came on board in Gaeta, Italy, are on the bridge wing with the captain. There's been a lot of scuttlebutt by the crew as to what their deal is. Any idea?"

"You're a radioman. Didn't you receive any traffic about them coming aboard and why?"

"Everything was in code. Yeah, we knew six government types were boarding when we reached Gaeta, but everything else was hush-hush."

"Well, the black dude looks like a SEAL to me. The dude with freckles looks like one of those military contractors, maybe the short guy, too. They are never dressed in dungarees or camouflage, like enlisted guys, or khakis, like the officers wear."

"You are the freakin' king of conspiracy theories, Cal," laughed Dakota as he looked up at a flock of seagulls that had decided to make the SPS-52 three-dimensional air search antenna a temporary resting place.

"Yeah? Who the hell do you think they are? Tourist guides? Do you see the blue berets those guys are wearing? Only SEALs wear them. Those other guys are not dressed like they're here for a joy ride. If they were politicians, then they would have worn suits and been onboard for an hour or two, got their photo-op, and got the hell off. Look at them coming out to the bridge wing to watch the chopper. It's entertainment for them. Besides, why would they board in Gaeta, Italy? If they were Senators or weapon's contractors they would have boarded in Rota, Spain or Civitavecchia, an hour drive from Rome. Naw, they are CIA and something's up."

"Whatever you say, Colombo," Dakota said with a chuckle.

"Alright, smart ass. Wasn't I right when I told you the Gunner's Mates were loading nukes onto the ship when we were doing ammo on-load in Charleston? The Gunner's Mates never wear those white outfits when loading missiles. They wear some kind of protective clothing."

"Okay, I give you that, but what would CIA guys be doing on the Charlie Deuce, a small, guided missile destroyer. I don't get it. What does SEAL stand for, anyway?"

"Sea, Air, and Land. They are a special operations force trained to engage in direct assaults on enemy targets," I said over the chuf-chuf-chuf of the chopper's rotary wing. "They conduct reconnaissance missions."

"How come you know so much about the SEALs?" asked Dakota.

"I wanted to become one, but I failed the preliminary swimming test. Those studs swim two miles in the open ocean, wearing a wetsuit and fins in cold, rough water, and they have to complete the swim in less than 75 minutes."

"Damn! What about the other two guys?"

"I'm guessing they are either CIA or military weapon's contractors," I said.

Two corpsmen could be seen carrying the wounded sailor on a stretcher to the landing pad near the fantail, on the aft of the ship. The cook's hand looked more like a club with the amount of bandage wrapped around it, and it was clear he was heavily sedated.

The HC-2 Fleet Angel helicopter approached the ship, trailing behind as the ship cruised at 25 knots. A crew dressed in yellow and green flight jackets stood by with cables and nets to lash, or secure, the wounded sailor once the chopper was stabilized.

As the chopper slowly maneuvered over the flight deck, the seagulls, whose peace and quiet had been interrupted, decided to leave for a location with less excitement. Circling the ship, the birds abruptly flew into the helicopter, penetrating the fiberglass fairings. One of the birds entered the cockpit, striking the pilot which disoriented him. The chopper pivoted drastically to the left and clipped the Mark 42 5"/54 caliber gun located in the aft section of the ship. A two-foot piece of the propeller broke off, flying towards the bridge wing at blinding speed, decapitating one of the mysterious visitors, tossing his head against the signalman's shack before his body had a chance to collapse on the deck.

TWO YEARS EARLIER

It was the summer of 1974, and it was the first time I was on a commercial airplane, and I was not off to a vacation in some warm, exotic location. Destination, Orlando, Florida. Warm, yes, exotic, no. I was on my way to boot camp. Originally, I was scheduled to do basic training in the Great Lakes in North Chicago, but when asked if I would rather do my basic training there, or Orlando, Florida, I foolishly chose the latter, thinking I could visit the newly opened Disney World on Cinderella Liberty. Like a typical knucklehead seventeen-year-old, I had no concept of how hot Florida is in July, August, and September!

There were several reasons why I enlisted in the Navy. After everything the country had gone through in Viet Nam, someone would have to have been insane to willingly join the military back in the mid-70s. The sanity thing may have been one of the reasons, but there were a few more. Here they are, in no particular order.

I was a true patriot. I had a deep love for my country and realized freedom is not inexpensive. Someone has to pay for it, so why not me? Although the war in Viet Nam was winding down (yes, *war*. Congress may never have issued a declaration of war on North Vietnam or the Viet Cong, but believe me, ask anyone who was there. It was a hell of a lot more than a "conflict"). Actually I was hoping it would fester long enough for me to see some combat action. I was a troubled teenager who struggled terribly with depression and self-confidence, and I was convinced my life was worthless. Dying for my country would seem an honorable way to exit with a bang, pun intended.

Secondly, I needed to find my moxie. Growing up, I seemed to be a good target for those wanting to take a shot. Being small for my age, I was beaten up habitually by the neighborhood bully known as Mongrel, and my teachers at school humiliated me in front of my peers for my consistent academic failures. I suffered from ADHD, which was not diagnosed in kids in the 60s and 70s. Courage seemed illusive for me as a child, and so my thinking was if I were forced into a "do or die" situation, I would have to "do."

My father, Thomas Lloyd, served in the 1st Marine Division during World War II. He fought in the Pacific Islands, including the horrific Guadalcanal campaign. He had guts. I wanted what my dad had. I attempted to follow in my father's footsteps by enlisting in the Marines; however, I was only seventeen, and being a minor, I needed my dad's signature. To my surprise, he said, "Calvin Lloyd, there is no way I will sign-off on this. Vietnam is not World War II. If you go into the marines, they will send you to Vietnam within a week of boot camp. A year from now you will be coming back in a flag-draped coffin. If you want to join the military, enlist in the Navy. At least you will get three meals a day and a place to sleep."

I was both angry and disappointed, but in retrospect, I knew my father did not want me to catch a North Vietnamese bullet before I got out of my teens. He did sign-off on the Navy.

Thirdly, the grades I received in high school eliminated college as an option. I never developed any skills to become a tradesman, so becoming a plumber or an electrician was not a feasible choice. The truth is, I had to get out of Dodge. Like Jonah, I was ready to sail to the other side of the globe to run away from my sordid past. I desperately needed a change of scenery, even if that meant strict compliance to a world of rules and regulations.

CHAPTER TWO

Naval Training Center/Recruit Training Command
Orlando, Florida
July 12, 1974

T he story I am about to describe is true, with more twists and turns than a roller coaster. It began when I arrived at boot camp.

Boot camp. Not something to which young men look forward, but I was different. I had enthusiastically waited for it, simply for the opportunity for a new start. I was now in a new location where no one knew me, or my past. It was an excellent opportunity to reinvent myself.

Conformity was not in my genes. I quickly discovered nonconformity is frowned upon in the military. Boot camp was all about discipline, and it began with the most mundane chores, like sweeping the barracks to make sure there were no ghost turds, those balls of dust and fluff that float about a room with the slightest movement of air. Assimilation into the Navy included learning the jargon, weapons training, learning to make a bed with hospital corners, and folding clothes to a fraction of their size so they fit in the shoebox called a locker. Boot camp for most sailors is eleven weeks of physical training. For me it included a little extracurricular activity. After evening chow, we were given one hour of "smoke and joke" time, an hour where we were allowed to have a cigarette, write letters home, and have conversations with other recruits. For nonconformists like me, that hour was spent at "Happy Hour."

Happy Hour's proper title was Intensive Training, or IT. For those of us who thought it necessary to question orders, or to share a little humorous sarcasm, it meant an hour of nonstop, extensive exercises. All I could think of when I was doing my "push-ups forever" was Robert Preston's song "Chicken Fat." "Push up every morning—ten times…Go, you chicken fat, go away!"

It was not my Company Commander (CC) with whom I had a problem; it was the CC's sidekick, Seaman Schon, a recent boot camp graduate who was given a cushy three-month assignment to assist the Company Commander, all because he won the award during his eleven-week training for being the biggest brownnoser. He was a Robin but acted more like a Batman-wannabe. Instead of addressing him as Seaman Schon, I repeatedly called him Seaman Schlong, a synonym for prick, putz, schmuck, or tadger. As recruits we were commanded to call this little weasel, "Sir!" It made my teeth itch and my skin crawl.

Give someone a little authority and he thinks he is Qin Shi Huang! Power *does* corrupt. Even a little power. This stinkin' weasel, Schlong, treated the recruits worse than the CC did. And there wasn't a damn thing any of us could do about it. Every morning this turd rudely awakened us with the slamming of a metal trash can. He would lift it high above his head and slam it down onto the barracks deck. "Get out of your racks, you worthless piss-ants. Muster on station."

Seaman Schlong had a particular dislike for me, most likely because of my difficulty assimilating to the rigidity of the military. My perception of inequity did not help either. Schlong had it out for me, and I had enough experience with injustice, having been picked on as a kid. I swore it would never happen again. But this was different. This was the military. Retaliation was not an option. This stinkin' piece of Spam went out of his way to make my life more miserable than boot camp already was, and yes, that was possible.

One morning, Schlong called the recruits to muster, and announced we were going for a two-hour march, something I thought was ridiculous. How marching in step with sixty other sailors was going to prepare us for the responsibilities on a ship was beyond my ability to fathom, but two hours of marching boredom inspired me to call an impromptu cadence.

"Your pants are loose, your belt too tight, your feet are moving from left to right, on your left, on your left, on your left, right, left, right, left."

The sailors on the march loved it, Schlong, not so much. When we got back to the barracks, Schlong called me into the Company Commander's office.

"Lloyd! Get your ass in the Commander's office. Now!" the weasel hollered.

My knock on the Commander's door was answered with, "Enter!" I walked into the office and stood at attention in front of the desk. The Commander was seated behind it, and Seaman Schlong stood next to the desk, like a prop.

"Seaman Recruit Lloyd, Seaman Schon has informed me he caught you sleeping on watch. Is that correct?"

I had always been an advocate for revenge on equal terms. In other words, let the punishment fit the crime. In this case, I was receiving a sledgehammer in response to a mosquito bite. Sure, I had been a smartass toward Schlong, but fabricating a story about sleeping on watch, which was an egregious act in the military, was well beyond what I deserved.

"No, Sir. I was not on watch, and I was not sleeping."

"Really? Well, you can explain that to Lieutenant Olson. Report to the Division Officer ASAP, Sailor!"

And so, I ran to the Division Officer's office (one was not permitted to walk anywhere within the Recruit Training Command grounds). Every recruit had to run from point A to point B, no matter where he was going. When I reached the office, some Petty Officer third class told me to stand at attention outside until I was called. I realized quickly the Lieutenant wanted to play a game of wills, a game I had invented. Standing at attention for an hour is actually more difficult than one may think. Standing at attention for an hour in ninety-six-degree heat, topped with a dollop of seventy percent humidity, should be considered cruel and unusual punishment, but I stood there. More than once my knees buckled, as I became drenched completely with sweat, but I did not cave to the senseless game.

My once-high spirits disappeared faster than hors d'oeuvres at a homeless shelter. I had always struggled with a poor self-image and failure, and this situation certainly did not help. I never bitched about being punished for something I did, but being framed for an imaginary offense was something that made my hackles rise. One of the reasons I joined the Navy was for a fresh start and I believed there was no better place to do that than a place where no one knew me. I could literally reinvent myself. But my reincarnation was off to a rough start.

To be falsely accused of disobeying an order was something that hit me below the belt. Dead center. My attitude was, *if you are going to convict me, or punish me, for crying out loud, do so for something for which I am actually guilty.* There was a potpourri of things I had done that would justify punishment, but to be tried for some fabricated falsehood? That was a cancer I could feel deteriorating my soul. Make no mistake, the Lieutenant would be prosecutor, judge and jury; there would be no appeal. That is the way it is in the Navy.

"Lloyd, the Lieutenant will see you now," the petty officer yelled out to me.

I actually left wet footprints on the sidewalk from my drenching sweat, as I squished my way into the air-conditioned office. It felt as though I had entered a walk-in freezer. To my surprise, the Lieutenant was a woman. I knew I was screwed. My intuition proved to be spot on, over and over again. Women who find themselves in a male-dominated profession will be much more difficult in negotiating. They fear any appearance of weakness would diminish their reputation, and they would not be taken seriously. That might be understandable, but in this case, I knew it would not end well for me.

"Seaman Lloyd, it says here you were caught sleeping on watch. What do you have to say for yourself?"

"Ma'am, I was not on watch. You can request the duty schedule and see that for yourself. Even if I were on watch, which I was not, I was awake all afternoon. We had just returned from a march." I thought I sounded quite convincing.

"Are you calling your CC a liar?"

Now, I found myself in a conundrum. Of course, my CC was a liar, or at the very least, he bought into Seaman Schlong's lie, but if I called a superior a liar, that just would not go well. On the other hand, if I said I was not calling his CC a liar, then I would be guilty as charged. I decided to go with the truth.

"Well, Lieutenant, what I am saying is the information you have been given is absolutely false, so if that makes the CC a liar, so be it."

"I'm setting you back a week. Retrieve your clothes, rifle and sea bag and report to company 4682 in quadrant 7. You will now have twelve weeks of basic training instead of eleven. You are dismissed."

This was my first indoctrination with RHIP, Rank Has Its Privilege. In other words, being a lowly seaman recruit, and she, a lieutenant, I was grossly outranked. She did not want to hear my story. This was not an innocent until proven guilty world. It was a "whatever a higher-ranking sailor said trumped anything a boot camp squid said" kind of world. I basically had no rights. Welcome to military life.

I wanted a clean start, but this is not what I had in mind. I wanted to excel in the military, despite my aversion to following rules. The military was a paradox for me. It was everything I loved, and everything I despised. I loved the challenge. I hated the chicken shit. I loved the violence. I hated the routine. I loved the adventure. I hated that I could not improvise. But I was a survivor, and I always ended up finding a creative way to deal with things. There is always more than one way to skin an armadillo.

I ran back to the barracks and began packing my sea bag. My bunkmate looked up from polishing his shoes and gave me a puzzled look.

"Where are you going," he said.

"They set me back a week. Schlong said I was sleeping on watch."

"Were you?"

"Hell, no! I wasn't even on watch!"

"He has it out for you, Cal. I'm really sorry. Keep your head up. Don't let him see that it bothers you. You can do another week of boot camp standing on your head," he said as he slapped me on the back. I knew he was blowing sunshine up my skirt, but it still felt good someone actually cared.

"See ya," I said as I threw the sea bag over my shoulder.

"See ya, Cal."

The feeling of rejection is possibly the worst feeling one can experience. One only discards something worthless, broken, or has no purpose anymore. The sailors who got set back in boot camp were either complete losers or guys nicknamed "rocks." Rocks are sailors who can't swim. The Navy would not let anyone out of boot camp until able to swim. Rocks went straight to the bottom of the pool. Some guys were in boot camp for six months trying to learn to swim.

I can endure some very unpleasant situations if I know there is a life expectancy to the situation. Boot camp was eleven weeks, which I could do while juggling on a unicycle, but for me, boot camp would be twelve weeks. Nonetheless, I did the time. There was even an upside to the daily hour of Intensive Training I was forced to do. I had gained significant muscle on my thin frame, and I was in the middle of a growing spurt. I was a late bloomer. I came out of boot camp looking like the statue of David; chiseled, with ripped pipes, and a sweet six-pack.

CHAPTER THREE

A few days before graduating from boot camp I received word my security clearance had been approved. Now, that was something that always confounded me. Not the need for a security clearance (I would be working with some highly sensitive material), but the background check revealed nothing that would disqualify me. I was amazed I actually *received* a security clearance! I wondered how inept the FBI really is. If they spoke to a half dozen people who really knew me, they would have discovered I smoked pot, dropped acid and snorted coke. But, to my surprise, I received the security clearance. I assumed they spoke only to my parents and Sunday school teacher.

Upon graduation from boot camp, I was promoted from Seaman Recruit, a rank lower than squid shit, to Seaman Apprentice, a rank equivalent to snail shit. I received orders to report to the Naval Technical Training Center, Corry Station, Pensacola, Florida. I was given travel expenses based on the mileage from Orlando to Pensacola and could have taken a commuter plane or a bus, but I decided to hitchhike and pocket the travel money. Back in the 70s, it was not difficult hitching a ride, especially if one were lugging a sea bag.

The drive from Orlando to Pensacola is only a little over six-hours non-stop, but since I would be hitching rides, it would take much longer than that. The good news was the Navy gave me three days of travel time to report. No matter how long it took to get there, I would not report a day earlier than I had to. A day off was a day off, and they did not come often enough for someone in the military!

I was able to catch a ride to Interstate 75 with an ensign who was heading to Tampa for the weekend to see his girlfriend. Once the ensign dropped me off at the entrance ramp to the interstate, I did not have to wait long before an 18-wheeler hauling oranges pulled over to pick me up.

"Where ya heading?" the man said as I threw my sea bag into the back of the cab and climbed in.

"Pensacola," I answered.

"Well, I can take you as far as Lake City, but you'll need to get on I-10 heading west from there," the man said. "You in the military?"

"Yes, sir. Just finished boot camp and now I'm heading to Corry Station for Electronic Warfare School before being assigned to a ship."

"You gonna go to Nam?" asked the trucker.

"Don't know," I answered. "I hope so."

"Well, you kill some of those slant-eyed, commie bastards for me, ya hear?"

"Yes, sir. I will."

The trucker held court, telling me everything from his take on the declining infrastructure across the country, to sharing a variety of government conspiracy theories. He was definitely scary, but not in a "life-threatening" sort of way. He said his name was Ray-Bob, which made me wonder if all southern boys' middle names were Bob.

"Never been to Pensacola. Only passed through. Ya know, Mobile ain't but an hour or so drive away. There's a little bar called Cindy-Sue's. Best wood-smoked barbecue in Florida, and that ain't the only thing that'll give you sticky fingers," Ray-Bob said with laughter that caused him to cough.

"Sir?"

"Behind Cindy-Sue's is an old red and white mobile home that's a whorehouse," Ray-Bob said with more laughter. "If you find yourself up there, make sure you ask for Beverly, ya hear? Tell her Ray-Bob sent you. Ya know, funny thing about the name Beverly. I once met an Englishman at the Dixie Travel Plaza in McLean, Illinois. He told me the original meaning of the name Beverly is *beaver stream.* Get it? BEAVER stream." The trucker laughed so hard the cab drifted to the shoulder of the road, spitting gravel across the highway and causing the trailer to whip behind us. It seemed Ray-Bob lost control of the rig for a second or two, but with a nonchalant response, the truck straightened as he cleared his throat, rolled down the window, and forcefully hocked a brownish green loogie.

The tractor trailer pulled off the interstate and slowed to a stop. Ray-Bob turned and looked at me and said, "Well, my friend, this is where we part. I'll be heading north; you, west. You be careful out there, ya here? There are some whack-jobs on the roads."

"Yes, sir," I said as I grabbed my sea bag and climbed down the steps till I felt the gravel in the road.

Ray-Bob let out a honk from his air horn as I watched him head on down the highway. The sun was beginning to set, and although I was getting pretty hungry, I thought it best to try and hitch another ride before it got dark. I knew my chances of hitching a ride would grow dim along with the light.

My shirt was glued to my back from perspiration. Florida was more than hot. As I looked down I-10, I could see the heat coming off the asphalt creating visible mirage-like wavy lines, like the old black and white TV at home when the aluminum foil would fall off the rabbit ears. My stomach reminded me I had not eaten since breakfast, and even though I was tempted to grab a bite, I had a more pressing need. If I did not get another ride that evening, I had no idea where I would spend the night. There was no motel in sight. I stuck my thumb out and watched the cars fly by.

My philosophy on hitchhiking was I needed to face the traffic and make sure I have a pleasant, non-threatening look on my face. I needed to debunk any perception that would prevent someone from giving me a ride. After facing the traffic for the better part of an hour, I started walking with my back towards the traffic and my left thumb and arm extended. I knew I would have better luck if the driver saw my face, that clean-cut, all-American young man with a baby face, but I needed to start walking. If I did not catch a ride, I at least had to make some progress towards Pensacola.

Fortunately, my hitchhiking luck continued as a purple AMC Gremlin slowed down just ahead of me. The driver turned her body to have a better look at me to make sure I did not appear like a serial killer. The car pulled over and the driver shoved the door open.

"Come on in, Sugar. You can lift the rear window and throw your bag in the back, darlin'," a sweet voice called out.

The driver, a pretty enough blond with shoulder-length hair, was wearing a yellow tank top and cut-off white jeans fraying well above her knees, but what really caught my eye were her breasts. They were large and she was braless. Her nipples clearly presented her in the friendliest fashion.

"Are you in the military, Sugar?" the girl asked.

"Yes. I'm in the Navy. I just finished basic training and now I'm heading to Pensacola for A-School."

"What kind of school?"

"A-School. That is what the Navy calls the school where one is sent before being given permanent duty station. Training in the specific field assigned. I was lucky and took some tests before I enlisted and qualified for Electronic Warfare School," I explained.

"Ooooh. It all sounds so important and . . . exciting," she said with a giggle. Do you excite easily, sailor?" she asked as she placed her hand on my knee.

"Well, it depends upon the circumstances," I responded with a half grin on my face.

"I bet it does," she said with a smile. "I'm Charlotte, darling. What's your name?"

"Cal."

"Moo," Charlotte said, then burst into hysterical laughter.

"Funny," I said, without a smile. "My name is Calvin. My friend's call me, Cal."

"Now, don't get sore, Sugar. I was just having some fun with you. Do you want to have some fun with me, Calvin?"

"You know I do," I said as I tossed her hair aside and cupped my hand against her neck.

"I live in Ponce de Leon. It's a little town on the other side of Tallahassee. Want to spend the night at my place?"

"That would be perfect. I had no idea where I would sleep tonight," I said.

"Well, Sugar, I can't guarantee you'll get much sleep, but you'll have a roof over your head," Charlotte said with another burst of laughter.

"Hey, I'm starving. Can we stop at that Biff Burger up ahead?" I said while pointing to the red, white and blue diamonds decorating the front of the restaurant.

"Sure, darlin'."

I felt a lot better after a greasy burger, fries and a shake. As we walked out of the restaurant towards the car, the darkness hid the aesthetically unpleasant visual of the parking lot, the gas station next door, and a scrap metal dump beside that. Darkness allowed neon signs and colorful reflections to make everything look better. Even people. Everyone looks better in low light. It hides imperfections, both physically, and in one's character. Perhaps it is because at the end of the day one is tired, not as sharp. Perhaps it is the desire to end the day on a positive note. Perhaps it is the fourth glass of wine.

We arrived at Charlotte's place an hour before midnight. She lived in a trailer park where every home on wheels sat on a postage stamp lot of the same dimensions. As we entered her abode, I wanted to ask if I could take a shower, but she was on me like ketchup on a white shirt. We undressed each other simultaneously, and clumsily stumbled onto her bed. Charlotte's body was soft and firm and had more curves than Lombard Street in San Francisco. We rocked and rolled until we both were weary. I slept better that night than I had in over six months.

The next morning, Charlotte walked in wearing a pink and white housecoat, carrying a cup of hot coffee. "Good morning sleepyhead," she said with a smile. "Here's some sugar and creamer, Sugar."

"Good morning," I said. "Wow. Thank you! That smells great."

"I brought your sea bag in from the car. My, that thing is heavy,"

"Yeah," I said. "It has my entire life belongings in it."

I was nearly finished with my coffee when I heard water running in the bathroom. "Your bath awaits," Charlotte said as she motioned towards the bathroom.

I got out of bed and walked into the bathroom already filled with steam. I put one foot in the tub and waited a few seconds to adjust to the hot water before fully committing my entire body. Charlotte let her housecoat fall off her. Clearly, she was going to join me. She slid into the bathtub like a baseball player approaching home plate. I sat back and tilted my head back as Charlotte began to bathe me. She used a soapy sponge to wash my neck before working her way south. At first, I felt a little uncomfortable being washed, but before long, I relaxed.

"There's a clean towel on the sink, darlin'," she said as she exited the bathroom.

I remained in the bathtub for a few more minutes enjoying both the warm water and the wonderful memories of the past twelve hours. When I opened the bathroom door I was met with the aroma of ham, home fries, eggs, and Charlotte. She said how she would love to do this for me forever. Those words are enough to make any eighteen-year-old boy run for the nearest ship heading anywhere. I had just celebrated my eighteenth birthday in boot camp.

Still needing to get a ride to the Navy base in Pensacola in two days, I figured I would play along and not give Charlotte a reality check, at least not yet. We jumped in her Gremlin and headed for Mullet Bay for a day at the beach. I was not sure if the beach was named for the ray-finned fish found in coastal temperate and tropical waters, or for the unusually high number of men sporting the non-aesthetically pleasing hairstyle in which the hair is cut shorter at the front, top and sides, but longer at the back.

We spread out a bed sheet on the sand and Charlotte handed me a beach towel with a large smiley face on it. She took off her flowered sarong which revealed an American flag-themed bikini which demanded a salute from my male member. In my peripheral vision, I saw men getting whiplash trying to get a glimpse of Charlotte's cha-chas which were overflowing from her top like one of those middle school vinegar and baking soda science experiment volcanoes.

Charlotte had packed sandwiches, chips and a six-pack of Old Milwaukee. I allowed Charlotte to talk, as she wanted to give me the *Reader's Digest* version of her life. I wondered how she could be in her late twenties and already be divorced, but who was I to judge? I had my own hamper-full of dirty decisions from my past.

That evening, Charlotte made me a classic southern fried dinner of fried chicken, lumpy white gravy, mashed potatoes, and corn on the cob. I viewed it as our "last supper" since I would have to report to my new assignment the next day. We decided to have *dessert* before having dessert. The next morning, Charlotte drove me to the Naval Technical Training Center, Corry Station, located in Pensacola.

When we reached the front gate of the base, the marine standing guard would not let Charlotte drive any farther. I leaned over to give her a quick kiss, but she latched onto me like a tick on a field dog. I indulged until I heard the marine say, "Take it over to the parking lot. I have to keep the gate clear."

"Gotta go, baby. I'll give you a call when I can. Just remember, the first couple of weeks is going to be hell. Probably won't have a free minute. I will call you when I can." I grabbed my sea bag and waved goodbye. Turning to the marine I asked, "I'm new here. Where do I report?"

"You need to go through processing. Go to the Administration Office at building H-16 with a copy of your orders. It will be on your left after the mess hall."

"Thanks," I said as I threw the sea bag over my shoulder.

CHAPTER FOUR

Processing was painless enough, other than the fact I made the grave error of calling the female sailor behind the processing desk a WAVE. She quickly schooled me on the acronym WAVE. It stands for Women Accepted for Volunteer Emergency Service—a division of the U.S. Navy created during World War II to free up male personnel for sea duty. Apparently, WAVES were disbanded in 1948 when President Roosevelt allowed women to receive regular permanent status in the armed forces. What did I know?

I was assigned a barrack and told to unpack my things, the mess hall would open at 1700 hours, and my bunkmates could tell me where it was located. With my sea bag over my shoulder, I walked down the main thoroughfare of the base. I looked around at the buildings and the layout of the base. Each building was clearly marked, and it was not long until I spotted barracks "C." I entered the building, climbed the stairs to the second floor, and found room 232. I knocked, then entered. Three sailors were in the four-man room.

Only four guys in a room? Sweet!

"Hey," I said to anyone listening. "I'm Cal Lloyd. I guess I'm your new…"

"Come on in. I'm Bret Jacobs," one of them said while extending a hand.

"I'm Jack Stranski," said a blonde-haired fellow, turning his head from his seated position at a desk positioned in the middle of the room.

"He's actually a California surfer impersonating an enlisted sailor. A real woman's man. Watch out for him. You can call me Croce," said the third sailor lying on his cot reading a Playboy magazine.

"His name is actually Anthony Rizzo, but we all call him Croce because he looks just like Jim Croce," said Bret.

He did look a lot like the popular singer-songwriter, with his dark curly hair, thick mustache, and a large Sicilian nose.

"You hungry?" asked Jack. "The food on this base is second only to what the bubbleheads get on their bases."

"Bubbleheads?" I asked.

"Submariners. You fresh out of boot camp?"

"Of course he is," said Croce. "Look at his hair. It hasn't had a chance to grow in yet."

"Guilty," I said with a chuckle.

"Come on with me. I'll show you where the mess hall is," said Jack.

While eating I talked about my assignment, Electronic Warfare School.

Electronic Countermeasures (ECM) is the use of devices or techniques intended to impair the operational effectiveness of enemy electronic equipment. It also is used to detect the presence of enemy counter activities. ECM are classified as 'active' or 'passive.' Passive ECM is the use of receiving equipment to intercept enemy radar and radio transmissions. Active ECM is the use of transmission equipment to jam the enemy transmission. It is designed to deceive or deceive radar, sonar, by relaying false targeting information to an enemy. The system is able to make multiple separate targets appear to the enemy, or make the real target appear to disappear. It is especially effective in protecting aircraft from guided missiles. The WLR-1H is the piece of classified equipment we use aboard ships for Over-The-Horizon Detection, Classification and Targeting area surveillance and threat warning.

There are two distinct parts of Electronic Warfare School. One is the electronics part. The students are expected to learn how to repair and maintain electronic warfare equipment.

The second characteristic of being an Electronic Warfare Technician (EW) is intelligence gathering and the operation of the equipment. EWs have access to a book classified as SECRET, which is filled with the parameters of hostile contacts. The Navy's official description is to control the electromagnetic spectrum (EMS) by exploiting, deceiving, or denying enemy use of the spectrum while ensuring its use by friendly forces. I excelled at this. The electronic repair part, not so much.

For me, learning how to electronically repair the EW equipment was harder than trying to do taxes with an abacus. Aptitude. One either has it or not, truth is, I didn't. That was a problem. If I were unable to pass this one-year course, I knew the Navy could very well stick me *anywhere* they wanted. I could end up peeling potatoes or cleaning the bilges for the next four years. To make things worse, one of my instructors was a prick.

EW1 (Electronic Warfare Petty Officer First Class) Braun, was a stammering, by-the-book, soft in the middle, lifer who never would have made it in civilian life. A lifer. A guy who stays in the Navy for twenty years, collects his pension, and probably becomes a greeter at Walmart. He was the typical "day late and a dollar short" type of guy. Making a career by working for the government was perfect for Braun. It is nearly impossible to be fired and one never really has to think. The Navy told everyone where to be and what to wear. Braun embraced the exact things unappealing to me.

When Braun saw I had difficulty grasping the nuances of electronic repair, he ridiculed me, and not privately.

"L-L-L-Lloyd, you failed the circuit continuity test, just like you failed the test on microcontrollers. You are an i-i-i-idiot. Why don't you just throw in the towel and accept you will be swabbing decks and chipping and painting for the next four years," Braun said loud enough so the entire class heard. The laughter in the classroom infuriated me, but I did not let it show.

I was tempted to get out of my seat, walk over to the asshole and deck him, but being court–martialed and spending time in the brig was a strong deterrent. I also considered embarrassing Braun for his stammering, but the last thing I wanted was to make unnecessary trouble. After being set back in boot camp, I did not want to cause any unnecessary waves.

If there is a nerve within me that, when pushed, creates an explosion, it is being ridiculed. In boot camp I took that stuff in stride.

Everyone was ridiculed. But instead of tutoring me and lending some assistance, Braun was contemptuous toward me and used dismissive language. My response was to say nothing.

When I first reported for duty at Corry Station, I was assigned as an assistant to Commander Buckingham while the next EW class began. The Commander was the complete opposite of Braun; he was a gentleman by all definitions of the word, always treating me with respect. I would have taken a bullet for that man. When it was clear I would fail the electronic part of the course, I decided to seek the Commander's advice.

"Sir, thank you for seeing me," I said.

"Of course, Lloyd. How is the training coming along?"

"Well, that's what I want to talk to you about. I only worked for you a couple of months, but I hope my actions prove I am a hard worker, and I love the Navy."

"I would agree with that," the Commander said.

"Well, I really wanted to be an Electronic Warfare Technician, but no matter how hard I study, I just cannot pick up electronics. I'm not wired that way, pun intended. I really did well on the intel evaluation and operations part of the course, but not the electronic repair. I think they are going to kick me out of school, and God knows where I will end up."

"Alright. Let me take a look at your service file and speak with a few people. You are a bright sailor, Lloyd. I want to make sure the Navy uses your talents productively. I'll be in touch."

"Thank you, sir," I said as I saluted and left his office.

I was placed in a holding status on the base and told not to attend class, but to report to the admin office every morning for duty. I was in limbo until they could decide what to do with me. My responsibilities changed daily, but I had become nothing more than a military gopher.

Retrieve this paperwork. Deliver this envelope across the base to some officer sitting behind a desk. Fun!

Like most of the enlisted men, I still had duty every six days. When a sailor is assigned duty, it is a twenty-four-hour shift; he has no liberty to leave the base at the end of the work day, and it consists of standing watch, waxing and buffing passageways, or cleaning toilets. But one day, I got wind of a different kind of duty.

Working in the admin office, I heard a lot of scuttlebutt. Most of it was of little value, but every once in a while, I would mine a real gem. One day a sailor reported for duty as the "Base Transportation Driver." The responsibilities were simple. He was given a base vehicle and ran errands around Jacksonville, mostly between the Naval Air Station and Corry Station. If that were not sweet enough, he had this specific duty only once every 28 days! It was such a guerdoned duty that those fortunate enough to be assigned to it kept it hidden from all the other sailors. A few inquiries and some of my God-given charm, I landed the gig. Unfortunately for me, there was a small catch.

Before being assigned as duty driver, I was asked a few questions by the Officer of the Day. The catch, the car was a stick, and not on the floor. I hid my reaction from the officer. *This was 1975! Who in the world bought cars with a stick on the column, for crying out loud?* Not only had I never driven a stick, one on the column was as alien to me as the electronics I had tried to learn.

"Can you drive a three-on-the-tree?" the duty officer asked.

"Sir?"

"Can you drive a car with a standard transmission? You know, a column-shift manual transmission."

I had to think quickly. If I said no, I would be back cleaning toilets and buffing passageways every six days. If I said yes, I had better be able to figure out how to manipulate a clutch pedal and gear shift. *How hard could that possibly be?*

"Yes, sir. Not a problem," I answered, thinking nothing was going to prevent me from having duty only once a month.

"Okay, your first day of duty will be Thursday," the officer said. "You have to report in your dress whites." The dress white uniform is what we wear for special occasions.

I always hated Thursdays. When I was younger, Thursdays were the days I had to deliver the local, weekly newspaper. With few exceptions, Thursdays were always the most windy, rainy, snowy or hottest days of the week! I hoped this Thursday would bring me better luck.

The next day was Saturday, and none of my bunkmates had duty. We all slept in till midmorning and went to chow together at noon. Someone I had not met walked to our table.

"Hey, a bunch of us are going to have a pick-up football game between the barracks, do you guys want to join us?" he asked.

"Yeah," answered Bret. "Count us in."

My three bunkmates and I finished our lunch and headed back to the room to change clothes. By the time we got outside there were a dozen sailors throwing a football. One of the guys suggested we line up to pick sides. That is when I saw him. Mongrel, my childhood nemesis, had not only joined the Navy, but was stationed at the same base as I. As I approached him, Mongrel recognized me.

"Cal, what the hell are you doing here?" he said, as if he were actually glad to see me.

I said nothing. With built up rage from the years of beatings I had received from Mongrel, I cold cocked my arch-enemy and threw a vicious punch that landed cleanly on Mongrel's eye. Mongrel fell in a heap.

"What the hell was that for," Mongrel said as he tried to compose himself.

"For the years you beat me up in high school," I said as I walked back to my bunkmates.

"Damn, Lloyd. You are a badass," Croce said with a laugh.

That evening, Croce, Bret, and Jack invited me to go out to their favorite bar for a few drinks. Since Croce owned a Harley, Bret and I would ride with Jack in his dark blue Nova. *The Cuddly Turtle* was popular with the local girls looking for a sailor to abduct as their boyfriend. In a Navy town, not all the women were fond of sailors, but these women were the exception. Although my bunkmates and I preferred rock and roll, we knew we would have to listen to a barrage of disco that evening. *The Cuddly Turtle* was a discotheque with a large dance floor and a mirror ball hanging above reflecting colored lights across the room. In the winter months, many of the young ladies who went to the disco were tourists, and they wanted to drink, dance, and get a little wild while away from home. The four of us were more than willing to accommodate.

We four amigos arrived at the disco a little after nine. The place had already started filling up and the ratio of girls to guys was approximately six to four, in favor of the minority males. Many of the local young men avoided discos because they preferred rock or country music, they simply despised disco, they couldn't dance, or they did not own the proper attire. Proper attire for me was a rust-colored leisure suit, platform shoes and a colorful kiana shirt. The ever popular kiana shirt was crafted from a cotton poplin fabric with 4% Elastane stretch. The two-way stretch allowed the shirt to be cut to a slim contemporary silhouette, perfect for my lean, but muscular body. The shirt was soft to the touch and did not compromise one's movement, ideal for dancing the hustle.

Soon after we commandeered a table, Jack's on again, off again, girlfriend, Peaches, walked over to us. Peaches was not her real name, but the name she used at the *Candy Cane Lounge*, a strip bar just outside the Navy base. She had long blonde hair and sharp features, but her appeal to men was her body, accentuated by her incredibly large breasts she purchased recently. Peaches wore a multi-colored Tuta mesh jumpsuit Fuzzi with large bell bottoms that swung in sync with her hips when she walked. She wanted the attention of every man, and the envy of every woman in the disco. She succeeded.

"I thought you were not going out tonight, Jackie," she said as I slid over to another seat allowing Peaches to be next to Jack.

"I changed my mind at the last minute. My bunkmates wanted to have a few drinks, and they needed a ride."

Croce leaned over and whispered into my ear. "She's high maintenance. A pain in the ass."

"What did you just say?" she said with disdain.

"I told Cal I was hoping you would strip and dance for us tonight," Croce said with a laugh.

"Keep hoping." Turning to Jack she said, "Let's get out of here. I don't like your friends."

"I am not leaving. I am their ride," Jack answered.

"They can get a taxi."

"Do you know how much a cab would cost from Jax Beach to the base? I'm not leaving."

"Are you choosing them over me?" she said, raising her voice.

With that, Croce and I got up and left the table. I approached a cute brunette and asked her to dance. Croce went to the bar and ordered another drink. As the hours passed, all four of us began to feel a bit inebriated. The evening went well, until it didn't. I had made great progress with the brunette vacationing from Canada, and Croce was trying his luck with a pretty barmaid when Jack walked up to him.

"Peaches wants to leave. I am going to give her a ride home," he announced.

"So, take her home and come back," suggested Croce.

"Her apartment is on the south side of town. I'm not coming all the way back here. You have your Harley. Cal and Bret will have to come with us, or they will have to find their own way back to the base," Jack said abruptly. "Where are they?"

"Bret is still back at the table. Cal is over there with that girl. I'll see what they want to do."

After a short discussion, we joined Jack and Peaches at the door. It was half past midnight.

Croce stayed back at the bar as Bret and I followed Jack and Peaches through the parking lot. Once inside the car, Peaches threw a barrage of accusations and insults toward Jack. He said nothing. In the backseat, Bret and I gave each other looks that needed no words. *When would Jack dump this chick and move on? He doesn't need this crap!*

By the time we reached downtown Jacksonville, Jack had had enough. Pulling the car to the curb, he walked to the passenger's door, opened it, and shouted, "Get the hell out of the car!"

"I'm not going anywhere!" Peaches yelled.

"Get out now, or I will make you get out!"

"I am not getting out, and you can't make me!"

Jack grabbed Peaches by the ankles and dragged her out of the car and onto the pavement. While on her back, Peaches let out a Banshee's scream, and kicked her leg high, landing her stiletto heel square into Jack's left eye. Jack joined Peaches' screams, and fell backwards, landing on the sidewalk. Once Peaches saw the blood streaming down Jack's face, her demeanor completely changed.

"Oh, baby. I'm sorry. I'm so sorry. Are you alright?"

"I swear I'll kill you, you crazy bitch!" Jack yelled, as he popped right back up, like a child's Bozo Bop Bag.

Peaches quickly took off her heels and ran down the sidewalk.

"Take me to the hospital," Jack groaned.

CHAPTER FIVE

Jack spent the next two days in the hospital. Croce and I took Jack's Nova to pick him up when he was released. He had a large white patch over his eye.

"What did they say?" I asked.

"I lost my freakin' eye. They couldn't save it," Jack said matter-of-factly.

"Damn!" Croce said.

"So, you get to wear a black patch like a pirate. That's kind of cool," I said.

Both Jack and Croce stood there looking at me with no emotion whatsoever, and then the three of us broke out laughing.

"Yeah," Jack said. "I guess that is kind of cool."

"So, from now on, you will be known as the One-eyed Jack," I added.

The three of us continued to laugh as we drove back to the base.

The next day I rose early, a habit I have never been able to break. No matter how late I would stay up the night before, I always get up before the sun does. My bunkmates were still asleep, so I decided to go to the mess hall and get myself something to eat. While walking to the mess hall, I began thinking how I would manage to drive a stick on the column for the first time.

When I returned to the barracks there was a note posted on the door informing me to report to Commander Buckingham's office. As

I walked outside the barracks, I looked around my surroundings. It was a beautiful day. The Florida sun sat behind the only cloud in the sky, giving me a temporary break from the heat. I assumed if the Commander had summoned my presence, it was news about my schooling. My time and options were running out, and I knew the Commander was my last hope.

While walking to the Commander's office, I thought about my Electronic Warfare schooling. Funny enough, I had excelled at the Intelligence part of the course, but it seemed I lacked the *intelligence* to grasp the electronic portion of the course. If Commander Buckingham could not come up with a solution to my schooling dilemma, I would spend the remaining four years of my enlistment in the bilges.

When I entered Commander Buckingham's office my eyes went immediately to my replacement, who sat in the same desk I had been assigned when I worked in that office. She was a beautiful brunette whose hair was pinned up in victory curls. Despite the knee length skirt her uniform required, the skirt rose considerably as she sat with her legs crossed.

"Hi. I am Seaman Lloyd," I announced.

"Oh, yes," she responded. "The commander is expecting you." Picking up the black phone on her desk, she announced my arrival. "Yes, Commander, Seaman Lloyd is here to see you. Yes, sir." Turning to me with a slight smile she said, "The Commander will see you."

"Thank you," I said, glancing at her a bit too long as I walked toward the Commander's office.

I knocked on the door. The Commander said, "Enter."

I entered the office and stood at attention. "At ease, Lloyd. How are you making out?"

Knowing the Commander understood my situation was precarious, I simply responded with, "I'm doing fine, Sir."

By his general demeanor, I thought he had some good news for me.

"I spoke with Captain Lankford, who runs the cryptology school, as well as Commander Dunleavy, who you know is the Commanding Officer of Corry Station. We reviewed your personnel file and your background before you joined the Navy. Your mother was Ukrainian, was she not?"

"Yes, Sir. Both my mother and my stepmother were born in Ukraine." I had no idea where this was going.

"Did they speak Ukrainian around the house?" he asked.

"Only when they were on the phone with their siblings and parents. When we had family gatherings, they would turn to Ukrainian if they didn't want us to understand what they were saying."

The Commander chuckled.

"Right," he said. "Do you speak or understand the language?"

"Very little, Sir."

. "Since you heard Ukrainian spoken frequently from a very young age, Commander Lankford believes that learning the language will come easier than you might think. He would like you to enroll in CTI school and study it. What do you think?"

I paused for a minute. I failed German in seventh grade, and it took me three years to get through two years of French. If I were to tell the Commander I did not have the aptitude to pick up languages, my stint in the Navy was going to be long and painful. I had to try and learn Ukrainian, if that was my only option.

"I'm willing to give it a try, Sir. Why Ukrainian and not Russian? Isn't Russia the real threat?" I asked.

The Commander paused for a moment, as if he were determining exactly how much to tell me. "There are activities going on in all of the Soviet bloc countries. We have people in all these countries. Let's just say some areas in the Soviet Union are more interesting to us than others. Ukraine is one of fifteen constituent republics composing the Soviet Union. Ukrainian is mainly a rural language. Russian has the perceived higher prestige and is mostly used by the educated urban society. There is some thought among our security agencies that we have neglected training individuals to be equipped for Ukrainian surveillance."

"May I ask what they want me to do?"

"Cryptologic Technicians Interpretive, what we call CTIs, are assigned according to the varying demand for the unique linguistic skills they possess. They utilize foreign language skills, and study regional and cultural traits. It is probably one of the most important and secretive rates in the Navy. CTIs intercept foreign language communications, transcribe, translate and interpret foreign language materials, and then analyze the information and exploit it. They locate and monitor worldwide threats. All this is to support national and fleet operations which includes special ops, air, surface and subsurface."

"Wow," I said. That sounds pretty impressive!"

"It is! Interested?"

"Yes, Sir," I answered enthusiastically.

"One last thing, Lloyd. This is a wonderful opportunity. With your understanding of operational Electronic Warfare, you could become somewhat of a hybrid. If you want the truth, you're being groomed; not quite sure for what. Actually, I'm not sure *they* know. But that's how they work. They look years ahead and prepare, and that includes people."

"Commander Buckingham, I want you to know I really appreciate all you have done for me."

"I believe in you, Lloyd. This is going to take a lot of work on your part. Don't let me down. Keep in touch," he said while getting up from behind his chair.

"Yes, sir. I will," I replied as I saluted the Commander and exited his office.

The next day felt like D-Day, the day I was assigned as the base Duty Driver. I confided in Croce, my roommate, that I never drove a three-on-the-tree transmission. Croce drew the shifting diagram on a piece of paper as a cheat-sheet for me.

"Remember, clutch in, shift, ease your foot off the clutch with your left foot as you put your right foot on the accelerator. Let me emphasize *ease. Nice and easy.* If you stall, make sure the stick is in neutral, otherwise, when you start the car again it will buck like a bronco. Got it?"

"Yeah, I think so," I answered.

I left the barracks and reported to the administration office wearing my dress whites as instructed.

"I'm Petty Officer Lloyd. I am the duty driver today," I said to the girl whose head was buried in paperwork.

"Okay. Sign in on this clipboard and have a seat over there. You're going to have to pick up some admiral at NAS Jacksonville at 1300 hours," she said matter-of-factly.

My first day as duty driver and I have to drive an admiral? I hope I get the hang of this three-on-the-tree, manual transmission on the column thing. But really, how hard can it be?

I watched the clock mounted on the wall behind me like an osprey anticipating its fish dinner. When the clock hit 1200 hours, I got up and walked over to the desk.

"May I have the keys, please?"

The girl behind the desk looked up at the clock and back at me.

"The admiral's plane doesn't land for an hour. It's only a twenty-minute drive to the air base," she said.

"Yeah, but you know how top brass are. I do not want to be late. Besides, those flights often arrive early."

"Here are the keys," she said, handing them to me. "It's the black Ambassador parked out front. There's a sign that says Official Base Vehicle Only."

Walking outside, I immediately saw the 1974 black, four-door sedan that had a front end so exaggeratedly long it looked like Jimmy Durante's nose. Ugly was not a descriptive enough adjective. Apparently, the government wanted to keep American Motors afloat, so they gave them the contract for a fleet of cars.

I settled into the driver's seat and looked at the drawing Croce gave me. It seemed easy enough. The drawing was a large "H". First gear down and to the left. Second, upper right. Third, down and to the right. I put my left foot on the clutch and turned on the car. So far, so good. I slid the stick up and to the left, putting the car in reverse. Releasing the clutch and giving it some gas, the car jerked violently backward and stalled. I looked around to see if I had an audience; thankfully, no one had seen the mishap, or so I thought. I tried again and got the same results.

A tap on the driver's window startled me. I turned to see Petty Officer Braun standing by the car, laughing. I rolled down the window.

"What the hell do you want?" I asked, already knowing the answer.

"You are such a p-p-p-putz," Braun said between bouts of laughter.

I felt coal-hot anger flowing throughout my body as I tried to put the car in gear. The third time was a charm. Off I was to pick up the admiral.

The Naval Air Station in Pensacola was much larger than the base at Corry Station. There, Navy pilots practice landing on an aircraft carrier. The USS Lexington, commissioned in 1943, was the landing platform for pilots in training. She set more records than any other Essex Class carrier in naval aviation history.

The marine standing guard at the gate gave me directions to the Public Affairs Office where I was to meet the admiral. In front of the square bland building was a parking spot with a sign that read OFFICIAL BUSINESS VEHICLE. Since putting the car in reverse had been a challenge, I decided to back the car into the parking spot to avoid any embarrassment when the admiral was in the car.

Walking into the building, I took my cover off and walked over to the clerk at a small desk. "I'm here to pick up Admiral Cartwright."

The sailor behind the desk picked up the phone and told someone the admiral's driver had arrived. A few minutes later a tall, lean gentleman with salt and pepper hair, dressed in khakis, came walking down the hallway. I stood at attention.

"At ease," said the admiral. "Are you my ride to Corry Station?"

"Yes, Sir," I answered.

As we walked outside the admiral put on his hat that had more scrambled eggs on it than a breakfast plate at Denny's.

"Thank you. What is your name and rate, sailor?"

"Seaman Lloyd, Sir. I am studying electronic warfare"

"Electronic warfare. Nice. Well, let's head over to Corry Station."

The beginning of the ride went fairly well. A little rough accelerating from a stop, but I was feeling more comfortable driving the car. The admiral was engaging and asked questions about my studies and was very interested in the hybrid schooling I was receiving.

"I have never heard of anyone trained in electronic warfare and as a cryptologic interpreter," the admiral said. "What language are you studying?"

"Ukrainian," I answered.

"Ukrainian. Now, that's very interesting. Good for you. You will be a uniquely qualified sailor. Your future is bright, Lloyd."

I was taken back at how engaging the admiral was. He was considerate, encouraging, and friendly. Then again, our interaction was fairly minimal.

The ride continued to go well until we reached a red light at the crest of the hill. *Here I sit in the flattest state in the country, and I find the only hill in the entire state.* I looked in the rear-view mirror and saw a car approaching. *Please turn green before that car gets here.* The light not only failed to turn green, but the car behind us stopped extremely close to our car. The light did change, but as I attempted to coordinate the clutch with the accelerator, the car stalled. I tried again, giving the admiral mild whiplash. The person behind us was blowing his horn. I could feel the sweat beading on the back of my neck.

"These Ambassadors are a piece of junk," I said, finally being able to get the car moving forward.

"I never have been a fan of these cars," the admiral said, knowing very well I was not accustomed to driving a stick on the column.

I dropped the admiral off at the Admin Office and went back to the barracks. I wished all officers were as decent as Vice Admiral Cartwright. The admiral could have made my life miserable, but he chose not to. He never criticized me, or my driving.

CHAPTER SIX

One-eyed jack was given a medical discharge, much to his disappointment. He was the fourth generation of Stranski's to have served in the Navy. He held no ill will towards his girlfriend, something I thought was remarkable.

A few weeks later, Croce approached me about a road trip.

"Hey, Cal. Next weekend is the Daytona 500. I'm taking the Harley. There will be tons of hot girls from all over the U.S. wearing skimpy clothes and looking to have a good time. Why don't you come with me?"

"On the back of your bike?"

"Yeah. It will be a blast!"

"How many freaking miles is it from here?"

"90 miles," Croce said. "Only an hour and a half."

"I dunno," I said with doubt in my voice. "I never feel comfortable on the back of a bike. Nothing personal. I know you are safety conscious on that beast. I always feel more relaxed when I am the one driving. Let me think it over."

"Alright, but if you never have been to the big race, you don't know what you are missing. It's not just the race. It is the whole experience."

"I know. I'll let you know in a few days."

Over the next couple of days, I kept trying to decide if I should go with Croce to the race. I wanted to, but there was something that kept nagging at me, telling me not to go. Man's intuition? I decided not to go. Croce did not seem upset and went by himself.

The next day I got a message to report to the admin office immediately. While walking to the office I was trying to figure out what I did wrong. I always expect the worst, that way, if it turns out nothing is wrong, I am pleasantly surprised. That is the way I operate. I had too many experiences of being surprised by bad news; too many instances where I was blindsided by unexpected disappointments. No more!

When I arrived at the admin office, I announced my arrival to the clerk at the desk and was told to have a seat. The Command Duty Officer soon opened the door and told me to come in.

"Lloyd, right?"

"Yes, sir."

"Your duty responsibility has changed. You will no longer be the monthly Duty Driver. You have been assigned guard duty at the security compound. That will be every six days. That's all."

I immediately thought of the bucking bronco ride I gave the admiral. I feared he decided to inform the office I had no idea how to drive a stick on the column and should not be driving anyone. "Sir, may I ask why the change?"

"Petty Officer First Class Braun said he needed another body for the rotating guard duty. He specifically asked for you," the officer said.

"Braun? He is the leading petty officer for Electronic Warfare. I am now assigned to the Cryptologic school," I argued.

"Whatever. Your first duty is Sunday. You are dismissed."

Braun! I swear I'm gonna kill that bastard! I am no longer assigned to the Electronic Warfare School where he had authority, and he is still trying to screw me!

That Sunday, I reported for my new watch duty. The compound was protected by a large chain link fence with rolls of barbed wire spiraling across the top of the fence like a slinky. I had been assigned to the 1700 to 2400 watch, the next to the worst time segment, the worst being the mid-watch, from midnight till 0400. I fully expected Braun to assign that watch in the future. I was supposed to check IDs for anyone wanting to enter the highly classified area, but there would be no foot traffic on a Sunday evening.

The sun had set as I stood in the telephone booth sized shelter. My boredom was replaced with stewing anger towards Braun. I realized I must have been channeling Braun, for somewhere in the darkness, I heard that familiar cackling. I turned from where the raucous sound was coming. Braun stepped into the light illuminating the entrance to the compound laughing as he said, "I s-s-s-s-see you have settled into your new d-d-d-duty, Lloyd."

"You stammering shithead!" I replied.

"Shithead? That is not nice. I should write you up."

"Go ahead, write me up. My word against yours."

"And I out-rank you. They will always believe me over a w-w-w-worm like you.

"What is it about you, Braun? Why do you have it out for me?"

"I really don't know. I just c-c-c-couldn't stand you from the first minute I met you. Besides, I get so much enjoyment abusing you."

"Get lost," I said.

"I think I will go over to the Enlisted Men's Club and have a beer. Want to come? Oh, that's r-r-r-right. You can't. You have d-d-d-duty. Well, Lloyd, this is your lucky day, because I am being transferred to temporary assigned d-d-d-duty for three months in Norfolk, Virginia, and then sea d-d-d-duty. I am really going to m-m-m-miss you," he said, laughing as he walked away.

I finished my watch and went straight to the barracks. Croce was at the Daytona 500, One-eyed Jack had been discharged, and Bret, my other roommate, was nowhere to be found. Probably out on the town. I was exhausted. I laid on my rack and quickly fell asleep.

Sometime in the middle of the night there was a hard knock on the door which startled me from a deep sleep.

"Cal, see who that is?" Bret said. "I got shit-faced last night."

I never heard Bret come in during the night. Another knock on the door. I got up and opened the door. A sailor I had never seen before stood there.

"Is this Seaman Rizzo's room?" the sailor asked.

"Yeah, but he's away for the weekend," I said as I began to close the door and go back to sleep.

"Well, we just received a phone call from the Florida State Police. Apparently, a car jumped the median strip on route 95 and hit his motorcycle head-on. He was killed instantly. I am sorry. The Officer of the Day told me to tell his bunkmates immediately."

I stood at the door, paralyzed with sadness. Bret stood behind me.

"You were supposed to go with him, weren't you?" Bret asked.

"Yeah. I cannot believe this," I mumbled. "First Jack, and now Croce."

"Unbelievable," Bret said. "Thank God I have only a few weeks left of school. I need to get out of this place.

"I hear you," I mumbled.

Over the next few months, I was consumed with my studies. I found the busier I was, the less I thought about Croce. Although I was still in Cryptologic Technician school, I was considered an Electronic Warfare Technician, not that it mattered to me. Commander Buckingham was right. Once I was stationed aboard a ship, I would be more valuable than the average enlisted sailor. Clout goes a long way on a Navy ship. I could not wait till school was finished, and I hit the seas.

Learning Ukrainian came much easier than I expected. The first time my eyes were permitted to gaze upon papers stamped SECRET, an unexpected sense of superiority swept over me. Knowing the masses would never see or know about this information placed me in an exclusive club. The sensation of supremacy increased as my security clearance increased. My security clearance would increase, or decrease, depending on what I was assigned to do at any given moment, but I would always hold the SECRET rating.

Specializing in the interpretive aspect of cryptology, I would be expected to utilize those language skills, collect, process, exploit, analyze and report all Ukrainian communications. Russia increasingly was adding more troops, missiles, and electronic surveillance equipment into the country. Ukraine's 2,782 kilometers of Black Sea shoreline was a major factor in Russia's decision.

Naval Intelligence reported Russia was installing new high-powered jamming systems to deceive NATO radar guided weapons systems. Now that I completed my schooling, I was assigned to a ship soon to be deployed to the Eastern Mediterranean where I would be able to utilize my newly developed skills.

Naval Intelligence. I will be the Intelligence Petty Officer on my ship. Me? Intelligence? Huh! How ironic!

Upon graduation from CT/EW school, I was promoted to third class petty officer and sent to SERE School in New Brunswick, Maine for 21 days before being assigned permanent duty on the *USS Charles F. Adams*, a guided missile destroyer. SERE is another military acronym, which stands for Survival, Evasion, Resistance, and Escape, a program that teaches how to conduct oneself if captured. The skills taught at the school included wilderness survival skills, how to evade capture, how to resist interrogation and how to escape if captured. We learned how to move safely and efficiently through various terrains, how to navigate from one point to another given point on the ground, and how to identify wild, edible plants, seeds, berries, and nuts. Little did I know all these skills would prove invaluable.

CHAPTER SEVEN

A s difficult as sere school was, I excelled. It was more a psychological challenge than a physical one. The physical challenge basically was dealing with open-handed slaps to the face and head, and periods of enforced hunger; what one would expect if he became a POW. The isolation in a prison cell, the verbal abuse, and techniques to demoralize take their toll. Some students began to believe they were actually prisoners, which had a despondent effect on them. Many of these students failed the course. For me, it was a mind over matter thing. I focused on surviving to the end, telling myself nothing lasts forever.

After graduation, I boarded a plane for Jacksonville, Florida. Grabbing my sea bag from the trunk of the taxi, I threw it over my shoulder, and gave the driver a sawbuck, telling him to keep the change. The Naval Station Mayport is located 15 miles east of Jacksonville, Florida, at the mouth of the St. Johns River. It was a short distance from the Atlantic Ocean, near the small fishing village of Mayport. Over thirty Navy ships were stationed at the base, although nearly a third were out at sea when I arrived at the USS *Charles F. Adams*. Named for Charles Francis Adams III (Secretary of the Navy from 1929 to 1933), she was the first of her class of guided missile destroyers. Although small by military ship standards, the *Adams* was both versatile and dependable, with its mission being primarily air defense and anti-submarine warfare.

I stood on the dock admiring my new floating home, my eyes scanning every nuance of her, as if she were a Playboy centerfold. The *Adams* was an impressive fighting ship, equipped with Surface-to-Air TARTAR Missiles, MK42 MOD 10 5"/54-gun system, a gun-fire control system with a forward looking infra-red sensor, a laser ranging unit, and a Mark 16 ASROC (Anti-Submarine Rocket). I felt like I was falling in love. This would be the beginning of what I dreamed of, actively serving on a Navy fighting ship.

There was another attraction to turning the page on the next chapter, a fresh start. But I would find out, relocating to a place where no one knows me, in an attempt to reinvent myself, the biggest obstacle is trying to forget who I was. I wrestled with imposter syndrome. The absurdity of it all is, this is where the memory is most keen. It never forgets who one is, no matter how hard he tries. *I am not that person. I am not that person. I am not...*

My objective to reinvent myself was more than a desire; it was an obsession. I realized those opportunities are rare. I had been picked on throughout my childhood. Teachers ridiculed me for my undiagnosed ADHD and poor grades. I was an easy target for the bullies of the neighborhood since I was short for my age. But my physical demeanor changed over 15 months in the Navy. The extensive physical activities of boot camp which included "Intensive Training," coupled with my commitment to daily workouts, and the fact I had grown an additional two and a half inches and gained fifteen pounds of muscle made me look physically impressive. Like a dog being trained for dogfighting, I had spent most of my life on a short, heavy, psychological chain. My greatest asset, if I could manage it, was my anger. I would no longer be anyone's punching bag, no matter what the cost.

I walked over to the bow, where the officer of the day stood dressed in khakis and wearing a pisscutter. A pisscutter is Navy slang for a garrison cap originally to facilitate the wearing of radio headsets. I saluted him and said, "Permission to come aboard, Sir."

"Permission granted," the officer said, returning the salute.

If living on a 437-foot floating hunk of metal, painted in 4 shades of gray, occupied by 354 young men whose testosterone is like a tea kettle needing to expel steam, and sharing a bedroom with 60 of those guys sleeping in a bunk bed stacked three high, working from midnight to 7 am, and then again from noon to 5 pm, or the idea of dressing exactly like hundreds of other people, is to your liking, then welcome to the Navy! For me it was exactly what I needed, whether I knew it or not.

I assimilated easily to ship life. There were mundane responsibilities for which I was responsible, but my assigned duty of both Electronic Warfare operations and Cryptologic Intelligence was both challenging and exciting. The classified information to which I was privy was intoxicating. Top secret photographs of Soviet and Chinese platforms that included land-based, surface, sub-surface and aircraft had me marvel at the risks American spies took to snap those pictures.

I immediately took a liking to the Operations Officer who was the department head for much of Combat Information Center (CIC), where I would report during battle stations. Lt. Mark Kiggans was a short, but handsome man, with chestnut brown hair and a pyramidal mustache that made him look more like a porn star than a Naval officer. Lt. Kiggans took an interest in my unique hybrid training of both Electronic Warfare and cryptology. The lieutenant assigned me as the Intelligence Petty Officer of the ship and spent time teaching me how to operate a sophisticated 35 mm camera with a high-powered zoom lens. I was responsible for taking photographs of enemy platforms whenever the *Adams* was in close proximity to them.

As much as I took a liking to Lt. Kiggans, the opposite was true with the Executive Officer (XO), the second in command of the ship. LCDR Peter Lynch had a chip on his shoulder, probably because he resented being number two. Like a box elder tree which spreads an endless amount of pollen in springtime, coating everything in thick yellow-green powder, the XO spread hate and discontent wherever he went; he triggered horrendous allergies to morale.

A few weeks after my arrival on the ship, I was eating chow on the mess deck when a sailor sat down across from me.

"Is anyone sitting here?" the sailor asked.

"No. Have a seat," I said.

"You must be new here. I am Ron Womack. Everyone calls me Dakota."

"Hi. My name is Cal Lloyd. How did you get the nickname Dakota?"

"I am from South Dakota."

I laughed. "I guess that makes sense. What rate are you?"

"I am a radioman. I work in Radio Central. Are you an EW? I saw you with the other Electronic Warfare guys at muster the other morning."

"I am, but I was trained also as a Cryptologic Technician, interpreter."

"Now that is very cool! What language do you speak? Russian? Chinese?"

"Ukrainian."

"Ukrainian? That is a little bizarre." Dakota said.

"I guess they want people trained in every Soviet bloc language. My mom and stepmom were both Ukrainian. It came pretty easily to me. What does a radioman do?"

"We manage voice and code communications between ships and aircraft. Like you, we must have a security clearance," Dakota said.

Dakota was a tall young man, with strawberry blond hair and a square jaw that complimented his boyish face. Raised on a farm, he had the type of muscles that come from demanding work, not from the gym; a towering portrait of a man painted with gentle strokes.

It took no time at all for the two of us to become good friends, despite our vastly diverse backgrounds. He was from the Black Hills of South Dakota, and I was from the swarming city of Philadelphia, but we both had a passion for the expanse of nature. We would often talk about our love for hunting and fishing, sharing stories of our largest catch or the deer we had bagged.

The next morning at muster, Lt. Kiggans spoke to the men under his command.

"Men, we have a new LPO for Electronic Warfare. I will let him introduce himself," Kiggans said.

I could not believe my bad luck. Of all the ships in the US Navy, what were the chances that my antagonist from EW school, Braun, would be assigned to the same ship?

Braun stepped forward from the ranks and said, "Good morning. I am EW1 B-B-B-Braun."

"Is that with one B, or five?" I yelled out.

The entire company of sailors laughed hysterically. Lt. Kiggans tried desperately to hold back his laughter.

"Ahhhh, Petty Officer Lloyd. I see you are the s-s-s-s-same undisciplined sailor you were in Pensacola," Braun said.

"Okay men, you are dismissed," the lieutenant said, trying to diffuse the situation. "Proceed to your work stations."

I climbed the ladder to the Upper Electronic Countermeasures (ECM) work space. Braun was already there.

"Okay. I n-n-n-need two volunteers, Lloyd, and someone else," Braun said.

"I didn't volunteer," I said.

"Oh, yes you did," responded Braun.

"I want you and Simpson to start chipping and painting the outside of Upper ECM. In fact, Simpson, you s-s-s-stay here with us. Lloyd can manage it by himself. Lloyd, go down to the equipment locker and sign out a d-d-d-deck grinder and whatever else you will need. You will b-b-b-be doing that all day."

"Fine by me," I said, trying to hide my growing animosity.

Petty Officer Braun continued to make life miserable for me at every opportunity. Being both creative and resourceful, I was pondering how I could retaliate. I decided to be patient, waiting for the perfect situation, the perfect time to act. That time was just not now.

When I worked with classified information, Lt. Kiggans, and even the Commanding Officer (CO) noted my exceptional analysis. I dreamed of being able to demonstrate my skills in a real-time, hostile situation, and that dream would soon come true. There was scuttlebutt among the crew that we were going on a six-month Mediterranean cruise in December. I had been brushing up on what Soviet ships we might encounter, and the armament those ships carried. Top Secret documents revealed the Soviets had just launched their latest ship, the *Kirov*. The *Kirov* was an anti-submarine warfare cruiser and would soon leave the Black Sea on her maiden voyage to conduct operations in the Mediterranean, North Atlantic, and Norwegian Sea. There was immense national pride in this newest addition to the Soviet fleet. I knew the ship had the latest technology. I was anxious to get overseas and try to discover by electronic surveillance the parameters of their new surface-to-surface missile guidance systems. This is what I trained to do. This is the excitement I craved.

The next day, Signalman First Class Towles walked up to me. We had not been close even though we both worked on the 03 level of the ship. Towles was a lifer, someone who planned on spending twenty plus years in the Navy. He followed the rules and regulations to the letter. He was ten years older than I and sported a thick black beard to match his hair, wore Navy-issued glasses, and was not a very attractive man. Towles was a nice enough guy, just a bit of a dweeb.

"Hello, Lloyd," the signalman said.

"Hey, Towles. What's up?"

"My sister is coming down to visit my wife and me for a week. She arrives on Saturday. She is a nurse at a hospital in Buffalo. I think she is around your age. Would you do me a favor and give her a tour of the ship? Maybe spend some time with her? I really do not have much in common with her due to our age difference. Maybe you could show her around while she is here."

Several thoughts swirled around my head. First of all, shouldn't there be a law preventing people from having more than one ugly kid? If this girl looked anything like Towles, I wanted nothing to do with her. Would I be nice to her? Of course, but I certainly did not want to commit to a week of being her escort.

"I would like to, Towles, but I think I have duty tomorrow," I said apologetically.

"Oh. Okay. Well, just let me know," Towles said as he walked back towards the signalman's shack.

The next day, Saturday, only a few sailors were found onboard the ship, which was typical for a weekend moored at our home port. Anyone who was not on duty was on shore. I was assigned ship security that afternoon as Petty Officer of the Watch (POOW), a position of managing the gangway and watching everyone who comes and goes.

When the ship was in port, a food truck made stops at each ship so the sailors could purchase sandwiches and snacks. As with all things in the Navy, there is a proper way to do everything. The Navy's way of announcing the arrival of the food truck over the 1MC system was "The Mobile Canteen is on the pier." Being bored, I decided to deviate from the norm. I announced, "the roach coach has made its approach." Throughout the ship, the crew laughed hysterically; however, the Officer of the Day was not amused. I was written up, a disciplinary action usually resulting in being restricted to the ship for three days. No liberty for three days was a typical punishment.

As my watch was ending, I saw Towles approaching the ship with his wife and sister. The closer they got to the ship, the more I could not believe my eyes. Towles' sister was stunning. *How could both Towles and this beautiful creature come from the same gene pool? Is this biologically possible? What else in the universe has something grotesque and something beautiful coming from the same source? A gargoyle and an angel can both adorn the same cathedral. Bitter-sweet.*

"Permission to come aboard," Towles said.

Not waiting for the Officer of the day to respond, I said, "Permission granted. And this must be your sister, Debbie. My name is Cal, as in Calvin. Welcome to Florida, and welcome to the *USS Charles F. Adams*. We call her the Charlie Deuce since her hull number is two. How was your flight?"

"It was good. I am happy to meet you, Cal,"

"Hey, I am getting off watch in ten minutes. May I give you a private tour of our ship?"

"I would like that," Debbie said.

My personally guided tour lasted over an hour, but Towles and his wife did not mind. They were delighted Debbie was having an enjoyable time and they would not have to entertain her during the week she was visiting.

The next day I was invited to the Towles' home for dinner. I dodged a bullet when I stood before the XO for my creative announcement about the "roach coach," and was given a verbal warning not to deviate from the Navy way of doing things. Dinner at Towles' place was on.

Over dinner, the conversation came easily, and the evening passed quickly. Towles told me it was late, and he would rather not have to take me back to the ship. His wife brought me some bed sheets, a blanket and a pillow so I could sleep on the couch. Towles and his wife excused themselves and retired for the evening. Debbie and I remained on the couch, talking and laughing.

The next morning, Debbie and I were naked and in an embrace when Towles woke me up.

"Lloyd, it is time to get up. We have to leave for the ship in 30 minutes."

It took me a few seconds to remember where I was and to assess the situation. I felt embarrassed. *Should I apologize? Should I pretend nothing happened? I cannot believe we fell asleep! Hey, we are two grown-ups. It is not my fault. Crap, this is more than awkward.*

Debbie gathered her clothes and frantically put them on under the bed sheet as Towles was in the kitchen making coffee.

"Please give me your address before I leave this morning," I whispered to Debbie. "Just in case I don't see you before you leave to go home, I want to make sure we stay in touch. I had a wonderful evening. Thank you."

"I did, too," Debbie answered as she grabbed the bed sheets and left the room. A few minutes later she returned with a piece of paper in her hand. "Here is my address. Please write to me."

"I will."

There was minimal conversation on the ride back to the ship. Nothing was said about how the morning began. Not then, not ever.

It was common for the *Adams* to get underway for a week of sea-ops. The ship would sail up and down the coast of Florida and Georgia, performing drills in preparation for the upcoming cruise. On this particular day, the crew was told we were only going out for the day. To most of the crew, it did not seem worth the trouble to go out to sea and back to port in one day, that is, until they received clarification from their Department Officers. Several civilians were seen boarding the ship before it left port. Soon after they boarded, a flag-draped coffin was carried aboard and placed respectfully on the fantail. There would be a burial at sea.

"Who is in the box?" I asked Dakota, as we both stared at the coffin.

"It isn't some young guy who was on active duty. Someone said it is a Master Chief. He died of old age. Ever think when and how you will die?"

"I try not to, but yeah, I do at times. Especially at funerals."

The ship sailed east till the skyline of Jacksonville evaporated into the sea. A Navy chaplain escorted the family to the fantail. Five Gunner's Mates in their dress whites stood at attention with their M16s resting on their right shoulders. Two other sailors stood at attention by the head of the casket. The family, CO and XO were all seated facing the port side of the ship. Dakota and I could not hear what the chaplain was saying, but it was obvious to us he was reading from the Scriptures.

Neither Dakota nor I ever witnessed a burial at sea. We were mesmerized by what we saw and impressed with the precision of our shipmates. The flag was folded and handed to the woman we assumed was the deceased man's wife. The two sailors standing by the casket lifted the board beneath the head of the casket so it could slide off into the ocean. The five Gunner's Mates proceeded with a 21-gun salute.

"Do you know why they chose 21-gun blasts instead of another number?" asked Dakota.

"No, but I'm sure you'll tell me."

"The 21-gun salute stands for the sum of the numbers in the year 1776."

"Now, that is very cool. Didn't know that. I have one for you. Do you know why the flag is folded in a specific way?"

"Well," Dakota said, thinking it was quite obvious. "There are 13 folds, so I guess that represents the 13 original colonies."

"Wrong-o, my little friend. Have a seat. School is in session.'

"Oh, boy! Here we go," snickered Dakota.

"It actually embodies the principles upon which this country was founded. One nation, under God. The first fold of the flag is a symbol of life. The second fold is a symbol of the belief in eternal life. The third fold is made in honor and remembrance of the veterans departing the ranks who gave a portion of their lives for the defense of the country to attain peace throughout the world."

"By the way, that coffin isn't sinking," I said as my eyes were transfixed on the bobbing brown box.

"It will," said Dakota. "Go on. What does the fourth fold represent?"

"The fourth fold represents the weaker nature, for as American citizens trusting in God, it is to Him we turn in times of peace as well as in time of war for His divine guidance. The fifth fold is a tribute to our country, for in the words of Stephen Decatur, 'Our Country, in dealing with other countries, may she always be right; but it is still our country, right or wrong.' The sixth fold represents where people's hearts lie. It is with their heart they pledge allegiance to the flag of the United States of America, and the Republic for which it stands, 'one Nation under God, indivisible, with Liberty and Justice for all.' The seventh fold is a tribute to its Armed Forces, for it is the Armed Forces that protect our country and our flag against all her enemies, whether they be found within or without the boundaries of our republic. The eighth fold is a tribute to the one who entered into the valley of the shadow of death, that we might see the light of day."

I interrupted myself to say, "The coffin still isn't sinking. Look, they are leading the family inside the skin of the ship."

"They can't let that thing bob across the ocean like a message in a bottle, can they?" asked Dakota.

"If they do, someone is going to get a pretty disturbing message when they open that box!" I replied.

"Okay, the ninth fold is a tribute to womanhood, and mothers. For it has been through their faith, their love, loyalty, and devotion that the character of the men and women who have made this country great has been molded. The tenth is a tribute to the father, for he, too, has given his sons and daughters for the defense of their country since they were first born. The eleventh fold represents the lower portion of the seal of King David and King Solomon and glorifies in the Hebrews eyes, the God of Abraham, Isaac, and Jacob. The twelfth fold represents an emblem of eternity and glorifies, in Christian's eyes, God the Father, the Son and Holy Spirit, and, drum roll, please."

Dakota obliged, offering his verbal rendition of a drum roll of the tongue.

"The thirteenth and when the flag is completely folded, the stars are uppermost, reminding us of our nation's motto, 'In God We Trust.'"

"Not too shabby!" Dakota said. "I am impressed, and I am not easily impressed. Cal, you are a walking encyclopedia."

The conversation was interrupted by a barrage of gunfire.

"Crap, they are trying to put holes in that casket so it will sink!" I said.

"Damn! No wonder they wanted the family out of there," responded Dakota. Changing the subject he said, "Hey, they are serving chow. I'm hungry. Let's go grab a bite."

While standing in line for chow, Seaman Jackson, a nasty S.O.B., decided to butt in line, just in front of Dakota and me. Jackson was built like a fire hydrant, short and thick, with a body as hard as cast iron. In his youth, Jackson lifted more weights than he had books.

"Leaning over to me, Dakota whispered, "That bar stool is missing a leg."

"You're telling me," I whispered back. "He is squirrely."

Hating injustice, and not giving it any thought, I turned to Jackson and said, "Get in the back of the line like everyone else, Jackson."

Jackson turned around and hit me hard in the center of my chest. I gasped for air as I could hear mild laughter coming from a few of the witnesses in line. Jackson smiled, showing his front gold tooth, then turned back to his friend as if nothing had happened. No one challenged Jackson. No one! I am sure some of the sailors were thinking I would be a fool to take on this beast.

"Are you alright?" whispered Dakota. "Jackson is an animal."

It took a while till I could catch my breath. My chest ached, but the embarrassment of being crippled by one punch hurt more. On the mess deck, we filled our trays and found somewhere to sit. My thoughts were consumed with what had just happened.

I have been picked on all my childhood, from an abusive stepmother to ridicule of teachers, to being the target of the neighborhood bully, I always found myself swimming upstream. But unlike the salmon, who do so to ensure the survival of their offspring, I did it for self-preservation. Now that I have graduated from "Raw Deal U" with a degree in Street Smarts, I am never going to put up with anyone's shit ever again.

"Hey, Cal, do you have any leave left?" Dakota asked.

"Hold that thought," I said as I stood up and walked over to where Seaman Jackson was sitting. Without any warning, I threw the hardest punch I could marshal, and landed it squarely on Jackson's mouth, causing him to fall backwards onto the deck.

"Now we are even," I said as I walked back to Dakota.

Jackson's mouth was bleeding profusely as he crawled on his hands and knees trying to find the gold tooth I had knocked out.

"Shit, Cal! You are freakin' crazy!"

"Yeah, I know. Now, what were you asking me?"

"Damn! I forgot. Oh, whether you have any of your leave left for the year."

"Yeah, I have two weeks left. Why?"

"Well, it is fall, and in South Dakota fall means elk hunting. Want to take a week and go home with me. I have an extra rifle."

"Absolutely, but I don't want a gun. I want to use a bow."

"Bow? So this city boy is an archer? You never stop amazing me."

CHAPTER EIGHT

A s the plane approached the airport I could see Black Elk Peak, the second highest point east of the Rocky Mountains. The plane touched down at the exact time the sun did. It had taken the entire day, three airplanes and two connections to arrive in South Dakota. Rapid City Regional Airport was insignificant compared to Philadelphia International, the airport closest to where I grew up.

Dakota's sister came to pick us up. She was blonde and slender, with an athletic build. She wore her hair in braids which, along with her black and yellow checked flannel shirt, made her look like the farm girl she was. She had the kind of natural beauty that required no makeup.

"Hey there, Ronnie," she said as she threw her arms around Dakota's neck, giving him a peck on his cheek.

"Ronnie?" I asked.

"Cal, this is my sister Rhonda, and don't even think about it," Dakota said.

"Ron and Rhonda? How funny. Hi, happy to meet you, Rhonda. Dakota never told me he had such a beautiful sister."

"Hello Cal," Rhonda said with an approving smile. "I hear you boys are going after elk."

"Yes! I really have been looking forward to this."

"Well, you have come to the right place."

The three of us got into the Ford Bronco and began the 45-minute drive to Dakota's farm. When we arrived at the farm, Dakota's mother had dinner waiting for us. After eating, both Dakota and I were exhausted. We would be getting up very early the next day, so we decided to have one last beer and call it a night.

The next morning we woke up to the smell of coffee and bacon sizzling in a large iron skillet. Dakota's mother stood by the stove in her housecoat and slippers, cracking eggs and standing watch over a pan of home fries.

"You didn't have to get up and make us breakfast, Mrs. Womack," I said, even though I was delighted she had.

"You boys cannot go hunting all day on an empty stomach. I also made you sandwiches."

"Thank you. That was truly kind of you."

"Good morning," Dakota said as he entered the room. "Cal, my dad borrowed his cousin's bow for you. After breakfast we'll go out to the barn so you can get used to it. We have plenty of bales of hay you can shoot into."

We finished eating and headed to the barn. Dakota handed me the Jennings Model T compound bow his father borrowed. I marveled at the design of the bow. The compound bow concept was still relatively new, and I shot only recurve bows. Dakota placed a bale of hay on top of another and fastened a small rag in the middle as a target.

"This thing is beautiful," I said. "The arrow travels at a much higher speed with these compound bows than a recurve."

I notched an arrow into the string, pulled it back to my ear, took aim, and released it. The arrow landed flawlessly in the middle of the rag.

"Oh, this baby is unbelievable. Let's go get ourselves an elk!"

After a few more practice shots, Dakota and I threw our backpacks and the game cart into the bed of the truck and headed toward the foothills of the mountains. It was still dark when we reached the spot where we would hunt. The air was chilly and felt even colder to me having spent the past year in subtropical Florida. There would be plenty of hiking ahead of us to warm us as we would need to get relatively close to where the elk were located.

"Listen," Dakota whispered. "Hear that?"

A bugling sound echoed down from a wooded hillside. "I did," I answered.

"That is a bull elk. They are in rut. He is advertising his fitness to cow elk and to show off to other bulls he is a stud. It tells the other boys to back off. Once the sun rises, we are not going to hear much of that. It came from up there. Let's try to get closer." Dakota shone his flashlight low, so he would not alert the elk. Quietly, we climbed the steep hillside. We entered a heavily wooded area and stopped at a large fallen tree.

"Position yourself between those two limbs. You will have enough cover there. I am going over to the wood's edge. I will have a broader view and can take much longer shots than you, since I have a rifle. Good luck!" Dakota said as he walked into the darkness.

With each bugle I heard, the faster my heart beat. One bugle kept getting closer. Twilight arrived, and I began to see through the trees. A northern saw-whet owl flew low and close to where I was sitting. A soft swooshing sound followed the owl. Soon, the chirps and songs by other birds filled the air, announcing the arrival of the sun.

A slight movement off at a distance caught my attention. I froze, keeping my eyes fixed on something I could not quite make out. Within minutes, I was sure it was either a large deer or an elk. Whatever it was, it was much larger than the white-tailed deer of Pennsylvania, and this cervid had much larger antlers. The animal changed its direction and headed down a path close to where I was hiding. I realized it was a mule deer, a nice buck with a symmetric rack, four points on either side. I pulled back my bow and aimed. I had a clear shot but decided not to take the deer. I came to South Dakota for an elk.

By mid-morning, I saw nothing else, besides an abundance of squirrels and chipmunks and one American pygmy shrew that crawled across my pant leg. Suddenly, a gunshot disrupted the silence. Then another shot rang out. *Had Dakota killed an elk?* Within minutes, a harem of cow elk trotted through the woods looking for cover from their two-legged predator. I carefully watched them trot by me. None of them was worth taking a shot; I was waiting, and hoping, for a bull elk with a respectable rack. My patience paid off.

The gang of cow elk kept looking back over their shoulders, an indication something was behind them that demanded their attention. It could have been the fear of the gunfire, but I knew from my years of whitetail hunting a male was most probably tailing them. Bucks and bull elk are smart; let the female make sure the coast is clear before proceeding. That may sound cowardly to the non-wildlife person, but this is actually a way to ensure the breed's long-term survival. One bull can service 20-40 cows.

Suddenly, an impressive bull elk appeared between some ponderosa pine trees. An elk's eyesight is not very good and, although they have good hearing, they make enough noise when they walk through a forest. It is their nose that guides the elk. They always travel into the wind so they can sense danger ahead of them. The mountain winds flowed downhill in the evening when the air cooled. The elk fed themselves down low during the night and were heading back uphill at morning light with the wind in their face. The bull came closer, calculatingly. Its rack was a beautiful 6 x 6.

When the elk was within 30 yards, it lowered its head to eat something. Although elk do not eat the needles of ponderosa pines, they do feed on the understory species. When its head was down, I took the opportunity to pull the bowstring back. I held the string back for what seemed like an hour, waiting for the elk to lift his head and turn back to its right. The elk obliged, giving me a perfect broadside view. I released the arrow and saw it enter just below the elk's shoulder, where both the heart and lungs are located. The elk jumped awkwardly, then ran off, beyond my sight. A stomping sound from the direction the elk came gained my attention. It was Dakota.

"Hey, was that you who fired twice?"

"Yeah. Something spooked them, and they ran across the field just below me. It was a pretty far shot, but I thought I would give it a try. I didn't hit anything," Dakota said.

"Well, I did," I said, while I maneuvered myself out of the fallen tree. "Over there."

We walked over to where the elk was hit. Blood and tissue could be found on a low hanging limb of a tree. "There is a blood trail!"

"Wow! Excellent! You freakin' bagged an elk with a bow! You are the man!" Dakota said with unbridled excitement.

I smiled. "It has been thirty minutes since it was hit. Let's follow the blood trail."

Small spots of blood could be found on dried leaves, twigs, and stones. Every so often we came across a pool of blood. We knew the elk could not have gone very far. About 40 yards from where I took the shot, we found the fletching and nock end of the broken arrow. We walked another 75 yards and found the elk lying in a small ravine. Dakota gave it a kick with his boot. It was dead.

Dakota pulled a small camera from his backpack and took several pictures of me posing with my trophy. It took several hours for us to field-dress and quarter the elk. While I was finishing the task, Dakota went back to the truck to retrieve the game cart. After we loaded the cart with the boned meat, we each took a handle and began the slow trek back to the truck. Thankfully, most of the trek was downhill. By the time we reached Dakota's farm, it was dark.

While we were taking our showers and changing clothes, Dakota's mother cut some thick steaks from the elk's loin and started preparing a feast for the two of us. We were famished. She served the elk steaks with a wild gooseberry sauce that complimented the wild game perfectly. That is how the day had been, perfect!

A week after Dakota and I returned to our ship, it set sail for Charleston, South Carolina in early November for ammo on-load. All available crew spent the day carrying 5-inch shells and powder casings for the rumored Mediterranean cruise. Gunner-mates were busy loading missiles aboard for the Tarter surface-to-air missile system. I noticed the all-white jumpers they wore, something unusual.

The scuttlebutt was made official when word came from the Captain that the *Adams* would, indeed, leave Mayport for a 7-month Mediterranean cruise on December 26. Although the married sailors were never happy about a long deployment, they were ecstatic they would be able to spend Christmas with their families. Holidays were always difficult for sailors far from home. When the ship was at its home port, the married sailors were able to spend it with loved ones. The single sailors suffered the most.

There were only a few holidays difficult for me to spend alone on the ship. Thanksgiving was one of them. No telling what kind of bird the cooks would serve up. Maybe seagulls or, if we were *lucky,* turkey log. There is not enough cranberry sauce in America to make a turkey log edible. Dakota was on the fence as to whether or not he should accept an invitation for Thanksgiving Day dinner from Patty, a girl he started dating. The dilemma was that the dinner would be at Patty's parents' house.

Having a home cooked Thanksgiving Day feast when away from home is incredibly attractive. Problem is, when one has dinner at a girl's parents' house there is an unspoken edict that the relationship is serious. If Dakota was to meet her parents, then both Patty and her folks might hear wedding bells. This relationship was not serious, at least not for Dakota, but since the *Adams* would be leaving for seven months, Dakota decided to accept the dinner invitation. The long absence from Patty would be an acceptable excuse why the relationship did not work out. That left me with little to no options. That is, until Lt. Kiggans approached me.

"Lloyd, what are your plans for Thanksgiving?"

"To be honest with you, sir, I am trying not to think of it. The thought of eating Thanksgiving on the ship is frightening. Maybe I'll fill up on potatoes and gravy and watch some football; that is, if they can pipe it into the berthing compartment," I said.

"How would you like to join my wife and I for dinner tomorrow? We do not have any children, and my wife is an excellent cook. Problem is, she doesn't know how to cook a turkey for two people, or three, for that matter. If your large appetite doesn't join us, I'll be eating leftovers for a month," the lieutenant said with a chuckle.

"That would be great, sir! Thank you!"

"Good," said the lieutenant. "I'll pick you up in front of the ship at noon."

The next day the lieutenant pulled up in his dark blue corvette. I thought about the pay difference between Kiggans and me. *It certainly is a lot better being an officer in the Navy than an enlisted squid!*

Although the lieutenant could have settled for base housing, he and his wife elected to live off base. It was a short ride as the lieutenant pulled up to the rented yellow and white ranch house. Red and white flowers lined the driveway, and several pigmy palms gave a Floridian-look to the well-manicured lawn. When we entered the house, I was surprised to see a Chinese woman standing over the stove. At first, it did not register to me that this woman was Kiggan's wife. The woman turned around, put the wooden spoon down, and wiped her hands on her apron. With a big smile, she said, "You must be Calvin Lloyd. Welcome! My name is Hua. If that is hard for you to pronounce, you can call me Rose. Hua means flower."

"Hello. No, Hua is fine. Thank you for inviting me to join you and the lieutenant for Thanksgiving. It is very kind of you," I said.

"When we are in my house, you call me Mark. Don't you dare call me that outside of here. Got that," he said with a smile.

"Yes, sir. I mean, Mark," I said, returning the smile.

While Hua was cooking dinner, the conversation covered several topics, including where and how Hua and Mark met. Lt. Kiggans was stationed in Saigon during the Vietnam conflict. He served as a Naval Intelligence Liaison Officer, whose primary duty entailed gathering intelligence on North Vietnamese and Viet Cong combat units and strongholds and the movement of supplies in the Mekong Delta. While serving in that role, he met Hua who worked in her father's small restaurant just off base. After Hua married Lt. Kiggans, she came to the States, became a citizen, and got a job as an Operations Research Analyst to the Assistant Secretary of Defense for Networks and Information Integration.

Hua called me into the kitchen to demonstrate how to velvet chicken.

"If you hang around Hua too much, you will have to change your rate from EW/CT to cook!" the lieutenant said with a chuckle.

"I would end up eating half of what I would make, so that's probably not a good idea," I said.

"Let's watch some football while the chef finishes preparing dinner," the lieutenant said. "The Bills are playing the Lions."

I followed the lieutenant into the living room. As we sat on the couch, I could not help but think of the odd match Hua and the lieutenant are. Hua was a delightful lady, but one with unalluring looks. A large mole on her forehead made it difficult for my eyes not to concentrate on it whenever I looked at her. It was not that she was ugly, so much, as it was that she was not nearly as attractive as the lieutenant was. It happens that way in love sometimes. Love has no boundaries, no rules.

The universe always prefers a balance of attractiveness, as if there were some unwritten etiquette. The scale is tipped awkwardly when one of the couple is much more attractive than the other. It throws the universe off balance, and it gives others the false impression they would have had a chance at catching an extremely attractive man or woman. It throws the entire well-being of happy relationships off kilter. People begin questioning whether they had "settled" for their partner. They wonder if they had exercised patience, they would have ended up with a more attractive mate. It is, really, quite a terrible thing, but apparently, the lieutenant was happy with Hua, and I guess that was enough of an explanation. It showed the integrity the lieutenant has. He was not shallow like most men. He saw beneath the outward appearance of Hua and fell in love with her inner beauty and talents. She may have been "plain," but she was also one helluva chef.

Hua prepared a feast which was nothing short of a culinary delight. Besides the traditional turkey, stuffing, and sweet potatoes, she prepared a few Vietnamese delicacies. The culinary festivities began with some Hors d'Oeuvres which included homemade spring rolls.

"These are called nem rán," Hua told me.

"Honey, spring rolls will do. Cal can speak Ukrainian, but I do not think Vietnamese was part of his linguistic studies," the lieutenant said.

"That's okay. I enjoy learning about other cultures and learning a few new words and phrases. You never know when I might be able to use them," I said.

"Well, there are several Vietnamese restaurants near the larger Navy bases around the country. There is one in Jacksonville, near the Naval Air Station. You can order in Vietnamese and impress your friends," the lieutenant said.

The Thanksgiving appetizer was Mì Quảng, part soup, part salad that included bright yellow noodles infused with turmeric and peanut oil. I especially liked the Bánh Căn, savory bite-sized pancakes made from a combination of rice batter, a cracked quail egg, and green onions. For dessert, Hua made good old fashioned American Apple Pie.

"Hua, this apple pie is incredible. Johnny Appleseed would be proud!" I said.

"Who is this Johnny Appleseed?" asked Hua.

"He is an American legend. In the early 1800s, Johnny was an American pioneer nurseryman who introduced apple trees to large parts of Pennsylvania, my home state, as well as Ohio, Indiana, Illinois, and West Virginia."

"Is this man true or fable?"

"True. He really existed," I said.

"This reminds me of a Chinese story my mother used to tell me as a child. Have you ever heard the story of the Five Chinese Brothers?"

"Hua," interrupted the lieutenant. "Cal does not want to hear old Chinese bedtime stories."

"No, lieutenant. I mean, Mark. I love stories that originated in other cultures," I said.

"Good," said Hua, giving her husband a "see, I knew Cal would be interested in a story from my heritage" look accompanied with a smile. "Calvin, this is not a true story, but it was always one of my favorites. 'The Five Chinese Brothers' is actually an American adaptation of the Chinese folktale, 'Ten Brothers.'"

"Once upon a time, in the Imperial China of the Qing dynasty, there were five brothers who all looked exactly alike. Each was given a special talent. The first brother could swallow the sea, the second had an unbreakable iron neck, the third could stretch his legs to astonishing lengths, the fourth was immune to burning, and the fifth could hold his breath forever. The five brothers lived with their mother by the sea."

'The first brother was a fisherman and was able to catch exceptional fish that sold very well at the local market. It gave his family a comfortable living. One day, he agreed to let a young boy accompany him on his fishing trip. He was able to hold the entire sea in his mouth allowing the boy to fetch fish and other sea treasures like sea glass, shark's teeth, sand dollars, and starfish from the seabed. When the first brother could no longer hold in the sea, he frantically signaled for the boy to return to shore, but the boy ignored him. The man was forced to expel the water which caused the boy to drown."

"The first brother returned home where he was accused of murder. The judge sentenced him to death; however, his four identical brothers came to his rescue by assuming his identity at four separate attempts to execute him. They each were able to deceive the judge by convincing him to allow them to go home and bid farewell to their mother before each execution was administered."

"Due to each of their special talents, the brothers cannot be executed. The second brother, with his iron neck, cannot be beheaded. The third brother, with his special talent allowing him to stretch his legs all the way to the bottom of the ocean, cannot drown. The fourth brother, with his immunity to burning, is unscathed at the stake, and the fifth brother, with his ability to hold his breath, survives overnight in an oven full of whipped cream. Finally, the judge decides since the man survived all four attempts to execute him, he must have been innocent. The man is released, and all five brothers and their mother live happily ever after."

"I love it!" I said. "Perhaps a little dark, but I love it!"

"Ah, that story has always been my favorite," Hua said.

"Well, Cal, I should be getting you back to the ship," the lieutenant said.

"Hua, I cannot thank you enough for the pleasant day. I thought I was going to have a miserable day onboard the ship, but you and the lieutenant made this a wonderful day. I really appreciate it."

"You are very welcome, Calvin. Have a safe cruise and make sure my husband does not get into any trouble," Hua said with a laugh.

"I promise," I said.

It was dark when I returned to the nearly abandoned ship. There was only a skeleton crew aboard for the holiday. Seaman Jackson was on the stern contemplating some sort of evil. He gave me an ominous look and spit a brown gob of snuff over the side of the ship. I went down to my berthing compartment where I grabbed a towel and a bar of soap and headed for the showers.

After my shower, I laid on my rack, reviewing the events of the day. The lieutenant and his wife could not have treated me better. Even though Petty Officer Braun was trying to make my life a living hell aboard the ship, friends like Dakota and Lieutenant Kiggans made my life enjoyable.

CHAPTER NINE

A few days before Christmas, the sailors who were single, appeared even more anxious than normal for mail call. The entire crew was hoping for letters and goodies from home. To my delight, I received a care package from Debbie that included Rice Krispie marshmallow treats, a package of red licorice, and a cassette tape, a verbal love letter. I opened the Rice Krispie treats and ate one. The sweet gooeyness was my culinary dream come true and a dentist's nightmare. Before I could realize it, LPO Braun picked up the box of Rice Krispie treats, and passed them around to the other sailors.

"Here Boys. Lloyd is one generous S.O.B.," he announced with that cackle of his.

The box returned to me empty. I enjoyed only one of the squares.

"What the hell, Braun?" I said.

"I thought you w-w-w-wanted to share, Lloyd," Braun said. "You weren't thinking of h-h-h-hoarding them all for yourself, w-w-w-ere you?"

"As a matter of fact, yes I was, dickhead," I said as I walked out of the compartment.

Christmas came and went with little fanfare for Dakota and me. Both of us decided to make some extra cash by subbing for married guys who were scheduled for duty. For an extra $50, we willingly stood watch. The next day we would be leaving Mayport for the Mediterranean, a cruise that would forever change my life.

The *Adams* slowly pulled away from the pier in Mayport with dozens of wives and girlfriends in tears, waving to their sailor who they would not see for seven months. No wonder sailors have the highest divorce rate. Maintaining a healthy relationship can be difficult enough without being separated for seven months.

The ship proceeded down the St. Johns River and into the Atlantic as her sonar attracted a pod of dolphins which escorted us out to sea. They took turns jumping and surfing the bow wave and the wake created by the ship.

I was not assigned to watch, so I took my portable radio-cassette player and turned on the Jacksonville radio station WAIV-FM. The WAVE, as it is fondly called, plays rock and roll. A *Foreigner* song just ended when the disc jockey announced that *Styx*, my favorite group, just released a new album entitled *The Grand Illusion*. The disc jockey then began playing a song from that album, *Come Sail Away*.

It doesn't get better than this! We are heading to a variety of countries where I have never been. I am going to be able to use my skill set and demonstrate my expertise to impress the brass! Dolphins put on a dance recital that deserved a standing ovation, and Styx wrote the perfect song to send us on our way. Sometimes, although rare, a day can be absolutely beyond compare!

By the second day at sea, the *Adams* joined other ships that became Task Force 60.2, which consisted of one aircraft carrier, the *USS Saratoga*, two guided missile cruisers, four guided missile destroyers, and a supply ship. Once she entered the Straits of Gibraltar, the *Adams* would join the Sixth Fleet which operated as part of United States Naval Forces Europe-Africa.

By day three at sea, the water began to change, and not for the better. The size of the waves doubled within a few hours. A tropical depression formed off the coast of the Cape Verdean islands of West Africa, which was a bit unusual for late December. Because hurricane season officially ends at the end of November, the two star admiral of the task force was not overly concerned. The thought was it would fall apart once it got out to sea, but that is not what happened.

The tropical storm became problematic when it took an abrupt turn north and the winds increased to 48 mph. The *Adams* was the smallest of the ships in the task force and, although it was tossed about in the storm, it maneuvered quite well. The fourth day crossing the Atlantic, however, concern turned to anxious worry when the task force, attempting to outrun the storm, found itself smack in the middle of a class 2 hurricane with winds exceeding 100 mph.

On the mess decks, we were served what would be the last hot meal for several days. The tossing of the ship made it impossible to cook, and the thought of cooks in the kitchen carrying sharp knives while desperately trying to keep upright was enough reason to shut it down. I knew lunch meat sandwiches, dry cereal, apples and potato chips would be breakfast, lunch and dinner till the hurricane passed.

There was no chow line when I got to the mess deck, and only a handful of sailors were eating dinner. Highly unusual, but an increasing number of the crew was seasick. Even Dakota, who never got sick at sea, retired to his rack after he announced he was not feeling well. Dinner consisted of spaghetti with meat sauce, garlic bread, tossed salad, and some undefinable cookie for dessert. I filled my tray and took a seat at one of the empty tables. Minutes later, a redheaded Operations Specialist sat at the same table. When I said hello to the sailor, I noticed that unmistakable green tint in the man's face. Before I had a chance to ask if he was alright, the sailor violently leaned forward sending the forceful retrograde expulsion of gastric contents across the table. I promptly lifted my tray, which had avoided the yellow wave, and found another table.

Green water was flowing over the flight deck of the *Saratoga*, some fifty feet above the surface of the ocean. Communication received on the *Adams* in the middle of the night reported a F-14 Tomcat secured on the flight deck of the *Saratoga*, was ripped off the ship and thrown into the sea by a gargantuan wave. Aboard the *Adams*, the Captain ordered anyone not on watch, to strap himself into his rack. Even though as sailors we established sea legs, adapting to the ship's movements in this kind of storm was impossible. Water poured through the ventilation system flooding the berthing compartment with a few feet of water.

I laid on my rack, feeling the ship's pitch against the waves. As the ship curtseyed to each massive wave, fifty feet of water covered the ship's bow, submerging it into the sea. There were times when the ship pitched drastically to one side, and would pause, for what seemed like forever, before pitching to the other side. With each drastic pitch, I was certain the ship would capsize.

It was dark and stormy for days, but the next morning it was the proverbial calm after the storm. The prodigal sun finally made its appearance like a reluctant groundhog peeking its head out of its hole. I walked outside the skin of the ship and looked across the expanse of the ocean. Nothing but blue water as far as the eye could see. There were no landmarks to judge the distance traveled, or how close the destination. My thoughts swirled like a tidal basin. My anticipation of the unknown acted like the gravitational forces exerted on the tides by the moon. I was running from my past, but like gazing out at the sea, the future looked too much like the past. This new road trip in my life had just begun, and the road ahead was going to be full of potholes.

After seven days crossing the Atlantic, land was spotted at the horizon. It took two days longer to reach Spain, due to the hurricane. The *Adams* approached a narrow peninsula that formed the Bay of Cádiz as it approached Naval Station Rota. The port city, founded in 1100 BC as a Phoenician trading colony, became an important geographical U.S. Navy base which gave support for U.S. and NATO ships, and provided safe and efficient movement of U.S. Navy ships and aircraft in the European theater of operations.

Several ships within the task force needed to go into the Rota shipyard for repairs because of damage caused by the hurricane, nautical hell. As a result, the needed repairs put the task force in a difficult position. We were minus two ships. The last thing anyone wanted.

After the nightmarish ordeal of crossing the Atlantic, everyone aboard the ship was more than ready for mail call. Unfortunately, before we could open mail, we had a more pressing need. Once the

Adams was moored in Rota, all hands were on deck to help replenish supplies. Large fuel lines were dragged from the pier to refuel the ship, as the majority of the crew carried boxes of food and other supplies aboard the ship. The replenishment took the better part of the morning.

When the crew finished carrying the last crate aboard the ship, they gathered around the Postal Clerk as he began calling out names. The longer a sailor waited without his name being called, the more he feared there was no mail for him. When it came to girlfriends left behind in the States, the last thing anyone wanted was for the "out of sight, out of mind" thing to become a reality. When I heard my name called, I hoped it was something from Debbie, but it was from my sister. More names were read. Then, the PC held a shoebox-sized box and said, "Lloyd!" Debbie had not let me down.

I was mindful of the swarm of locusts that devoured the last care package I received from Debbie. That would not happen this time. I could feel the dozen or more sets of eyes focusing on my box of treasures, like a coalition of cheetahs eyeing a gazelle. I stood with my back to the corner and slowly opened the box. There was a letter from Debbie that I stuck in my pocket; I would read it later. I then pulled out a cassette tape of Styx's new album I never would have been able to purchase overseas. *Debbie remembered how much I love Styx!* Finally, I removed a stack of Rice Krispie squares covered in saran wrap and a smoked kielbasa. I knew these food items were open prey.

"Hey, Cal. Are you g-g-g-going to share?" Braun said, laughing as he walked toward Cal.

"Sure," Cal said. "But first, I need to anoint the food."

"Anoint?" asked Braun.

A few more sailors joined the gathering in the berthing compartment like a cackle of hyenas, licking their lips in preparation for a free meal. With all eyes focused on me and my box of goodies, I dropped my drawers, pulled out my cyclops, and began touching all the food items with it.

"That is disgusting!" Braun said. "You are s-s-s-sick!"

I threw back my head and laughed hysterically. "Now, does anyone want a Rice Krispie square? A slice of kielbasa?"

The crowd dispersed.

CHAPTER TEN

T he next day Dakota and I had liberty, and we were more than excited to explore Spain. Neither of us had been to a foreign country, except Canada. We walked down the pier with no specific plans. There was no place we had to be. It was the true definition of liberty for two young single sailors who yearned for autonomy.

Seaman Jackson was waiting for his drinking buddy. He had no intention of absorbing local culture or historical sites. He would spend his entire liberty drinking at the first bar he could find, and the extent of his experiencing local culture would be to find a Spanish hooker.

"You better watch your back, Lloyd. You, too, farm boy," Jackson said as he took a pinch of snuff and placed it between his cheek and gums.

"Screw off, Jackson," Dakota said as we walked past the boatswain's mate.

Dakota and I walked down the narrow streets taking in the ambiance of the town. Paint peeled off the brightly colored buildings as we investigated the small shops carved out of the oyster stone. Vendors had set up folding tables, selling everything from bienmesabe, a popular adobo-fried fish served in paper cones, to shrimp tortillas. We passed a man shucking fresh oysters as we walked down the El Paseo Maritimo, a boardwalk that runs along Rota's beautiful beach: Playa de la Costilla. This is where the townspeople were. A flurry of people sat at bars and restaurants dining al fresco, while others strolled along the boardwalk.

We grabbed seats at an outside cafe and, after asking the waiter what the locals ate and drank, ordered freshly caught sardines sprinkled with olive oil, and rebujito, an alcoholic punch made with dry fino sherry, lemon soda, mint, and ice.

"I love seafood," Dakota said. "I should become a fish mongrel."

"Monger," I said.

"What?"

"It's a fishmonger. It is not a half fish, half canine, mixed breed."

"Whatever," Dakota said with a relaxed tone.

Dakota and I were in sailor's heaven. Eating fresh seafood, rather than the frozen squares of some unknown fish prepared aboard the ship, having a drink native to the area, and enjoying the aesthetics, highlighted by the beautiful curvy coastline that matched the curves of the beautiful Spanish girls, made the day perfect. The aesthetics, however, were about to improve.

"It doesn't get better than this," Dakota commented.

"Oh, yes it does!" I said with a nod of my head, directing Dakota's sight to two girls who took a seat at the table next to us. In a near whisper, I leaned toward Dakota and said, "She is the most beautiful woman I have ever had the pleasure to rest my eyes on."

"They both are beautiful," Dakota said with a smile.

Polite or not, I stared. I had to. I was transfixed on one of the two girls. Her beauty was so stunning that, although the other girl was very attractive, she appeared mundane compared to my ideal girl.

"I have to speak to her.".

"She's out of your league; besides, she probably doesn't even speak English."

"She is obviously out of my league, but she is out of *everyone's* league! No man alive is worthy of being her escort, let alone husband or boyfriend. If I live to be 100, I will regret not introducing myself to her."

"Go for it," Dakota said with a smile.

The young lady's beauty mesmerized me. She had olive skin, high cheekbones, full lips, and a beautiful body. The young lady's breasts were large, but not overly so, as to be disproportionate to her frame.

"I have to come up with an opening line. It has to be good. I have only one shot at a woman like her. You know…first impressions."

"Well, you better come up with one fast. If you spend the next hour thinking of a come-on line, this beauty and her friend are going to walk away with your fantasy. Hey, I have one for you?"

"Let's hear it."

"You walk up to her and say, excuse me, but did you sit in a pile of sugar? Cause you sure have a sweet ass!" Dakota said, followed by a prodigious belly-laugh.

"Funny," I said, not appreciating Dakota's humor. "How about, heaven must be missing an angel, because you're here with me right now."

"Well, you better hope she has never heard any Tavares songs. If so, she'll shoot you for lack of originality."

"Alright. Wish me luck," I said as I got up from the table and walked towards the girl. *Sometimes one just needs to jump in with both feet and hope the water is warm.*

As I approached the young lady, our eyes met, and she gave me a reassuring smile. That was all the encouragement I needed.

"Hola! Mi nombre es Calvin y ese es todo el español que sé," I said.

Both girls responded with a laugh.

"Well, if that is all the Spanish you know, you may want to take more Spanish lessons," the girl said.

"Okay, since you speak English, I think I will stick with that. My name is Calvin, and my friend over there is Ron."

The gorgeous girl turned to her friend and said something that made her giggle. I had no clue what she said, but my heart sank a bit. This was not going as well as I had hoped.

"My name is Paula, and her name is Lucia. Happy to meet you, Calvin. Did you arrive on that American ship?"

"Yes, I did. We are only going to be here for five days, so I am looking for a tour guide, and I was hoping that might be you," I said with what confidence I still had.

"Me? I do not date sailors. They have a girl in every port and just when the relationship begins to progress, they leave you and go back out to sea," Paula said.

"I do not have a girl in any port. I am very selective."

The girls got up from their table and started walking away. Paula turned her head over her shoulder and said, "Well, Calvin, I hope you find your girl."

I walked back to Dakota.

"Well, that went well, don't you think?"

"She shot you down, huh?"

"She is absolutely stunning. Hey, I gave it a try."

Dakota and I spent the rest of the days exploring the sights and having a great time, but my mind could not shake Paula. Late that night, when I was back on the ship and lying on my rack, this girl consumed my thoughts. *I would give anything to have one more chance to get a date with her. Heck, I would be happy just to gaze into that goddess' face one more time.*

The next day I was scheduled to stand watch, but I paid another sailor to take my place. I was hoping, even though I knew my chances were slim, I would see Paula again. I had no idea where she lived, where she worked, or how I could find her. Regardless of my slim chances, I was going to be prepared if I ever did see her again. *Paula will want to know my motives. If she thinks I simply want to bed her, then jump on my ship and never see her again, she will decline any request. But that is not my motive. What is my motive? Did I fall in love at first sight? I don't even know her!*

Think this through. Be honest. Be kind. Smile. Make her laugh.

Dakota met me on the fantail. We decided to explore the waters of Cadiz Bay by taking a fishing trip. We found a skipper at the local marina and, after several minutes of negotiating an agreeable price, set out to catch some fish. The mid-morning sun was warm and the seas calm. We caught a few croakers and several sea bream, when Dakota hooked into a nice sized pink dentex, a fish unknown to us. The fish is a dark shade of red with black spots, and looks a little like the snapper we catch back in Florida. The skipper told us they are delicious and most of the local restaurants are happy to cook it for us, so when we returned to the marina, we decided to search for a restaurant with the fish in hand.

As we walked through town, we saw a small restaurant with a wooden sign shaped into a fish hanging out front. We thought it was a good omen. Dakota waited outside with the fish, as I went in to see if the chef would cook our fish. The place was completely empty inside, which is not what you want to see when you go into a restaurant in a city where you have never been, but then I realized it was only late afternoon. Spaniards do not eat dinner till at least 2100 hours, 9 o'clock. I heard pots and pans being moved around in the kitchen, so I called out, "Hola!" A nice-looking man in his 40s came out of the kitchen wiping his hands on his apron.

"Sí? Puedo ayudarle?" the man said.

"I'm sorry. My Spanish is poor. Do you speak any English?"

"Yes. How can I help you?"

"My friend and I were fishing in Cadiz Bay today, and we were successful. Would you be willing to cook the fish for us?"

"Yes, of course. Bring the fish into the kitchen."

I went outside to summon Dakota who was busy entertaining a young lady.

"Hey, Romeo. They will cook our fish for us."

"Here," Dakota said, handing me the net bag with the fish. "As you can see, I'm busy."

The man in the restaurant took the bag of fish and held it up and said something in Spanish, then turned to me and said, "This is a lot of fish for two people."

"I know," I said. "Why don't you prepare us the pink dentex, and you can have the other fish for your trouble."

"Ah, you are a generous man. My name is Emiliano. My wife and I own this restaurant. Please come back at nine tonight. You will not be disappointed."

Outside, Dakota was finishing his conversation with the cute senorita. "They will prepare the fish for us, but we need to come back at 2100 hours."

"My stomach will shrink by then," Dakota said. "But that should work. The lovely young lady told me about a discotheque in town that opens about then. We'll have a wonderfully fresh fish dinner and dance the remainder of the night with Spanish mermaids."

"Sounds good. Let's get back to the ship and shit, shower and shave. We'll change our clothes and be back here in plenty of time.

Dakota and I left the ship, passing a line of taxis lined up at the end of the pier. It was a fairly long walk to the center of town, but paying for a taxi meant less money to spend on more important things in town, like dinner and drinks. The activity in town began to increase after looking deserted during the afternoon siesta. When we reached the restaurant where Emiliano was to prepare our fish, the place was already half full. When Emiliano saw us enter, he hurried to greet us.

"Hello, my friends! I have a table reserved for you over here. What would you like to drink?"

We both ordered a beer and sat at the small table. The restaurant crowd was mostly couples, except for three older ladies sitting at a table near us. The table next to us was vacant, but had a RESERVED sign on it. An attractive young lady brought us warm bread and poured olive oil on two small plates.

"Where's the butter?" Dakota asked.

"I think the olive oil is supposed to take the place of butter," I said.

"You're kidding me?"

"Hey, when in Rome…"

I dipped a piece of bread into the olive oil and was surprised how good it tasted. A little while later, Emiliano brought us the pink dentex prepared on skewers with tomatoes, bay leaves and green capsicums. The fish was absolutely delicious. I had just taken another bite of bread when Dakota punched me on the arm and said, "Look who just came into the restaurant!"

I began choking on the bread when I saw Paula's gorgeous face.

"Hey, are you alright?" Dakota said as he slapped me on the back. "She is going to be the death of you!"

"Well, I doubt it. Look who's with her."

A tall, dark, handsome man accompanied Paula. He was dressed well, sported a neatly trimmed beard, and was obviously in great shape. His broad shoulders tapered to a narrow waist. My heart sank faster than a rowboat filled with water.

Paula apparently did not see us as she and her friend sat at the last open table conveniently next to ours. Once seated, she turned and caught me staring at the two of them.

"Are you following me?" Paula asked with a sheepish smile.

"I was going to ask you the same question. We were here first," I replied.

"Alejandro, this is Calvin and his friend…" Paula paused, looking for me to finish her sentence.

"Ron," I said. "But he goes by Dakota."

"They are American sailors," she said.

"I make it a habit not to follow ladies who already have a boyfriend," I stated. "Especially one who is bigger than I am."

Paula and Alejandro laughed.

"Alejandro is not my boyfriend. He is my brother," Paula said with an appealing smile.

My mood had gone from disappointment to pure joy in a matter of seconds.

"Well, that changes everything. You know, this is fate. You are meant to go on a date with me," I said, returning the smile. "Paula, I simply would like to get to know you better. That's all. If you would like to bring Alejandro as a chaperone, that's fine."

Paula laughed. "Well, maybe," she said.

"This is the first time I have been to your lovely country. I am in need of a tour guide…but not any tour guide," I said, trying to draw her in.

"Oh, and what characteristics must this guide have?" Paula asked with that same curious smile.

"Well, the guide cannot be a man. Men do not have the ability to see the nuances of the surroundings. They tend to overlook the little things that make something special or unique. For example, tell me something about that building on the corner over there," I said, pointing to the building across the street.

Paula turned and looked at a nondescript building that had obviously been there a very long time.

"Ah, that building! Sí. That building once was a brothel that catered to sailors, like yourself. A local bishop, under the cloak of darkness, was known to frequent the establishment."

I threw my head back and laughed. "See, this is what I mean. You just shared a tidbit of information which made that old building come to life!"

"What do you mean, tidbit?"

"A tasty morsel. A small piece of information that is juicy."

"And what other personality traits does this tour guide need?"

"Well, she must be a local."

"Of course."

"She must be beautiful, able to speak English, and stand about this tall," I said, offering my hand for Paula to stand.

She responded to my gesture and stood. I then raised my hand to the top of Paula's head. "This tall."

"Go ahead and show him the town," Alejandro said. "His motives seem pure to me."

"Hmmmm," Paula said. "So, must I interview for this position?"

"You just did, and you are hired, my fine lady," I said.

Paula and her brother joined my laughter as Dakota watched in amazement.

"Well, my fine sir, meet me in front of the restaurant where we first met. I will be there at 9 o'clock tomorrow morning for your guided tour."

"I look forward to it." Not wanting to push my luck I added, "I will let the two of you eat your dinner."

I walked back to Dakota who had just paid our bill. He wore the largest smile I ever saw on his face.

"You nailed it!" Dakota whispered. "Damn! She is gorgeous!"

"On a scale from 1-10, she's a 25," I said, as if in a trance.

Dakota walked and I floated as we left the restaurant.

The next day, I arrived at the cafe at 0830 hours. I was not going to be late. The chairs were still upside down on the tables that provided al fresco dining. I sat on a stone wall overlooking the bay, dotted with sailboats. All the fishing boats had gone out for their catch much earlier in the morning leaving only luxury craft in port. The adjacent pier housed supply ships and barges.

I repeatedly checked my watch. When it reached 3 minutes till 9, I began to feel anxious. *Has Paula been playing me? Has she reconsidered?* My worries subsided when I saw her walking toward the cafe. Or was she floating? She wore a blue and white striped nautical off-shoulder swing dress that enhanced her feminine curves.

"Good morning, Calvin," Paula said as she nonchalantly threw her hair back with a nudge.

"Good morning, Paula. You look absolutely lovely," I said with an inviting smile.

"Thank you, as do you. Since you are a sailor, I decided to wear this outfit. Come with me," she said as she took my hand.

We walked down the narrow-cobbled streets past white-washed buildings, passing the 19th-century Cádiz Cathedral and other grand churches. We walked through the Plaza de Abastos, where flowers, fruit and produce were beautifully displayed for purchase. I wanted to purchase a bouquet of flowers for Paula, but I thought better of it. *If I move too fast, I will lose her. Easy does it.*

We stopped at interesting shops and paid a visit to the fish market at the harbor of Pesquero Astaroth. According to Paula, it was known as the most famous fish market on the Cádiz coast. Cannons dating back to the Napoleonic Wars found a new purpose as guardrails, positioned upright on corners to protect buildings from speeding cars. The morning passed quickly. Too quickly.

We walked along the long stone promenade that lines the coast, stopping just to enjoy the view. I turned to Paula and asked, "Is there a place where we can rent a sailboat?"

"Of course. Down there by the yellow building."

"Tomorrow I would like to take you sailing," I said, taking a gamble.

"How romantic!" Paula said with a smile.

We walked some more and stopped at a little cafe and found the last table available. I held Paula's chair for her and watched how she made sitting in a chair an art form. She personified gracefulness. She had the kind of beauty that makes a man feel simple; like he is grateful she allows him to share the same oxygen with her. I did not feel worthy, at least, not yet. Paula never expressed the slightest sign of vanity or superciliousness. She was confident with the absence of haughtiness. *She was perfect!*

"Let me order lunch," Paula said. "The food in this region is the best in all of Spain."

We sat sipping glasses of fruity sangria and watched people walk their dogs along the adjacent park. The waiter came with a large plate of aged ham, and payoyo cheese, made from the milk of a goat unique to the region. Another plate followed with arranque roteño, a dish of mashed tomatoes, green peppers and garlic, and yet another plate of homemade foie-gras served with a sweet jelly, gingerbread, and toast points.

"This is more like dinner than lunch," I said as I took a sip of sangria.

"It *is* our dinner. Our supper is normally a lighter meal, unless someone is going out to eat. Our late meal is much later than your American dinner. Restaurants do not even reopen until 8 o'clock."

I listened, and daydreamed, as Paula spoke. I listened because everything Paula said, no matter how mundane and ordinary, was incredibly interesting to me. I daydreamed because that is what one does when he is living a fairytale. Paula was a goddess among mere humans. I daydreamed about those few instances when gods married mortals. Perseus, son of Zeus (king of the gods), fell in love with the mortal princess Danae. Zeus also had a relationship with Alcmene, a mortal woman, and Zethes, son of Boreas (the Greek god of the cold north wind and the bringer of winter), fell in love with Oreithyia, daughter of King Erechtheus of Athens. I liked my chances.

At 3 pm, the wait-staff began wiping down tables and putting chairs upon them.

"They look like they are closing for the day. It is a bit early for that, isn't it?" I asked.

"Like elsewhere in Spain, Cádiz largely shuts down between 2 o'clock and 5 o'clock for siesta. Time to rest," Paula explained.

"That makes sense."

The remainder of the day seemed like a mirage. When it was time for me to return to the ship, I looked deeply into Paula's eyes, smiled, and deliberately moved towards her lips. I never knew a simple kiss could be so memorable. Our kiss was short and relaxed, soft and deep, firm yet tender. A part of me that was dormant, awakened. It was something much more potent than simply feeling amorous. The kiss spoke volumes. It said, "You make me feel more than happy. I cherish this moment we are experiencing…together."

The weather did not cooperate with our sailing plans. A steady drizzle brought people indoors. The streets were mostly empty, save for a few individuals walking their dogs. I waited inside the cafe where we had agreed to meet.

"Calvin! I am so glad you are here. I was afraid you would not come since it is raining," Paula said. She smelled like fresh gardenias.

"Nothing could have kept me from coming today, Paula. I had a wonderful time yesterday. I don't think sailing is going to happen today."

"No, of course not. Tomorrow we will go sailing. Do you enjoy art?"

I hesitated. I was not a fan of modern art, and I was aware that Picasso was Spanish. I never cared for Picasso and his bizarre "masterpieces." I had to be careful how I answered Paula's question. I wanted to do nothing to push Paula away. My favorite artist is Andrew Wyeth who lived in Chadds Ford, Pennsylvania, an hour from where I grew up. I appreciated the artist's realism style of hardscrabble rural life.

"Oh, yes, I do enjoy art. My favorite American artist is Andrew Wyeth," I said with enthusiasm.

"Andrew Wyeth is highly respected in Spain. The Wyeth family has a wealth of artistic talent flowing through their veins. Andrew was the son of N. C. Wyeth, and father of Jamie Wyeth. All three are wonderful artists."

"How do you know so much about art?"

"My father is an art dealer. I get to travel throughout Europe procuring select pieces for him. Sevilla is only a 90-minute drive from here, and it is a treasure chest of art. Tourists do not realize how artistically rich that area is. Everyone flocks to Barcelona, Madrid or Figueres, but Sevilla has some wonderful art. Would you like to spend the day there since it is raining?"

"But, of course," I said, extending my hand to Paula.

Paula hired a driver, and we headed to Seville. Even in the rain, the scenery was striking. A Mediterranean triad of olive groves, wheat fields, and vineyards dotted the landscape along the way. Once we arrived in Seville, Paula served as the perfect tour guide, of course. She could have taken me to the Siberian mining city of Norilsk, Russia, and I would have enjoyed it. Being with Paula was like a movie that transitions from black and white to color, kindred to *The Wizard of Oz*. She painted my black and white life with brilliant color.

Paula explained that Seville is known for its cultural immersion, flamenco traditions, vibrant festivals, and energy. We spent the morning viewing sculptures. Paula took me to see the 15th century Altarpiece of the Virgin of the Pomegranate, by Andrea della Robia, one of Florence's greatest 15th century artists. From there we went to the San Hermenegildo chapel, site of the remarkable Tomb of Cardinal Cervantes by Lorenzo Mercadante in 1458.

We stepped into a small cafe for lunch where we sipped Vermouth del Grifo as Paula ordered Cazón en Adobo, cubed-sized boneless dogfish, marinated and fried. Montadito de Pringá, a pork sandwich which reminded me of the steak sandwiches I ordered from Jim's Steaks on South Street in Philly, followed. For dessert we had Tortitas de Aceite, a popular pastry made mostly from flour, virgin olive oil, sugar, and different kinds of seeds.

After lunch, Paula showed me the ceiling fresco of Apotheosis of Hercules by Pacheco at The Casa de Pilatos, and the impressive Apotheosis of St Thomas Aquinas by Zurbarán located in the Fine Arts Museum of Seville.

"Who is the greatest Spanish artist?" I asked.

"Most people who are not art enthusiasts would say either Pablo Picasso or Salvador Dalí, and no doubt, they have left their mark on the world, but I believe that Diego Velázquez stands alone as the master of Spanish art. If you love Andrew Wyeth, you will certainly appreciate Velázquez's work, specifically for his mastery of the naturalistic style. Most of his popular pieces are located either in London or Madrid, but there are some fine works by the maestro here. Come, I will show you."

The remainder of the afternoon was dedicated to Velázquez's paintings. Of all the pieces Paula showed me, I especially enjoyed the Portrait of Cristóbal Suárez de Ribera, the robust priest.

"It is too bad that you are not going to be in Spain longer. You really should see Madrid," Paula said.

"Well, I will just have to come back then, won't I?

CHAPTER ELEVEN

The next day provided bright sunshine that glistened off the water. Paula brought a picnic basket and her alluring smile for a day of sailing. She wore a multicolored boho-style dress of red, purple, and yellow. It was backless and strapless, framing a luscious decolletage. The dress had a breezy look pleading for a day of sailing in the Bay of Cádiz.

We walked along the el Paseo Maritimo, the boardwalk that runs along Rota's most beautiful beach, Playa de la Costilla. We passed the cluster of bars and restaurants, hand in hand, while enjoying the flurry of activity, with people walking their dogs, dining al fresco, or strolling down the el Paseo Maritimo.

"Here is the man who will rent you a sailboat," Paula said, pointing to a young, bearded man with an open white linen shirt. "I am sure you must be a wonderful sailor."

I gazed upon the blue and white Mistral 16, a beautiful, 16-foot open dinghy. It was exactly what I imagined, when dreaming of the two of us cutting through the water with Paula's hair dancing in the wind. I am a romantic and a dreamer, but I am also very resourceful. If one can turn his dreams into reality, life can be good, very good. There was, however, one problem with my perfectly planned date. Just because I am in the Navy does not mean I know the first thing about sailing! I had no idea how to sail; a small detail when trying to impress a girl. Just like when I contemplated the challenge of driving a stick on the column, I wondered *how hard can it be?*

The man explained, in excellent English, that the Mistral had a fractional sloop rig, a spooned, slightly raked stem, a plumb transom, and a transom-hung rudder controlled by a tiller and a folding centreboard, all of which meant nothing to me. The man pushed the boat off the beach and waved to us as he shouted, "Adios mis queridos amantes!"

I asked Paula for an explanation. She accommodated with a smile, "Farewell, my dear lovers. Is it that obvious?"

"It must be."

"We are entering laja de la sal," Paula said.

"What is the English translation?"

The best Paula could translate was "the smell of salt."

Getting the sailboat to open water was not a problem. The winds were cooperative, and I handled the sails with erase as we caught the wind which propelled the boat forward. I never realized there is a special connection to nature while sailing. We embraced the sea, feeling the currents move about us. It was another idyllic moment. The wind, the sea, and the most beautiful woman in the world, a wondrous combination, a moment in time I wanted to remain.

The feeling of complete bliss was interrupted by my fear of getting the boat back to the beach. I experimented with ways to turn the boat when the winds did not cooperate. When we left the beach, the wind was coming from behind the boat, pushing against the sail and shoving the boat forward. A few hours later, the wind shifted and was coming from the side of the boat, flowing around both sides of the sail which pulled the boat forward. Trying to sail into the wind proved more difficult than I anticipated.

"Are you hungry, my beau?"

"Yes. I'm starving."

Paula opened the wicker picnic basket and removed Spanish Jamón, Queso y Chorizo con Pan, but this was no ordinary ham and cheese sandwich. I unwrapped the butcher paper and took a bite. The manchego cheese, jamon, and chorizo on a crusty baguette was exceptional.

"This is the best sandwich I have ever eaten. The ham actually tastes like prosciutto."

"Jardon is a very special ham. It comes from acorn-fed Ibérico Bellota pigs and has a long curing stage. Would you like a little wine?" Paula asked as she poured a glass of Campo Viejo Cava Brut Reserva.

The time flowed by as quickly as the wind, and what was midmorning a few minutes ago became late afternoon. "Don't you think we better head in?" asked Paula.

Little did she know I had been trying to get the sailboat to shore for the past several hours. Or maybe she knew, but did not want to embarrass me.

"Of course," I said. "I guess I have been taking my time getting us back. I think it is because I did not want the day to end."

I discovered tacking by trial and error. How does a boat make progress sailing toward the wind? I realized by maneuvering the bow of the boat through the wind, the wind would change from one side of the vessel to the other side. During the first attempt at tacking, I was almost knocked into the sea when the boom began to swing. The wind was blowing over the port side, and the boat was on a port tack. That's when the boom swung hard and fast. I caught the movement in the corner of my eye and ducked just in time to miss the boom. Paula had apparently been adept at sailing, as she was always aware of where the boom was.

With persistence and resolve, I was able to return the sailboat to shore.

"I thought you two lovebirds were going to take my boat to America," laughed the man while tethering the boat to the dock.

"We thought about it, but we decided it was just a bit too small," I said.

We left the dock and walked up the road which took us to the town center.

"Paula, my ship is leaving tomorrow, which means I am leaving. I want you to know how much I have enjoyed the past few days. I want to see you again. I am a realist. I understand how difficult long-distance relationships can be, but I know we can make this happen if we want to. I can get leave and come back to Spain, or you can meet me at . . ."

"See? This is what I was worried about," Paula interrupted. "This was the only reason I did not want to go out with you, Calvin. You charmed me into being very fond of you, and now you are leaving. I never should have said I would date you."

My heart hurt. She was right, of course. What was I thinking? *Maybe, just maybe, we can keep this flicker of a relationship burning. We will write and as soon as I get some leave, I will return to Spain.*

"Paula, maintaining a relationship will be difficult, you are correct, but it is not impossible. You are a special lady, and I do not want this to be good-bye. I promise you I will come back to you as soon as I possibly can. Meanwhile, we can write. If we both are committed to giving this a serious try, I believe we can make this work. I am not going to be in the Navy forever. I have only 16 months left on my enlistment." I hoped I did not sound desperate.

Paula looked at me for what seemed like an hour. Then she said, "I am willing to try if you are."

"I am. Most definitely. I wish I could stay here just for one more week."

Paula placed her finger on my lips to silence me. "Hush, my darling. I know your ship is leaving tomorrow, but I refuse to think about it. I surprised myself with the feelings I have for you, Calvin. This is not what I expected. I thought I would show you the sights and that would be that. But the more time I spend with you, the more time I want to spend with you. Calvin, we have tonight, and I will take you to my casa adosada, my townhouse. Tomorrow may never come. This evening is ours."

I had been floating, rather than walking, ever since I met Paula. My perspective on life, my expectations, my confidence, had all changed like springtime awakening from its slumber. The bad things in life did not seem as bad, and the pleasant aspects of life seemed sweeter. Pesky barnacle colonies attached to pier pilings appeared like exhibitionists, displaying artistic formations in a wide variety of colors including pink, yellow, green and brown. The sunrise was even more spectacular, and birds sang in three-part harmony.

As the *Adams* got underway, there on the pier stood one woman, waving to one sailor, Paula, bidding me farewell. But my merriment was dashed and replaced with fear and doubt. *Will she write to me? Will this become "out of sight, out of mind" for her? Is this nothing more than a summer romance taking place in the winter? A love that is intense, exciting, but fleeting?* I needed reassurance. For now, the fact that Paula came down to the pier to see me off, will have to suffice.

I stood on the 03 level of the ship staring at the shoreline until it slowly evaporated into the sea. I would soon have to report for my watch station, and then whatever worthless task LPO Braun conjured up for me to do.

The *Adams* passed through the Strait of Gibraltar which narrowed to 8 miles in width between Point Marroquí, Spain, and Point Cires, Morocco. We could look on the port side of the ship and see Europe, and turn to the starboard side and see Africa. The ship passed through the Straits of Gibraltar when I reported to lower ECM to stand watch. I scanned the frequency band on the WLR-1, a receiver that required a security clearance to operate. The contacts I received while on watch were mostly from Algeria. It was a boring watch. After my watch, I reported to Braun to see what shit job he had for me.

"Lloyd, grab a Cadillac and swab the passageways."

A Cadillac is Navy slang to describe a mop bucket with wheels and a ringer. I went down to the storage closet and grabbed the bucket and mop. It was not the menial task that upset me; it was the fact Braun never had any of the other sailors in our unit do the shitty jobs. Even sailors junior to me in rank were not given the degrading tasks. I had become an indentured servant. After the swabbing, I proceeded to wax and buff the passageway. When I was finished with my work, I met Dakota on the mess deck.

"I received some info which might be of great interest to you, my friend," Dakota said. "We will be pulling into Tunis, Tunisia on the 22nd of the month, Palermo, Sicily on the 3rd of February, and Civitavecchia, Italy on the 11th."

When deployed, the *Adams* location at any given time was confidential, not that the information was that closely a guarded secret. The crew was told only the ports of call they would visit, but not necessarily when. In letters sent home, sailors often told their loved ones where they were heading. Dakota, being a radioman, was privy to dates and locations of the ship's movements.

"How far is Civitavecchia from Rome?" I asked.

"About an hour drive. Why?"

"I was wondering if Paula could meet me there. I'm going to write her a letter and ask her."

"Speaking of letters, we are supposed to have mid-ships highline sometime tonight. Besides loading supplies and refueling at sea, we should be getting some mail," Dakota said.

That evening, at 2330 hours, the *USS Kalamazoo* (AOR-6), approached the *Adams*. Replenishment at sea (RAS), was the method of transferring fuel, munitions, and stores from one ship to another while underway. Both ships were traveling at 16 knots. The *Adams* came alongside the *Kalamazoo* at a distance of approximately 70 yards. A Gunner's Mate fired an M-14 rifle that had an adapter kit attached to it, sending a heavy bean bag with a light line attached to it. The messenger line was then used to pull across various equipment including the transfer rig lines.

Replenishment at sea is a dangerous operation. The possibility of a line or hose snapping and swinging freely is very real. On a small ship like the *Adams*, all enlisted personnel, (specifically Third-Class Petty Officers and under) not on watch, were required to participate. Replacement parts for onboard equipment needing repair, mail and dry goods were transferred to the *Adams*, while refueling was taking place. Food items including powder eggs, dehydrated potatoes, canned bacon, and boxes of beef steaks marked "for military and penitentiary use only" were carried down to the mess deck. I have always been ever-hopeful and I foresaw an opportunity. I waited for a specific food item to come across the mid-ships highline, and when I saw it, I seized my chance to covet the prize.

Within days of the ship having been replenished with food items, whether in port or at sea, the best flavors of mini cereals disappeared. Those small boxes consumers buy in an 8-pack, were served at breakfast onboard the ship as an alternative to the powdered eggs and canned bacon. Within a few days, the only cereal that remained were corn flakes, shredded wheat, or bran flakes. I was on the lookout for a large cardboard carton containing 200 boxes of cereal. An hour into the replenishment, I saw a seaman carrying the award-winning culinary treats.

"Here, I will take that from you," I said, flexing the little bit of rank I had over the sailor. "Help out over there with that pallet of machinery parts."

I took the box from the sailor and made a slight detour on my way to the mess deck. I stopped by a fan room located close to my work center, opened the cardboard box, and began rummaging for the treasure. I removed every Sugar Pops, Frosted Flakes, Sugar Smacks, and Trix and hid them in the fan room. I would be having the choice cereals for weeks when the other crew were forced to settle for those cereals that tasted like birdseed. I carried out my heist with aplomb.

The next morning there was mail call. Dakota received a letter from his sister and a package that contained chocolate chip cookies, elk jerky, and red licorice. I was hoping for a letter from Paula, but instead there was one from Debbie.

"Want some jerky from the elk you bagged?" Dakota asked.

"Yeah! If you are going to dick your treats in front of the guys, do me a favor and give me a few more pieces of the licorice, too," I said while opening Debbie's letter.

"I am not going to touch my food with my cock, Cal. I will take my chances. Is that a letter from Princess Paula?"

"I wish. It is from Debbie, and it is a 'Dear Calvin' letter'."

"She's dumping you?" Dakota said in a bout of laughter.

"You think that's funny? I knew it wouldn't work, but I was hoping it would linger for a little longer. It really doesn't matter. I have always viewed women as I do trout fishing. Catch and release, or at least I used to have that philosophy, until I met Paula."

Dakota laughed. "Look, Man, you just traded a Gremlin for a Corvette. Forget about her."

"Yeah, I will, but I am sure going to miss her care packages."

I had some free time before I had to report for my next watch assignment. I went down to my berthing compartment and wrote a letter to Paula, asking her to meet me in Rome.

The next month was fairly uneventful. The three-day port of call in Tunis was the polar opposite of Rota. Although a handsome city with a blend of ancient Arab souks and mosques and contemporary-style office buildings, the Muslim majority provided little entertainment for the American sailors. Alcohol was hard to find and any conversation with young ladies was impossible. In fact, if a woman was walking alone and saw an American sailor, she would cross the street so as not to come in close contact with her perceived degenerates.

Before the ship left Tunis, I realized I had misplaced my buck knife, probably somewhere in Combat Information Center. I entered lower CIC, the brains of the ship. When the ship was underway, CIC would be bustling with officers and crew operating dozens of highly sensitive equipment. In port, it was more like a ghost town. I looked around the room but could not find my knife. I thought it may have fallen out of my pocket while I was on watch, so I pulled back the chair and crawled under the mounted electronic equipment on my hands and feet. There I saw the knife all the way back towards the bulkhead. As I crawled under the equipment, I heard voices entering CIC. I immediately recognized the first voice as belonging to the XO.

"Lt. Kiggans seems to think Lloyd is an asset to both Combat Information Center and the Electronic Warfare team."

"Well, he knows the Soviet Intel stuff, b-b-b-but why should he be rewarded for n-n-n-not knowing how to repair the equipment. That is the mundane part of the job. It is not the sexy part of b-b-b-being an EW.'

The stammering immediately identified the speaker as Braun.

"Look, he works for you. If he gives you any shit, make his life miserable. I do not put up with any cocky subordinates. If Lloyd screws up, write him up. When he comes before me, I will make his life more miserable than it is," the XO said.

"Alright, Sir, I am g-g-g-glad we are on the same page."

When the two men left the compartment, I crawled out from under the equipment and stood there stewing. It was time to retaliate. Time for a preemptive strike.

The next port of call, Palermo, Sicily, was a great reprieve from the restrictive Tunisia, and a lot more fun, but I had difficulty living in the moment. Literally, *everything* I did was seasoned with the anticipation of being with Paula once again. I was holding on to the hope she would agree to meet me in Rome.

Once the ship left the port of Palermo, she continued to steam toward the eastern part of the Mediterranean. The work space where I stood watch was completely dark, except for the lights that lit up electronic warfare equipment like a Christmas tree. The contacts on my screen were all friendly, but I still had to log everything I identified.

When my watch ended, I had some rare free time that afternoon and decided to read a paperback outside. I needed something to occupy my mind besides Paula. The weather was too nice to be locked up inside, besides, in a few hours I would be back on watch for 7 hours.

CHAPTER TWELVE

H aving been exiled to the mid-watch from midnight to 0700 hours, I had plenty of time to ponder my situation. The XO was a prick, but retaliation was nearly impossible. Any obvious attempts at vengeance would create serious consequences I was not willing to risk. Braun, on the other hand, might be an easier target. I desperately wanted to fight to free myself from my despotic leading petty officer. There had to be a way to seek revenge for the miseries inflicted on me by both the XO and Petty Officer Braun.

Diligently, I scanned the frequency on my WLR-1 for any contacts, foreign or domestic. A bleep on the screen indicates a contact; ship, aircraft, land based or submarine, anything that transmits a signal. My thoughts wandered. Only Rocky the flying squirrel could fly undetected. Credibility with my two antagonists would soar if I were to identify an enemy contact and log its parameters. No such luck. It was a quiet evening.

I felt the need to drop the kids off at the pool, but I needed someone to cover for me when I went to the head to relieve myself. Suddenly, I had an idea. It was risky, but I thought it could be relatively easy to execute my plan in the middle of the night. There was only a skeleton crew on watch at 0330 hours. I saw a legal pad sitting on the desk beside me. I would need the cardboard at the back of the pad to accomplish my prank. Tearing off the cardboard and stuffing it under my shirt, I walked into the Combat Information Center and asked the LPO on watch if someone could stand watch for me in the Electronic Warfare corner of CIC while I went to the head. The Petty Officer obliged.

The bridge was adjacent to CIC and just outside the bridge there was a small one urinal head. A short walk from the head was Officer's

Country, where officers have their berthing compartments. Unlike the enlisted men, the lower rank officers were assigned two men staterooms. Higher rank officers had their own staterooms. The passageway, strictly off limits to enlisted personnel, was dark, lit only by a red light. I entered the compact, one-man head and dropped my drawers. I did not have to urinate, I had to drop a stool. I folded the cardboard in half and dropped my excrement onto the crease in the cardboard. Slowly, I opened the door to the head to make sure the coast was clear. So far, so good. Quickly, I walked down to Officer's Country. Without hesitation, I turned the cardboard upside down and the night soil plopped in the middle of the passageway. I quickly exited the area and, on my way back to my watch, threw the cardboard into a file 13 (a euphemism for the trash can). Sitting in front of my EW equipment, I laughed hysterically as I pictured the XO stepping on the dung and sliding halfway down the darkened passageway, like a penguin on ice skates.

As far as I was concerned, the XO was a turd so this retaliation was most appropriate. It may have been stooping pretty low, but when one is way down on the food chain and stuck on a tin can in the middle of the ocean, his opportunities and resources are limited. I had to get creative, and creative is one thing I am.

Nothing remains a secret onboard a floating city, that is, unless it is literally classified material, and it did not take long for the scuttlebutt on the ship to spread that there was a "Mad-Shitter" on the ship who dropped a depth charge in Officer's Country. It was a subject of delight for the crew. Now I just needed to find the appropriate punishment for Braun. An eye for an eye…

Mail call provided a letter from Paula. Going outside the skin of the ship, I found a quiet place on the 03 level and sat with my back against the bulkhead. As I held the letter, I gazed out at the calm sea. Eight miles from the ship, a fair-weather waterspout formed along the dark flat base of a line of developing cumulus clouds. It looked exactly like a tornado, thrusting water upward from the surface of the sea to the overhead cloud. The spray vortex rose several hundred feet creating a magnificent funnel. I wondered what would happen if the *Adams* ever got caught in a waterspout. *Maybe the ship would be beamed up into the universe like some Star Trek episode.*

I opened the letter from Paula and read the good news. She expressed her enthusiasm for meeting me in Rome and added she often travels to the Eternal City and knows the city well. She would go to Rome a few times a year to acquire art for her father. Paula suggested meeting in the colorful Trastevere district in Rome, an artsy area that embraces its centuries-old, working-class roots. She gave me the address of a trattoria where she would meet me.

When the *Adams* arrived in Civitavecchia, I could not get off the ship fast enough. Although a bus was hired to take sailors into Rome, it was not scheduled to leave till noon. Dakota and I, along with a few friends, decided to hire a driver to take us into town. If we split the cost it was going to be cheaper than taking the bus. While the other sailors in the car discussed seeing the Coliseum, the Pantheon, and St. Peter's Basilica, Paula dominated my thoughts. I convinced the others to have the driver drop me off in the Trastevere district before Trevi Fountain, where the others wanted to begin their tour of the sites. Trastevere is the area where Paula suggested we meet, and it would save me time and money if I did not have to traverse through Rome.

Rome was everything I had expected. Historic architecture, fountains and aqueducts, obelisks and columns, statues, catacombs and bridges dotted the city. The metropolis lifeblood of fashion, entertainment and cuisine was evident everywhere I looked and... it was romantic.

When I got out of the cab, my friends wished me luck as the car sped off to Quirinale Hill, the historic center of Rome. I scanned the crowd of people looking for Paula, but did not see her. At a small stand, I purchased an Italian-English dictionary. An older gentleman in a newsboy flat cap, walking a small black dog with white paws, stopped next to me to purchase a pack of cigarettes. I opened my new literary translation guide and decided to give it a try.

"Il tuo cane dovrebbe mordermi?" I asked the man.

The man burst into laughter. "I believe your Italian needs a little work my friend. I think you wanted to say, il tuo cane morde? You said, your dog should bite me," he said, laughing again.

I joined in the laughter. "Well, yes, I guess my Italian needs some work."

"A man who loves dogs is a man who is compassionate, loyal, and dependable," a woman's voice said behind me.

"Paula!" I said as I wrapped my arms around her. "You came!"

"But of course I did. Nothing in the world could keep me from you, my dear Calvin. I think the old adage is true. Absence makes the heart grow fonder."

The old man gave me an approving pat on the back and continued to walk his dog.

"That is a very rare dog," Paula said. "It is a Volpino Italiano."

"You are knowledgeable about art, dogs, what don't you know?"

"I don't know enough about you. I need to know everything about you, about your home, your family, your job..."

"And about my three-legged dog," I said with a laugh.

"Three legged?"

"She was hit by a car and the Vet had to amputate the back right leg, but she has adapted wonderfully. She can run almost as well as before the accident."

"That is amazing. You know, Calvin, the fact we are both canophiles might just be an omen we belong together."

I had no idea what a canophile was, but I surmised it was a dog lover.

"I want your world to eclipse my world. I want to get that close to who you are," Paula said. "I want to know *everything* about you, Calvin. I don't want you to hold anything from me. If this relationship is to work, we must be completely transparent. The good *and* the bad.

I do not want to find out something about you months from now, something I should have known from the beginning. I do not want to be hurt."

"I'm not holding anything back, Paula. I told you I cannot discuss my job, and I am not even supposed to tell you where the ship is heading, but I want to see you so badly I must tell you we will be in Piraeus, Greece, in a few months. Piraeus is only eight kilometers from Athens. I want you to meet me in Athens, Paula."

"When?"

"That is the problem. We will not be there till the third week of March."

"Oh, that is such a long time, my Calvin, but yes, of course I will meet you."

"You are an angel," I said.

We decided to avoid the crowds and touristy things and explore other parts of the city. We went to Teatro di Marcello, the understated sister of the Colosseum which seats 11,000 people. Unlike the Colosseum, there were no crowds. After stopping by a small Alimentari to purchase some fresh, crusty bread, cured meats, and cheese, we took the short walk to Park Caffarella, a sanctuary from the city's chaos.

The vast park included pastureland, flocks of sheep and goats, and 18th century old farms. We found a small pond and sat in the grass to enjoy our lunch. While we were enjoying our lunch, a fox rushed by, as if late for an appointment.

After lunch, we walked back to Paula's hotel, made love, and fell fast asleep.

When I awakened, Paula was still asleep. The sun was nearly in bed as the lights in the city showed through the thin curtains gently moving to the beat of the wind. I lay there lionizing Paula's body. It was mannequin-like perfection. Every centimeter of her body was firm and taut, as if she were an athlete or ballerina. Those areas of her body which are typically flaccid on the average woman's body, the derrière, breasts, tummy and thighs, were as tight as an Etruscan shrew's ass.

I gently glided my hand down Paula's back, to the smooth valley that separated her back from her derrière, ending at her perfectly round cheeks. It was like spreading butter on a warm bagel.

"Ahhhhhhh...I will give you an hour to quit doing that," Paula said in a half-asleep tone.

I kissed her from her valley to her neck. "It is getting dark. Should we find a place for dinner?"

"If you keep kissing me on my neck, we are not going anywhere," she whispered.

I smiled as I got out of bed.

We got dressed and walked the short distance to a trattoria known for its suckling pig. We entered the small building on a corner of an unassuming neighborhood. Crammed tables, bare-brick walls, and old copper pots hanging from the ceiling gave the restaurant a homey feel. We took a table by the large window and the waitress brought us a bottle of sparkling water.

As we were enjoying the moment, I saw Lt. Kiggans and Hua getting out of a taxi.

Pointing to them I said, "That is my division officer and his wife. They are wonderful people. They invited me to their home for Thanksgiving dinner."

"Go and invite them to join us," Paula said.

I was a bit torn. It would be fun to have them join us, but a selfish part of me did not want to share Paula with anyone. On the other hand, I wanted to show the world my girlfriend. "Okay," I said as I got up and walked outside.

"Lieutenant Kiggans!" I called out.

The lieutenant and Hua turned at the same time.

"Calvin!" Hua said as she gave me a warm embrace. "What a surprise."

"Hello, Cal," the lieutenant said. "Are you enjoying Rome?"

"Yes, I am," I answered. Turning to Hua I said, "I didn't know you were going to meet the lieutenant in Rome. It's so good to see you,

Hua. Hey, my girlfriend flew in from Spain and we are about to order dinner. Would you like to join us?"

Hua turned to the lieutenant and said, "That would be delightful."

We entered the restaurant, and I introduced Paula to them.

"Paula, this is Hua and Lt. Kiggans—eh, I mean, Mark," I said.

"Hello," Hua said.

"Hello, Paula," the lieutenant said.

"It is good to meet you both," Paula said with a smile. "I hope you don't mind, but I took the liberty of ordering a bottle of red wine and misto affettati."

"I give up," I said. "What is misto affettati?"

"It is a plate of cured meats and cheeses," said Paula. "I added a ball of mozzarella di bufala," Paula said.

"It is to die for," Kiggans said.

As the wine flowed, so did the conversation. The four of us spoke as if we were long lost friends. Laughter complimented the remarkable food. The second course consisted of fresh homemade carbonara, which came topped with a raw egg yolk and shaved black truffle. The main event was the maialino al forno, suckling pig served with roast potatoes. The crispy skin kept the meat juicy, tender and succulent.

After dinner, I excused myself and went to the bathroom. As I walked back from the bathroom I saw Hua and Kiggans leaning forward on the table, intently listening to something Paula was telling them. When I arrived at the table, the conversation stopped abruptly.

"Don't stop on my account," I said with a slight smile. "I assume you were talking about me?"

"We were talking about how difficult it is to be married to a sailor," Hua said. "Having a lover disappear for seven months of the year is poignant, but it can work if the love for each other is stronger than the elements at work against the couple."

"Well, I am not staying in the Navy for life," I said. "I have less than a year and a half left on my enlistment, then I am a civilian."

The evening could not have gone better. The most hospitable owner, the ambiance of his establishment, and the mouth-watering cuisine underscored the event. Any stranger observing our camaraderie and conversation would conclude the four of us were friends for a very long time.

On the way back to the hotel, I turned to face Paula.

"You look very serious," she said.

"Paula, I know we have not known each other for very long, but our time together has been magical. I think it is safe to say we have something special. I do not want to lose that."

"And neither do I, my dear Calvin."

"I have been doing a lot of thinking about us. I would like you to come with me to the States when I get discharged."

"Oh, my darling, Calvin. I would love to, but I could never leave my family. I do love you madly. You know that."

I tried to hide my disappointment, but I did not persist. Instead, I would have to try and live in the moment. Every moment with Paula was pure joy.

When we got back to the hotel, we discussed if it were possible to meet somewhere before Athens. Istanbul was a possibility, but Kiggans told me there were several high security operations taking place once the ship reached the eastern Mediterranean, so that did not seem feasible. We decided Athens made the most sense, although our meeting would not be for another couple of months.

It was late when I returned to the ship. I got undressed to my skivvies and laid on my rack replaying the events of the day. It was another day of perfection, but then again, every day with Paula is perfect. She filled in all the colors for my paint-by-numbers kit.

CHAPTER THIRTEEN

T he *adams* got underway first thing in the morning, leaving Rome in its wake. The crew was assigned port and starboard watch, which for me meant I would be in CIC between 1200 and 1700 hours, and once again from midnight to 0700 hours. Before the midwatch, I went to the mess deck for midrats, rations specifically for sailors who worked the night shift. When I arrived, Dakota was already seated with his tray.

"You will see her again," Dakota said with a smile.

"I am fine," I said, without looking up from my chili and rice.

"Not according to your demeanor."

"Wow. You are using big words this evening."

"Ah, and you are acting a little pissy."

"I told you I am fine."

"Really? The way you stand, the way you talk, your facial expressions, all say you are not okay."

"I'm sorry, Dakota. I am so in love with Paula that each time I am away from her I miss her more than the last time, and now I will not see her for over two stinking months. That is enough time for her to meet someone, fall in love, get married and have three kids."

Dakota laughed. "Well, maybe only two kids. Hey, absence makes the heart grow fonder."

"Yeah, that is what she said, but no cliches, please?"

"Alright. Cheer up, my friend. I hate seeing you like this. I have to go. I need to check the radio traffic from the previous watch."

As Dakota was walking away, I said, "Dakota?"

Dakota stopped and turned around.

"Thanks."

I walked to the forward part of the ship and climbed the ladder that took me to CIC. I relieved the sailor on watch and took the seat in front of the EW equipment. In a few days the electromagnetic spectrum would begin to light up the screen before me. The spectrum is the range of all types of electromagnetic radiation, radio waves that come from all platforms, air, subsurface, surface (ship), or land based. The closer the *Adams* sailed toward hostile platforms, the busier electronic warfare technicians become.

The problem with standing watch alone in the middle of the night is too much uninterrupted time to think. And think, I did. I thought of the long wait to see Paula. I thought about losing Paula; after all, any man alive would want to call her his girlfriend. I thought of Braun and the XO. All less than positive thoughts. Those thoughts moved me, physically and psychologically. Negative thoughts on XO prompted a call to action.

Walking into CIC, I asked for someone to cover for me while I relieved myself in the head. Opportunity knocked once again, as I dropped a stool on a piece of cardboard and deposited it in the hallway of Officer's Country. Nonchalantly, I returned to my watch.

The next morning, the ordure was all the talk among the crew. Apparently, the XO had not seen the brown pile in the dimly lit passageway, stepped on it, and slid enough for him to lose his balance and fall backwards into the human skat. When I reached the mess deck after my watch, the crew was in unusually high spirits.

"Did you hear the latest?" a sailor asked me in the chow line.

"No, what?"

"The Mad-Shitter struck again," the sailor said, then burst into hysterical laughter. "I don't know who the culprit is, but he should be awarded the Navy Cross!"

I began laughing and could not stop.

"I know. Brillant!" I said.

After breakfast, I reported to my work space where Braun was waiting for me.

"Lloyd, someone left the c-c-c-coffee pot on all night with nothing in the p-p-p-pot. It cracked the glass pot and n-n-n-now we can't make coffee."

"Thank you for sharing that," I said, "b-b-b-but it wasn't m-m-m-me, and besides, Mr. Coffeemaker makes shit coffee."

"Why you little shit! Just wait and see what I have planned for you," Braun said. "After your mid-watch I want you to begin chipping paint. You can begin with the outside of the work compartment."

"I just have one question, Petty Officer Braun. Are you the Mad-shitter?"

"Get out of here!" Braun yelled.

That evening, before I had to report for my watch detail, I went down to my berthing compartment and was asked to join in a poker game already in progress. Dakota, an Operation Specialist named Lockhart, another radioman, Robinson, and a signalman nicknamed Dante, were seated at the small table eating some geedunk, a term sailors use for vending machine food.

"Who's winning?" I asked.

"Lockhart," Dante said. "But he cheats."

"Deal me in," I said.

I have always been a gambler-type in life. I did not hesitate to take calculated risks. No risk, no reward, or as the saying went among sailors, no balls, no blue chips. The cards were dealt, and I held a Jack-high hand after receiving three new cards. I bluffed and raised the ante twice, with Dakota, Robinson, and Dante folding. Lockhart was pondering whether to join the other three or call my bet.

"Let's go, Lockhart! We don't have all night! I have the mid-watch, for crying out loud!" I said.

"Okay, okay," Lockhart said.

"Ever wonder where the word okay came from?" I asked. "Contrary to popular opinion, that term has its roots in Boston, originally a substitute for 'oll korrect' or 'all correct.' It actually is of American Indian origin. Choctaw to be exact."

"You are a wealth of insignificant trivia, Lloyd," Dante said.

"Yeah, God-forbid you actually broaden that intellectually, miniscule brain of yours," I said. "Are you going to fold or call, Lockhart?"

"Cal is the king of trivia. You have no idea," Dakota said. "Ask him what the average weight of an elephant's foreskin weighs."

"Well, Lloyd, how much does it weigh?" Dante asked.

"9.6 pounds. Pass me some of that geedunk."

"Hey, does anyone know who those six VIP guys are who came aboard when we were in Gaeta?" Lockhart asked.

"Maybe defense contractors," Robinson answered.

"I doubt it," I said. "I'll bet they are CIA."

"What in the world would CIA guys be doing on our ship?"

"Who knows. It's your turn to deal, Dante said."

"Did I ever tell you guys about my vending machine disaster when I was in Southeast Asia?" Robinson asked.

"No, but I'm sure you will tell us," said Lockhart.

"It was unbearably hot and humid, and the air conditioning on the ship went down. At night I was lying on my rack in a puddle of sweat. I decided to go to the vending machine to buy one of those chocolate bars with crisped rice. Well, I unwrapped the bar and ate half of it before realizing the rice was moving. It was filled with maggots!"

"On second thought, I don't want any geedunk," I said.

Lockhart folded, and I pulled the red, white and blue chips to my corner of the table.

"I gotta go see a man about a dog," I said.

"What?" Dante asked with a look of bewilderment.

"He has to go take a crap," Lockhart said. "If you are going to hang around this guy, you better get hip with his Lloydisms. He has a library full of them."

I took my winnings and went to the head to do my business, then tried to do a little reading before I reported for my watch that evening. After reading the same paragraph three times, I put down the book. It was 2230 hours. The seas were fairly calm, so I decided to take a walk outside the skin of the ship for some fresh air.

It was a beautiful night with the skies filled with so many stars it looked as though someone had taken a paintbrush dipped in white paint and spattered it against a black canvas. I walked down the starboard side of the ship to the fantail. I saw someone else had the same idea. He was standing by the stern of the ship, smoking a cigarette and looking out at the wake. The smoking lamp was lit within the skin of the ship, but it was strictly forbidden outside. The burning cherry at the end of a cigarette can be seen for a long distance at sea, and military ships never want to be visually detected at night. Whoever it was, he was breaking a cardinal rule.

As I got closer to the sailor, I saw it was Braun. *This jerk is quick to punish me for the smallest infraction, and here he is having a smoke outside, at night!* Without much thought, I quietly walked behind Braun, lifted my leg, and kicked my nemesis hard in the hollow of his back. I heard a distant splash as the ship continued at a brisk 30 knots. The perfectly placed target of the kick knocked the wind out of Braun's lungs, making it impossible for him to yell for help. *This was too easy. I should do the same to the XO, but I guess two sailors lost at sea would be too much of a coincidence.* I turned around and reported for my watch.

No one reported Braun missing until muster the next morning. A search was made of the ship, and when it was confirmed he was nowhere to be found, the ship turned around and went into "man overboard" mode. Captain Stansbury called the *Saratoga* requesting air assistance in the search.

After searching for 24 hours, Braun's search was canceled. Troubling the crew was how he could have fallen overboard in relatively calm seas. Nonetheless, life on board continued as usual while the squadron moved closer to the eastern part of the Mediterranean. Even the missing Braun did not interfere with the Captain calling a meeting in CIC to discuss a high security mission. Only those who held a secret clearance or higher, and who had a need-to-know, were in the meeting.

"Men, we have a very special opportunity. The Soviets just launched a new battlecruiser called the *Kirov*. She is a nuclear-powered, guided-missile cruiser and the largest and heaviest surface combatant warship in the world. She was designed as a multi-purpose warship with a focus on anti-ship and anti-aircraft warfare. It will also provide long range strike support in amphibious landings, and she is loaded with guns, missiles, rockets, and torpedoes, along with advanced electronics. We have intelligence that she will be in Kythira anchorage, and we are going to sneak up on her and gather as much information as possible."

The Soviets' anchorage was off the island of Kythira, between the southeast tip of Peloponnesus and northwest Crete. The Aegean Sea is of vital importance to the Soviets as a passageway for their ships sailing between the Black Sea and the Mediterranean. Kythira is known as the Isle of the Goddess of Love, Aphrodite. According to the ancient myth, when Cronus severed his father, Uranus' genitals, and threw them into the sea, it created the two rocks rising out of the sea.

Electronic intelligence, known in the espionage business as ELINT, is critically important, enabling weapons and personnel the ability to accomplish even greater feats for America's fleet. As the Cold War continued, the U.S. Navy was an enthusiastic participant in the secret war against the Communist bloc. For decades, the Navy waged a daily struggle against enemy air and surface defenses to gain desperately needed intelligence regarding the military capabilities of the Soviet Union and its Communist allies.

"The only photographs we have of the *Kirov* is of it still being built as it sat in dry-dock," continued the Captain. "They had installed their new missile guidance system on this ship, but we have no information of its electromagnetic spectrum or any other critical data. That is where Electronic Warfare Technicians come into play. Lt. Kiggans is the Intelligence Officer on the *Adams* and Petty Officer Lloyd is the Intelligence Petty Officer. Lloyd, I would like you to explain what you will be searching, electronically speaking."

I was not expecting the Captain to call on me, but this was my expertise. I was *good* at this. As Intelligence Petty Officer, I was trained to analyze top-secret information, interpret electronic parameters, and photograph hostile platforms. While others may see nothing, Lt. Kiggans and I would be able to use my keen analytical abilities to perceive vital intelligence.

"The electromagnetic (EM) spectrum is the range of all types of EM radiation," I explained. "Radiation is energy that travels and spreads out as it goes. For example, light from a flashlight and the radio waves that come from a radio station are two types of electromagnetic radiation. What we are interested in is the EM radiation from the *Kirov's* new missile guidance system," I said, impressing my peers and even the XO.

"Captain, may I ask how you plan on sneaking up on the Soviets?" They certainly know the parameters of most of our radars and would see us, electronically, long before we are visibly on the horizon."

"We are going to do something very unorthodox. We will go into radio silence at nightfall. We will anchor a hundred miles from Kythira anchorage. There we will paint over our hull number, and we will string white lights from the stern to the top of the mast and from the pigstick to the bow. We will play rock n' roll over the speakers."

The look on the faces of everyone in the room was as if the Captain had stripped off his clothes, bent over, and played *Wipeout* on his butt cheeks.

"Brilliant!" I exclaimed. "So, the Soviets are going to think we are a cruise ship until it is too late, and we have gathered the intelligence we are after!

"Exactly," the Captain said over the laughter and chatter from everyone in the compartment.

The scuttlebutt spread throughout the ship, and the entire crew was visibly excited about the Captain's plan. The ship anchored in fairly calm seas as some boatswain's mates constructed a hanging scaffold so they could paint over the hull number. Other sailors were busy stringing lights across the superstructure of the ship. A few officers rummaged through a selection of cassette tapes trying to decide what pop music they would play as they snuck up on the unexpecting Soviet cruiser. I had my own idea of the perfect song when we were approaching the enemy ship. I went down to my locker and retrieved the cassette tape.

When the preparations were complete, the *Adams* began cruising toward Kythira anchorage.

Up on the bridge the XO walked up to Lt. Kiggans to voice his objection of me dominating the EW watch. "Kiggans, I would rather Petty Officer Benitez take the watch."

"I understand, Sir, but Lloyd is the best we have at this particular skill set. He may not be able to repair the equipment he operates, but he is one hell of an EW operator, and he has extensive training in Soviet Intelligence, which Benitez does not. I really want Lloyd to take the lead here. If he gets tired and needs to be relieved, you can select whomever you would like to replace him." The XO paused to ponder the lieutenant's request.

"Alright. It's your call," he said.

Kiggans wondered why the XO has disdain for me.

I sat at my electronic warfare equipment, the AN/WLR-1, a radar warning receiver designed for real-time intercept of signals, direction-finding, processing, and evaluation of radio-frequency signal emitters. There would be no designated watch for me. I had decided I would not leave my post until I intercepted the *Kirov's* new missile guidance radar system, no matter how long it took. Even if the radar was in standby position, it would leak an electronic transmission, but it would be much harder for me to intercept.

Aboard the *Kirov*, a contact appeared on the surface search radar screen. That contact was actually the *Adams*. The Operations Specialist aboard the Soviet ship only picked up a surface search radar, the only radar the *Adams* was transmitting. Every boat had a surface search radar aboard, even a small pleasure craft, and so it was ignored.

"Kapitan-leytenant, new contact 239," the sailor said to the Conning Officer over an internal phone.

"What is its bearing and distance?" the officer asked.

"Bearing of N84°W. Distance 67 kilometers," answered the sailor.

"Let me know its course and whether other contacts appear on your screen. There is an American task group cruising in the Eastern Mediterranean. If this is a lone contact, it is not part of that task group. They travel as a group. I want a report every 5 minutes," the officer said.

"Yes, Kapitan-leytenant."

"Sonar," the Kapitan-leytenant said, "Be alert. Listen for any marine chatter."

Thanks to a lot of coffee, I had been on watch for over 20 hours searching for the electronic parameters of the Soviet's new missile guidance system. I came up empty. I did, however, detect a Soviet Juliett class submarine's surface search radar transmission when it surfaced. This class of Soviet submarine could travel 9,000 miles and remain submerged, utilizing only the snorkel to replenish the air and recharge the batteries. Operating close to the Soviet anchorage and under the cloak of darkness, the submarine felt it was safe to surface without being detected.

It was a rare find, which I reported to the Officer of the Watch. The ship immediately sent a Top-Secret Raindrop Red Transmission to Washington, D.C. That would be celebrated in Washington and would be a feather in my Dixie Cup hat, but that was not for what I was searching.

"Lloyd, how is it going?" the Captain asked, startling me. I had no idea the Captain had walked up behind me.

"Captain Stansbury! Eh, well, nothing from the *Kirov*. I did find a Julliet Class sub, but that's not good enough."

"I heard you detected that sub. Absolutely excellent work, Lloyd. You have been at this for a while. Why don't you let someone relieve you so you can get a little shut eye. I'll have someone wake you when we are within sight of the *Kirov*."

"Sir, if it is all the same to you, I want to see this through. I want to nail these Commies."

"Very well. Your commitment is duly noted, Lloyd."

"Sir?"

"Yes?"

"I do have one request. Would you play the Brothers Johnson's *Strawberry Letter 23* when we are approaching the Soviets? It's the best disco song ever! It's a perfect song for a cruise ship. I just so happen to have a cassette with the song on it right here," as I reached into my pocket.

Laughing, the Captain said," Sure."

Noise travels well in water. Aboard the *Kirov,* the sonar technician detected music, *Bohemian Rhapsody* by Queen, coming through his headphones. The young Soviet sailor loved the interruption from his mundane life.

"Sonar, are you picking up anything from the target that was reported?" Asked the Conning Officer on the bridge.

"Yes, Sir. It is a cruise liner. I can hear music and laughter."

"Let me know immediately if there are any changes," the officer said.

"Yes, Sir," the sailor said. "Sir? I was thinking, is it not strange they are playing music at 0400 hours?"

"No one asked you to think," the officer said. "Just do your job." Changing telephone lines, the officer wanted positional information on the contact that was the *Adams*. "Operations, what is the update on that contact?"

"Bearing is still N84°W, but it is closing. Distance is now 43 kilometers," answered the sailor.

"Keep me abreast as to its whereabouts. Do not make me ask for this information again!" the officer said arrogantly.

"Aye aye, Kapitan-leytenant."

Meanwhile, the sonar technician was enjoying the musical interlude, anxiously waiting for the next song to come over his headphones. This time it was *Dancing Queen* by ABBA, causing the sailor to begin bobbing his head and shoulders to the music. Clearly, this was the best watch the sailor ever had. Everything was going well, until it was not. When *Strawberry Letter 23* began to play, the sailor moved his hips and began dancing in his seat.

"Comrade! Do you have a case of the crabs?" a junior officer asked.

"No, Sir," the sailor said as he sat erect in his seat. "It is just that the cruise liner we picked up is playing very good disco music."

"The Imperialist's music is decadent and culturally corruptive, Comrade. Dance again and you will spend a month in the brig. Understood?"

"Yes, Sir," the sailor said.

My eyes widened and my posture leaned toward the screen of the electronic equipment.

"We got it!" I screamed loud enough for everyone in Combat Information Center to stop what he was doing and look my way. Lt. Kiggans, the mid-watch officer, quickly walked over to the Electronic Countermeasures area where I had captured the *Kirov's* new, top secret missile guidance system's electromagnetic spectrum.

"Lloyd, are you sure it is the *Kirov*?"

"Yes, sir. The signal is weak. I am guessing the guidance system is in standby mode, but it always leaks some transmissions. I knew the frequency had to be somewhere between 4 to 18 gigahertz. As I scanned that range, I kept narrowing my search as the faint signal appeared."

"Outstanding, sailor! Quickly log all that info before it is lost. I am going to wake up the XO, and I will let the Captain know," the lieutenant said.

I grabbed the green bound logbook and began to write down the critical information. I finished logging all the data when Captain Stansbury walked in.

"I hear congratulations are in order, Lloyd."

"Thank you, Sir. I wanted this badly!"

"Bravo! We will send another Raindrop Red Transmission to Washington immediately. They are going to love this! I think you have earned your keep today, Sailor," the Captain said.

Having achieved our objective, Captain Stansbury appeared on the bridge and gave the quartermaster orders to increase speed to 30 knots as the *Adams* cruised toward Kythira anchorage. The eastern nautical twilight sky was bathed in a warm, ethereal glow as daybreak quickly approached.

Walking over to the XO, the Captain said, "We captured the parameters of the *Kirov's* guided missile system. Intelligence indicated they have SS-N-12 Sandbox anti-ship missiles aboard. Let's say hello to these Red Fleet Mariners." Turning to the boatswain's mate, he said, "We will circle the *Kirov* at a safe distance. When we get close enough, I want you to play *Back in the U.S.S.R* over the speaker system."

Yes, Sir," the sailor said with a huge smile on his face.

The *Adams* joined the sun as both made their appearances over the horizon. The Kapitan of the *Kirov* stood on the wing of the bridge and looked at the *Adams* through high-powered binoculars. He knew he had been hoodwinked. Turning to his XO, he screamed, "Why did we not detect the Americans?"

"Kapitan, the Imperialists only generated their surface-search radar, nothing else. They also played dance music which made the officer of the day believe it was a cruise ship," the XO said.

"Idioty!"

The *Adams* got within 100 meters of the *Kirov* when *Back in the U.S.S.R* began blaring over the speakers. The entire crew not on watch gathered on deck as enthusiastic spectators, including me and Dakota. I manned the 35 mm intelligence camera with a powerful zoom lens so I could capture photographs of the *Kirov,* and its weapons and radars.

The *Kirov* was built in the traditional Soviet Naval style. It was top-heavy, having two of almost every radar and weaponry. Unlike the U.S. Navy, the Soviets had little trust in their crew who were not college-educated officers. Instead of training them to repair equipment while out at sea, the Soviets employed two of every vital piece of equipment. If one broke down, they had another, two surface-search radars, two air search radars, two surface to air missile launchers, and so on.

"Launch the helicopter and have it circle the American ship," the Kapitan ordered. "Have it swing dangerously close and wildly around their superstructure."

"Aye, aye, Kapitan," the XO said.

The Kremlin may not have liked The Beatles, but the crew of the *Kirov* loved the western music. They laughed and smiled when the lyrics mentioned Ukrainian, Moscow and Georgia girls, to the anger of the commissioned officers aboard the *Kirov.*

The Kamov Ka-25, a naval helicopter nicknamed the Hormone Bravo, transitioned off the ship and quickly hovered closely to the *Adams.* I was on the main deck with the camera taking photos of the *Kirov* when I changed my focus to the helicopter. The door of the Hormone Bravo swung open, and a sailor began taking photographs of the *Adams.* In a defiant response, the crew grabbed their crotches and flipped the bird to the pilot and photographer.

Suddenly, the helicopter maneuvered wildly, causing the photographer to frantically grab the sides to the open door to keep from falling into the water. When he did, he dropped his camera into the sea. The entire crew of the *Adams* laughed hysterically.

"That sailor is going to spend the next 10 years in Siberia," Dakota said with a cackle.

"For sure," I said, joining him in laughter.

CHAPTER FOURTEEN

T he next few weeks were uneventful, if not boring, compared to everything that went on at Kythira. Idol time was my enemy; too much time to think, and think I did, mostly about Paula. I had received a flurry of letters from my love, but a fear of losing her to another always followed me, like my shadow when the sun appeared low in the sky. Mail call, however, did more than ease my mind.

I received another letter from Paula, and what I read made me jump out of my chair. Time has a way of changing one's perspective and, in this case, absence *did* make the heart grow fonder. In the letter, Paula stated she wants to go to America with me when my enlistment is up. I reread that portion of the letter a dozen times.

I want to be wherever you are, Calvin! Anywhere in the world. I do not want to continually be separated from you. I adore you!

At first, the thought of marriage scared me. I was only 21, but after massaging the thought, I knew I would never find a girl who measured up to Paula, in her beauty, her kindness, and most of all, in how she loved me.

The *Adams* would be docking in Istanbul as the next port of call. Istanbul is the world's only city straddling two continents, Europe, and Asia. This unique city offers excitement and fascination for visitors; however, for the crew, it presents several problems.

The Turks' welcome was mixed. They were warm and friendly and enjoyed the tourist business the sailors brought. There was also curiosity and suspicion when it came to Americans. Some sailors had rocks thrown at them by children as they walked the streets. Clearly they were executing what they learned at home, that Americans should not be trusted.

Dakota and I spent the first two days visiting the blue Mosque, the Grand Bazaar, and Galata Tower. When we returned to the ship the second evening, there was a clear presence of anxiety among our shipmates.

"Did you hear what happened to Harrison and Manzello?" the Petty Officer of the Watch asked us.

"No. What?" I asked.

"They bought some hash from some guy on the street and were busted by the Turkish police. The XO contacted the US Embassy, and they are over at police headquarters now trying to get them out."

"Shit!" Dakota said. "Turkey is not Italy. It's not going to be easy getting them out of this!"

"Maybe, if the XO tells them the two sailors will be restricted to the ship for the duration of our stay, and then face American justice, they will agree to release them," I added.

"Maybe," the petty officer said. "Maybe not."

The next day would be our last day in Istanbul. Dakota and I decided to take the ferry across the Bosphorus to the Anatolian side, or Asian side, which is home to waterfront attractions, including the ornate Beylerbeyi Palace. On the way back to the ship, I ordered a Turkish tea onboard the ferry, while Dakota had another beer.

"Hey, look who it is," Dakota said, pointing to the XO who was seated with the Weapons Officer, Lieutenant Commander Golan.

As if on cue, the XO turned and looked directly at the two of us. We both nodded in unison, which was returned with a scowl by the XO.

"How weird was that?" Dakota asked.

"Very," I responded. "Hey, I don't feel very well."

"What's wrong," asked Dakota.

"I am dizzy, and I feel like throwing up. I feel wasted."

"But you had only, what, two beers?"

An announcement in Turkish came over the speaker system as the ferry approached the dock.

"Yeah. I'm not drunk. Dakota, someone drugged my tea. I can hardly stand," I said as I stumbled into Dakota's arms.

"Damn! You are serious! Don't worry, buddy. I will get you back to the ship," Dakota promised.

As Dakota was helping me off the ferry, the XO approached us.

"You better tell your friend if he cannot hold his liquor, he should go back to drinking milk when he is on liberty," the XO said dismissively.

Dakota said nothing in response.

The next morning, I felt better, but I was still trying to shake a cloud of grogginess; nothing a few extra cups of Navy coffee could not correct. I went up to the mess deck to grab some breakfast. While in the serving line, Dakota ran up to me.

"Cal, I have to talk to you about something. By the way, how are you feeling?"

"Like I am in a cloud. I don't know what someone put in my tea, but it was some ass-kicking narcotic. Freakin' Turkey! What do you have to tell me?"

"Last night, someone must have gone into Radio Central and sent an encrypted message, but it was sent to an unknown location. I can tell you it was not sent to one of our ships or to Washington," Dakota said. "I found it by mere chance when I was looking for the logistics report I had accidentally transmitted to the *Saratoga*. I tried to decipher the transmission, but what is weird is that the typed data did not mesh with our code sheet from that day."

"Maybe it was one of those CIA guys who came aboard in Gaeta. They have their own special codes," I said.

"Maybe."

The *Adams* left Turkey before noon and proceeded up the Bosphorus Strait on its way to Constanta, Romania. After exiting the strait, the ship was in the Black Sea, an area not seen by many American ships.

Those onboard the *Adams* with security clearances were briefed on the Black Sea, the U.S.S.R's interests in the region, and reminded they should approach all they do as if in hostile waters. I studied the intelligence I received and was well prepared for the numerous tattletale boats that would shadow the *Adams*. Tattletale boats are disguised as fishing vessels; however, they are void of actual fishing equipment. Instead of fishing nets and gaffs, these tattletale boats have nearly a dozen communication gathering antennas. A typical fishing boat has one radar aboard, a simple surface search radar. Tattletale boats are laden with electronic gear used to glean as much information as possible while an American ship is in their backyard. They collect data from NATO ships and tattletale the intelligence back to Moscow.

After reviewing the intelligence report one more time, I realized how exhausted I was. Knowing the next few days would be active with Soviet contacts, I went to my bunk and tried to get a few hours of much needed sleep.

After muster the next morning, there was a short, unexpected award ceremony on the main deck. All hands not on watch were required to be present. To my surprise, I was given a Letter of Commendation by the sixth fleet admiral for discovering the parameters of the *Kirov's* guided missile system. Although I was thrilled about the recognition of my efforts, I was more excited for the challenges sailing in hostile waters of the Black Sea might bring. I should be more careful when I wish. Little did I know the next few months would deliver excitement in spades.

After the award ceremony, I had a little free time, so I decided to head to the mess deck and grab some lunch. Mystery meat hamburgers, cold french fries, stale potato chips, and bug juice were the culinary treats offered. I settled on a salad instead.

I took a few bites of my salad when a horrific scream echoed from the galley. One of the cooks ran out from behind the serving line, holding his hand with his apron covered in blood. Someone summoned the hospital corpsman who placed pressure on the sailor's wounded hand and led him to sick bay.

I lost my appetite and decided to go outside and grab some fresh air on the main deck. Dakota just finished his watch detail and must have had the same idea.

"Did you hear what just happened?" I asked.

"Yeah, Robinson just told me. Damn! Did the cook lose his entire hand?"

"I don't know, but blood was everywhere."

"Well, a chopper from the *Saratoga* has been summoned and it should be arriving to medivac the poor guy to the aircraft carrier. They are better equipped to manage this kind of thing."

Staring up at the SPS-52 three-dimensional air search antenna, Dakota said, "Look at those seagulls resting up there? They better not crap all over the place."

"Well, with no land in sight, I guess they thought the ship was a good place to take a break."

"I see those VIP visitors that came aboard in Gaeta are enjoying the action. They are standing on the bridge wing with the Captain. Hey, there it is!" Dakota said as he pointed to a helicopter that appeared on the horizon.

Dakota and I continued conversing without taking our eyes off the chopper. When it reached a stone's throw away from us, the whirlybird turned and approached the ship from the stern.

As the chopper slowly maneuvered over the flight deck, the seagulls, whose peace and quiet had been interrupted, decided to leave for a location with less excitement. Circling the ship, the birds abruptly flew into the helicopter, penetrating the fiberglass fairings. One of the birds entered the cockpit, striking the pilot which disoriented him. The chopper pivoted drastically to the left and clipped the Mark 42 5"/54 caliber gun located in the aft section of the ship. A two-foot piece of the propeller broke off, flying towards the bridge wing at blinding speed, decapitating one of the mysterious visitors, tossing his head against the signalman's shack before his body had a chance to collapse on the deck.

The ship was in organized chaos. Chaos, but on a U.S. military ship, even under the most stressful, chaotic situations, everyone knows where to go and what to do. Everyone has a responsibility when it comes to damage control, from the Commanding Officer down to the lowest seaman recruit. Even in the worst situations, chaos is always handled in the most efficient, organized way.

The helicopter crashed into the sea and the ship's motor whaleboat was launched in an attempt to rescue the crew of four, plus two hospital corpsmen. Over the 1 Main Circuit (1MC), the shipboard public address circuit, an alarm sounded, followed by "This is not a drill. This is not a drill. General quarters, general quarters. All hands man your battle stations. Damage Control team report to the flight deck immediately! Chopper down, port, aft."

The motor whaleboat reached the helicopter in a reasonably short time. Only two of the six men who went down with the chopper were wearing life preservers. Two men were treading water, one with a nasty gash across his forehead. One of the corpsmen was holding on to the sinking chopper with one hand, and with the other hand he was holding onto the body of a floating corpse. The boatswain's mates and corpsman aboard the motor whaleboat got all six men aboard and headed back to the Adams.

"What the hell happened?" asked the Petty Officer First Class who was navigating the boat.

"All I know is we were on approach when a flock of seagulls appeared from nowhere. One shattered the cockpit, and Dex must have gotten disoriented. We tipped hard to the port side and clipped the gun mount. We swerved around and went down. I thought we were all okay until I found a piece of the prop had hit Dex in the chest."

"Who is Dex?"

"Lieutenant Dexter Manning, the pilot."

"Well, he's not the only one to get whacked by the prop. The civilians who came on board in Gaeta were standing on the bridge wing area of the ship and one was beheaded."

"No shit?"

"Oh, plenty of shit, and it's going to hit the fan. You assholes are going to be covered with it."

By the time the motor whaleboat reached the *Adams* and was secured, General Quarters had been relaxed and the commanding officer called all available officers and the six guests to the wardroom for an emergency meeting. The guests consisted of four SEALs, Chief Petty Officer Noah Harrington, Petty Officer Samuel Deerstone, Petty Officer Brock Brudzinski, and LTJG Jim Kovacs. The other two were from the CIA, Chip Paxton and Richard Houston.

"Men, I do not need to tell you we have a royal mess here. We are going to keep level heads and make sure every detail is either resolved or has a plan of action. First off, Peter, did they retrieve Mr. Mayfield's head and where is his body now?" asked the Commanding Officer, Commander Stansbury.

The XO took a swallow of coffee and put down his cup.

"The head did not go overboard. It was found on the O2 level. Mr. Mayfield's body, and his head, have been wrapped and taken to the walk-in freezer."

"Okay and how is the poor steward who lost his fingers?"

"He was given more morphine. He's in stable condition and another chopper has been called from *Saratoga*. It should be here in...seven minutes," he said as he looked at his watch.

"I understand the pilot of the Sea Stallion was killed." stated the Captain. "How are the other crewmen?"

"They have been rescued and given a change of clothes. We'll have them on the next bird back to their ship, sir," said the XO.

"Alright. Contact the *Saratoga* and find out how and when they are going to retrieve the downed chopper. We have to remain with her. Soviet ships are in the area."

"Everyone is dismissed other than Mr. Lynch and our guests." The Captain turned to the Communications Officer. "Mr. Comolli, get me the CO of the *Saratoga* on the line," ordered the Captain.

"Yes, sir." The remaining department heads left the wardroom.

Turning to Richard Houston, one of the CIA agents, the CO said, "Houston, we have a problem."

"Yes, Sir, we certainly have a problem. Mayfield was assigned to this mission because he was fluent in Ukrainian. He spoke with no accent. That is crucial. We don't have time to fly a replacement from the States. We're going to have to abort the mission, and Washington is going to be more than pissed."

The captain walked over to a map of the Eastern Mediterranean and stood with his back facing the men. "Maybe not," he said as he walked over to a hand carved mahogany library armchair, the back in the shape of a ship's transom carved with the ship's insignia.

"What are you thinking?" asked Houston.

"We have a sailor aboard, a third-class petty officer, who is fluent in Ukrainian. Both his mother and stepmother are native Ukrainians. He's smart and was trained in both Electronic Warfare *and* as a Cryptologic Technician, interpreter. He has a secret security clearance which can be upgraded on a need-to-know basis. Why not use him?"

There was a silence that seemed to last a dog year. "Captain, even if this sailor speaks the language flawlessly, he would need to be able to execute an acting job worthy of an Academy Award. He must be steadfast under extreme pressure. If he acts nervous or cracks, he can get us all killed."

"Do you have a better idea?"

"No, I don't. We have to get Meiyang Fang out of Ukraine. He is one of the top Biochemical Engineers in China, and now a dissident. By now, he's probably in Kiev with our agent. We can't leave him stranded or he will be captured and executed. Langley has been planning this for months. We will have to use the sailor you suggested. What's his name?" Houston said with a reticence in his voice.

"Lloyd. Calvin Lloyd. Lt. Kiggans is our Operations Officer, Lloyd's Division Officer. Let's get him up here and bring him up to speed on our change of plans. Then we will call for Lloyd and see if he's up to it."

CHAPTER FIFTEEN

T he atmosphere on the *Adams* was tense as Lt. Kiggans walked into the boardroom and surveyed the room. He did not have to be told the current situation was precarious. The atmosphere in the room was thick with tension, like the men were trying to swim through peanut butter.

"Sir, you called for me," the lieutenant said with a salute.

The Captain returned the salute indifferently. "Kiggans, we have a situation. The man who was killed by the chopper blade was essential for this mission in Ukraine. You are aware of the peripheral areas of this mission, but I will fill you in on the blanks. You know these men are CIA and SEALs. They are to exfiltrate a Chinese dissident, Meiyang Fang, and return him to the *Adams*. He is a biochemist with extensive knowledge of China's biological and chemical weapon program and Washington wants him brought safely to the States before Zhongnanhai knows he is missing. The CIA has an agent who is handling him and is to bring him to a location in Kiliia, a rendezvous point where these men are to meet him. Kiliia is a town in southwestern Ukraine that sits on the Danube River. Across the river lies the town of Chilia Veche in Romania. The mission was to launch when we arrive in Constanta, Romania."

"What can I do to help?" asked Kiggans.

"The problem is, Mayfield was the only one who spoke fluent Ukrainian, and he is dead. He was to meet the agent in a pub and find out where Fang is stashed." Motioning toward the SEALs and CIA agents at the table, the captain continued. "Mayfield was to return to where these men would be waiting and together they would retrieve Fang."

"Doesn't the agent speak English?" asked Kiggans.

"Not really. Only a few words. Mayfield was to grab a seat at the bar and use a code phrase when he asks the bartender for a drink. That, obviously, would have to be said in Ukrainian, and without much of an accent. That code would tell our Ukrainian agent Mayfield was his contact. None of us know who our agent is or what he looks like. We are thinking Petty Officer Lloyd is our only chance of pulling this off. Fang has already left China and is in Ukraine. We cannot delay this mission an additional couple of days until a replacement for Mayfield arrives from the States. Do you think Lloyd can pull it off?"

"Lloyd?" Kiggans said, as he searched for the words to answer the Captain's question. "Lloyd has an irreverent sense of humor, but I can tell you he's an outstanding intel Petty Officer. Stellar. He does not have the knack for electronics, so as an Electronic Warfare Technician, he focuses on operations instead of electronic repair. He was going to be yanked from A-School because of his failure in electronics, but an astute commander got him into Cryptologic Technician Interpretive School, CTI. He finished the course in half the time it takes the average student. Corry Station had only two schools, both highly classified," Kiggans explained.

"I don't like it, Captain," the XO said. "We're putting a kid into a potential barn fire. What if something goes wrong? What if he is forced to improvise? What if he panics?"

"None of us is crazy about this, Peter," the Captain said. "We are forced to improvise. The alternative is we abandon Fang in Ukraine, which will get both him and our agent killed."

"I think we need to abort the mission," the XO said. "We can't just wing it. Can't our agent be used as an escort to get Fang out of Ukraine?'

"No!" said Mr. Paxton emphatically. "If our agent disappears for days while he is getting Fang out of Ukraine, his cover will be blown. He has worked for years establishing his cover, and he is planted in an extremely sensitive position. Over the past four years he has provided critical information on the Soviets for us. If we do not go through this, then we will lose both Fang and our agent. We cannot just abandon them."

"Lloyd is a pirate looking for a mutiny," XO continued. "His LPO, Braun, God rest his soul, could not stand him. He is a wise ass and always thinks there is a better way of doing things."

"So, he thinks outside the box. That is not necessarily a bad thing." the Captain said. "We just need to pull him in a little." Turning toward the only commissioned officer among the SEALs, the Captain said, "Make sure he follows orders, Mr. Kovacs."

"Not a problem," Kovacs said.

The Captain looked at Lt. Kiggans and asked, "Mark, do you think Lloyd is the type of sailor who would panic?"

"Actually, no." Lt. Kiggans answered, "He certainly has balls. Mr. Lynch, you may recall Lloyd appeared before you at Captain's Mast. He knocked out Seaman Jackson's tooth in retaliation for Jackson's cutting in on the chow line."

The XO finally smiled. "Yeah, and Jackson is no one I would want to mess with. Can the kid pull off a little acting? He'll need to. He will have to act the part in the pub, even though he'll probably be in there for only 15 minutes."

"Act?" the lieutenant said laughing. "Believe me, the kid was born to act!"

"Get Lloyd up here," the Captain said. "We will tell him just what he needs to know and keep the danger part at a bare minimum."

"I just have a bad feeling about this," the XO said.

Silence fell upon the boardroom like a funeral held in a library. Each man's thoughts swirled about, but each man landed in the exact same spot. No choice. And so, I was summoned. Each of them knew the mission would have a greater chance of success if I were willing to participate rather than being forced to do so.

Instead of summoning me to report to the wardroom over the 1MC, which would have drawn the attention of the entire crew, Kiggans had a steward locate me and bring me to the wardroom. The steward found me playing cards in the berthing compartment.

My game was interrupted with, "Lloyd, get your ass to the wardroom. Now."

Before I could question why, the steward turned his back and walked away.

"What the hell did you do now?" asked Dakota, as he placed his two pair on the table.

My thoughts bounced around in my head like a pinball, considering every possibility of having disobeyed an order. "I have no idea, but this can't be good, can it? Maybe they want to give me a medal for the work I did at Kythira Anchorage."

"You are an optimist," Dakota said. "Well, you sure as hell aren't being invited to have dinner with the CO!"

I folded my cards and stood. "Well, this should be interesting," I said as I climbed the ladder to the main deck.

I knocked on the wardroom door. The XO opened the hatch. "Sir, I was told…"

"Come in, Lloyd," The XO said interrupting.

I stood at attention, but my eyes moved rapidly around the room. An uneasiness swept over me like the waves that had recently covered the ship during the hurricane. The plain-clothed men and the unidentified sailors in uniform were all there. The captain spoke first.

"At ease, Lloyd. Thank you for coming up here." Like I had a choice.

"Of course, Sir."

"We have a problem we believe you can help us with," the Captain said.

I had a look of confusion on my face as I, once again, surveyed the room.

"The man who was killed in the helicopter accident was from the CIA. His name was James Mayfield," the Captain explained.

I knew it! What the hell does this have to do with me?

"He was an essential part of a top-secret mission. That is why these men are here. I'll explain more in a minute, but let me first introduce you to everyone. The first couple of men are SEALs; they are with the Naval Special Warfare Command. This is Chief Petty Officer Noah Harrington, Petty Officer Samuel Deerstone, Petty Officer Brock Brudzinski, and LTJG Jim Kovacs."

One by one, each of them stepped forward and shook my hand as I took notice of each man's mien. Noah Harrington was tall, with broad shoulders, and skin the color of coffee. Samuel Deerstone had hair the color of pepper, and skin the color of burnt umber. Brock Brudzinski was thick across his chest with huge hands and forearms. Although I had a man's handshake, firm with a tight grip, Brudzinski nearly broke my fingers when we shook hands. Jim Kovacs looked like one of the Beach Boys, tan with blonde hair. He was tall and lean.

"These two gentlemen are with the CIA," continued the Captain. "Chip Paxton and Richard Houston."

Both men simply nodded when they were introduced. Chip Paxton was clearly in excellent shape. His auburn hair and freckles made him look very unassuming, a good trait to have when you want to lull and disarm someone. Richard Houston, a short, stocky man, who looked more like a high school math teacher than an agent, wore what appeared to me a permanent scowl.

"Lloyd," the Captain said, "You have a secret clearance which can be upgraded to Top Secret on a need-to-know basis. What I am about to tell you is Top Secret. Your secret clearance has just been upgraded to Top Secret since you will certainly have a need to know the details. This mission is considered SAP—Special Access Program."

"You are not to share this with *anyone,* and I mean *anyone!* Do you understand me?" added the XO.

"Yes, sir," I responded.

"Mr. Mayfield spoke fluent Ukrainian. He was the only one on the team that did. That is our problem. An intricate part of the mission is someone who has that linguistic skill."

"That is where I come in," I said.

"Correct. I understand you speak Ukrainian with no accent."

"Так. I мама, і мачуха народилися в Україні. Yes, both my mother and stepmother were born in Ukraine."

"Perfect!" responded the Captain. "Mr. Paxton, why don't you explain the part of the mission Lloyd needs to know."

The lead CIA agent got up and walked over to me, pointing at the map laid out on the table.

"The *Adams* is scheduled to pull into Constanta, Romania on Tuesday. We'll be there for five days as a mission of goodwill between our countries. For most of the crew, it will be simply a port of call. However, unlike other ports, the crew will have to wear full dress uniforms while on land. The Romanian officials want to be sure our men can be identified easily at all times."

Mr. Paxton looked up to make sure I was listening intently. I was.

"The seven of us will take two motorized rafts up the Danube River which separates Romania from Ukraine. We leave on Thursday under the cloak of darkness as soon as the sun sets. When we get to our destination, we will camouflage our rafts and make our way to a designated location not far from where you will meet our agent. We have selected our launch date to coincide with the welcoming dinner-dance to which the mayor of Constanta and some military brass have invited the crew. That evening will be the perfect time to launch the rafts, leave Constanta undetected, and head to the river."

Paxton paused and looked at the captain, then the other men. My stomach began to feel like it did on my favorite rollercoaster ride at Willow Grove Park back home. The difference was, after every roller coaster, I always felt exhilarated. I gave the CIA agent a look of, *"Well, tell me the terrifying part."*

"We need you to go into the town by yourself, to a pub called *The Drunken Mouflon*. We will give you a coded phrase you will say to the bartender. It will sound very natural, but our contact will be in the bar listening for that phrase. He will take a seat next to you at the bar and give you a message you will relay to us when you come back to our rendezvous point. Unless there is a glitch, we should be back on board this ship in 36 hours. That's it. Simple. Okay?"

Okay? Glitch? Simple? What is your definition of simple? There is more to this story than I am not being told. Should I tell them unless they fill in all the blanks for me, they can count me out?

"What's a mouflon?" I asked.

"What?" Agent Paxton responded.

"The bar. You said it was called *The Drunken Mouflon*. What is a mouflon?"

"It's a wild sheep, like our Bighorn Sheep."

"We *need* you, Lloyd," Lt. Kiggans said, having been speechless up to this point. "Quite literally, lives are at stake here. If you refuse our request to join the team on this mission, then several important men will die. The Captain is also offering you 30 days leave after the mission, which will not count against your annually allocated 30 days leave."

"Is this an order, sir?" I asked.

Silence permeated the room. Everyone was waiting for the Captain to speak.

"No. I will not order you to join this mission…"

"Captain?" interrupted Paxton.

The captain raised his hand to quiet the agent.

"Lloyd," the Captain continued, "Your country needs you. This is your moment. Never would I send you into any situation if I did not believe you were capable. I completely believe in the success of this mission."

Well, I wanted an opportunity to prove my moxie. I was pissed off when Nam ended. All those things for which I volunteered were elementary school stuff. This is the real thing.

"Count me in," I said, instituting a chorus of exhales from everyone in the room that sounded more like the hiss from a train's brakes.

The men stood and one by one, they patted me on the back and shook my hand, all except the XO, that is. He had walked over to the large map of Romania, Moldova and Ukraine spread over the table.

"Mr. Kiggans," said the XO. "Have a cryptic message sent to our agent in Kiev. He needs to know we are still a go, and the planned date is still on."

"That's Kiev, Sir." I said, correcting the XO.

"What did you say?" barked the XO.

"It's pronounced Keeve. You said Kee-ev……sir."

"Why, you little shit!"

The CO chuckled, but quickly controlled himself as he quickly diffused the situation by interjecting, "That is exactly why you have been called here, Petty Officer. You know the native language."

Having traveled 372 miles from Istanbul, the *Adams* was scheduled to pull into Constanta, Romania the next day. There was an uptick in morale, and a little more chatter from the crew caused by the anticipation of visiting a port not open to U.S. ships for decades. There was a sense of mystic suspense about the communist country. It was different from other ports of call with which the crew was familiar. The Socialist Republic of Romania was more like a forbidden land.

I had just finished the port and starboard mid-watch, from midnight to 0700 hours. After being relieved from my watch, I went down to the mess deck for breakfast. Dakota was already in line.

"Did you just get off watch?" asked Dakota.

"Yeah. I'm beat.".

"What did the Captain want with you yesterday?"

"It's a long story. I'll fill you in later. They needed someone who can speak Ukrainian."

"That's weird. Hey, listen, I wasn't on watch, but I went into Radio Central to try and figure out who sent that cryptic message and where they sent it. I'm getting close to figuring it out," Dakota said with a hushed tone. "We always use a symmetric key algorithm, and that changes every day. The print-out showed what was sent, and I checked the algorithm for that day, the day before, and the day after the transmission. It wasn't even close. In fact, the code was not just letters and numbers, it used many symbols. One of the CIA guys sent a message, and I double-checked it after he left Radio Central, and they use the same algorithms we use, so it wasn't one of them."

"Damn! You need to bring this to Lt. Kiggans' attention. Now! Do not share this with other radiomen or LPO. One of them could be the culprit, and he could turn around and blame you. Kiggans is your department head, and he should know what you discovered. He can be trusted. The lieutenant should be able to cover your butt if something goes off the rails."

"Already did. I'm not stupid. Kiggans is cool. He's one of the few officers I like. He gave me the go-ahead to continue my investigation, but to do so quietly. He said if I were to make some noise about this, my LPO or the XO could shut it all down. He also told me to come to him first if I find anything, and we would present it to the Captain and XO."

"Ya know what? That is particularly good advice. I'm telling you, I don't trust the XO."

"Yeah. There's something squirrely about the guy. We have to nip this in the butt. Gotta go. My watch starts at 0800 and I need to shit, shower, and shave."

"Are you kidding me? Nip it in the butt? It's bud! Nipping it in the bud. Nipping something in the bud means putting an end to it before it has a chance to grow."

"Whatever. Gotta go."

As soon as Dakota left, Robinson, a radioman who worked with Dakota, walked up to me.

"What were you and Dakota whispering about?" Robinson asked.

"Nothing."

"Hmmmmm. It didn't seem like nothing, but whatever," Robinson said as he walked away.

I had an uneasy feeling about Robinson. He was a little too nosey for my liking.

CHAPTER SIXTEEN

T he port city of Constanta came into focus as the *Adams* slowed to 7 knots. The two breakwaters located northwards and southwards sheltering the port, created protection for port activities. The Casino Promenade, once considered Romania's Monte Carlo, stood as a beautiful welcome to the crew. It was the venue for the dinner-dance.

I felt a chill as I raised the collar of my peacoat to cover my neck. The skies had turned from blue to gray to synchronize with the increasing winds, like a young lady who changes her steps to oblige her dance partner. Winter overstays its welcome in the Baltic countries. Reaching into my breast coat pocket, I pulled out a pack of cigarettes and lit one up.

"So, you never did tell me what the Captain wanted?" I had not heard Dakota walk up behind me. "Don't tell me you screwed up and are restricted to the ship. I am looking forward to accommodating the desires of a few sexually deprived Romanian ladies. Are you in?"

"No. I'm not in any trouble. He asked me to do a favor for him." I said as I turned back towards the approaching shoreline.

"Favor? Yeah, right."

"I am serious.'

"Well? Are you going to give me details, or am I going to have to flip you upside down and dangle you over the side of the ship?" Dakota asked as he chuckled. "You said he needed someone who could speak Ukrainian. I know Ukraine borders Romania. Are there going to be some Ukrainian dignitaries at the dinner-dance, and they want you to be their translator?"

"No, it's nothing like that. I can't talk about it, but I won't have any liberty in Constanta."

"What? So, you *are* restricted to the ship. Damn, Cal!" Dakota said as he gave me a friendly shove in my chest.

"No! I told you I am not restricted, asshole. I will be going somewhere with some of those guys who boarded in Gaeta and both tonight and tomorrow I am supposed to be briefed," I said with a raised voice.

"Hey, you don't have to be a jerk about it," Dakota said. "Going somewhere? Like, in Romania?"

"I'm sorry, Dakota. I'm just bummed I can't hit the town with you. That's all. Actually, I don't know the details. All I know is they need an interpreter, one who speaks Ukrainian. Do not say anything to anyone! You will get me court-martialed if you do!"

"You know you can trust me. On another subject, I am almost sure I have figured out who sent that encrypted message. I do not know to whom he sent it, but I do know it was sent to someone working for the People's Republic of China. It is probably the last person you would expect. If I am correct, it is..."

"Men?"

Neither of us saw the XO walk up behind us.

"Yes, sir," Dakota and I said in unison.

"Don't let me interrupt your conversation," the XO said.

"No, Sir. We were just wondering what Romanian women look like," Dakota said, hoping that would suffice.

"I have never been to Romania, but eastern European women tend to be beautiful," the XO said. "We will be the first US Navy ship to visit Romania in over 40 years. This is both an honor and privilege. Don't do anything to bring shame upon your country, your Navy, or your ship."

"Yes, Sir. Understood," responded Dakota.

"Well, I am needed on the bridge. We are about to secure the mooring lines. Lloyd, why don't you join me," the XO said.

"What an asshole," mumbled Dakota to himself. "I need to tell Cal who the traitor is."

By the time the Adams moored at pier number six in Constanta, it was nearly dark. The lights in the port city began to speckle the night in random fashion, like fireflies on a hot, Pennsylvania summer night. I was restricted to the ship, not as a penalty, but as ordered by the Captain and the mission crew. They did not want to risk it. I watched as a flood of crewmen dressed in their Navy-blue crackerjack uniforms anxiously disembark on their way to have some fun while on liberty. There would be no fun for me.

There was only a skeleton crew onboard; only those assigned duty. I was to report to the officer's wardroom the next morning after chow for more briefing on the mission, but tonight there was little to occupy my time. I decided to go down to my berthing compartment and do a little reading to distract from the mission. The more I thought about the next few days, the more anxious I became.

Two sailors were watching the close circuit television when I arrived in the lounge area of the compartment. *On Her Majesty's Secret Service* was playing for the umpteenth time.

They really need to get some new VHS tapes on this tin can. But how appropriate. James Bond. I am going somewhere, doing something, which I will accomplish somehow. I sure hope they fill me in more on the details of this mission, but I doubt they will. Spies don't usually give a thorough run-through before a mission, do they? Something tells me I am going into this with blinders on. Not good!

Instead of watching the rerun, I picked up a dog-eared copy of Joseph Wambaugh's, *The Onion Field*, lay on my rack, and began to read. I had no idea when I had fallen asleep.

The next morning, I went up to the mess deck for some breakfast. I looked around for Dakota, wanting to know who he thought the traitor was, but I could not find him anywhere. *Maybe he got lucky while on liberty in Constanta. He's probably hung over and sleeping it off.* Meanwhile, in the officer's wardroom, the group of SEALs, CIA, and the top brass were meeting before I was to report.

"Mr. Paxton, let's review how this will be going down," said the Captain.

The lead CIA agent stood and looked at each of his men seated at the table. "The name of this mission is *Dental Appointment.* Gentlemen, you have a dental appointment; however, you will be the dentist. You are going to extract a biochemist, rather than a tooth. The Chinese dissident is Dr. Meiyang Fang who worked at The Wuhan Institute of Virology for the past seven years. We believe China has been developing new biological pathogens for at least several years. Our destination is Kiliia, Ukraine. Captain, I think it best we do not let Petty Officer Lloyd know the intricate details of the mission. As our plans unfold, we will let him know more. The last thing we need is for him to have second thoughts, or to have unnecessary fear. There will be enough going on that will force him to battle nervousness. Hell, we all have to confront those feelings."

"Agreed. Lloyd only will be told on a need-to-know basis," the Captain said.

"The 1972 Biological Weapons Convention bans the development, production, acquisition, transfer, stockpiling and use of biological weapons, but that doesn't seem to matter to the Chinese, or the Russians, for that matter," continued Mr. Paxton. "Gentlemen, biological weapons are deadly and highly contagious. Unlike conventional weapons, they are not confined to national borders and can easily spread around the world…rapidly."

"The Chinese have been known to use biological weapons in the past, haven't they, Mr. Paxton," asked the XO.

"If I may, Chip," the second CIA agent, Mr. Houston interjected. "Dozens of our military who were POWs captured during the Korean War were used for biological and medical experiments in a secret Chinese facility in Northeastern China. They were tortured and used as human guinea pigs for germ warfare research. And if I may add one more unpleasant detail, the Chinese are aggressively working on entomological warfare, a type of biological warfare that uses insects to deliver a biological agent. Essentially, the enemy infects insects with a pathogen and then releases them over a target area, infecting anything they bite, man or beast."

"Correct," responded Mr. Paxton. "Thanks for adding that, Rick. Biological warfare, or germ warfare, is the use of biological toxins or infectious agents such as bacteria, viruses, and fungi with the intent to kill, harm or incapacitate humans, animals or plants. We also have intelligence that the Chinese have been developing entomological warfare as well."

"We will launch our rafts at sundown tomorrow, our second night in Constanta. Most of our brass and Constanta's, high-ranking officers, will be at the dinner-dance, along with the majority of our crew. It's important to note the Romanian noncommissioned military are not invited, so there will be plenty of eyes on our ship and the shoreline. It's a good 90 miles from Constanta to the mouth of the Danube, and we will need to travel another 50 miles up the river to Kiliia. We must reach Kiliia before the sun rises. If everything goes as planned, we will return to the *Adams* by daybreak on Saturday morning, a thirty-six-hour excursion."

A knock on the wardroom door caused everyone to turn their heads to see me enter.

"Enter. Ahhhhh, Lloyd, we're glad you are here. Take a seat," the Captain said, pointing to an open chair next to him. "Mr. Paxton was just saying everything is in order and the mission is sure to succeed. You should be back onboard the *Adams* in time for morning chow the day after tomorrow. Thirty-six hours."

"Petty Officer, we will be taking two rafts up the Danube River to a small port town. Again, all we need you to do is to meet a man in a pub, listen carefully to what he tells you, and come back to where we will be waiting for you. You will then give us a briefing of your meeting, including the location where we will find this high-ranking Chinese diplomat and bring him back to the ship," Mr. Paxton said.

"What is a high-ranking Chinese diplomat doing in Romania? Can't he just take a flight to the U.S.?" I asked after thinking I should have kept my mouth shut.

Another knock on the door interrupted the conversation. Lt. Kiggans walked in, to my relief. One ally.

"Excuse me, Gentlemen," Kiggans said as he walked over to the Captain. Bending over, he whispered into the CO's ear."

"Sir, Petty Officer Womack is AWOL. He did not report to muster this morning."

"Okay, keep me informed when he returns to the ship. He probably had a bit too much to drink last night and is sleeping it off at some young lady's apartment," the Captain said in less than a whisper. "This is not a place where we need any problems with the crew, and we certainly do not want to draw any unnecessary attention with this mission taking place."

Sitting next to the Captain, I heard what the lieutenant whispered and became unsettled. *Dakota has gotten drunk dozens of times on liberty, but never so much that he couldn't find his way back to the ship. With curfew set at midnight, and in a communist country, he never would have screwed up this badly. Something has gone terribly wrong.*

"Lloyd, are you paying attention," the XO said in a raised tone. "This information could save your life, or the life of any one of these men."

"Yes, sir. I'm sorry."

Shit. This wasn't supposed to be dangerous, but now we are talking about the risk of dying?

"This should be easy sailing," the Captain said.

Oh sure, easy sailing, like taking candy from a baby, easy-peasy-lemon-squeezy. My ass!

Again, there was a knock on the wardroom door. "Enter," the XO said. Robinson, the radioman of whom I was suspect, entered and stood at attention. "Sir, this transmission was just received. It's classified as Top Secret and addressed to Mr. Chip Paxton." The XO took the paper from the sailor and gave it to the CIA agent. He read it and handed it to Captain Stansbury.

"The location of the exfiltration has been changed. I find that a bit odd," Paxton said. "Maybe the original location had been compromised. I guess it really doesn't affect us since we have no idea where the location is. Lloyd will be the first of our team to find that out, but I am glad this agent is playing it smart...and safe!"

The Captain put the piece of paper through a shredder that sat behind him.

"That's all for now. The Captain has arranged for us to have a special dinner before we launch tomorrow evening. Relax today and make sure you get plenty of sleep tonight. You won't get any the following night," Chip Paxton said.

As the day passed, there was still no sign of Dakota. My thoughts grew more unsettled.

Dakota would have made it back by curfew, no matter what. He is smart, and he would never risk the punishment of losing three days of liberty for a few extra hours of fun. No, something bad has happened. Was Dakota injured and unable to make it back to the ship? Shit! I should have been on liberty with him! Was he kidnapped by the Romanian Intelligence Service? The Romanian version of the KGB? No. That's ridiculous. I'm getting paranoid. Whenever he did surface, there would be plenty of questions to answer and an inevitable punishment.

I thought Dakota would go to the head or berthing compartment first, to clean up before reporting to his LPO. But when 1200 hours arrived, and Dakota had not appeared, my concern grew into a panic. I decided to walk up to Radio Central to see if Dakota went straight to his work station. The door to Radio Central was always securely locked. When someone who does not hold a high enough clearance needs to contact someone from within, he would simply knock, but instead of opening the door, the radioman would open a small sliding window, reminiscent of a speakeasy door. I just didn't know if I would need a password, like the speakeasies required. I did not have to wait long for someone to open the window.

"Yeah?" Robinson answered. I always thought Robinson was a bit strange. He was a loner. A man who had no close friends, was not married, and never seemed to participate in any fun the rest of the crew experienced in ports of call.

"Hey, Robinson, has Dakota shown up?"

"Not yet. He is in a world of shit! If he's lucky, he'll only get restricted for 3 days. I know you two are good friends, but I have to tell you, Lloyd, he may get thrown in the brig. Being a few hours late for muster is one thing, but if he is stupid enough to take a vacation for a couple of days in a foreign port, he deserves whatever he gets."

"Screw off, Robinson. The one thing Dakota is not is stupid. You, however . . ."

Robinson shut the sliding window, and I stood there for a minute not knowing exactly what to do. I decided to get some fresh air on the focsle.

CHAPTER SEVENTEEN

T he worst thing about being involved in a clandestine mission is being sworn to secrecy and forbidden to share the details with anyone, even decades later. It becomes a secret stored in that little memory room, kept locked in the hope those memories don't return to haunt.

I was invited to the wardroom for evening chow, an honor never bestowed upon an enlisted man. The men who would leave on the mission that evening were to meet in the wardroom at 1700 hours, an hour earlier than when dinner was normally served. The early serving would allow the stewards the opportunity to join the rest of their shipmates for the dinner-dance and besides, the mission crew needed to launch soon after sun down.

I went outside the skin of the ship to take in the sights of the port, hoping to see Dakota walking down the pier toward the ship. There was no Dakota, just the noise from the machinist mates and enginemen, commonly called snipes, who were finishing some maintenance on the propeller shaft and connected gear box.

I walked to the forward part of the ship and climbed the ladder to the level where the officer's wardroom is located. By the time my foot reached the third rung, a wonderful smell filled the air, causing my stomach to remind me I had skipped lunch. As soon as I reached the wardroom door, LTJG Kovacs, one of the SEALs, was just opening the door.

"Hey, Lloyd. Does that smell good, or what? I'm starving!"

"I am, too!" I said.

The other five men of the mission crew were seated at the table where seven salads were patiently waiting to be devoured.

"It's about time, boys!" Petty Officer Brudzinski said, looking up at Mr. Kovacs and me. "What were you doing, powdering your noses?

The men at the table laughed, as if on cue.

"You see, Lloyd, this is Lance's weak attempt at humor. Before any mission, we tend to joke around a bit. It relaxes us before the need to focus on the task at hand. Just want to warn you. You're free game and fresh meat," Brudzinski said.

"Wait, I thought your first name was Brock?" I said to Brudzinski.

"It is," responded Petty Officer Deerstone. "We all have nicknames. His nickname is Lance, as in Lance-Romance. You should see this guy with the ladies, smooth as Louisiana soft serve! Smoke, will you please do the honors? The lettuce is freakin' wilting!"

The black Chief Petty Officer bowed his head, and everyone else followed suit. "Dear Heavenly Father, we are grateful for this food. Please nourish our bodies, sharpen our minds, and strengthen our courage on this mission in which we are about to partake. Please bring us all back safely. In Jesus' name…"

The chorus of men concluded," Amen."

"Smoke is our preacher. His mom and dad's names are Mary and Joseph. He's the only one of us who has two nicknames, Smoke and Preacher," said Lance. "Use whichever one suits the occasion, Kid. Out of respect, we watch our language around the Preacher. At least he practices what he preaches, not like the rest of us pricks."

"No shit? Oh, sorry Preacher," I said, already forgetting about the use of foul language around the SEAL. "Your mom and dad's names are really Mary and Joseph?"

"Yep, go figure. I guess if I were Hispanic they would have named me Jesús."

The room exploded in laughter.

"They call you Smoke because you are black?" I asked.

"That, and because the enemy does not want to mess with him. He'll smoke them. Waste them. Wipe them out!" explained Lance, as he took another forkful of salad.

"Over here we have the leopard," LTJG Kovacs said as he pointed to the CIA agent, Paxton.

"How did you get the name Leopard?" I asked as my fork stabbed into my salad.

The entire room laughed. Even the steward, who brought a large carving knife to a small side table, chuckled.

"Ain't it obvious?" Lance said. "You can see that Chip is covered with freckles, right? That's the obvious part, but he's one mean SOB. He is stealth. He creeps up on his prey like a cat. In Libya, he crept up on our target, severed the man's jugular vein, causing rapid exsanguination. That target was dead before he hit the ground. You poke a leopard and it will rip your head off!"

Leopard raised his eyebrows nonchalantly. "And Mr. Kovacs here, we like to call Salmon, because he always swims upstream. He should be a commander by now, but he tends to buck the traffic. He has a tendency to piss off his superiors because he thinks outside the box. The bottom line is, he always finds a way to get the job done. He is the guy you want on a mission like this, because, if the well laid-out plans go haywire, you need someone who can improvise…quickly."

Lance turned towards me with a more serious look and said, "You would be surprised if you knew everything the CIA has done. Not all of it is spy vs. spy. Have you ever seen the movie, *Dr. Zhivago*? It is a love story set against the backdrop of the Russian Revolution, written by renowned Russian author Boris Pasternak. The CIA clandestinely published the book."

"You are kidding me," I said.

"Nope. It's true. There is something else, Kid," said Lance. "We do things a little unorthodox. We don't follow Navy regs, and we don't discuss any deviation with our superiors when we return."

"Oh, we'll get along just fine then," I said.

"Unorthodox? CIA spooks like to follow their daddy's orders down to when you can scratch an itch. Shit, you would think *they* were the ones in the military, not us SEALs. You see, the CIA frowns upon independent thought. It's not valued," Smoke said.

"Lloyd, the reason Houston and I are assigned to this task in the first place is because these squids can't do it by themselves. Oh sure, they are strong mothers, and are trained killers, but don't ask them to think," Leopard said.

"Easy, boys. We don't want any bloodshed before we even leave the ship," said Deerstone.

"We do not want bloodshed *at all* on this mission," Houston said.

"Exactly," Smoke said in an agreeable tone.

"And over here we have Vegas," Leopard said, giving a head nod in the direction of CIA agent Richard Houston. "We once had a bad experience in Houston, Texas, so none of us like the name Houston. We went through a bunch of city names till we decided on Vegas. If you get pissed at him, call him Charlotte, right Tonto?"

"That's cold," I said, recognizing that Samuel Deerstone was obviously an Indigenous American.

"That's okay, Kid. Leopard knows I'll scalp him in his sleep if he pushes me too far."

"Seriously," Leopard said, "Tonto is an Apsáalooke, a Crow Indian. Tracking and marksmanship is in his blood. He is the best!"

The steward walked in from the kitchen carrying a large steamship round of beef on a cutting board. He placed the roast on a small side table where a carving knife was waiting. Another steward brought in a large bowl of mashed potatoes and green beans with almond slivers scattered on top. It was abundantly clear to me that officers ate much better than enlisted slobs. The mashed potatoes were even made with real potatoes. In the enlisted men's mess, the mashed potatoes were dehydrated potato flakes, and a steamship round of beef would never make its way down to where the enlisted men eat.

"Now that's what I call a roast," said Smoke as the steward placed several slices on his plate.

"Why do I feel like this is the last supper?" I asked anyone who was listening.

Vegas chuckled and said, "Everything will be fine, Kid."

"You don't know that! I know less about this mission than anyone. How am I to know everything will be fine? And stop calling me Kid!" I said with a tone that surprised me.

"Oooooh! The Kid's got some fire! I like that!" Lance said.

"The Kid's right, though. We need to find him a nickname," Tonto said.

"While you all are eating, let me give you a little history lesson on where we are heading," Leopard said. "Kiliia has been controlled by more countries than Lance has had wives. Let me see if I can get this right. Back in the 14th century it was ruled by Hungary, then by Moldova, then Romania, back to Moldova, then Hungry again, and back to Moldova before falling to Turkey. Are you following the little bouncing ball?"

"No, we aren't. Pass the beans," Tonto said.

"When it was a Turkish port, it was plundered by the Cossacks, until the Russo-Turkish war, when it was held by the Russian Empire in 1812. After the Crimean war, it was returned to Turkey but was ceded once again to Russia. After the First World War, it was ceded to Romania. Now, Kiliia is a city in Izmail Raion, Odessa Oblast, southwestern Ukraine."

Wait a minute! No one said we were going into Ukraine! Shit! What is going on here? There is a hell of a lot more to this mission than what they are telling me!

"Thanks for the history lesson, but what the hell is the mission all about? I feel like a freakin' mushroom! Everyone keeps feeding me bullshit and you are keeping me in the dark!" I said.

"That's it! That will be his nickname!" shouted Tonto.

"What?" asked Salmon. "Bullshit?'

"No, Shroom!"

The table exploded with laughter at the same time the wardroom door opened. The Captain walked in. The SEALs seated at the table all began to stand when the Captain told them to be at ease.

"Really? That's the best you can come up with?" I asked. "Seriously, I told you I am in. I am willing to do whatever it takes to help this mission be successful, but you have kept me in the dark. So much for appreciating me for stepping in for the man who was killed by that flying prop."

"Mayfield. His name was James Mayfield, and you are right," Vegas said. "You deserve to know more details about our mission. Leopard?"

"Don't look at me. You seem to be on a roll," Leopard said. "Tell Shroom the particulars. He needs to know the code phrase anyway."

Vegas leaned forward and placed both hands on the table. His demeanor, serious. "Look Lloyd, I know you were thrown into this cold, but like the Captain told you earlier, this is your opportunity. Your time has arrived. You could be like one of those clones whose biggest adrenaline rush they will ever get will be setting off some fireworks on the 4th of July. They live to be 80 and yet never really lived. They've always taken the easy road. The safe road. You are actually doing something that matters. Yeah, you're right. They should have been square with you, but they weren't. So what are you going to do about it?"

I looked at Vegas for what seemed like an hour and said nothing. I looked around the table and back to Vegas in a way that communicated I wanted Vegas to continue.

"It is very important you say these exact words to the bartender. Give me a vodka and a tarhun. The tarhun first. That's the code phrase to inform our agent you are his, or her, contact. Repeat it back to me verbatim."

"Give me a vodka and a tarhun. The tarhun first," I said.

"Good. Our sleeper will take a seat next to you at the bar and will say, 'Nobody orders tarhun and vodka on Saturday.' You will respond, "I thought it was Sunday."

"What in the world is a tarhun?" Captain Stansbury asked.

"It is a carbonated soft drink flavored with tarragon," I said. "What is a sleeper?"

"A sleeper is an agent or spy living as an ordinary citizen in a foreign country," answered Vegas. "He or she is active only when directed by his or her home agency. Your contact, the sleeper, will tell you something in code. It may not make sense to you, but it will tell us where our agent stashed Fang, the biochemist. Like a dentist, we are going to extract him and bring him back to the ship. That's why the mission is code-named *The Dental Appointment*. The correct term is Exfiltration Operation. It is a clandestine rescue operation designed to bring the defector and his, or her, family out of harm's way. Fang is a bachelor, so that should make our job easier. Oh, and one more thing. Fang should be referred to as Cowbird. That is his code name."

"This kind of encrypted language is in case anyone tries to eavesdrop. This agent has been working for the U.S. for nearly a decade. I'm told this agent is one of our best. The agent will make sure he, or she, was not followed on his or her way to the tavern. You need to do the same when returning to where we will wait for you. Stop in front of shops and look in the reflection of the windows. Look to see if anyone is behind you. Stop to tie your shoe and look behind you. Zig zag around different streets to work your way back to your team. Do NOT rush back. Take your time. This will be easier than you think if you follow our instructions. Do you understand?"

So he is no senior diplomat. He is a biochemist. What more don't I know?

"Yes, sir," I said. "He, or *she?*"

"Don't call me sir," Vegas said. "We have no idea if the agent is a man or woman. Langley either forgot to tell us, or most likely, wanted to keep even that hush-hush. I cannot emphasize enough how sensitive this mission is."

"Be aware your contact may be a woman. Women make the best spies. Think about it. They spend their entire life lying to protect the frail ego of their husbands or boyfriends. 'Oh, yes, dear. You are the absolute best lover,' she says as she fakes another orgasm, or 'Yes, my love, you are so very smart.' She has to stifle her own ambition to elevate the man's. She has to act less intelligent at parties, so she doesn't upstage the man. They spend their lives *acting* in front of a male audience. Need I go on?"

"So, I assume all of you will have weapons?" I asked.

"Yes," answered Leopard. "You will be well-protected."

"But no one will be with me when I walk to the pub, while I am in the pub, and while I clandestinely snake my way back to our rendezvous point. Do I have that correct?"

"You do," said Vegas.

"Well, that is a problem. I need a gun. The 'everything should go smoothly' shit works fine until everything does not go smoothly, and my experience has been that something always goes wrong." I said with a raised voice.

Vegas looked at Leopard and then Salmon.

"The problem with that is, civilians are not permitted to own or carry a gun in the USSR. If the KGB or military police sense you have a gun on you, you will be thrown in some cell for the next 20 years," Vegas said.

"Rick, give him the pen," Leopard said to Vegas,

Vegas thought for a moment, then turned and walked over to the corner of the room to retrieve a metallic briefcase.

"This pen is a weapon, it is a single-shot gun with a safety notch, and it is designed to be carried in a shirt pocket. The .38 Short Colt bullet is a low-velocity, black powder cartridge." Vegas said, handing me the pen.

"Wait, you said *single shot?*

"Yes. It should be used only in the most dire circumstances," Leopard said.

Suddenly, the wardroom door burst open and the XO walked in. A pain-stricken look was on their faces. The XO looked at the men gathered at the table and back to the Captain, as if he were trying to decide whether or not to whisper the news he needed to convey. He decided not to.

"Captain, the enginemen were finishing some maintenance on the propeller shaft and they had to turn props for a few minutes. A body floated to the surface. It is Radioman Second Class Womack. The sailor who was reported AWOL."

I stood and yelled, "Dakota?"

Everyone turned and looked at me, then back to the Captain.

"Does it seem to be an accident? Did he come back to ship drunk from liberty and fall off the side?"

"Maybe. He has a nasty gash on the back of his head, probably caused by the propeller," the XO said.

I was devastated. I tried desperately to hold back my tears. Needing to talk to someone, I leaned over to Smoke. "He was my best friend. We were brothers." Turning to the Captain, I said, "Captain, this was no accident. Dakota, I mean Womack was murdered."

"What makes you say that, Lloyd?"

"He told me weeks ago someone sent an encrypted message from Radio Central in a format he had never seen before. It was sent to a recipient's numeric signature, also something he had never seen. He believed someone on this ship was communicating with the Chinese. He told me the day we pulled into port that he was getting very close to figuring out who sent the message, but he needed to confirm a few things."

After I had spoken, I regretted it. Not telling the Captain what Dakota's suspicions were, but rather I had told him in front of the XO.

"Peter," the Captain said, turning to the XO. "Do you know anything about this?"

"No, sir, but he may have told Lt. Kiggans. Kiggans is his department head."

"Okay. Tell Mr. Kiggans to come up here, and Peter, since we have two divers aboard the ship, send them down to where they pulled Womack's body. See if they can find anything."

"Aye eye, Captain."

I got up and walked toward the door.

"Where are you going, Lloyd? We have more to go over," Salmon said.

I ignored the question and left the room.

After I left the wardroom, I was the topic of conversation. From what Smoke told me later, it went something like this.

Turning toward Salmon, Smoke offered an explanation for my abrupt departure. "He told me the dead sailor was his best friend. He's pretty shook up."

"That is just great! Well, he better become un-shook in a hurry. We don't need him to screw this mission up for the rest of us. As it is, I don't like bringing him into this. He's never done this type of thing before, and he is not trained for it."

"He'll be fine. We just need to keep him relaxed," Lance said.

I went to the stern where a crowd of sailors had gathered. Several Romanian port workers walked over to see what the commotion was about. A frogman was sitting on the pier, putting on his mask and fins. Dakota's body was lying on the pier. There was a bloodstained slit in Dakota's shirt with a marlin spike sticking out of his chest. His body was clearly swollen, and his mouth and nose were discharging blood containing foam. Horrified, I turned and vomited off the pier. A crow had joined the chorus of seagulls in singing a requiem for Dakota's soul.

Two boatswain mates were covering the body when I heard a large splash. Two divers had entered the water.

"Lloyd, I'm sorry. I know you two were close," said a sailor standing behind me. I sat down, never turning to see who had given me his condolences.

I didn't even notice the XO who had parted the crowd. Walking towards me, he put his hand on my shoulder.

"Lloyd, I know this is upsetting, but we need you to finish preparations for tonight. We'll get to the bottom of this, and I will make sure his body is treated with respect and returned to the States and given to his family."

Could it be I misjudged the XO? Maybe he is a good guy.

"Thank you, sir. I just want a few more minutes to see if the divers find anything."

"Okay. I'd like to see that, as well."

It did not take long before one of the divers surfaced with something in his right hand. Swimming over to the edge of the pier he called out to one of the boatswain's mates.

"Hey, grab this chain. Get someone to help you pull this onto the pier. It's heavy."

The XO and I stepped closer to see what it was they were bringing up. Within a few minutes, a Kevlar lifeline appeared to have been fastened to Dakota's belt, and then attached to a deck grinder to weigh the body down. A deck grinder is a heavy machine used to strip the many layers of non-skid paint on the ship's deck. A kevlar lifeline has multiple strands of rope and acts as a fence that goes around the outside of a ship, so people don't fall overboard. When the props had been turned, it stirred the water enough to help loosen the chain from the belt, causing the body to surface.

"This is now a homicide," the XO said. "Come on. You need to get back to the wardroom. We will secure the area and have someone from NCIS fly out here from the U.S. Naval Support Activity, Naples, Italy."

The XO and I boarded the ship and walked toward the boardroom. Neither of us spoke a word, but we were consumed with thoughts about what we had just witnessed. When we entered the wardroom, the abundant chatter ceased. There was a deafening silence as the men waited for either of us to detail what we had seen.

"One of our sailors was murdered," the XO said.

"You have got to be kidding me?" Salmon said.

"No, I am not kidding. This is the last thing we need. We do not want any added attention focused on us, or the ship. I'm going to my stateroom to change my clothes. If the Captain comes back, tell him where I am. I am sure he will want to discuss things," the XO said.

"Will do," Salmon said.

A steward was standing at the table, waiting for an opportunity to speak. "Lloyd, I kept your plate warm." He set plates in front of me, but I pushed the plate away.

"You have to eat, Lloyd," Lance said. "We probably will not eat again for close to 18 hours, and even then it will be C-rations."

"I'm not hungry," I said. My thoughts were dissecting everyone who might have had a reason to kill my friend. Dakota's death had ruined me.

"Lloyd, you must eat," Tonto said. "We have a mission requiring all of us to be at our best. A good meal does more than nourish your body, it also nourishes the mind. Poor nutrition hinders your focus, it hinders your ability to handle stress, and it distracts you from your goals."

I said nothing, but I did pull my plate toward me and motioned the steward for another slice of beef. I *will* focus on the mission, and I *will* find out who killed Dakota. The agent I was to meet in the Ukrainian pub may have some clue who from my ship may have communicated with the Chinese, and who may have received the transmission. Hypothetically, only the agent, the men in the wardroom, a few select people at Langley CIA headquarters, the Captain and XO, knew of this mission.

Watch everyone carefully. Listen to every word spoken and how it is said. Even the most careful individuals will slip-up, especially when they do not think they are being watched.

The Captain and XO walked into the wardroom in their dress whites. The shoulder boards, black with gold stripes, mimicked the colors on the officers' hats, a black bill with gold scrambled eggs.

"We are off to the dinner-dance," the Captain announced. "Your mission has been well-planned. Be focused. Good luck and Godspeed."

CHAPTER EIGHTEEN

"Alright, men, we have exactly 23 minutes before launch," Leopard said. Reaching into a sea bag he pulled out some civilian clothes. "Lloyd, take off all your clothes, even your underwear and put these on. And take off your dog tags."

I looked at the rest of the men in the room. They were all dressed in black, from head to toe, including black balaclavas. I looked at the clothes Leopard gave me and mumbled, "This is what they are wearing in Ukraine?"

"You're supposed to be a commoner. A laborer. You don't have extra money to waste on stylish clothes," responded Leopard.

"But I have money to drink at a pub?"

"Everyone in the Soviet Bloc drinks…to excess. You would, too, if you lived in a country that stifles your personal freedom and human rights."

"Whatever," I said. "I hope you have thought about *every* little detail. I don't want to get strung out to dry."

"We never go into any mission without going over every little nuance. We give a lot of thought into all the 'what ifs.'"

The six men were inspecting their firearms of choice. Leopard was carrying the High Standard HDM/S, a suppressed .22 pistol, small enough to be carried stealthily. He also had another gun that appeared as though the barrel was much too narrow to shoot a bullet.

"I see you packed a .22, but what type of gun is that?" I asked, pointing to the other gun.

"It is a heart attack gun," Leopard said with a smile. "I love this gun. It shoots darts that are designed to barely leave a mark. It causes the victim to have a heart attack. I doubt I will need it on this mission, but it has come in handy in the past."

Vegas, Salmon, and Lance each carried a Browning HP-35, a pistol that could be chambered in 9 mm and .40. Smoke and Tonto both preferred carrying Glock 19.

"Let's head down to the main deck," Leopard said. "The rafts have been prepared and the cargo nets have been dropped on the starboard side of the ship."

We quietly went down to mid-ships where two rafts were sitting, waiting to become wet with purpose. The waves were slapping against the hull of the ship in perfect half notes, like a cymbal clapping monkey. The pier was dark and absent of any activity. Lights from the Casino Promenade stirred my imagination of what was going on inside, women, music, food, and dance. *Dakota and I should be enjoying the hospitality of our Romanian hosts, but instead, Dakota is dead, and I was off on a top-secret mission no one thought would include me just three days earlier.*

The rafts were lowered one at a time over the side of the ship as we climbed down the cargo nets. Lance, Tonto, and Smoke were in the front raft. I was assigned a raft with Vegas, Tonto and Salmon. The inflatable rafts whispered against the flow of the current, singing a lullaby-like water song. I turned to Vegas and said, "It sounds like a bad joke. A Jew, an Indian, and a Black man, all board a raft..."

"You think this is a joke, Shroom," Salmon said with more than a little attitude in his voice.

"No, I don't. What I do find funny is you expect me to believe this is no big deal. Just a short and simple little side-trip, and yet, all of you are as rigid and focused as copperheads stalking a field mouse. Contrary to your thinking, I am not stupid, and I am very observant. I don't know all the details of this mission, but I do know it is much more than I was led to believe."

They were the last words spoken for the next 97 miles as we quietly cruised north, staying a few miles off of the coastline. There was very little traffic in that part of the Black Sea. A few cargo ships could be seen well out to sea, but the seven of us were more concerned about the KGB agents on board the tattletale ships.

After traveling for about five hours, our rafts reached the mouth of the Danube River. The rafts had no military markings on them, yet it would be impossible for them to proceed up the river undetected. Traveling under the cloak of darkness should eliminate any identification or raise suspicion about our destination and purpose.

The weather seemed as confused as I was, not sure what was coming, and suspect of every little change in its surroundings. It had been warm enough to send a soaking dew across the riverbank, but the temperature began to drop as night settled and welcomed frost to appear.

A sliver of light from a waxing crescent moon coaxed fragile white crystals to sparkle, a valid attempt to mimic the stars above the rafts. The rafts are constructed in such a way to minimize the amount of wake they produce, even at 25 knots. The small engine was surprisingly quiet. The rafts are made for silence and stealth.

After traveling several hours up the river, the two rafts drifted toward the shore between a white poplar and a willow tree. Heavy brush aided in hiding the rafts from any curious eyes that may wander down the shoreline. Everyone had a job to do, and each did it with precision. That was comforting to me. *These guys know what they are doing. These are the world's best! I am part of an elite team! They need me!! Everything will go smoothly.*

"It is almost light," Salmon whispered loud enough for everyone to hear. "There is a small farm on the outside of town where we will spend the day. When the sun sets, Shroom will head to the pub. Let's go. We are running out of dark cover."

We climbed the riverbank and walked through an overgrown picnic area, toward the street. To avoid the appearance of a large group of men walking together, we separated into two groups. Vegas, Tonto Salmon and I crossed the street and walked a block behind the others. By the time we reached the edge of town, first light dispersed in the upper atmosphere, ushering in the morning.

We then walked together down a road, badly in need of resurfacing. The chill in the air just before dawn caused fleeting, misty clouds to escape from our mouths and nostrils. A farm appeared around the bend in the road, its silo bearing a secret sign that this was the correct location to safely wait till dark. The "sign" was actually a bright light pointed directly toward us, as if someone were pointing a spotlight on us.

"That light is actually a small mirror angled perfectly so the rising sun reflects toward the bend in the road," Leopard said. "In another 20 minutes, the sun will move enough so that the reflection will be off the road. This is our safe house. We will wait out the day. Shroom will leave for the pub at 1630 hours. It will take him about 40 minutes to walk there."

We approached the farmhouse, a small, white-washed building with a thatched roof. Smoke was billowing out of the chimney. A flickering light from a small window informed us the house was occupied. The welcoming smell of fresh-baked bread reached each of us at the same time. My stomach spoke, yet I remained quiet.

"Shroom. I'm going to knock on the door. When someone answers, say, 'the prodigal son has come home,'" Vegas said.

"Wow," I responded. "There may be a lot of truth to that statement."

A steady knock on the door interrupted a crow announcing daybreak. A sleepy rooster followed. The door opened and an elderly lady bent over at the waist appeared. She was dressed in a blue and white dress. Had she been able to stand up straight she still would have been barely taller than Smoke's waist.

"Tak?"

"Bludnyy syn pryyshov dodomu," I said.

"Ahhhhh, uviydit'," the lady replied as she held the door open for us to enter.

We walked into the cottage and took off our hats, as a sign of respect. We followed the woman into the kitchen where our eyes rested upon three loaves of challah sitting on an embroidered towel. She picked up a loaf, broke it in two, and handed it to Lance and Salmon, motioning them to share it with the rest of us. A large iron skillet with melted lard sat on the stove, waiting for the old lady to retrieve the basket of fresh brown eggs that rested on the table. The woman obliged, as she began cracking eggs with one hand as she stirred a pot of red beets with the other.

Assuming I was the only one in our group who spoke and understood Ukrainian, the lady became talkative. She told me she did not get many visitors. I politely listened as she continued cooking. The lady pointed to a shelf and asked me to collect seven plates. As if she were used to being a short-order cook in a diner, she methodically placed the eggs and a small piece of ham on each plate, handed one to each of us, and then took off her apron and went outside.

"Now this is Ukrainian hospitality," Smoke said. "I wasn't expecting this!"

"Take a look at this map," Salmon said as he picked it up and unfolded it. "It's pretty old, but it does show the layout of Kiliia. There is little detail. Where's the old lady?"

"She went out to the barn to do some work," I said. "She is alone now. She said her son was killed in Vietnam. The Soviet Union only sent about 3,000 troops to Nam; her son was one of them. He was training the North Vietnamese on how to use surface-to-air missiles the Chinese were incapable of producing. She told me a few years ago her husband was taken away by the Committee for State Security, or KGB if you would rather, accusing him of plotting with some other men to overthrow the government."

"Come on. Let's help her with the chores," Leopard said as he took the last bite of his breakfast and got up from the table.

"I will get some water from the pump outside and wash the dishes. I'll meet you in the barn when I am finished here," said Lance.

When we entered the barn we saw the old lady with a baling hook in her hand, trying to pull a bale of hay down from the loft.

"Here. I've got this," Smoke said, knowing the lady could not understand him. But she did understand. She climbed down the ladder, handed Smoke the baling hook and patted him on the shoulder as if to say, "thank you!"

The old lady moved a small stool over to a cow that looked like, if milked, would only give cottage cheese. Tonto approached the cow and forced its mouth open.

"Ol' Betsy is about 9 years old," Tonto said.

"How do you know that, and how do you know the cow's name is Betsy?" asked Salmon.

"You city boys need to get out of the concrete jungle. You tell a cow's age by its teeth. The corner teeth show considerable wear, and they have become nearly straight. I know her name is Betsy, because I just named her," Tonto said as he motioned for the old lady to let him sit at the milking stool. The lady looked surprised, then got up and stood there waiting to see if the Indian could make the pail sing. He did.

Tonto sat on the stool and leaned forward, under the cow's belly. Squeezing with his thumb and first finger as high up as possible on the udder, he then pulled down on the teats squirting the milk into a bucket. The old lady threw her head back and laughed, then patted Tonto on the back.

"I will help her feed the chickens," I said as I took the feed bucket from the woman's hands.

The chicken coop had been patched up so many times it resembled my favorite jeans I wore in high school. Sheet metal had been welded together in odd shaped pieces to create a roof. Plywood planks and solid wood sheathing made up the walls. The fence posts were made from nearby linden trees, as confirmed by the old lady. I asked her about the grove of linden trees just beyond a pond. Picking up a leaf from a linden tree she handed it to me. "It is heart-shaped," she said in her native tongue. "The tree represents the 'Sacred Heart.'"

She told me the Holodomer, the man-made famine in the 1930s that killed millions of Ukrainians, also took two of her sisters, a brother, and her father. Now, she tills the fields, milks the cow, gathers the eggs, and bales the hay. Her life had never been easy.

After helping the lady with her chores, we decided to spend the remainder of the day in the barn. We could not risk being seen outside, and we wanted to give the old lady some privacy. We settled in, resting against bales of hay and the sacks of feed. Everyone seemed unusually pensive. I was feeling much more confident as I realized how much the men were relying on me.

Turning to Smoke, I said, "If you are so religious, why don't you have a problem with killing?"

"There's a time for everything...a time to kill and a time to heal," Smoke said.

"Preach it, brother!" shouted Salmon.

"Ecclesiastes Chapter 3," I said. "Beloved, never avenge yourselves, but leave it to the wrath of God, for it is written, "Vengeance is mine, I will repay, says the Lord.""

"Ahhhh, very good! Romans Chapter 12. You know your Bible," responded Smoke.

"I was raised in the church. You could find me there for at least four services a week."

"Well, if we do not stop evil, it will spread like chicken pox," Smoke said.

Another long lull in conversation ensued. Hurry up and wait was the military way. Killing time was harder than killing the enemy. Tonto reached into his small shoulder sack and pulled out a long sleeve undershirt and a poncho liner used to trap body heat. He took off his jacket and his shirt, revealing several small circle tattoos across his chest and back.

"What do those tattoos mean," I asked.

"I am of the Apsáalooke tribe, which means people with many tattoos," Tonto said as he turned his body to show a tattoo with black and red stripes with a circle resting on top. "The seven stripes each represent one of the seven medicines of life. The circle is black on the bottom, because that is where the heart is. This triangle signifies the way one should always begin a prayer. 'Hey-so-no-ne-hoe.' Great Spirit, that's the way I want it."

"That's rich," I said. "Hey Lance, do you have any ink?"

"I'm Jewish. Jews don't get tattoos?"

"They don't?"

"When my ancestors had to endure the holocaust, demeaned to nothing but a number tattooed on the arm, I do not voluntarily get tattoos. My parents were deported from the Theresienstadt ghetto to Auschwitz. My father was tattooed with the number 158941."

"I'm sorry, Lance. I should have known better," I said, feeling pretty stupid for asking the question in the first place.

"No worries, Shroom. We're good."

"You know, I have profound respect for Jews. The world's greatest accomplishments were from Jews," I said.

"Yeah, they gave the world Matzo ball soup and potato latkes," Smoke said.

"No, really. There are fewer than 15 million Jews worldwide. That is something like 0.2% of the world population. Jews have won 22% of all Nobel Prizes ever awarded. Albert Einstein, Sigmund Freud, John von Neumann, all Jews."

"Oy Vey," Salmon said. "Are you sure you are not Jewish?"

"Nope," I said laughing. "I had a good friend who was. Hey, Smoke. Can I ask you a question?"

"Do I have a choice?" answered Smoke.

"Not really. Why do some black college students elect to be branded when they join Omega Psi Phi fraternity? I would think blacks would abhor getting branded, just as Jews would avoid getting tattooed."

"And that is the 64-million-dollar question. You're right, Shroom. Colonial slave owners often branded their slaves. Sometimes the slaves would wear several brandings. They might receive one of the Portuguese crown, or whoever kidnapped them from their homeland, and then they might receive more from each of their private owners, or perhaps an extra cross after they were baptized. So, why in the world would they voluntarily get branded? It is a combination of things. For the young black men, it forges a connection. It simply states, 'if I am willing to endure pain and permanency of branding simply to be associated with this group, then I am literally willing to die for any member of the group.'"

I stared at Smoke without responding.

"Look, I didn't say it made sense, I am just answering your question. Personally, I think if more of these young men would study in depth their own American Black History, they would never choose to be branded, but I have learned long ago, my opinion matters little to others."

"Enough with the ethnic accomplishments," Leopard said. "The only accomplishment I care about is this mission. Let's get this done and put it in the accomplished file."

There was no more conversation for a while. Tonto was whittling a piece of wood, while it appeared Vegas and Salmon were taking naps. It was Lance who broke the silence.

"Hey, Tonto, what do you want to be when you grow up?"

"A coyote," he said without hesitation.

"A what?"

"A coyote. You know, the wild dog resembling the wolf and is native to North America."

"I know what the hell a coyote is. I just don't know why that's your answer. Is that an Indian thing?" Lance asked.

"It's an Indian thing," answered Tonto as he continued his whittling without looking up.

"Care to elaborate?"

"Not really, but I have the feeling you won't leave it alone. Old Man Coyote is the Crow Indian deity. It is a long story, but Old Man Coyote was alone in a large ocean when he met two male ducks. He encourages one of the ducks to dive deep into the water. After a long wait, the duck surfaces with a root. The duck goes down a second time and brings up some mud. Old Man Coyote creates the first island out of the mud and creates vegetation from the root."

"Is that a Dr. Seuss story, Tonto?" asked Salmon.

"Screw you. I thought you were asleep," said Tonto.

"When you speak, I am all ears, oh, great one from the children of the large-beaked bird."

"How about you, Lance," asked Tonto. "What do you want to do when you get out of the Navy?"

"I want to be a pimp and own the largest whorehouse in New York City."

"Always reaching high on that sewer ladder, Lance. I'm proud of you," laughed Smoke.

"I thought he would want to own a kosher deli in Brooklyn," said Leopard, who had awakened from his nap.

"What about you, Shroom. What do you want to be when you grow up?" asked Vegas.

"Either a hand model or a corsetiere," I answered.

Then the men, in unison, broke into hysteria.

"Hand model?" asked Vegas.

"What the hell is a corsetiere?" Asked Smoke.

"I thought you pretty CIA boys would appreciate an aesthetically-pleasing, perfect hand. Look at my freakin' hands. They're beautiful!" I said.

"Shroom must be feeling pretty comfortable around us. He just busted on our two ghosts," said Salmon.

"As for your second question..." I said, ". . . a corsetiere is a professional bra fitter."

There was a pause for about five seconds, then the men broke into hysteria in unison.

"Hey, there is an underappreciated artistry in marrying a pair of breasts with the perfect brassiere, and gentlemen, I am uniquely qualified for such a profession," I added.

"Absolutely beautiful," responded Lance.

"Enough with the exploration of ethnicity and humor. What time is it?" asked Leopard.

"1320 hours," answered Salmon.

"I hate the wait. It is the worst part of the job."

"You're telling me? Well, if everything goes as planned, we will be enjoying a late breakfast on the *Adams*," Leopard said.

"All this talk of food is making me hungry," Lance said. "When we get back to Norfolk, the first thing I am going to do is go to that Vietnamese restaurant on Water Street and order a big plate of Com tấm."

"Order me some nem rán," I added.

"This is a South Vietnamese restaurant. It's called chả giò. Only the North Vietnamese call it nem rán."

"Stop talking about food!" shouted Leopard. "Damn, I do hate the waiting."

"Half of my time in the Navy has been waiting for someone or something, it seems," I said. "Hey, do you think China will retaliate once they realize this scientist defected to the U.S.?"

"Of course," Lance said. "In one way or another. It's a game they play. A one-upmanship thing."

"Why didn't he defect to one of our allies in Europe? Wouldn't that have been easier?"

"Other than Great Britain, our European allies are a bunch of pussies waiting for America to pay their debts, fight their battles, and wipe their noses," Tonto said. "We couldn't trust any of them to stick their necks out that far."

"And now most of Europe is embracing Socialism, in one way or another," Smoke said. "If the U.S. wants something done right, she needs to get it done. Socialism has not worked anywhere in the world, but everyone wants to give it a try. A couple more decades and it will be a burning ember in America, and all an ember needs to turn into a raging fire is a little wind. Liberal politicians have plenty of wind."

"You really think socialism will be accepted in the U.S.?" I asked.

"Everything begins in Europe and travels westward. Twiggy, fashion, socialism. You can quote me; socialism and lawlessness will be the norm and common sense will be abnormal. Politicians will be elected, not on their experience, but by how the media paints them. The masses are sheep. All they want is to be led, doesn't matter where."

"So, let me ask you this," I said. "You are a black man in America. Wouldn't the idea of socialism be attractive to you? Redistribution of wealth?"

"You insult me, but I know you did not mean to. So, what you are actually saying is that African Americans need to be coddled and given freebies because we are too stupid or lazy to earn our own living or to be highly educated."

"No! That is not what I meant," I said, thinking I should stop talking. It seemed I was not very sensitive with some of the subjects I broached. I guess it was the result of feeling nervous about the mission. Nervous talk.

"I know what you meant, Shroom. It's cool. Look, government handouts are not the way to help people out of poverty. It has not worked in the past and will not in the future. It does, however, buy votes. The party who keeps giving away stuff for free actually buys the vote of the black man."

"You want to crawl out of the ghetto? You take a page from the Jewish playbook. Education! Education! Education! Jews preach education to their children. They tell their children they are the minority the world hates. No one is going to give them anything. Study hard. Work hard, and that is what my parents taught me. That, and keeping the family together. Did you know that fewer than 10% of children living with two parents live below the poverty level?"

No one spoke for a few minutes, then Smoke continued, "The sheep will begin to run the country, and that, my friend, is frightening. I have been shot at by combatants all over the globe, and that shit doesn't scare me. The future of the United States scares the hell out of me."

"Well, that was some synopsis, Nostradamus," Salmon said.

"Smoke is spot on," Vegas said. "Winston Churchill said it best. "Socialism is a philosophy of failure, the creed of ignorance, and the gospel of envy; its inherent virtue is the equal sharing of misery."

CHAPTER NINETEEN

T he day moved on reluctantly, as if it needed help remembering bedtime was approaching, albeit, one minute later than the day before. Conversation sputtered like bumper-to-bumper traffic. It would happen, then it wouldn't.

Bored to death, I turned to Vegas and said, "It's not a popular time in America to be in the military."

"No, it isn't," responded Vegas. "We probably should never have been involved in Vietnam in the first place, but if the government is going to send tens of thousands of troops to risk their lives, there must be a plan in place to win the damn war. You don't win anything with a half-assed approach. You don't win a game of Parcheesi, you don't win a football game, and you sure as hell can't win a war with a half-hearted effort. We should have learned that lesson when we were in Korea. We should have known better in Vietnam."

I knew he had hit a nerve, and didn't know whether to continue the conversation or let it die. Conversation won. It made the time go faster.

"You are right. Things are changing back home, and it's not just the draft dodgers and hippies. Our country is beginning to lose consciousness and forget upon what our republic was formed," I said.

"How old are you, Shroom?" asked Leopard.

"Twenty-one."

"You sound like an old man. And that's a good thing. Where do you get your insight?"

"I read newspapers. Smoke is right. The sheep in our country believe what they are told to believe. I read and decide for myself what is right and what is wrong. I used to believe in my country right or wrong, but I have moved away from that stance," I said.

"Watergate will do that to you," said Lance.

"Do you remember what the prophet Nikita Khrushchev said about the future of America?" Lance asked. "He said 'We will take America without firing a shot . . . we will bury you! We can't expect the American people to jump from capitalism to communism, but we can assist their elected leaders in giving them small doses of socialism, until they awaken one day to find that they have communism. We do not have to invade the United States, we will destroy you from within.'"

"Leave it to a shoe-banging, crazy Ruskie to make sense of America's future," Tonto said. "Take the German people, for example. It's the proverbial frog in the boiling water. They sat around and watched Hitler become more powerful and evil while they picked their noses. Are you telling me they couldn't recognize Hitler for who he was? If it walks like a duck and talks like a duck..."

"Three things worked to Hitler's advantage. First, the populace was told Germany did not lose the First World War. The masses were told their country was betrayed into losing the war by leftists and that the Jews betrayed them. The American public is being told their government betrayed them. There is a mistrust being fed to them by those on the left and colleges across the nation."

"Second, the Weimar Republic, set up after the First World War, was hopelessly unmanageable and inefficient. The U.S. Government is becoming too top heavy. Our government is getting bigger. Big mistake! Our founding fathers stressed the importance of State rights. Let the States decide. What California wants may not be what Georgia wants."

"Third, the German people love organization and hate disorder. Germany after the First World War was chaotic. An autocratic regime brought law and order, and it was welcomed with open arms. Racial riots and war protests are bringing chaos to America. Keep it up and Americans will welcome anything and anyone who will bring calm and order."

"And you thought Tonto was only the model for the Indian head nickel," said Smoke.

"Funny," responded Tonto.

"You are spot on, Tonto," said Salmon. "The naivety of the American public; they just want to stay fat and happy. No one studies history. The German public were *intentionally* oblivious. They made that choice. If the American public doesn't wake up, the same will happen to us."

"Even England tried to eat the load of crap Hitler was dishing out," added Leopard. "Beware with whom you make alliances. Hell, even thieves know that! Prime Minister Chamberlain thought a deal with the devil would be chiseled in granite. Hell, it wasn't written in granite, it was written in sand, and as soon as the first hot wind of Nazi breath blew over the English Channel, the sandy agreement was illegible."

"Well, the American public wants their freedom, but they sure as hell don't want to know where or how it is achieved," said Salmon.

"Speaking of the Germans, I grew up in Pennsylvania," I said. "We have one of the nation's largest Amish populations located in Lancaster County, about an hour and a half drive from where I grew up. The Amish left Germany due to religious persecution and a desire to practice their faith freely. So they ran to America, where freedom rings from shore to shore. Problem is, they never have been willing to pay for that freedom. They took, but never gave. They refuse to serve in the military, the same military that paid, and continues to pay, the high cost freedom charges. Without the military, none of us would have that freedom. Freedom is expensive, and we should all contribute to that expense."

"Now look who's preaching!" laughed Smoke. "You bring up an excellent point," Leopard said. "There is an expense to freedom. Funny thing is, there is also a monetary cost to freedom. We need Congress to finance our covert operations, but after a couple of clandestine missions became public, it has become increasingly difficult to get financial backing from our own government!"

"What the masses do not know is that our government has, and continues to have, secret wars. They are secret for several reasons. First, and probably the real reason, is that the public would never approve of the majority of these clandestine "wars." The American public demands their freedom and their prosperity, but they do not want to know what it costs. No, they prefer to plead ignorance and accept the spoils of war."

"The second reason the public should never know of these secret wars has to do with secrecy. Secrecy is imperative for a mission's success. It is another reason the public must remain in the dark. Even if the Senate and/or Congress knew of these plans, the missions would surely be doomed. Most politicians cannot be trusted with a secret. That has been proven time and time again. Leaks to the press are inevitable, and then failure in these missions is guaranteed."

"Everything has to be clandestine today. After Nam and the public discovered we were in Cambodia, the public does not want our military any-freakin'-where. Everything we do now has to be on the Q.T., but we gotta keep doing it. As long as Americans can live in their safe little bubbles, have their 2.5 kids, and have their 3 weeks vacation, they are happy."

"Well, I guess they will be building another bridge in Minnesota. Right, Leopard?" Leopard laughed. "I guess so."

" Huh? Bridge in Minnesota?" I asked with obvious confusion on my face.

"Okay, a little social studies and political lesson for you, Shroom," said Salmon. "Thanks to the Rockefeller Commission and the Church and Pike committee, Congress cut off funds for military and paramilitary clandestine operations. Leopard and I were just in Angola. I know, why were we in Angola? Well, according to the American public, we weren't. But we were. The quick answer is we were there to stop the spread of communism and to protect American oil interests in the region. America staunchly opposed the left-wing, ruling party in Angola, the Popular Movement for the Liberation of Angola (PMLA), a Soviet aligned group. Leopard and I were sent there to assassinate the Cuban backed leader of the PMLA, but he pissed off so many people that one of his people got to him first."

"What Salmon is trying to say is when the CIA needs to conduct a clandestine operation somewhere in the world, they need to convince a senator to have Congress allocate funds for a major project, like building a bridge in Minnesota. The funds never make it anywhere near the land of 10,000 lakes. It's funneled through the CIA to fund our missions."

"Do you really believe the CIA is ever going to stop clandestine operations around the world?" asked Vegas. "Just because some career politician thinks a national crisis is limited to a fabric snag on his custom-tailored suit, does not mean we can stop gathering intelligence on our enemies and thwarting their efforts. The CIA is different from Special Forces. They often go in with a bang. We go in with a whisper. If we do it right, no one is aware we were there."

"It's getting late. Shroom, are you ready? What are you going to say when you walk up to the bar?" asked the Leopard.

"Give me a vodka and a tarhun. The tarhun first," I said.

"Good. It's going to take you about 40 minutes to walk to the bar. Look at this map. Just three turns once you walk down the farm road. The *Drunken Mouflon* is located on Vulytsya Kahul's'ka. Right here," Leopard said while pointing to a spot on the open map. "Got it," I said.

"Any questions?" asked the Leopard.

"Nope. I'm good."

"Alright then. Come back here after you leave the pub. Remember, zig zag. Stop occasionally and look behind you. Use reflections in the store windows."

"I know. I have it. I won't let you guys down."

"We know you won't, Shroom," Salmon said. "See you in a couple of hours."

A slight breeze blew across the naked fields giving me a chill down my spine. Remnants of corn stalks bent over as if to pay homage to the soldier marching off to war. I could envision the old lady harvesting the corn and shucking it for her livestock's feed. I pitied her. *No one deserves such a hard life. Stop! Focus! No distractions!*

The directions to the pub were simple enough. I made the second of the three turns and began to pass stores closing for the day. A baker was unloading a sack of flour from a truck that coughed black smoke from its exhaust. A few blocks farther, there was a light on in a butcher shop. I stopped and watched a man in a white apron skin rabbits. He did so with such precision and grace, like a maître d' helping a lady remove her stole; one gentle movement.

Making my last turn onto the town's main street, the pedestrian traffic picked up. It gave me a calm feeling to mesh into the busyness of the residents hurrying home for dinner, or in my case, to grab a quick shot or two at the pub before heading home. A wooden sign with an engraving of a species of sheep with large horns curled around its face moved back and forth as the wind blew sporadically. The mouflon's eyes looked tired and inebriated. Small bubbles retreated from the sheep's portrait towards the letters that spelled *The Drunken Mouflon*.

I could hear music escaping with the cigarette smoke as a portly man exited the pub. I caught the door before it closed and entered the pub. To my surprise, no one looked up from his perch. For some reason, I envisioned everyone stopping in mid-sentence and silence engulfing the patrons as soon as I walked into the pub. *I have watched too many Westerns!*

Another surprise was the type of music being played. American blues! At the end of the sixties, thousands of high-school and college students in the Soviet Union became amateur ham radio operators recording and then broadcasting popular Western music. The KGB interpreted this as "radio hooliganism" and concluded anti-Soviet behavior was stimulated by western pop culture. Nonetheless, western music grew in popularity.

A stage not measuring more than 8 x 10 was nestled in the back of the room, and a three-piece band was playing. A bass player with sunglasses and a sixpence cap stood next to an upright piano. Although the pianist could not speak a word in English, he had memorized the English words and sang them fairly well:

> *You made my dinner, yes, you made my bed,*
> *You shared secrets, that I swore I wouldn't tell,*
> *I heard 'I love you,' that is what you said.*
> *This sure ain't heaven, so it's gotta be hell.*

The music was not half bad and was an unexpected comfort even though my heart began mimicking the song *Wipeout*. As I walked over to the half-filled bar. A poorly taxidermied wolf head with snarling teeth guarded the bottles of liquor that lined the bar, reminiscent of *Werewolves of London*. I took a seat at the bar, an empty seat to my left. The man to my right downed a shot of vodka then slammed the glass on the counter signaling the bartender for a refill. Assuming I would order vodka as well, the bartender looked at me and asked, "Shcho ty matymesh?"

In Ukrainian, I answered, "Give me a vodka and a tarhun. The tarhun first."

The bartender poured the vodka, then turned away to retrieve the tarhun.

"Nobody orders tarhun and vodka on Saturday," a voice behind me declared. I had not seen the man approach the bar. Turning my head, I saw a slender middle-aged man with wire rimmed glasses, dark hair, and a thick mustache to match.

"I thought it was Sunday," I responded.

"Every day blends into the next anymore," the man said as he pulled a deck of dog-eared playing cards from his coat pocket. "Want to see a card trick?"

"Sure," I answered as the music continued.

> *You fed me meatballs of lard and ground bread,*
> *you have me captured under your witchy spell,*
> *you stood there laughing while I sat and bled,*
> *this sure ain't heaven, so it's gotta be hell.*

The man shuffled the cards. I cut the deck and selected a card which he placed in the middle of the deck. It was the King of Hearts, the suicide king. *How appropriate,* I thought. The man made some hand movements above the deck and turned over the top card. It was the King of Hearts. Several more times I took a card, buried it in the deck, only to have it surface as the top card.

"Impressive," I said.

"One more time," the man said.

After sliding the card randomly into the deck, the man turned over the top card, and it was the Five of Spades.

"Ah ha!" I said. "It didn't work this time."

"Look in your right coat pocket," the man said.

I reached into my pocket and pulled out the King of Hearts. "Well done!"

"It's called the Ambitious Card Routine. Keep the card. It will come in handy. There is an abandoned Olympic training facility just west of town. You will find your Cowbird at the skeet and trap range." With that, the man finished his drink, patted me on the shoulder, and left the pub.

I sipped on my tarhun, and then took one more shot of courage. Not wanting to leave the pub too soon after the man left, I turned and faced the band as they continued to play.

I sat here cryin' in my beer.
tears coming, a bottomless well,
You stood there laughing at my tears,
This sure ain't heaven, so it must be hell.

I stayed for one more song, placed a ruble and a 50 kopeck on the counter, and left *The Drunken Mouflon*.

It was not very late in the evening when I walked out of the pub. People were just finishing dinner in Kiliia. Black choking clouds of smoke from coal being burned in homes filled the air. Those who could not afford coal burned wood. When the clouds were low, as they were tonight, the smoke stayed below an imaginary horizontal stick in the air, as if it were playing limbo. Street lamps lined the main thoroughfare, but once I started my zig zagging by alternating right and left turns onto other streets, lighting became sporadic. I could hear people coughing from the chimney smoke, and yet I did not see anyone. It gave me a feeling of uneasiness.

At one point, I walked completely around the block, then entered a park, walking diagonally through its center. A mammoth statue of Elizabeth Petrovna, Empress of Russia on her horse looked out of place, icicles clinging to the horse's mane. The smell of the chimney smoke, the lingering taste of tarhun, the sensation of the cold breeze on my cheeks and lips and the silence accentuated all my senses. The slightest movement of a tumbling leaf captured my vision; a cracking noise heightened my scrutiny. *Broken twig. Someone is following me!*

I paused and studied the statue, looking back to see if someone was behind me. Two dark figures were roosting on a park bench like a couple of sparrows waiting for breadcrumbs to be tossed their way. Both figures were slight in build, with one of them markedly short in stature. I evaluated the situation.

They are just a couple of ladies out for a walk. But at night? Are they KGB informants passing on information as to my destination? I cannot blow this! Great, there are two of them, and I have this stupid pen that fires only one shot. Am I simply paranoid? Would it look odd if I turned around and walked back the way I came, passing them? I could get a better look at them.

I decided to do just that, thinking their reaction would give me some idea as to whether they might be following me. As soon as I turned and started walking their way, both figures quickly got up off the bench and walked away with their backs to me.

Okay. This isn't good. Coincidence? Maybe, but I'm not taking the chance.

I exited the park and turned down a side street out of the vision of the two figures. I quickly ducked into a small entryway to a cobbler's shop. As I expected, the two figures passed by without noticing me. The lack of light prevented me from getting a good look at the couple stalking me. I waited several minutes before walking in the opposite direction. *Shit! Am I lost?* Gathering my thoughts, I assessed my surroundings, looking for a landmark as I continued to walk, consciously keeping my pace at a normal stride. That alone seemed to be a challenge as my instincts told me to run.

Making another turn down a street, I saw the butcher shop where the man had been skinning rabbits. The shop was now dark and closed for the evening, but it gave me my bearings. I used the reflection in the store's window to look for the two figures. I saw nothing but an overweight man smoking a cigarette, walking in the opposite direction. I continued to cross streets, turn down side streets and alleys until I reached the lonely street where the smallholder farm was located. A small light was a welcoming beacon, like a lighthouse guiding a sailor to a safe harbor. Snow had begun to fall which gave me more concern. My footprints would be a map for anyone pursuing me.

Flurries are not going to do the trick. It needs to snow harder to cover my tracks!

I turned off the road and onto a first trail toward the farm. I approached the barn, knocked twice and slid the large barn door open. I was welcomed by six guns pointing at me.

"That's a warm welcome," I said.

"We will not shoot you until we're heading back to the ship," laughed Lance.

CHAPTER TWENTY

"How did it go?" asked Leopard.

"It went fine, except I am convinced two people were following me. That's what took me so long to get back. I ducked into a store entryway and they passed me. Then I doubled back. I definitely lost them."

"That's not good," Salmon said. "Not that you lost them. The fact that you were being followed."

"Where are we to rendezvous with the Biochemist?" Leopard asked.

"He told me there is an abandoned Olympic training facility just west of town. Oh, and he gave me this playing card," I said, handing the card to Leopard. "Is someone going to fill in the blanks? I want to know everything. I'm entitled to that, aren't I? I swear, I feel like the Lone Ranger!"

"Hey, you hear that, Tonto? You need to start calling Shroom, Kemosabe," Lance said.

"Funny," Tonto mumbled.

"Is there some significance with the King of Hearts?" I asked.

"No," answered Vegas, "but there is a message concealed within this playing card. Tonto, would you take this pail and put a little water in it? There's a well pump by the farmhouse."

Tonto grabbed the rusty pail from Vegas and left the barn.

"There's an abandoned Olympic facility around here? I didn't see that on the map we studied back at the ship," Smoke said.

"Yeah," answered Leopard. "When the facility was built decades ago, a shitload of mistakes were made due to the rushed construction. In particular, the stadium was aligned along an east-west axis instead of the standard north-south. After living with the poorly constructed facility for decades, a replacement stadium was built a few years ago. While renovations were taking place this location in Kiliia was used as the Olympic training for their athletes, but now it just sits there as a concrete ghost."

Tonto returned with a bucket of water. Vegas dipped the card into the pail. Words gradually appeared on the card, reminding me of those blank pieces of paper I would get as a kid that magically manifested an image when I rubbed a pencil across the paper. Tonto read the words out loud. They were brief, but disconcerting.

Archery Range.
Cowbird in danger. Being pursued by C & R. Move quickly.

"Shit! That's all we need," Salmon said. "Both the Chinese and Russians are in hot pursuit of Fang. Alright, we need to get moving. We go to the Olympic Training Facility, retrieve the Cowbird and get the hell out of here. Suit up!"

I leaned over to Smoke and asked, "Why is the code word for the biochemist cowbird? I know you guys like to use symbolism."

"The cowbird is a brood parasite. It does not build a nest. Since the biochemist will be homeless and looking for a nest, someone thought it was a good code word."

The men grabbed their weapons, and we exited the barn. The wind bit at our faces, like a gentle slap to awaken the senses, not that we needed any awakening. We all were acutely focused. The other team members knew their assignment and were more than ready to execute their plan and get back to the ship. It seemed like years since I left the *Adams.*

The abandoned Olympic village was just a few miles from the farm. We would get there in under thirty minutes. Leopard led the way using a flashlight that radiated a red light. It did not illuminate very well in front of him, but it also could not be seen from a distance.

The rest of us followed closely in pairs. I was teamed with Smoke. Vegas and Salmon brought up the rear, constantly watching to make sure we were not being followed.

There was no sign at the entrance to the Olympic facility. Graffiti was splattered randomly on anything that would accept the unsolicited paint. No windows were left unbroken, and doors had either been removed or, where they had been padlocked, forced open by removing the hinges. The only sound was the wind whistling between the buildings. It not only looked like a ghost town, it felt like one, too.

"Shroom, what does that sign say?" Leopard asked, pointing to a placard with discolored lettering and an arrow pointing to the right.

"I speak Ukrainian, I can't read it," I answered.

"What direction should we head?" Tonto asked.

"Vegas, Lance and Tonto, follow that sign. We'll go this way. The Cowbird was supposed to be at the skeet and trap range. According to the playing card, that has been changed to the archery range. If you find it, use your walkie-talkie, but keep audio traffic to a minimum."

The two teams went our separate ways, but it did not take long before Vegas received a transmission from Leopard.

"We found the range. Double-back and take the same route we took. At the fork, bear left."

The three men turned around and headed for the archery range where they would rendezvous with the rest of us. After finding the biochemist we would head back to the rafts, and then to the ship. We were still on schedule. When we arrived at the range, they immediately saw our tense expressions.

What's the matter?" asked Tonto.

"We can't find the Cowbird," answered Salmon.

"He may be scared and afraid to come out of hiding. He's around here somewhere," Tonto said.

"He knows we are coming to pick him up, right? I get that he did not want to stand in the open and wait for us, but when he saw us walking around, wouldn't he show himself?" Smoke asked.

"He knows the plan. Look, we are wasting time, and we need to get back to the rafts and head back to the ship no later than 2300 hours. We're going to split up into three groups this time. Smoke and Shroom, search the skeet and trap range thoroughly. There are storage areas over there. Look everywhere. Tonto and Vegas, stay here in case

Cowbird shows up. Salmon, Lance and I will walk the perimeter to see if he strayed off a bit. Maybe he got spooked," Leopard said.

"Stay with me," Smoke told me. "I don't want us to be separated."

"Neither do I. Remember, you are the one with the gun," I said.

We walked to the skeet range where a trench sat in front of the shooting stands concealing a dozen or so traps. Shattered clay pigeons littered the course. The Cowbird, Fang, was nowhere to be found.

"He's obviously not here," said Smoke. Let's go back to the entrance and wait for the others. They probably found him and will be back soon. Time is our enemy at this point."

Smoke and I stood at the entrance to the shooting range waiting. I noticed Smoke was unusually edgy. Thirty minutes seemed like hours. Smoke reached for his walkie-talkie. He would not have wanted to create any transmission noise over the frequency, but there were few options. He wanted to get the group back together and hopefully, with the Cowbird.

"Adams 6 to Adams 1, what is your position, over?"

Nothing but static could be heard from the walkie-talkie.

"Adams 6, this is Adams 1, can you read me?"

Nothing.

"Something is wrong. We need to get out of here and see what is keeping them," Smoke said.

The high-pitched squeal of rubbing metal surfaces broke the silence. Instinctively, Smoke reached into his vest and pulled out a Colt M1911A1 .45 ACP, a pistol best-known for its short recoil. I felt naked and vulnerable without a weapon. The one-shot pen I had was worthless if a gunfight materialized.

We approached the amphitheater, littered with red, yellow, blue, and white- lettered graffiti. *There is something the world shares, a senseless act of self-expression. The artist's brush, a spray can. The canvas, a wall. An illicit art gallery.*

Our senses were in hyperactive mode. We could hear a raindrop a mile away, or smell gunpowder just as far. A scurrying of feet brought both of us to a standstill.

"Did you hear that?" I asked.

"Yeah. It came from over there," answered Smoke. "Quiet. Follow me."

With our backs to the painted mural, we took short steps toward the corner of the building. Smoke took a quick peak around the building. He saw a dark figure at least a hundred meters away running the opposite direction.

"Someone is high tailing it from the far entrance to the amphitheater. I couldn't tell if it was one of our guys. Come on. Let's see what he was running from," Smoke said.

The Aquatic Center with large panes of broken glass stood before us. Even from a distance we could see the rusted high-dive platform for the Olympic swimming pool. As we entered the building, I saw the tiled sides of the pool and the painted lines to help the athletes stay straight while swimming. Near the end of the pool, the lines formed a T-shape that alerted the swimmers they were nearing the end of the pool. A cushioned office chair on wheels was ectopically positioned in the deep end of the pool. Sitting in the chair was Salmon with his head hanging off the back of the chair. As we got closer, we saw a fish wedged in his mouth. Smoke jumped into the dry pool and ran to the lifeless body. A solitary crow with its glossy black plumage was perched on the diving board, barking with its raucous voice, as if calling for more witnesses to the scene of the crime.

"Shit," Smoke whispered.

"Someone knew where we were to meet the cowbird," I whispered, startling Smoke, who never heard me enter the pool behind him.

"For sure, but something else is going on here. They didn't just kill Salmon. They were sending a message. Why the hell stick a fish in his mouth? There is definitely a message here. I just don't know what that message is."

"A friend of mine from back home is Italian. He said his grandfather was in the mafia. I never really believed him, but once told me back in the day, the mafia allegedly would put a fish on someone's stoop to warn the homeowner if he did not stop what he was doing, or if he would not leave town, he would end up sleeping with the fishes," I shared as I looked back up at the crow.

Crows! Tonto was from the Crow Tribe. Coincidence? No, I am just paranoid.

"Well, we are not dealing with the mafia," Smoke said. "I guess there's the Russian mafia, but I don't know what they would want with us, or Cowbird. Let's find the rest of the team."

Smoke and I left the Aquatic Center and walked to the west side of the Olympic Training Facility. Smoke took his walkie-talkie and spoke into it.

"Adams 1, this is Adams 6, do you copy?"

The response was only crackling and hissing noises. The two of us walked until we reached the podium for winners of the games, the faded Olympic rings standing behind it as a reminder of dreams fulfilled and dreams shattered. I was beginning to think any dreams I had might fall into the latter category.

Why a winner's podium if this was only a training facility? Maybe it was for the athletes to envision what it would be like to reach the pinnacle of success.

Focus!

I turned and started walking toward something hanging from a railing. As I got closer I could tell it was one of our crew's backpacks.

"Over here," I whispered as loudly as I could.

Smoke walked over to me and took the back pack from my hands.

"It's Lance's," Smoke said.

"Is that Lance over there?" I asked while pointing towards a raised platform adjacent to the podium.

Behind an overgrown kalyna bush at the far side of the complex, I could see what appeared to be the back of Lance's head.

"Lance!" Smoke called out; a bit louder than I wished he had. "Brudzinski?" Turning to me, Smoke said, "He can't hear us from this distance, and I don't want to yell any louder. We are going to have to go around the back of those grandstands in order to reach him."

There was no direct access to where Lance was standing. Smoke and I had to walk around the backside of the podium and take the walkway around the north side of the complex. On the far side of the podium, we took steps going down to ground level. From there we could approach Lance's left flank.

As we got closer to Lance, the kalyna bush became less of a camouflage. We both saw it at the same time and stopped, as if our shoes were in quicksand. Lance's decapitated head was impaled on a spike, his torso was lying close by with his hands bound behind him and feet tied with a white cord. Neither of us said a word. The silence was deafening.

I picked up Lance's revolver next to the torso and looked at Smoke. Neither of us said a word. We stared at each other for what seemed like an Olympic marathon. One obscure thought came to mind. *This sure ain't heaven, so it must be hell!*

Smoke broke the silence. "Salmon, Lance and Leopard left together." Let's hope Leopard is still alive."

I picked up a fallen sign with a map of the Olympic Training Complex. I studied it for a minute.

"They said they were going to walk the perimeter. The Aquatic Center is here, and the podium is also on the perimeter, right here. Logically, the next stop would be at this lake, where training for canoeing, kayaking, sailing, and rowing took place."

"Alright, let's head over there," Smoke said in agreement.

The lake was on the east side of the complex. The north shore was sheltered by woodland that included birch, elm and poplar trees. The far east side of the lake was scattered with large estates where party leaders had built summer homes. The south and west sides of the lake demarcated the Olympic Training Facility. The absence of any boats made the scene look incomplete, as if an artist had not yet completed his painting. Empty, rusty, boat racks sat waiting for a canoe to grip the gunwales where they could rest, waiting for the next race.

A caw from the familiar crow informed us it was not only following us, but arrived at the lake before we did. It directed our attention to a dock which had capitulated to the elements and was partially submerged in the lake. On the dock was a rack that would have held six canoes. It leaned toward the water. There was one object lying on the rack, but it was not a canoe. It was Leopard.

Leopard was lying prone on his back. His eyes were wide open, as was his mouth. His mouth was filled with water. Smoke walked over to the body to inspect it for the cause of death.

"There are no wounds on the body. He drowned. Leopard was an all-American swimmer in college. Someone held him under the water. There is no way he drowned without someone's help," Smoke said. "What a cluster. Let's hope Tonto and Vegas are okay."

"And that they found the Cowbird," I added. "This is messed up."

Morning twilight promised dawn was not far off. Neither were thoughts of my possible demise.

Even if we find Cowbird, and meet up with Vegas and Tonto, our plans will have to change. We will not be able to navigate the Danube and skirt the Black Sea during daylight.

Smoke and I walked cautiously back toward the archery range where our two remaining team members had been searching for the Cowbird. The only sound was the morning wind repeating the same message, danger was still lurking around every turn. The silence was short lived, however. We heard a hideous scream from a building a hundred meters in front of us.

"What the hell was that?" I asked, as a cold chill met the sweat dripping down my spine.

"I don't know, but it came from that building. Make sure that piece is at the ready," Smoke said as he nodded toward the gun in my hand.

Another scream; this time with a prolonged tone of agony. The only obvious certainty, it was a male voice. A small trail of smoke rose against the rising sun.

"Something is burning over there," I said.

Outside the building was what appeared to be a heap of trash, with small flames gyrating at the wind's command. The two of us cautiously approached the smoldering mass. The closer we got to it, the more confused we were of what was burning. It was not until we were standing next to the burning item until we realized it was the badly burnt corpse of Vegas. That left only Tonto.

"Oh my God! Help us!" I mumbled.

"We are a step behind them. Whoever is responsible for this cannot be far from here," Smoke said.

The building where we were standing was the cafeteria where the athletes were once fed. A door was open just wide enough for one person to enter at a time. Smoke entered first, with his gun drawn. I followed.

The dawn provided little light within the large room. A row of long tables with fixed chairs attached to them scattered the cafeteria. The serving line with a combination of hot food wells and cold food compartments stood at the front of the room. Behind the serving line were two large-capacity sinks where another one of our team's backpacks had been placed.

"This is Tonto's," Smoke said.

Walking over to some swinging doors leading to the kitchen, Smoke whispered, "I'll go in high; you go in low. If anyone starts firing, take cover behind a piece of equipment or the counter."

Smoke pushed the door open just a crack. Peeking inside, he saw no one. Smoke slowly opened the door and entered. As instructed, I crouched as I entered the kitchen behind him. An island prep table stood in the middle of the room with various pots and pans hanging above it, like Spanish moss dangling from a cypress tree. Four large gas stoves lined the far wall. Three of the four ovens were open. A walkie-talkie was on the floor near the stoves. I picked it up and showed Smoke. Neither of us spoke a word.

Instinctively, I walked over to the one oven not open. One end of a rope was tied around the handle, the other end of it tied to the stove's leg so it could not open. I walked over to the prep table and looked in several drawers.

"What are you looking for?" whispered Smoke.

"A knife. That last oven is tied shut."

"Here," Smoke said as he handed me his Survival Rescue Knife.

I took the knife and cut the cord tied to the oven handle. I pulled the oven open, then immediately fell backward, as if having been pushed unexpectedly. Tonto's body was crammed into the oven in a fetal position. And then there were two.

"Let's get out of here, Smoke said. Because we kept moving we were spared the same fate as our teammates. We'll take one more look around the archery range. If the Cowbird isn't there, we will get out of here and head back to the rafts."

When we walked back outside, I heard a commotion in a naked linden tree. The solitary crow was joined by a murder of crows, laughing in unison as they expressed their unanimous approval.

As Smoke and I walked back towards the archery range, thoughts rushed through my mind like water gushing through a compromised dike. A children's counting rhyme I had not heard, or thought of for years, played in my head.

> *Ten little Indians standin' in a line,*
> *One toddled home and then there were nine.*
> *Nine little Indians swingin' on a gate,*
> *One tumbled off and then there were eight.*
> *Eight little Indians gayest under heav'n.*
> *One went to sleep and then there were seven;*
> *Seven little Indians cuttin' up their tricks,*
> *One broke his neck and then there were six.*
> *Six little Indians all alive,*
> *One kicked the bucket and then there were five;*
> *Five little Indians on a cellar door,*
> *One tumbled in and then there were four.*
> *Four little Indians up on a spree,*
> *One got fuddled and then there were three;*
> *Three little Indians out on a canoe,*
> *One tumbled overboard and then there were two.*
> *Two little Indians foolin' with a gun,*
> *One shot t'other and then there was one;*
> *One little Indian livin' all alone,*
> *He got married and then there were none.*

The archery range was not the original rendezvous point for retrieving the Cowbird, but Smoke thought perhaps, the biochemist got confused as to which firing range he was to wait for us. Perhaps he went to the skeet range first, then headed for the archery range. Archery had disappeared from the Olympics for 40 years but made its return at the 1972 Munich games. The United States won two gold medals with Poland and Sweden taking silvers and Finland and

Russia taking bronze. Walking over to a large wooden box, I inspected the pile of broken bows and arrows. I picked up one of the bows. It was a recurve bow, with which I was familiar, but instead of a brush rest, it had a feather rest.

Targets were littered across the shooting range, some torn with straw sticking out like the bristles of a broom. A wall behind the targets had collapsed, causing large slabs of concrete to slope precipitously. Smoke leaned against part of the broken wall and tried to gather his thoughts. I let him ponder the situation before I spoke.

"Smoke, why were each of the men killed differently? Why not simply shoot them?"

"I asked myself the same question. It doesn't make sense. Clearly, someone was sending a message, but there is a more pressing question. Who is the traitor? No one knew where we were to meet Cowbird. In fact, it was a secret our agent did not verbally reveal. He gave us the playing card that had to be soaked with water before it showed us where we were to find Cowbird. It could have been someone on the ship, but he would have had to be in communication with either the Chinese, Russians, or Russian-controlled Ukrainians."

"Stay here. I'm going to make sure Cowbird is not hiding in one of those two small sheds over there. If he isn't there, we need to head for where we stashed the rafts and wait till sundown before heading back to the ship. We will have lost a full day. The *Adams* is leaving Romania tomorrow morning, so our window of time is closing."

I watched Smoke walk towards the two storage sheds. I was not going to let him out of my sight. Five of the seven who left the ship were dead. If something were to happen to Smoke, I knew I would be next.

What was it Leopard said when we were in the wardroom on the ship? *If everything goes as planned, we will return to the Adams by daybreak on Saturday morning, a 36-hour excursion. This should be plain sailing.* Right! Smooth sailing until dismasting occurs. In this case, the high winds and storm that broke the mast for hoisting the sails was not caused by the weather. *Superman, where are you now?*

Smoke stealthily opened the door to the first shed. A metal rake, a shovel and burlap bags of straw filled the small space. As soon as he reached the door of the second shed, a man with a handgun burst out of the shed, knocking Smoke's gun out of his hand. Smoke instantly grabbed the man's wrist and repeatedly smashed it against the door, causing him to drop his gun. The assailant kicked hard, landing his foot on the outside of Smoke's thigh, targeting the nerve running down the outside of the leg, a favorite technique of Muay Thai fighters. Smoke fell in a heap.

The assailant turned in an attempt to retrieve his gun, but Smoke grabbed his foot and twisted it violently, causing the man to stumble and fall on one knee. By the time the man was able to stand again, Smoke had already gotten up and landed several hard blows to the man's face. The man responded with several blows. Although Smoke was at least 25 pounds heavier, the man was more than holding his own.

I aimed Lance's handgun at the assailant, waiting for an open shot, careful not to endanger Smoke. When I finally had an opening, I squeezed the trigger, but nothing happened. The gun jammed. I decided to enter the fight, but as I ran towards it, I had an idea. I stopped at the pile of bows I saw earlier. I picked up one with the string attached. The majority of aluminum arrows were either bent or missing a fletch. Quickly rummaging through the pile, I found an arrow intact. I aligned the slot in the nock with the string and pulled the bow back to my ear.

The man, although badly beaten, was able to pick up his gun. Just as he lifted it to shoot Smoke, I released the arrow striking the assailant between his ribs. The man fell on both knees and grabbed the arrow in his hands. With his eyes wide open, he fell on his face, dead.

Smoke seemed as surprised as the man appeared to be.

"Though they intended evil against You, and devised a plot, they will not succeed.

For You will make them turn their backs. You will aim with Your bowstrings at their faces," Smoke said.

"That has to be a Psalm," I said.

"Psalm 21:11-12. I wish Tonto were here to have witnessed how you handled that bow," Smoke said as he turned the body over to look at his face. "I owe you, Shroom! You saved my life."

"You don't owe me anything, other than getting me back to the ship safely," I said.

"This guy is Chinese," Smoke said. "They must have sent agents to Ukraine to retrieve Cowbird. I wonder if the Soviets are in on this too. It really doesn't make sense, but then again, not much has made sense today."

"The Soviets hate the Chinese. Strange. What is more perplexing, the KGB and China's Central Investigation Department working together. The People's Republic of China is considered a dangerous adversary of the Soviet Union. Very strange. But then again, when enemies have a common goal, they often join forces, temporarily. Strange bedfellows."

"This was supposed to be *easy!* That is what everyone kept telling me," I said.

"How do you think I feel, Shroom? I just lost three friends with whom I fought, ate and drank. They were family! I knew more about them than I do my own brothers and sisters." Looking at the dead man's face again, he said, "This guy is definitely Chinese. No surprise there. They will do anything to keep Cowbird from defecting."

"Okay, let's get going. It's already light. We need to move the rafts to a safer location. About a mile upstream there is a cluster of boathouses. We will take one of the rafts up there and convince someone to let us store it until sundown. I'll give them my knife for their trouble. Believe me, that will be more than enough payment. I'll need you to do the talking, that is, unless they speak English or Spanish, which I doubt will be the case."

The two of us left the Olympic Training Compound and started walking back to where the rafts were hidden. The streets were sprinkled with people going about their morning chores or heading to work. The busyness of the streets was a welcome sight. It was easier for us to blend into the pedestrian traffic.

By the time we reached the river, barges were already making their way north upriver to where ports were located. There, longshoremen would unload the cargo. When it appeared as though no one was paying attention to us, we hurried down the bank of the river to where the brush was camouflaging the rafts. Immediately it was clear to us someone found the rafts and made a poor attempt to cover them with the brush.

"I hope to God whoever found these rafts was just a curious dockworker or stevedore," Smoke said.

I removed a few branches only to reveal that one of the rafts was deflated, like a child's party balloon that had lost its helium.

"Someone sabotaged the raft," Smoke said.

"There's a large slit in the side," I said, lifting the edge of the raft.

Smoke and I dragged the raft that had not been slit into the water. I got in first, with Smoke taking the stern. Smoke yanked the pull start cord, but the engine only coughed. He tried pulling the cord again, with the same results.

"Someone has screwed with the engine," Smoke said as he opened the lid to the gas tank.

Looking around, he found an undershirt caught on a branch by the water's edge. Tearing a piece off the shirt, he wrapped it around his index finger and put it into the gas tank, swirling his finger. He pulled his finger out and inspected the piece of cloth.

"Ground glass. It wasn't a river worker who did this. Whoever leaked the confidential information about our mission had plenty of help here in Ukraine. We have been sabotaged at every turn. We are going to need some help. Our agent is based out of Izmail, about 19 nautical miles from where we are now. I'm going there. Hopefully, he has the biochemist and they are waiting for the dust to settle before making a move. Maybe they realized the mission was compromised, and the agent decided to take the Cowbird back to Izmail until it was safe. I am going to our agent's Central Investigation Safe House. I'll hitch a ride on a cargo-carrying motor barge. I want you to head back to the farm and wait for me there."

"Let me go with you," I said.

"No. One person will not draw too much attention. Two people doubles our chance of detection. We have no raft to return to the ship, and even if we did, the *Adams* is setting sail in less than twelve hours. If I am not back by dawn, you need to get the hell out of here. Make your way down to Greece. The ship is due in Piraeus, Greece on the twenty-third of the month. That is nearly two weeks. It will give you the time you need to get there safely, even if you have to lie low somewhere for a day or two. You'll need to go through Romania and Bulgaria."

"You're kidding right? How am I supposed to travel hundreds of miles, undetected? I have no map, no money, no identification, and no weapon. Do you have an extra gun you can give me?"

"No, but even if I did, I would not give it to you. The problem is you have to travel under the guise of a student. No civilian is permitted to carry a gun in the USSR. If you are stopped and asked to show your papers, you can act surprised when you can't find them. You can say they were stolen. You can always plead you are nothing but a stupid college student who got lost traveling in the north of Greece. But if a military guard or KGB frisks you and finds a weapon, you're screwed. Do you still have that pen-gun," Smoke asked.

"Yeah, one shot. One worthless shot," I said.

"One shot is all you need. Listen, you are a good sailor. You are resourceful. I know you can do it. You can steal a map at any train depot, or gas station. As far as money goes, ask the old lady at the farm for some money. Tell her our agent will repay her tenfold. I will inform him to do so when I meet up with him. Obviously, you can always steal some cash from someone, but you cannot raise any commotion that would bring the military guard. There was that map in the kitchen of the farmhouse. Take it with you. Shroom, you can do this. Be smart. Don't trust anyone. Keep your head."

"But you're coming back, right?" I asked with little assurance.

"I hope so, but we always prepare for the 'what ifs.' We never want to be surprised. God be with you, Shroom," Smoke said.

"And with you," I responded.

I walked nonchalantly through town and towards the farm. My stomach reminded me I had not eaten anything in nearly twenty-four hours, but I knew the generous old lady would provide a meal. As I approached the farm, the sun was reflecting off a piece of sheet metal used to patch a hole in the roof of the farmhouse. Although still at a distance, the bright reflection was like a lighthouse, giving direction to this long-lost sailor.

As I got closer to the farm, I saw the old lady, the most welcoming thing I had seen since leaving the ship. She was standing with her back to the barn, as if being propped up by it. Her posture was not unusual for the elderly. As one ages, any support is welcome. Her knees appeared slightly buckled. I knew if I could spend the night there, be fed, get some shut eye, I would be in a better state of mind. At least I hoped so.

As I approached the woman, I stopped abruptly. My body became paralyzed, as if I had spent the last day packed in dry ice. A sickening feeling came over my empty stomach. A pitchfork stuck through the old lady pinning her against the barn. Her eyes were wide open and blood dripped from her mouth. I closed the woman's eyes, gave her a kiss on the cheek, and cautiously entered the barn. Inside, the cow was lying dead, a bullet hole between its eyes. I grabbed a sickle off the barn wall and headed to the farmhouse. It would have to suffice as a weapon.

Nothing had gone as planned. The mission was supposed to be…. *easy*. Everything is peaches and cream until the cream sours and it certainly was rank!

The door to the farmhouse had been kicked open. A muddy footprint was strategically placed just below the doorknob. I knew I could not stay at the farm and wait for Smoke to return. I did a quick search of the house and prepared for anyone who wanted to erase me. The house was empty. I looked around for anything to aid me on my journey. When I put the sickle down on the kitchen table, I saw the map was still lying on the chair where Salmon had put it. A half loaf of day-old bread was sitting on the counter. I rummaged through the cabinets and found strips of dried meat which I stuffed in my backpack. There were jars of pickled beets in the cupboard. Because of the weight of the jars, I was limited to taking only one. I had no canteen, so I emptied one of the jars and filled it with water from the outside pump.

I walked over to the old lady and removed the pitchfork someone used to pin her against the barn wall. Her body slid down the side of the barn, lubricated by the blood-soaked boards. There was no time to bury her properly, so I dragged her inside the barn and placed her body gently on a bed of hay. I placed her hands in her lap, said a prayer, and left.

CHAPTER TWENTY-ONE

B ack onboard the USS Charles F. Adams, tensions had reached uncomfortable levels. Captain Stansbury, XO Lynch, and LT Kiggans gathered in the wardroom.

"We have to get underway in less than an hour, and they still have not shown up," the Captain said. "Was Washington and Langley notified we have not heard from the team?"

"Yes, sir," responded LT Kiggans.

"God, I hate to leave them behind," said the Captain as he stared at the map on the wall.

"I know, but we don't have a choice," the XO said. "If we were docked anywhere but Romania, we could request an extra day or two to stay in port, but there is no chance of that happening here."

LT. Kiggans chimed in. "They know we are scheduled to be in Piraeus in thirteen days. If anyone can figure out a way to get there safely, it is these men. Other than Greece, the nearest friendly country to where they are in Ukraine would be Austria. Brumowski Air Base is located in eastern Austria. The problem getting there is travel would be completely over land, and through either Slovakia or Hungary. I am guessing they would rather be as close to the shoreline as possible. It would be easier for them to stay undetected."

"The crew is preparing to get underway, Captain," the XO said, stating the obvious.

"We will get underway at 1000 hours, as planned," the Captain said.

In Kiev, the KGB, and two representatives of the Chinese State Security Ministry (IPA), evaluated the status of their mission. The IPA is the principal civilian intelligence, security and secret police agency of the People's Republic of China, responsible for foreign intelligence, counterintelligence, and the political security of the Chinese Communist Party (CCP).

"Have all the combatants been eliminated?" the man who was clearly in charge asked.

"No, the negro, Harrington, and the young Electronic Warfare sailor, Lloyd, escaped from the Olympic Training facility," the second man responded.

"Beijing told us to let Lloyd go, at least for now. Their ship left Constanta this morning. He will certainly try to make his way to Athens. His ship is due in Piraeus in less than two weeks. Everything is in place for him to take the fall for the deaths of his teammates and for the intelligence leak. This way we can keep our double agent on the *USS Adams*. Lloyd will not make it back to his ship. We made sure of that. Before he is killed, we will make sure he is completely discredited, and that evidence will prove he is the guilty party. That will keep our governments out of this."

"What about Harrington, sir."

"As far as we know, he is not with Lloyd." Turning to one of the KGB agents, he asked, "The KGB is sure to capture Harrington, right?"

"How hard should it be for us to find the only negro in Ukraine? You do not have to worry about us. It is your intelligence community that has a bad track record," the KGB agent said, exposing his obvious disliking for the Chinese.

Turning to his subordinate, the Chinese IPA agent said, "Listen to me carefully, there have been several intelligence embarrassments over the past few years. This will not be one of them! We must not fail!

I am to report to President Yen Chia-kan in three days. I want to be able to tell him our mission was a complete success."

"But, of course, Sir. It will be a success."

I was able to convince a small water taxi to take me over to the Romanian side of the Danube in exchange for a pair of wool socks. Before I could board the boat, a Ukrainian military officer spotted me.

"You! Come over here. Where are you heading?" the officer asked.

I knew this was one of those moments where my answer could seal my fate. My response was quick and confident. Leaning toward the man, I spoke quietly.

"I met a girl last week at *The Drunken Mouflon*, the daughter of a Romanian official. She is absolutely gorgeous, my friend. I just have to see her again."

The officer's expression never changed. "Where are you from?" he asked.

My mind was racing, trying to think of the small village where my stepmother grew up.

"Pidlisnyi Mukariv," I responded.

"Comrade! Pidlisnyi Mukariv is my hometown! It is such a small village. I never meet anyone from there! Is not this crazy?" The officer said as he embraced me and kissed me on both cheeks. The embrace was just long enough for me to inconspicuously lift the man's wallet with a near-expert sleight of hand.

"If you are from Pidlisnyi Mukariv, you must know Bohdan Shevchenko. He is about the same age as you."

"Oh, yes. Pidlisnyi! What a character!" I responded with a terrible feeling stirring in my stomach.

"It was horrible what happened to his parents," the man said.

"It just wasn't fair," I said.

"Life is not fair. You should know that, my friend. Go and charm that girl into bed. Be careful when you return. Most military guards will not be so agreeable with your plans of romance."

"I will. Dyakuyu!" I said with gratitude.

I boarded the small boat and was dropped off on the Romanian bank of the Danube. Paranoid I would be followed and soon have the same fate as my fallen comrades, I decided to travel country roads, away from the curious eyes of military guards and police.

The western side of the Danube is considerably warmer than in Ukraine, which gave me some comfort. No doubt, I would have to spend nights sleeping outside with no sleeping bag. Besides getting decent sleep, there were other challenges undoubtedly I would face. One was more immediate. My stomach reminded me I had not eaten for nearly a day. I could easily go several days without food, but with the amount of walking I would be doing, I needed sustenance. Being well-nourished would give energy and aid in keeping me warm. I tore off a small piece of stale bread and ate it quickly.

As I walked the country roads, I began scanning the surrounding woodland for edible plants or nuts. If at all possible, I would need to conserve what little food I had taken from the old lady's house. Although a poor student in high school, I loved studying field biology and botany. I also learned about edible wild plants and mushrooms at SERE school. That knowledge proved to be invaluable.

In a clearing I found some sea kale, a coastal European perennial whose tender young leafstalks can be cooked and eaten like asparagus. However, I did not have a pot in which to cook the sea kale. Not knowing when or from where sustenance would come, I pulled several of the leafstalks and placed them in my backpack.

The wooded area made way for sprawling fields. It was too early for any planting, and the snow melt left the ground muddy and difficult for walking, so I decided to travel on the road. I walked for hours, leaving the wooded area far behind. A hamlet of houses appeared over a hill, the sun illuminating them in a postcard setting. It reminded me of the tiny houses that decorated the train set my father set up at Christmas time. Home. I wondered if I would ever make it back there again. I also wondered if I would ever see Paula again.

The events of the past few days were so hectic I had no time to think of Paula. Perhaps it was a good thing. I could not afford to be distracted by anything. I had to remain focused on my objective and attentive to any danger around me. With the way things transpired over the past few days, it would not have surprised me if Paula would not be at the hotel in Athens when I arrived. If I arrived. I reminisced about better times, the times I held her, kissed her, made love with her.

As I got closer to the village I smelled a wonderful, unmistakable aroma coming from a house with a thatched roof. In this timber-scarce area, wattle-and-daub construction was the norm. The homes in the hamlet were not built close to each other, which allowed each to have a small farmstead. I found that very helpful. Neighbors have a tendency to monitor any activity outside. I walked carefully toward the house from where the aroma was coming. If I could beg, borrow, or steal something to eat, the day would be a success, but avoiding human contact would be better yet.

Common with Ukrainian village houses, the door of the house did not face the road, which also pleased me. The last thing I needed was for some farmer to see me trespassing on his property, and for me to end up like the poor old lady, with a pitchfork in my chest. The farmstead was divided into a people area and an animal area. The animal section contained the outhouse and the bathhouse, considered the "unclean" part of the farmstead.

Walking along the side of the house, I saw a partially open window, and what lifted me to ambrosial heights. Three small yavorivs'kiy pies were cooling on the window sill. My Ukrainian stepmother made similar pies, adding pieces of savory ham, but I knew there would be no meat in this pie. Meat was expensive in Soviet Ukraine and would be served only for major holidays. As I approached the window, I saw a rushnyky, dancing with the breeze to some unheard music. The ritual embroidered pieces of cloth were considered to have potency, as they were believed to protect residents of the home from evil.

I carefully removed one of the pies from the window. It had cooled just enough not to burn my hands. Placing the pie into my backpack, I turned away from the house and headed back to the road, all the while looking for a safe place to sit and devour the pie.

Farther down the road I saw an elderly gentleman pumping water from a well into a bucket. The age of the man suggested he had experienced plenty of oppression by the communist regime and maybe, just maybe he might be a bit hospitable towards me. I hoped the man understood Ukrainian.

"Hello," I said while still a distance from the man, not wanting to startle him.

"Hello," the man said in broken Ukrainian. "I no speak Ukrainian good."

"That is alright. I do not speak Romanian at all," I said with a smile. "May I have a drink from your well?"

"Yes, of course," the man said while handing me a ladle and the bucket he had filled with spring water.

"You....," the man could not come up with the words he wanted to articulate, but he made motions with his hands and fingers that I understood to mean whether I was traveling a distance.

"Tak," I answered affirmatively. "To Greece."

"You sleep here," the man said, pointing to a large shed.

"Tak. Dyakuyu," I responded with gratitude.

The sun was low over the horizon and the cooler evening air had suddenly arrived. The man went back into his small house and closed the door. My fear was the man might be an informant and would contact authorities, but the more I thought about it, the more convinced I became there was little chance of that. I saw no electrical wires going into the house. The man would have no telephone, and he was too feeble to walk into town to report my appearance at his home.

I entered the shed and sat on the cold ground, resting my back on a burlap bag stuffed with shelled maize. Reaching into my pocket, I retrieved the wallet I stole from the Ukrainian guard. My stomach reminded me there was a yavorivs'kiy pie patiently waiting for me in my backpack. I took a bite of the pie. The silky mashed potatoes, the fried onion, and boiled buckwheat, tasted like I was eating at a three-star Michelin restaurant. A quick glance around the cluttered shed reminded me I was anywhere but at a serene city restaurant.

I opened the stolen wallet. A photograph of an attractive woman fell onto my lap. Either the man's wife, or a girlfriend, I thought. Girlfriend. My thoughts again went to Paula and how sweet it would be to wake up next to her every day. I wondered what our long-term chances were to preserve our romance, still in its infancy. The *Adams* would return to Mayport, Florida, in a few months. I knew how fragile long-distance relationships are from my own experience, as well as my shipmates. Divorce rates in the Navy are double that of their civilian counterparts. Going away on seven-month cruises often killed even the strongest relationships. It was either absence makes the heart grow fonder, or, out of sight, out of mind. There was no way I could afford flying to Spain several times a year, and even if Paula could fly to the States, my being granted leave depended upon the ship's schedule. Getting married at only twenty-one years old was also not part of my future plans, but I knew I would regret not marrying her.

There were fourteen rubles in the man's wallet, roughly twenty-three dollars. With that much cash I might be able to purchase a train ticket through Bulgaria to the Greek border. But first I would need to traverse Romania.

The next morning, I awakened with a chill that penetrated my bones. My body was stiff, and I had not slept very well. Every little noise had me at the ready. I picked up my backpack and opened the door to the shed. The sound of birds, busy with their morning chores, was the only thing I heard. It was time for me to cover some distance. I had a long way to go. Unfolding the map, I looked at the possible routes to Athens. There was a train I could catch in the border town of Ruse that would deliver me to the outskirts of the Rodopi mountain range. From there I could circumvent the mountains to the west and enter Greece. I threw my backpack over my shoulder and began walking down the deserted road.

CHAPTER TWENTY-TWO

S moke had a serious problem. A black man traveling through Ukraine stood out like Alfred Hitchcock in a Rockettes kick line. Drawing attention to himself was not what he needed, so he decided to head back to the farm till nightfall, then head to Izmail.

Smoke made it through the town and was approaching the farm. The looks he received from the townspeople confirmed he should travel by night only. He left the road and crossed a field to the barn. He decided with his change of plans he would take me to Izmail. My command of the native tongue would be essential, and it would be safer for both of us to make the trek to Greece.

Smoke's SEAL training taught him to have eyes that covered more ground than an owl. Too bad he could not turn his head 270 degrees, Smoke thought to himself. Smoke suddenly pulled his sidearm as he approached the barn. The weathered wood on the outside of the barn had a large bedabble of blood, as if someone took a bucket of crimson paint and splashed it against the barn. His first thought was I had succumbed to the same fate as the rest of the team.

Cautiously, Smoke entered the barn. His eyes had difficulty adjusting to the drastic change in light. He saw the old lady lying peacefully on a bed of hay. *They never would have laid her in this position. Shroom must have found her outside and brought her here.* Smoke walked over to the farmhouse hoping to find me.

Shroom decided to get the hell out of here. He should have waited. They had come to the farm and looked for the Cowbird, and us. When they realized we weren't there, they left. They won't be back. Damn, Shroom!

Smoke's brow was dripping with sweat even though a chilly northeast breeze abruptly announced twilight had arrived as he dug a hole not even six feet deep, but it would have to suffice. He gently laid the old lady in the grave.

"I lift up my eyes to the hills; from where will my help come? My help comes from the Lord, who made heaven and earth. Come to me, all you who are weary and burdened, and I will give you rest. Take my yoke upon you and learn from me, for I am gentle and humble in heart, and you will find rest for your souls," Smoke quoted the scripture from memory with his head bowed. Then he began shoveling the dirt into the grave.

I found train tracks positioned northeast to southwest. I continued to walk in the southwest direction hoping I would come across a small station where I could board a train heading south. I debated whether it would be safer to stay in the rural areas of Romania or try and get lost in the crowds of larger cities, like Bucharest. I needed to stay incognito. Invisible. My careful observations from the villagers of the small towns through which I traveled was that there was a deep distrust of the communist government and authorities the farther I got from the city. Just north of the route I was traveling, there had been the Jiu Valley miners' strike in the Transylvania region earlier that year. The strike was targeted against the Communist bureaucrats who administered the Valley and profited from the miners' labor, resulting in stifling the laborer's salaries.

Following the strike, the protesters were labeled "anarchist elements," and "worthless people." During the trial, they were given new designations that included gypsies, lowlifes, and infractors. Many of those who participated in the strike were either internally deported, hospitalized in psychiatric wards, or sentenced to correctional labor in prison.

It was impossible not to see the resentment of the people. On the surface, everything seemed copasetic, but like touching fresh paint, the experience left an impression upon me. I observed a man walking his dog who was being harassed for no apparent reason by the Securitate, the secret police agency of the Socialist Republic of Romania. Some of the Securitate wore military garb adopted from the Soviet-style uniforms, some wore bland suits, and still others wore street clothes to fit into the masses. There was fear and suspicion among neighbors, not knowing who was working for the government. Apparatchiks, those working full time for the communist state, could be anywhere.

I thought this could work to my advantage. If I needed assistance from a townsperson, like I did from the farmer who gave me a place to sleep, the response would probably be positive. Probably. As the train tracks bent wide around a steep incline, my spirits rose cautiously, but like a balloon trying to navigate tree limbs. A small hamlet was in sight, but like the balloon, the slightest wrong move and my hopes would burst.

A road came parallel to the train tracks as small shops appeared dotting the road. A butcher shop with two chickens, and what appeared to be half a carcass from a goat, hung in the storefront window. School age children dressed in uniforms walked hand-in-hand toward a nondescript building as an old man sat on a vegetable crate, rolling a cigarette. The small train station sat by itself, facing a police building standing watch across the street.

I walked into the train station hoping the person selling tickets would understand Ukrainian. He did not. The man behind the counter wreaked alcohol and looked decades older than his actual years. The glasses the man wore were covered with so many fingerprints I wondered if he could even see me. I grabbed a small pamphlet which had the schedules and train routes listed. Although written in Romanian, I recognized the names of several towns and cities listed on the schedule. Scrolling down with my index finger, my eyes kept looking for any stop in Bulgaria. I needed to get out of Romania, even though Bulgaria was also communist.

Pulling out the weathered map I had taken from the old lady's farm, I searched for the train route that could get me closer to Greece, closer to Paula, and closer to the *Adams*. I decided going through Bucharest, which would be the fastest route to Greece, would be an unnecessary risk. There was a train leaving in an hour traveling to Pitesti, then Slatina, then Craiova, and eventually to the Bulgarian border to the town of Sofia. Without any complications, I calculated I should be in Athens in six days. But it seemed there were always complications. Nothing had gone as planned.

Smoke arrived in Izmail a little before 0200 hours. He had difficulty locating the safe house. He had an address, and knew it was only a short distance from Old-believers St. Nicholas church, but that is all the information he had.

Izmail was the largest Ukrainian port in the Danube Delta, and the largest city of the Ukrainian Budjak area. Both the Ukrainian Navy and the Ukrainian Sea Guard units operating on the river were based there. Dozens of apartment buildings that could not be differentiated, stood next to each other as if they were soldiers lining up for inspection. The cookie cutter construction was designed for one purpose, to put a roof over the heads of as many people as possible.

After an hour of searching, Smoke found the safe house where he hoped to find both Fang and the agent. It was not really a "house" per se, but an apartment in a housing block nestled in Izmail. The complex was anything but complex. It was simple, square, and constructed with red bricks. It was dilapidated and dreary. The apartment building had no elevator, leaving Smoke to climb the five flights of stairs. Smoke was already exhausted from his ordeal since leaving the ship. As he reached the third floor, he mumbled, *"No elevator? Really? Of course not, and the agent's flat had to be on the fifth floor!"*

The absence of decent outside lighting at the housing complex provided the cover Smoke needed. As he approached the apartment, he did one more visual surveillance around the building. There was no one within sight. Cautiously, he tried to peek through the window of the apartment, but the drapes were drawn. He could see nothing. There were no lights on inside the flat. Smoke maneuvered around the recessed door only to find it had recently been kicked open. Although the door was closed, a splintered indentation was visible just below the door knob. Smoke pulled the handgun from his hip holster.

Slowly, he pushed the door open, but the attempt to do so quietly was thwarted when the door buckled. It was hanging precariously on only one of the hinges. Smoke froze. He heard nothing, and there was no movement inside the apartment. He decided to risk turning on the light. The lone lightbulb dangling from the ceiling provided enough light for Smoke to see the agent sitting alone in a chair. His badly beaten body registered everything Smoke needed to know. The agent was tortured for information about the mission, to where Smoke and I had escaped, and, most importantly to the Russians and Chinese, whether or not we had retrieved Meiyang Fang.

Knowing there was an excellent chance the apartment was being watched, Smoke got out of the apartment and headed for the stairs. He had no idea where I was. He thought, *If I did not experience any major problems, I probably had made it to Greece by now,* or so Smoke hoped, and decided the only option was to abort the mission and head to Greece himself.

When he reached the bottom of the stairs, Smoke once again scanned his surroundings for a sign of anyone. He saw a figure walking towards him, in the direction he wanted to go, so Smoke went the opposite way. He would simply walk around the block and head back the way he had intended; unfortunately, there were two more figures heading toward him in that direction, as well. *Three people out for a walk, hours before dawn?* Smoke turned back, once again, and walked toward the figure who was alone. He was confident he could defend himself against one assailant, probably two, but three was problematic. He crossed the street only to find all three figures did the same. Now there was no question who these people were. He ran.

The city was a maze to Smoke, and he felt as if he were the mouse trapped within it. He turned down an alley that led to a small playground. It was in a large open area which provided no place to hide. He needed to find a building where he could lose them. Smoke glanced over his shoulder to find the three figures, now running together, gaining ground on him. There was a road to his right lined with shops and offices. Reaching the road, he turned down another alleyway filled with boxes and trash. Quickly, he hid underneath a truck parked against a fence.

Smoke heard several footsteps enter the alleyway, and then muffled voices. It sounded like they were separating, trying to cover more ground in their search for him. One of the men could be heard kicking the empty boxes and moving some boards propped up against the building. Smoke watched the man's legs move as he approached the truck. The feet stopped at the side of the truck with the toes pointing toward Smoke. He was prepared when the man's face and a gun peered underneath the truck. Smoke grabbed the man by the throat and pulled him down on the ground. Rolling out from under the truck, Smoke wrestled on top of the man and with one swift movement, slit the man's throat. One down, two to go.

Smoke slid the dead body under the truck and doubled-back the way he came. When he turned the corner of the building, the barrel of a gun was pressed against his forehead. Within seconds, the other man appeared. Smoke was placed in handcuffs, thrown in a Russian made GAZ-24-24 vehicle, and driven away.

I purchased a train ticket which cost me just about everything I had in my pocket. I picked up a newspaper someone had left on a bench and pretended to read it. I was not interested in the local news and besides, I could not read Romanian, but it would shield my face from anyone looking for me. I knew I had to stay focused. When people get sloppy in executing plans they get in trouble. Even the most meticulous, well-thought out, plans go awry when focus is blurred. I struggled with my swirling thoughts distracting me. My heart sank whenever I thought of Dakota. I was unable to attend the funeral in South Dakota and knew my friend's family would have wondered why.

Who killed Dakota? He got too close to the flame and was burned. Dakota found out who the traitor was. The traitor was not going to allow anyone to jeopardize his plans. He realized Dakota, who fit the last piece of the puzzle in place, must be eliminated. But who was the traitor? It could have been anyone in Radio Central. All of the officers on board had legitimate reasons to be in that secured area, but the CO, the XO, and Lt. Kiggans spent most of their time there, due to their responsibilities.

If I do not get to Athens in the next six or seven days, Paula will assume I am not coming and will check out of the hotel and will go back to Spain. Swirling, distressing thoughts. Focus!

The newspaper was lying on my lap when a policeman meandered through the small crowd waiting for the approaching train. His eyes met mine before I had a chance to raise the newspaper. The policeman walked toward me. I felt a hot wave crash upon me, despite the chilly temperatures. Sweat beaded up on my neck and back.

Relax. The most convincing way to erase suspicion is to believe you are who you are pretending to be, and you belong here. Confidence! These officials who hunt people have a sixth sense and can smell fear like any predator in the animal kingdom. The last thing I want to become is a wildebeest for some starving lion.

The train whistle blew as it approached the station. I stood, hoping I could board before I would be questioned. When the policeman got a few steps from me, a woman ran up to him and anxiously asked a question. Whatever his answer, the woman was not satisfied and began pleading with the officer. I used the opportunity to assimilate quickly into the crowd and boarded the train. I walked through several coach cars with open seating, but they were congested with passengers. I squeezed between a boy and an older man, neither of whom were pleased by my interruption.

Time moved glacierly as the last passenger boarded. The woman finished her conversation with the policeman and went into the station. The officer walked briskly towards the train, looking at the passengers seated by the windows. When he reached the car in which I was seated, our eyes met once again, as the train pulled out of the station.

I decided to get up and find a better seat. Walking through the train, I came upon a sleeping car. A couchette would be perfect;

however, I had not paid for one and I did not want to fall asleep in a vacant couchette and have someone call for the authorities to straighten out why someone was in his paid compartment.

In the next car, there were compartments that opened into the corridor. A conductor was walking down the corridor, knocking on each compartment, asking to see passengers' tickets. I entered the compartment closest to me and stood at the door. A middle-aged lady occupied the compartment, and her look of mild surprise and the look on my face explained enough that when the conductor knocked and entered the compartment, the lady was prepared.

The lady handed the man her ticket. He glanced at it briefly, punched it, and returned the ticket to her. When I gave the conductor my ticket, I expected the man to escort me out of the compartment and put me in coach where there were no seats in the open seating format. The conductor looked at my ticket, then at me, and finally to the lady, who explained something to him in Romanian. Whatever she said, the man punched my ticket, said something to me I did not understand, and left the compartment.

"Dyakuyu," I said to the lady with a slight smile.

"Cu plăcere," the lady said. I assumed it meant something like "You are welcome" in Romanian.

The lady and I knew words could not be used to communicate, so facial and hand gestures would have to suffice. The lady placed an apple on her lap and then retrieved a knife with a 5" blade from her large bag. She quartered the apple and offered me one of the wedges, which happily I took. I sat on the bench seat opposite the lady as she surveyed me in such a way I wondered what she might be thinking. Clearly, she was no threat. She just saved me from, what could have been, a difficult situation.

I was exhausted. The train's slight sway and the soothing sound of the repetitious beat of the tracks beneath me was hypnotizing. The more I fought to stay awake, the more futile the effort, and without knowing it, I fell fast asleep.

The sound of the cabin door opening abruptly awakened me from a deep sleep. Momentarily confused, unaware of my surroundings, and having no idea I had slept for nearly three hours as the train sped towards southern Bulgaria, I sat up and suddenly all came into focus. There standing in the doorway was a Securitate dressed in military uniform. The Romanian Militia officer's uniform was gray, with buttons of a light grayish-blue, and four pockets. He wore high military boots, and his cap ornament consisted of the letters, R.P.R., which stand for Romanian People's Republic.

The Securitate asked for our papers, evident by the documents the lady gave him. When the officer turned to me, his voice rose as he motioned for me to provide my documentation. I had none. I stood, reached into my pocket, and looked surprised my nonexistent papers were not there. I shrugged my shoulders and extended my arms with open hands as if to say, "I must have lost my documentation papers." My first thought was to push the guard aside and run for it. But where? I was on a moving city traveling nearly 50 miles per hour. The Securitate was standing so close to me I could feel, and smell, his warm, stale breath.

I grabbed the soldier by the neck and pushed him against the doorframe. With one hand around the man's throat, I extended my other hand behind me and opened my palm, hoping the lady would understand. She completely understood the unspoken request. The lady picked up the knife she had used to pare the apple and placed the handle in my hand. With a quick swinging motion, I thrust the knife into the man's stomach and turned the blade so it pointed up, at which point I pulled the knife up toward the man's chin, tearing through his stomach and up to the sternum. The man's knees buckled, then he collapsed on the floor, his life slowly ebbing away from him. Like a leaky faucet, the Securitate's blood flowed red into a puddle by my feet.

I turned and looked at the lady. Her eyes were wide with amazement but shared the same anxiousness with me. I carefully pulled the sliding doors open and stuck my head out to check to see if the corridor was clear. Other than a lady who was entering the bathroom, there was no sign of anyone. I grabbed the Securitate underneath his arms and dragged him out of the train car, to the gangway connecting one car to another. I pulled, then pushed, the body off the train. By the time I returned to my car, the lady had cleaned up most of the blood. She handed me the towel she used and motioned for me to get rid of it. I looked down at my blood-soaked shirt. There would be no way of hiding that stain. I leaned over, kissed the lady on the cheek, and left the cabin.

Returning to the gangway, I knew I had only one option. I threw my backpack off the train and immediately followed, rolling as soon as my feet hit the ground. I laid at the bottom of a small trench listening to the fading sound of the train and waiting for my body to relay to my brain what part of my body hurt the most. One limb at a time, I assessed the damage by slowing moving and rotating each appendage. Although bruised and wearing a few nasty scratches, I appeared to be fine.

Déjà vu. Here I was once again. I had hardly any money, had no idea where I was, could not speak the native tongue, and was both tired and hungry. A commotion began in my stomach as it protested the lack of food. I figured my options to find something to eat were, once again, to beg, borrow, or steal, with the first two being impossible. I did not have enough money to purchase another ticket for a train to the Greek border and, besides, the authorities would, no doubt, be on the alert for a murderer traveling by train. Walking and hitchhiking may be the better alternative.

I spotted a European Beech tree and sat down, propping my back against the trunk. The rolling hills of farmland, its various shades of green and yellow, lingering spots of snow, and the low sun casting indiscriminate shadows along the landscape, provided a much-needed calming effect. The mountains in the distance framed the beautiful scene. It reminded me of South Dakota and, more so, of my friend who I missed terribly.

CHAPTER TWENTY-THREE

O nce again, i did not sleep well. Every nocturnal animal that scurried near where I made my bed, and the other sounds of the night, all shook me from my sleep. I slept in spurts and was not well rested by the morning. My hip hurt due to my jump from the train, and I was hungry. Very hungry.

Winter wheat had begun to sprout, and fields had been plowed for planting. Since a road paralleled the train tracks, I considered using the tracks as a compass towards Bulgaria, but I would have to be mindful of any traffic coming down the road. I did not love that alternative, but I had little choice. My decision, however, was short lived. It took only one military vehicle driving down the road, to make me scramble for cover in an overgrown ditch alongside the road. Close calls were not what I needed.

I saw a heavily wooded area just ahead and decided that it provided better cover for my clandestine journey. The sunset was stunning, a little beauty in what otherwise was an ugly situation. Darkness also provided cover, so I decided to walk through the night and sleep during the day. I entered the woods, thankful a full moon illuminated my path. A Eurasian scops-owl sang a monotone song as my growling stomach attempted to play bass. The apple wedge was not enough. A cauldron of bats momentarily diverted my focus on my stomach as I watched them dart about, shifting their focus from one meal to the next.

That evening was the warmest it had been since our team left the *Adams*. It was still cool, but the bite of the late winter chill had disappeared. I continued walking through the woods, in what I hoped was the correct direction. I found myself at Makaza, a pass in the Eastern Rhodope Mountains connecting southernmost central

Bulgaria with north-easternmost Greece. I listened to the night insects trilling and appraised my current situation and reviewed the events of the past few days. One by one, the faces of those I lost appeared, Tonto, Lance, Salmon, Leopard, Vegas, and Dakota.

The specific ways in which each of them died is key. Why not just shoot them all and be done with it, or, if they did not want to create attention with a gunshot, sneak up behind them and cut their throats? Why were each killed in a unique way? What is the significance?

My thoughts ceased abruptly. Up ahead I saw what appeared to be the glow of a fire that cracked through the darkness like a newborn chick that penetrated its eggshell to break free. Clandestinely, I crept closer to see the source of the light. As I got nearer the fire, I heard music, and then voices. Assuming these were signs of a party, or family gathering, I let my guard down and continued walking towards the fire and music. Where there is laughter and music, there is food, and food was by now a desperate objective.

It was not till a twig snapped under my foot, I was reminded of my imminent danger, but it was too late. Someone yelled something and the music stopped. I froze, waiting for something to indicate the coast was clear. That was when I felt the sharp point of a knife in my neck, and the trickle of blood that followed. A less than welcoming voice said something in Bulgarian as I felt a shove for me to walk towards the gathering.

When we reached the fire, I saw a group of about 25 gypsies, commonly called Romani. I was shoved to the ground. A man asked him something, but again, I did not understand, so I spoke in Ukrainian.

"I mean no harm to anyone," I said. "I am traveling alone and trying to get to Greece to meet up with my girlfriend."

A man took a step from the crowd and said, "You are Ukrainian?"

"Yes," I said, thinking Ukrainian might be received better than American. "I was attacked by a Securitate on the train, and I feared for my life."

Knowing the Romani are nomadic people, and not well received in Romania, Bulgaria, Hungary or Slovakia, I thought that sharing my anti-establishment, "Enemy of the State," persona would be the best way to go.

"I can see you had a confrontation. Is that your blood or the Securitate's?" the man asked, pointing to a blood blotch on my shirt.

"His," I answered.

With that, the man slapped me on the back and motioned me to join them.

"Excellent! We speak either Bulgarian or Turkish. I am the only one who speaks Ukrainian. My father was Ukrainian. My Name is Georgi. Are you hungry?"

"I am starving. I have had only an apple wedge the past three days," I said.

"Sit, my friend. Sit."

A woman walked over to a large black pot on the fire where she was cooking something that smelled divine. She took a ladle and scooped a vegetable stew, called ghivetch, into an earthen bowl. The stew was made with potatoes, cabbage, grape leaves, onion, carrots, and some kind of meat. She brought the stew over to me, along with some banitza, a type of bread she demonstrated was to be dipped into the honey she also offered me. I thanked her and began eating rapidly. The food was delicious, but spicy.

"Her name is Nikol. Pretty, yes?"

"Yes! Very pretty," I said as I took another mouthful of stew.

"Careful," Georgi said to me. "You have not eaten in three days. If you do not slow down, your stomach will revolt."

"This ghivetch is delicious, but I cannot quite figure out what type of meat is in it."

Georgi could not find the English word, and I could not understand the Ukrainian word he used. Frustrated, Georgi raised his index finger telling me to wait a minute. He walked over to the far side of camp, and then returned with a black feather.

"Bopoha!" he said, handing me the feather.

It then dawned on me what Georgi was trying to tell me. It gave a whole new meaning to the phrase "Eating crow!"

As I ate, the music resumed. A zurna (oboe), a tupan (two-headed drum), a violin, and a squeezebox began playing rhythmic tunes as several Romani danced around the fire.

"You are tired. I can see this. Over here. Lie down. You are safe here, my friend," Georgi said, while handing me a blanket.

It took no time for me to fall into a deep sleep. I dreamt I was falling, but not with fear or with the anticipation my landing would be my demise; this falling was more like a floating. Clouds of blue cotton candy and white, puffy sheep meandered by. Dakota and Paula were ahead of me, motioning me to follow them. I tried to catch up with them by adopting a swimming-type motion. My two friends floated on a pink river that moved them along with no effort from either of them. The river curled behind them, like a surfer's wave, and their speed down the river quickened. Precipitously, the pink river thrust Dakota and Paula into the mouth of a hideous monster.

I sat up abruptly, breathing heavily. The fire was burning low, and the woods were still. For a minute, I wondered if the gypsies, the music and the food had all been part of the same dream, but the soft snoring from someone nearby, clarified things. I laid back down and eventually fell back to sleep.

The morning air was wet with dew. It had been my best night's sleep since I began my execrable journey. Georgi walked up to me with a cup of tea and some bread.

"You sleep good?" the man asked, accompanied by a large smile.

"Yes. Very well."

"You want to go to Greece? The green border is very hard to cross. Danger. But there is a place in the fence where you can get through, if you are strong. You are strong young man. You will need to climb fence at a post. No barb wire there. I will walk with you to the road. A farmer come and give you ride close to fence."

"Thank you," I said.

"I draw you a map. Look. Here. This is where you cross border. Nowhere else."

"Okay. I understand," I said.

I followed Georgi through the woods for an hour before we came to the edge of the forest. The sound of a horse, neighing and whinnying could be heard as we approached the edge of the woods.

"There," Georgi said, pointing to the horse-drawn wagon. "He is expecting you. "For your trip," he said while handing me some dried meat and a piece of hard bread. "God bless you, my friend."

"Thank you for everything, Georgi," I said.

I walked down a dirt path to the road. A farmer who was hauling hay harvested the previous autumn was approaching. No doubt he was on his way to sell the hay to someone who had not calculated the amount of fodder needed to make it through the long winter. Livestock must eat, or they become deadstock. Thanks to Georgi and the gypsies, I was not deadstock.

The horse-drawn wagon seemed a bit primitive for the 1970s, but that is what socialism does. I was reminded of Vegas quoting Churchill. ". . . the philosophy of failure, the creed of ignorance, and the gospel of envy, its inherent virtue is the equal sharing of misery." Yes, ignorance and misery. Why use the modern technology of tractors when medieval technology of horse labor is available?

I stood by the road and watched as the farmer drew near. The wagon stopped. The farmer said nothing, but once I was on the wagon, he made a clicking noise with his mouth and the horse began walking once again. The pile of hay was the softest thing upon which my body rested in quite a while. I laid back and watched the countryside disappear behind me.

The temporary charity of tranquility was rudely interrupted when the farmer turned and said something in an anxious tone. Peeking around the farmer's body, I could see a checkpoint orchestrated by men in military garb. I wondered if it were simply a routine checkpoint, or if they were looking for the man who murdered the Securitate in Romania? The farmer turned around and motioned for me to conceal myself in the hay.

A conversation ensued where the voice of one of the men was clearly authoritative and stern, the other, reserved. The voice of authority approached. He was so close I thought he was going to hop on the bed of the wagon and join me, but something much more disconcerting was in store. Without warning, the tines of a pitchfork were plunged alarmingly close to where I was hiding. I found myself in a difficult conundrum.

Damn! Should I surrender and take my chances with the Bulgarians? Being imprisoned in Bulgaria or dead in a pile of hay; not much of a choice. Another stab at the hay brought the tines within inches of my head. *Stay calm!* Apparently, the man was satisfied there was no contraband under the hay because, without any more conversation between the two men, the wagon began moving again.

I whispered a thankful prayer. *Please tell me that was the last test. Please help me cross the border. Please get me safely to Athens.* If I could navigate through the border undetected, I should be able to arrive in Athens in time to meet Paula, and my ship.

It was already late afternoon when the wagon reached its destination. Although we traveled fewer than 20 miles, it took most of the day. The farm where the hay was to be delivered had a surprisingly large livestock population. Most farms in eastern bloc countries are small, family run farmsteads. I worried this could be, perhaps, a state-run farm and, if so, I would be ruined. And yet, the border was only a few kilometers away. I decided to attempt to cross the border as soon as there was the cover of darkness.

I spent the hours before dusk walking around the working area of the farm. For the most part, the workers ignored me. As much as I tried to relax, my thoughts were consumed with the last obstacle standing between me and Paula. The "green" border.

Unlike its counterpart in Berlin, the impenetrable "green" border between communist Bulgaria, and both Greece and Turkey, was made mostly of barbed wire. It ran through the woods near the Black Sea and the halcyon Rhodope Mountains along the Greek border. It was fabricated with restricted zones, state-of-the art surveillance equipment, and heavily armed guards with vicious dogs. As much as I was concerned about the locals who might be coerced to report and spy on outsiders, there was something else bothering me. The border appeared to be deceptively easy to cross.

Darkness fell upon the Bulgarian hills. As I looked at the map Georgi drew for me, I found it was surprisingly easy for me to understand. He added landmarks including a well with a water pump, a large Baikushev white fir that stood by itself, and an abandoned truck with vegetation growing high around it. Crawling on my belly, I approached the post where I was to cross. Someone had fastened small pieces of a tree limb to various parts of the fence with wire, as if to provide steps for climbing the fence. At the top, the barbwire had been cut, enabling someone to roll back enough of the razor-sharp barbs.

Timing was an issue, as guards patrolled the area. I would have to attempt to scale the fence as soon as the nearest guard turned his back to walk the other way. I first needed to calculate how much time I had before the guard turned and began walking back in my direction. As the guard turned, I began counting. *One - one thousand, two–one thousand…*

I had 43 seconds to scale the fence and disappear on the other side. Doable. When the guard turned away from me, once again, I began to scale the fence.

Once I began climbing, I understood why someone had fastened the pieces of wood to the fence. When my weight was applied to the sections of the fence where I placed my feet, the fence became unstable. It pulled the fence backwards so my head and torso were much farther from the fence than my legs and feet. It took tremendous upper body strength to reach the top of the fence. *Eighteen–one thousand.* Now I just had to move the barb wire back carefully and swing my first leg over to the other side. *Twenty-six–one thousand.*

I held onto the post with one hand, the fence with my other, and lifted my leg high to clear the fence. My foot cleared the fence, but my pants were caught on the barbed wire. *Thirty-four–one thousand.* The guard would be turning back my way soon. Trying to negotiate the pants stuck to the wire was hopeless. *Forty–one thousand.* I untied my boots and threw them over the fence. Then I unbuckled my pants, slid out of them and left them hanging on the barbed wire as I made it to the other side of the fence. The thin metal of the fence dug deeply into my stocking feet. *Forty-three–one thousand.* The guard turned around.

"Halt," the guard yelled, as he raised his flashlight and shined it on me.

I jumped from the fence. Just as I bent over to pick up my boots, a shot rang out. And then another. I ran like a glutton to a smorgasbord. When I reached the high grass, I dove for the ground, crawling until I reached the relatively safe woods of northern Greece.

Smoke sat in the dark room, his hands cuffed behind him. There were no windows, no heat, and water was dripping from an overhead pipe. The Russian interrogation room was empty except for himself and the chair upon which he sat. Hours passed before several men entered.

"Chief Petty Officer Noah Harrington," the man said in surprisingly good English. "What brought you to Ukraine? Were you hungry for some Holubtsi?" The man asked, causing the other man to chuckle. A woman of Chinese descent stood beside the two men, observing.

"If you cooperate and answer all of our questions truthfully, you will receive food, a shower, and a comfortable cot so you can get some sleep. Are you tired, Mr. Harrington?"

Smoke was more than exhausted. The Russians use sleep deprivation as their first tool to obtain information from prisoners. To those who have never experienced this torture, it sounds fairly benign, but forced sleeplessness is a horrid thing to endure. When sleep is deprived for days on end, the mind becomes befuddled, and chisels away at one's will to reason. The individual ceases to be himself. Smoke remained speechless.

After four hours of questioning Smoke, the KGB interrogators, and the woman, left the room. Smoke fell immediately to sleep, but his rest was short lived. Twenty minutes later, a doctor, escorted by a military guard, entered the room. The soldier kicked the chair to which Smoke was handcuffed, waking him up.

The doctor pulled a small flashlight out of his white lab coat and looked into Smoke's puffy and bloodshot eyes. They had already begun to spasm and twitch. Reaching into his black bag, the doctor retrieved several vials and a needle. Having used a variety of truth serums in the past, including scopolamine, 3-quinuclidinyl benzilate, and sodium pentothal, the Soviets developed a more effective truth drug code-named SP-17. The newly developed truth serum was not only used on "Enemies of the State," it was also used on their own agents to confirm their agents' loyalty. Lacking both scent and taste, it was impossible for an agent to know a serum was slipped into his beverage. The doctor injected the SP-17 into Smoke's arm.

I was freezing, having left my pants on the border fence. If I don't find some trousers soon, my body will lose heat faster than it can produce it. Hypothermia causes a progressive mental and physical collapse, and death would be close behind. I wrapped my jacket around my midsection the best I could, but it did little to keep me warm. I had to keep walking.

After traveling several miles in the countryside, I came across a small hamlet. Finding a pair of pants, jockeyed over my need to find some food, as my number one priority. Where there are people, there are trousers. I knew I certainly could not walk the city streets without pants.

At the town's edge were a few scattered apartment buildings. I snuck around as carefully as possible on my scavenger hunt. It did not take long before I found the prize, clothes hanging out on a line to dry. A pair of men's pants dangled in the morning breeze, along with a few shirts, a dress, and an assortment of undergarments. The problem was the clothesline spread across two buildings three floors above. There was no way to reach the clothing without entering the building.

Standing under two buildings, I looked ridiculous. Thankfully, it was still early enough that no one was stirring, at least, not yet. I knew that entering the building would be too risky. Besides the possibility someone would call the police. I knew that an angry tenant might not appreciate me stealing a pair of trousers. I did not need a confrontation. I was in Greece, a friendly country, but the authorities would not be friendly if I were caught stealing. Looking around the wide alleyway, I picked up several baseball-sized stones. The pants were secured only by a few wooden clothespins. A well-aimed throw with one of these stones and the pants would fly off the clothesline.

The first throw missed the trousers and hit a pair of women's panties, causing them to wrap around the stone as it flew away from the clothesline. The second stone landed perfectly at the zippered fly of the pants, releasing them from the clothespin and dropping them to the ground. I put on the pants. Other than being a little baggy, they fit just fine.

A door opened from a first-floor apartment off to my right. I froze, hoping no one saw me commandeering the trousers. The lady placed a bowl of something on the step of her apartment and made a clicking sound with her mouth. A feral cat appeared from nowhere and ran towards the lady and the bowl. She went back into the apartment and closed the door. Quickly I ran over and shooed the cat away, picked up the bowl and began eating its contents. As much as I could gather, the impromptu meal was a combination of dried fish, egg, and yogurt.

My luck continued when I spotted a bicycle leaning against the apartment building. It was secured with a chain and a small padlock. I reached into my coat pocket and pulled out the bobby pin I took from the old lady's farmhouse and broke the pin in two. I applied pressure to the wavy part of the bobby pin, using it as a rake pick. Using the straight pin, I wiggled it up and down and in and out until the internal pins of the lock became set, and the lock opened. I jumped on the bicycle and continued heading south towards Athens.

I rode all day and through the night. Cars, trucks, and buses passed me with no one paying much attention to me. I blended into the background as naturally as a Greek off to run some errands. My route took me back into a rural area and as dawn hinted at its arrival, I began searching for a place to sleep. At a distance, lights from a small village began appearing, like fireflies randomly illuminating the morning twilight. Although there were no wooded areas nearby, there were groups of trees with bushes congregating around their trunks, a short distance away. Positioning my backpack as a makeshift pillow, I made sure I was concealed from sight and fell fast asleep.

The next morning, I pulled the map from my backpack and tried to get my bearings. The Greek town of Komotini was just kilometers away. As I straddled the bicycle, my buttocks and thighs quickly rebelled from the previous day's ride. I was unbelievably sore. I decided to ditch the bike and walk towards the approaching town.

I walked down the main street in Komotinia, a town strongly influenced by Muslim culture. It was a city of contrasts. Modern cars shared the road with horse-pulled carts. Shops displaying both stylish clothing and traditional items used for centuries lined the streets. I gazed into the various shops, as I walked down the street, now busy with pedestrians. A linen store displayed a colorful collection of ladies' headscarves and a bakirtzi displaying an impressive assortment of bronze and silver-colored Turkish coffee pots, round baking pans, and teapots.

The smell of freshly baked bread got the attention of my empty stomach, but I had little money to purchase a meal. I was about to use the last of what I had to buy a loaf of bread when I realized that rubles would probably not be accepted as payment. While standing in front of the bakery, I turned and saw a kafenion, a traditional Greek café, the social hub in villages. In the window men were playing backgammon, a game my friend, Perry, from back home, taught me. I learned the game in no time at all and was good at it. Some money was sitting on the table where the men were playing, making it obvious this was more than just a friendly game. I walked into the cafe to confirm they were gambling on the game and if I could challenge the winner.

Several men were standing around the table watching the two men finish their game. One of the men looked up at me and said something in Greek, which I assumed had to do with the game.

"I'm sorry," I said. "I do not speak Greek."

"Ah, you are an American," one of the men said.

"Yes, I am. I'm trying to get to Athens."

"There is a bus that leaves every afternoon at 2 o'clock. You can catch it in front of the post office. Do you play backgammon?" the man asked.

"Yes," I responded.

"They are just about finished with this game. We play for money."

"I would love to play, but I have only a few rubles. No drachmas."

"Rubles?" the man asked with a look of confusion on his face.

"It's a long story."

"I will play you for that backpack you have there. If I win, I get your backpack. If you win, I will give you 180 drachmas," the man said.

I smiled and sat at the table. "Let's play."

I won that game and the next two, pocketing 720 drachmas, more than enough for the bus fare to Athens. I didn't even have to purchase any food since the kafenion served meze, or free snacks, that included saganaki (a fried cheese appetizer), kolokythokeftedes (zucchini fritters), and moussaka (eggplant lasagna). My new friends bought me ouzo with beer chasers each time I won.

In the hour and a half I was in the kafenion, I became a legend, having beaten the three best backgammon players in the village. The men gathered outside the cafe to bid me farewell, making me promise I would return someday and spend more than a few hours with them.

The bus arrived nearly an hour after it was scheduled. What I expected to be a leisurely ride to Athens, was anything but. The bus was overcrowded, and any hope of catching a little shut eye was pointless. I had to shove my backside onto a two-person bench seat that already had two people on it, but that was the norm for the bus. It made the bus ride aggravating, but at least I did not have to worry about my safety. Babies were crying and a couple argued incessantly making the long bus ride even longer. I got a whiff of a horrendous smell that nearly made me dry heave. Looking at the woman seated next to me, I thought, *Doesn't this woman ever take a shower? Does she have any idea what deodorant is?* Suddenly, it dawned on me that the offensive odor was coming from me.

But none of this really mattered. I could see there was a beautiful bright light at the end of this horrific tunnel. The story I lived for the past couple of weeks was coming to an end, and I was more than ready for the happy ending.

CHAPTER TWENTY-FOUR

I t was dark when the bus arrived in Athens. I was anxious, fearing
Paula may not be at the hotel where we were to meet. The *Adams*
would not arrive in Piraeus for another day, which would give
me a little quality time with her, if she were there. I had never been to
Athens, and I had no idea where the hotel was, but I had money in my
pocket from my winnings playing backgammon, and so I hailed a taxi.
The hotel's name was easy to remember, Hypnos, named after the
Greek god of sleep.

The taxi driver knew the hotel and after a thirty-minute drive with
more turns than a mouse can find in a maze, we pulled up to the hotel.
Located in the lively Psyrri district of Athens, the boutique hotel was
a beautifully restored 1920s townhouse with only six uniquely
designed suites. It was small, intimate, and stylish, the exact type of
hotel I would expect Paula to have chosen. It also had a rooftop terrace
with stunning views of Ancient Greece. But sightseeing was not what
I had on my mind. A shower and Paula were the only things I needed.

I was filthy and very self-conscious about the odor exuding from
my body. I felt embarrassed to enter the hotel, but nothing was going
to keep me from Paula. When I walked up to the front desk, the clerk
was gracious and polite, yet was obviously appalled by my
appearance.

"I'm sorry for my appearance. I had a mishap on my journey
here," I said apologetically.

"Not at all, Sir. We do not have showers, but every suite has a
large bathtub," the clerk said. "Checking in?"

"My girlfriend made a reservation. Has Miss Delgado checked
in?"

"Yes, she has. I will buzz her suite and let her know you have arrived, Mr....."

"Lloyd. Just tell her Calvin has arrived."

The clerk picked up the phone on the counter and dialed a few numbers.

"Good evening, Miss Delgado. Mr. Lloyd has arrived and said you are expecting him. Very well." The clerk hung up and looked up at me. "Miss Delgado is in suite 206. She is expecting you. The elevator is behind you and to the left."

I pushed the button for the elevator, but when it did not open immediately, I took the stairs, sprinting three steps at a time. Suite 206 was at the end of the hallway. With nervous anticipation, I knocked on the door. The door opened and before I saw Paula, the smell of fresh gardenias reached me, reminding me of our first date.

"My beloved, handsome sailor," Paula said with her arms wide open, inviting me to come into them."

We embraced with passionate firmness. I broke the embrace and said, "I am filthy. I just had two weeks of hell."

"You are handsome no matter how dirty you may be. Come, I will run you a bath and I will wash you. After we make love, I will go to a boutique and get you some clean clothes, but you will not need them for a while," she said with a luscious smile.

"You are the best!" I said as she entered the bathroom.

Steam emerged from the bathroom as Paula filled the bathtub.

"Have a drink, my love. The bar is well-stocked," Paula called out from the bathroom.

I poured myself a glass of Fino sherry and took a swallow. I let the fresh almond aftertaste rest on my tongue.

"Come, my love. Your bath is ready. Allow me to wash you," Paula said. "Now, tell me about your horrid journey. I want to know everything."

I slid into the tub like a sea lion gliding into the water. Paula washed me gently with a soapy sponge, listening to all the events of my disastrous trip.

"Five of the seven men who left your ship are dead? They were murdered?" asked Paula with a look of astonishment on her face. "You killed one of the bad men with a bow and arrow?"

"Yes, I am actually better with a bow than I am with a gun, and I am pretty good with a gun. The fact that each was killed differently is what baffles me. It's like the assassins were trying to make some statement. If I can figure out the significance of those murders, the way each was killed, I may be able to find who the traitor is aboard the *Adams.*"

"What about the sixth man? Mr. Smoke? Where is he?"

"I last saw him on the bank of the Danube in Ukraine. We decided to separate. Smoke went to the safe house in Izmail, trying to find Fang and our agent. I'm guessing he made it back to the ship. I had to work my way back here, traveling from Ukraine, then through Romania and Bulgaria with no money or weapons. It was far from easy."

"It must have been frightful. You are my hero, Calvin," Paula said as she picked up a towel and began drying me. "Come to my bed, my love."

We made glorious love, the type of lovemaking that makes everything right with the world, even though the world may be crumbling. Afterwards, I fell quickly to sleep. When I awakened, slacks, a shirt, underwear and Italian shoes were lying on the ottoman positioned at the foot of the bed. Paula was on the phone, speaking softly.

"To whom were you speaking?"

"You are awake, my love. You were very tired. I was confirming my appointment tomorrow afternoon. I am looking to purchase some pieces from a gallery located in the Monastiraki section of the city."

A knock on the door interrupted our conversation. Paula opened the door allowing a young man to wheel in a cart filled with various foods.

The steward introduced each course one by one, lifting the silver cloche food domes that kept each dish warm. "Here we have souvlaki," he said as he lifted the domed lid long enough for Paula and me to see the delectable cuisine. Repeating the presentation he went on to each dish. "Grilled octopus, dolmades, and spanakopita.

Oh, and of course, tzatziki, the dish that makes everything in Greece taste better."

"Thank you," Paula said as she handed the steward a few drachmas. "It all looks wonderful."

"What is spanakopita?" I asked as I finished dressing.

"It is a delicious spinach and cheese feta wrapped in a flakey phyllo paste. You will absolutely love it."

Paula and I ate and talked, mostly about my ordeal.

"Did Mr. Smoke tell you where this safe house is? What neighborhood or whether it was a flat above a restaurant or shop?" asked Paula.

"No. We had no time for details. He just wanted to get to Izmail, and I needed as much time as possible to get all the way from Kiliia to Athens. This was supposed to be an easy, almost a routine, mission. It was anything but."

"This is all so terrible, Calvin. Whoever did this to your friends will have the same done to them, to show where the crayfish is wintering." Paula stopped speaking somewhat abruptly, as if she said too much. The words slipped from her mouth before she could retrieve them. Like a bullet leaving its chamber, once it is released, it's gone. The look on my face put Paula in damage control.

"Oh, that is an old Spanish saying my father used to say about men who would sell counterfeit art. It means…"

"It means to teach someone a lesson. To show someone what's what. It's often used as a threat," I said.

"Well, yes, you are correct."

"But that's not Spanish. That's a Ukrainian phrase unique to their culture. My Ukrainian stepmother always said that. You're not Spanish, are you? You are Ukrainian!"

"Calvin, dear," Paula said as she put her hands around my waist."

Something did not add up, and I was doing my best to give Paula the benefit of the doubt.

"Please, tell me the truth. Are you Ukrainian?" I asked.

"My mother was Ukrainian, my father Spanish," she replied.

My gut told me Paula was trying to deceive me. It was just then that I saw the mother of pearl grip of a pistol protruding from under her handbag on the desk. Paula realized I saw it and beat me to the desk and pointed the pistol at me.

"Who are you?" I said with anger in my voice. "You've been playing me, haven't you?"

"I'm sorry Calvin. I was really hoping we could continue our relationship."

Paula was a spider, and I was the fly, caught in her web. I had gambled my heart away.

"Relationship? It was all a lie! Did you ever love me?

"I actually found myself fighting off my affections for you, Calvin. But I have a bigger focus, a job to do."

"So, you work for the Russians?"

Paula's tone and demeanor quickly changed.

"I usually do, but have also worked for the highest bidder; I am always in high demand. Currently, I'm working with the Chinese. It's complicated, but we just could not let Meiyang Fang defect. The Americans cannot know what the Chinese are developing in their bio weapons lab. Biological weapons will be the preferred weapon in the future. The ultimate goal is to make a soldier, sailor or airman too sick to fight, not necessarily kill him. Killing a soldier only eliminates one target. Injuring a soldier, or making him violently sick, removes three soldiers off the battlefield, the injured, and two soldiers to carry the wounded man to safety."

"Did you kill the men on my team?"

"No, my dear Calvin, but it was a woman. Never underestimate the power of a woman. Men are so silly. They can be easily disarmed by the beauty and charm of a woman, or the promise of sex. Isn't that so, my koxaha?"

My posture sagged like a plant badly in need of water. "I am not your beloved. So what now? Are you going to kill me?"

"Sit down, Calvin," Paula said, motioning with her gun.

"You are good," I said, trying to conceal the pain that can only be caused by someone you really love. "You are one hell of a whore."

"Sexpionage, my dear Calvin. Patriots who would never think of betraying their country for money or power, will share the most sensitive secrets to a seductress. I will give you credit, Calvin. You would not share any of the confidential information I wanted. Bravo! You call me a whore. I am actually a Russian Federal Security Service-trained seduction agent. I am the most sought-after female agent for high priority clandestine missions."

"And I take it, your father is not an art dealer?" I asked.

"No. I loved art and wanted to study it in college, but at a young age I was hand-picked for a special government program for children of high-ranking officers. It is impossible for anyone to enter this program unless she has a family member who is a high-ranking officer. I was told to forget my dreams and serve the mother country. I had no other option. My father fought the Nazis during World War II and became a high-ranking officer in the Soviet army. A great feat for a Ukrainian born man."

"He was a Ukrainian who embraced Russia?" I asked. "Strange. Ukraine suffered greatly under Stalin's rule. The famine Ukraine suffered in the early 1930s, what was it called? The Holodomor. It killed nearly 4 million Ukrainians. Every Ukrainian I knew despised Russia, but you and your father prostitute yourselves to the Russian bear. I loved you, Paula," I said as I stood, trying to get close to Paula so I could disarm her.

"Stop right there, Calvin. Sit!"

I sat back down, like a dog obeying its master's commands.

"Why did you seduce me?" I asked.

"We have agents scattered all over your country. The land of the free gives the KGB full access to your most secretive interests," she said, throwing her head back and laughing. "In fact, we have an agent on your ship. A turncoat, I think, is how you say it. A U.S. Navy man who understands his government is corrupt and evil, a country who bullies to get what it wants by throwing its influence around the world."

"Our spy stationed on your ship told us you were someone we wanted to target. You were single, and you had access to some of the information for which we are looking. You are the Intelligence Petty Officer aboard the *Adams*. The U.S. capabilities in electronic countermeasures is a high priority to the Soviet Union. If we understand your country's capabilities, it will aid in our ability to produce weapons that circumvent them. I was told to befriend you and extract as much information as possible. I was to use seduction and persuasion to get information from the enemy target. When that CIA agent was killed in that helicopter incident, and you were selected to take his place, it was an unexpected bonus. But you, Calvin dear, are a tough shell to crack. I will give you credit. You are a true American patriot. I assume you are not willing to share some critical American Navy intelligence to save your life?"

"No! I would never turn my back on my country! So, tell me, how does China, of whom Russia has recently been very critical, ask for your assistance with this mission? Don't they have their own spies?"

"Yes, but when they realized Fang fled China and was already in Ukraine, they wanted a Ukrainian-Russian agent to assist them. The details are above my pay grade, as you Americans would say. It is amazing how two adversaries will suddenly work together when they have a common enemy and objective. By loaning me for this mission, China owes Russia a favor. Russia loves countries being indebted to them. Later, in strategic situations, Russia will come to collect on that debt."

"You never answered my question. Are you going to kill me?"

"You know too much. But before I kill you, you will need to do something, my love. You see, we would rather your people not have an investigation. That will get messy. They will demand answers, plenty of them. This is a much better plan. It will wrap everything neatly for your government. This way, all the blame is put on you. The authorities will assume you became overwhelmed with remorse and decided to commit suicide. Write down what I tell you and then sign the confession."

"They are not going to believe I would, or could have, pulled this off. You may forget, I was recruited for this mission at the eleventh hour," I said.

"Your people already think it is you who is the traitor. We made sure of that. There's a pen in the desk drawer."

"I have my own pen," I said. "Just tell me this, who is the traitor on the *Adams*?"

"Ah, our agent aboard your ship. A sleeper. But I do not know his real name, only the code name by which we refer to him. Thrasher."

"As in the bird? A Brown Thrasher?"

"Very good, my love," Paula said. "You really are a nature enthusiast."

"Do not call me your love. The Brown Thrasher is in the family Mimidae, so named because of their incredible ability to mimic other species. The Brown Thrasher can sing up to 2,000 different songs," I said. "And this traitor impersonates a patriotic American sailor."

"Correct. Now sign this letter. I do not have much time," Paula said, pointing the gun at my head.

I reached into the pocket of my dirty shirt that was lying on the floor and pulled out the pen Vegas gave me.

"I find it more than a coincidence you people named the piece of shit traitor after a bird, just as we named Fang the cowbird. You were mocking us," I said.

"Like a mockingbird," Paula said with a chuckle. "Just sign the confession, Calvin. I do not have much time."

I took the pen in my hand. I looked up at Paula, pointed the pen at her, as if to demonstrate something, and pushed the cam. The crisp sound of a gunshot interrupted the silence like an unexpected clap of thunder. Paula looked at me in dismay and astonishment. A blotch of blood appeared on her blouse, spreading slowly outward like pancake batter on a hot skillet. She reached out for me, dropped to her knees, and then collapsed on her face.

I knelt next to Paula and kissed her on the cheek.

"Wounds from a sincere friend are better than many kisses from an enemy," I said.

I never was happier to see the U.S.S. Charles F. Adams. The clothes Paula had bought me were contemporary European, and I looked a bit out of place when I arrived at the gangway. To my delight, Lt. Kiggans was the Officer of the Deck.

"Permission to come aboard?" I asked.

"Lloyd, you are alive!" the lieutenant said with a shocked look.

"I am. I guess everyone but I knew this was a suicide mission," I said with a bit of disgust.

"No, it's not that," Kiggans said. "When none of you returned to the ship after a few days, we all knew something had gone terribly wrong. Stay here on the quarterdeck. I have strict orders to let the Captain know when, and if, you report back to the ship."

I stood off to the side, wondering what was going on. It was odd I would be instructed to wait on the quarterdeck instead of reporting to the officer's wardroom or CIC. I did not have to wait long as the Captain, the XO, and two other men I did not recognize appeared.

The Captain did not speak. One of the unidentified men did.

"Petty Officer Lloyd?" the man asked.

"Yes, sir."

"I am Lieutenant Commander Jurgens with the Naval Criminal Investigative Service, NCIS. This is Special Agent Steen. Lloyd, please turn around. I have a warrant for your arrest."

"What? What the hell is going on here? You need to arrest whoever it was who set us up in Ukraine! We walked into a cluster! It was a freaking hornet's nest, and we all got stung! This is bullshit!"

"Lloyd, just go with them. Don't cause any trouble. We will get to the bottom of this, I promise," the Captain said. "There are a lot of unanswered questions."

"Captain, there is a traitor aboard this ship. They knew we were coming, and they killed everyone but Smoke, I mean Harrington, and me," I said as the two men led me off the ship.

The two NCIS officers escorted me down the pier and into a black sedan. I was handcuffed to one of the men. The car took us to Athens airport where we boarded a helicopter to Naples. Once we arrived in Naples, I was put on a military plane and flown back to the States.

CHAPTER TWENTY-FIVE

T he only thing worse than sitting in a jail cell is sitting in a jail cell for something I did not do. There I sat, falsely charged, and any evidence that would prove my innocence was destroyed. Even if there was any evidence, it was 4,500 miles away.

I looked around my new home. There were no bars in the cell, just bare walls. The interior decorator had adorned the small room with a bed, a toilet, a sink, a desk, a chair, and a locker. No matter one's image of prison, the reality is much worse. I guess if I had to be sent to prison, a military correctional facility would be the best bet. But like anything, there are pros and cons to serving a sentence in a brig. The pros are quite appealing. I don't have to worry about being raped and/or beaten by other inmates. Normally, my head does not have to be on a swivel. The confines are cleaner, and the food and medical care are much better. The less attractive aspect of serving time in a military prison, there is no chance of early parole. One serves every day of his sentence.

Originally, my pre-trial confinement was to be at Naval Air Station Jacksonville Brig, but it did not take long for some politician to catch a whiff of why I was arrested and thought it was best for me to be imprisoned in the northeast, for "logistical" reasons. *Logistics?* Bullshit! My case was very high-profile, and some people viewed it as a career booster. One congressman had a vacation home on Block Island, Rhode Island. Having me sent to Portsmouth, no doubt, would provide future opportunities for his parading on television for various photo ops so he could straighten his posture for the red, white, and blue. After all, each representative is habitually running for office. Once they are elected, they initiate the next two-year campaign. But I drifted on to another current. Back to my story.

I was in the Jacksonville brig for two days only when I was transferred to Portsmouth Naval Prison. Yes, the same one the public had been told closed three years earlier. Funny how when the U.S. government makes a statement, the press assumes it has to be valid, and the public accepts it as the god's honest truth. The public should have learned something about politicians and truth when it was proven President Nixon lied about the Watergate break-in.

The naval prison was aptly called "Alcatraz of the East," as it was modeled after the infamous military fortification, turned military prison, turned federal prison, situated off the coast of San Francisco. Portsmouth Naval Prison, situated on the border of Maine and New Hampshire, was also built on an island, Seavey Island. Tidal currents deterred any chance of escape. And here I sat.

It did not take long, once I was sent to prison, to enter into survival mode, something with which I had plenty of experience. I adjusted quickly. I looked around my new home, an 8 by 10-foot closet, disaster for the claustrophobic. Thinking spatially is beneficial. I was very good at visualizing an area of expanse. I pictured myself in the forests of Pennsylvania, archery hunting for whitetail deer. This was especially helpful because when I would archery hunt back home, I would be in a tree stand, often at dawn or dusk, sitting motionless for hours, waiting for a deer to walk by, oblivious of my presence.

The mental toll of being wrongfully imprisoned is very real. For many, the stressful weight can cause persistent personality changes, depression, and complex feelings of loss. Loss! I lost my best friend when he was murdered by the individual who should be sitting in the cell instead of me. I lost my girlfriend, or who I thought was my girlfriend. People who I considered friends, disappeared as quickly as the daily summer afternoon rains in Florida. Men with whom I worked so closely were gone, and the icing on the cake was I was being accused of a heinous crime and no one wanted to be associated with me.

I sat alone in my cell. Most of the other inmates had a cellmate, but I was viewed differently at the beginning of my confinement. I was charged with espionage and murder. One of the reasons I did not share the cell with anyone was for my own protection. At least that's what I was told, but those kinds of decisions change as fast as winter weather does.

In a military prison, like any other prison, there is a hierarchy based on the crime one committed. Those committing murder and armed robbery were at the top of the hierarchy. Their status is derived from reputation, toughness, and a propensity for violence. At the opposite side of the hierarchy were child molesters, rapists and ... traitors.

Every prisoner had a mother, sister or niece, and many had children of his own. The sex offenders were placed in protective custody, segregated from the other prisoners, but that was not the case for those accused of espionage. Personally, I would rather see the death penalty for child molesters, than I would for some murderers. Those worthless individuals are guilty of murder, only their victims are forced to go through life having their souls cut out of them.

I had been arrested and charged with espionage and murder. I was firmly placed on the lowest rung in the prison ladder of the hierarchy. There was no camaraderie. No one wanted to be a friend to a traitor.

My heart had broken into a thousand pieces. I felt like Humpty Dumpty; all the king's horses and all the king's men could never put me back together again. No one loved his country more than I, and I was more than willing to die for the cause of freedom. To be falsely charged with espionage was literally the worst possible scenario I could have imagined. There are dozens of things for which I could be accused, even convicted, but to be falsely accused, and of all things, espionage, gnawed at me like a beaver on a willow tree.

I picked up the prison jargon quickly by listening to other inmates. Portsmouth Naval Prison, was referred to as "the Castle." Correction Officers were sometimes called COs. I only knew CO to mean Commanding Officer. In my recent experience, that would be the captain of our ship, Commander Stansbury. The inmates, however, called the Correction Officers, zookeepers. They controlled the world in which we lived, like caged animals behind bars. The zookeepers and Petty Officers in charge were surprisingly more respectful and professional to the vast majority of inmates; not so much towards me.

On my third day in The Castle, a zookeeper opened my cell door.

"Good morning, Petty Officer Lloyd. Allow me to introduce myself. I am God. You see, I have the power to let you live or let you die. Confess to the crimes with which you have been charged, and I will make sure you get a life sentence. Refuse to cooperate, and you will hang and be labeled as a traitor. You'll be a disgrace to your family and country."

"That is certainly a generous offer," I said, "but I think I will pass. I am innocent. I am the fall guy here. There *is* a traitor on the *Adams,* but it is not me! If you want to keep me here until I am proven innocent, that's fine, but please, please, do not stop investigating who the real traitor is on my ship. Think about it. I didn't even have access to Radio Central. As far as the murders are concerned, once you find out who the traitor is, you will find out who was responsible for the deaths of my teammates."

"NCIS is investigating this, not me, but I can tell you now, since the murders were committed in Ukraine, they probably will never find out anything more. They already have enough on you. You will never be set free. Better get used to your new life, shit-bird."

As he was walking away, I yelled, "Hey, I still have not seen my lawyer!"

I demanded to see the warden, but my demands were ignored by the zookeepers. I was in prison for nearly two weeks and had not yet seen an attorney. I decided to get creative.

"Tell the warden I have some information of interest," I told one of the zookeepers.

"Tell me and I will pass it on to him," the guard said.

"No. I will share it only with the warden," I said.

Remarkably, I was escorted to the warden's office less than an hour later. Problem was, I had to come up with something more than

I had a legal right to an attorney and I would make sure it was known I was denied that right.

The warden's office was large, but nondescript, much like most government offices. An American flag stood in the corner and a photograph of the president, our fearless Commander in Chief, hung on the wall. The warden, a commander, sat behind an old heavy steel desk, painted one of the dozen shades of Navy gray.

"Lloyd, do you have something you want to share with me?" he said.

"Yes, Sir. Something NCIS may want to know for their investigation. When I met our agent in that bar in Ukraine, he said the original location of our meeting had to be changed because *after we had left the ship* someone had informed the Chinese or Soviets. I could not have done that, Sir. It had to be someone who was still on the *Adams* after the team left the ship."

"I will let them know this, but you will be meeting with them soon enough." Turning to the zookeeper standing behind me he said, "Take him back to his cell."

"Sir, one more thing," I said as I pushed the zookeeper's hand off my shoulder. "I have not yet seen my attorney. I was told the Defense Service Office is supposed to provide me with the highest quality legal representation in a timely manner. I'm sure the prosecution does not want this delay to be used as a possible argument for an acquittal."

The warden gave me a strange look, and then said, "I was not aware you have not met with your attorney. I will get you someone soon. Dismissed."

Every day in The Castle, one of the zookeepers inspected my room. My bed had to be made by military standards that included hospital corners, everything had to be orderly in my locker, and my cell had to be clean. I was finishing my daily housekeeping when an inmate and a zookeeper came to my cell.

"Today is your lucky day, Benny," the zookeeper said. You are getting a cellmate. The warden decided to pile all of the shit into one cell."

The inmate was a behemoth of a man, with a shaved head, tattoos covering every inch of his arms, massive biceps and a chest as large as

Texas. My first reaction was not that I would have someone to keep me company, but this monster could snap me in two with very little effort. First impressions are always important, so I extended the first olive branch.

"I'll move my stuff to the top rack," I said while gathering my pillow and linens.

"Hey, thanks. I appreciate that," the man said. "So, you are the new guy accused of espionage and murder.

"Yeah. I'm Cal," I said with my hand extended.

"I am Lloyd, but everyone calls me Bear," the man said as he shook my hand.

"Are you kidding me? My last name is Lloyd. That should add some confusion to things," I said. "Do you know why the zookeeper called me Benny?"

"Yeah, the other inmates gave you that name when you arrived. You know, Benny, as in Benedict Arnold."

"That's just great," I said. "I guess you will not believe me, but I am innocent."

"Okay, if you say so."

"No, I am serious! Really!"

"Well, if you are innocent, I hope they clear things up for you. My situation is hopeless,"

Bear said.

"Why? What did they say you did?" I asked.

"Fragging, and I admitted to it," Bear said.

"Fragging?

"Yeah. It is military slang coined during the Vietnam War, when someone would kill a fellow sailor or soldier with a fragmentation grenade, to make it appear the killing was accidental or during combat with the enemy. I got along with every man in my squad, that is, until I discovered my sergeant was screwing my wife.'

"My Marine Expeditionary Unit was in Nam and after experiencing a week of heavy fire from the Viet Cong, we went to the base at the rear of the battlefield for some rest and to recharge our batteries. The supplier officer dropped a bag of outgoing mail, and I helped him pick up the pile of letters. That is when I found a letter from my sergeant to my wife. I did not say a word. The next time we were in battle, I *accidentally* tossed a grenade by his feet."

"Damn! Well, I get it, Bear."

"Actually, you are also accused of fragging. Nowadays, fragging refers to the deliberate or attempted killing of a soldier by a fellow soldier."

"Wonderful!" I said.

"Well, here's the deal. The sentences are pretty severe for those who committed an act of espionage or fragging. Hell, even small-time crimes like theft can get a guy eight years in the military. Civilian courts actually are more lenient, in most cases and, of course, civilian courts offer parole," Bear said.

Even as a Petty Officer, I was still at the bottom of the food chain. There were plenty of people who ranked above me, and every one of them required a salute and a greeting of the day. It did not take me long to play the game. I stood at attention, looked senior officers in the eye, and said some pleasant greetings while I mopped the floors.

While waxing and buffing the passageway, a zookeeper came up to me to say my lawyer is here and wanted to talk with me. Finally! I was escorted to a room that had a table, several chairs, and a photograph of the current Commander and Chief on the wall. A lieutenant Junior Grade stood when I appeared. I saluted him since he was an officer.

"Petty Officer Lloyd?" the man asked.

"Yes, Sir," I responded.

"You don't have to call me sir. I want you to feel comfortable with me. My name is Jon Comeaux. I will be representing you."

He explained he would be my defense counsel, my lawyer, and a Judge Advocate General Corps (JAG) officer. JAG officers are normally prosecutors, but in cases with serious offenses, they are appointed as defense counsel. He asked me to explain everything that had happened, beginning with the moment I was asked to join the mission code named *The Dental Appointment*. I gave him even the most miniscule details, hoping a small detail could be the difference in proving my innocence.

"Alright. I need a list of everyone who had access to Radio Central," the Lt. JG said. "You never have been in that workspace, even for a few minutes?"

"No. I have no reason to be in there, which means I could not have warned the enemy the date we were to arrive in Ukraine had changed. I knew nothing. They fed me bits of information a little at a time. I knew less than anyone who was involved in this disaster. I am telling you, I was set up to be the fall guy."

"Okay. I have a friend who works for NCIS. I will see if he can help us. I am going to be honest with you, Lloyd, we are going to need all the help we can get. I will see you next week," Comeaux said as he gathered his papers and briefcase.

The walls of The Castle had witnessed thousands of inmates' prayers and pleas over the 66 years it was operational. I had many more prayers than pleas. I was told the last hundred or so inmates, I being one of them, would soon be transferred to The U.S. Disciplinary Barracks (USDB) in Ft. Leavenworth, Kansas, the nation's largest military prison. It was the morose home for over 1,400 inmates. The USDB would soon be the U.S. military's only maximum-security facility housing male service members convicted of court-martial for violations of the Uniform Code of Military Justice. Only "special" prisoners were sent to Leavenworth, I was told. Only enlisted prisoners with sentences over ten years, commissioned officers, and prisoners convicted of offenses related to national security had the honor of calling Leavenworth their home.

My hope was to be exonerated before being transferred anywhere, but I was a realist. Without solid evidence, I knew I would rot in prison. The one person who could testify I did not commit the murders was my friend, Smoke. My attorney said no one had heard from him and he was presumed dead.

Time slowly marched on. It truly is amazing how one can adapt to even the worst environments. Unlike the other prisoners, I was not assigned to any vocational programs to occupy my time. Other inmates were in programs to learn various skill sets, including automotive repairs, printing, carpentry, upholstery, and hotel and restaurant management. Other than swabbing the passageways, I was subject to forced workouts daily. That, I did not mind.

Although he was reluctant, my cellmate, Bear, gradually became more accepting of me and my situation. However, when we were with the general prison population, he would not show it. He needed to watch his reputation in The Castle. Bear did give me some guidance on the "dos and don'ts" of The Castle. The number one "do" is to mind my own business and keep my mouth shut.

The following week, my attorney showed up, as promised. My fear was he was a bit green, with little experience in trying a case, especially a case of this magnitude. To my chagrin, my case had been publicized in the press, making me America's villain.

"How are you holding up?" Comeaux asked.

"Okay. I am trying to search for a crumb of hope, but there really isn't much of one," I said. "Has anyone heard from Smoke? I mean Chief Petty Officer Harrington?"

"No. They fear he had the same fate as the others on your mission. Lloyd, I have an idea I want you to consider," Comeaux said.

"I am listening," I said.

"If you are honestly not guilty, I think you should take a Polygraph."

"Fine. I have nothing to hide."

"Good. I will set it up. You need to make sure you are relaxed and calm. Do not think of the injustice you have suffered, or really anything that would get you riled up. The polygraph will measure your different physiological responses, heart rate, blood pressure, respiration, and skin conductivity, when answering questions."

"Got it," I said, hoping the test would be the first of many positive developments to come.

CHAPTER TWENTY-SIX

T he polygraph was scheduled for that afternoon. The more I tried to relax, the more anxious I became. My swirling thoughts made me sick to my stomach like the "Around the World in 90 seconds" ride at Willow Grove Park," the amusement park near where I grew up. Just as the centripetal force kept me standing still as the ride spun at a great speed, the force of rejection made me unable to move as the false accusations spun around me. I felt like I was searching for a missing word for a crossword puzzle. I could find no answers.

My mind raced even faster than that ride. I can handle pain, both physical and emotional pain, when I know there will be an eventual end to my suffering, but I could see no resolution to this debacle. Loneliness, I was accustomed. Hell, I wore that Lone Ranger thing as a badge of honor, but the "me against the world" thing was starting to take its toll. Was anyone on my side?

I was ushered into a room, similar to the room where I had been meeting my attorney, except the temperature in this space was freezing. I had to wonder if that was a deliberate attempt to make me uncomfortable. I was given a "stim test," a test where I was asked to deliberately lie so the tester could report he was able to detect the lie. When the actual test began, the questions asked were irrelevant, like "Are you a Second-Class Petty Officer?" Those questions were followed by diagnostic questions, and then the remainder of the test had relevant questions in which the tester was really interested.

I was passing the test with flying colors until I was asked, "Did you kill anyone who was not a hostile combatant?" I answered "no," but the lie detector spiked, showing deception. The problem was that I had killed Braun, of course. Even if that murder had not taken place, there was my killing Paula. She was a hostile combatant, but my mind did not look at her that way. I had a love for Paula. Strangely, I still do. Except for that final day I saw her in Athens, when I killed her, she was nothing but kind, encouraging, loving and supportive. My mind unexpectedly returned to the good memories I had with Paula.

When the test was complete, I waited outside the room for my attorney to give me the results.

"The test was inconclusive. Apparently, they detected some deception by you on one important question. All of your other answers seemed to be answered truthfully," Comeaux said.

I was ushered back to my cell where I contemplated my recent setback. Not even the lie detector could help me. I was not scheduled to see Mr. Comeaux for another week, so when I was told he had arrived at the prison, I was hoping he had some good news. As I walked into the room, I tried to determine the disposition of the news by the look on his face, but the look was deadpan. He would have made a good poker player.

"I have some good news and bad news, Lloyd. The good news is they found Chief Petty Officer Harrington. The bad news is he has been captured by the Soviets and is being held in Vladivostok."

Reading from a press release, Comeaux continued. "Russia's RIA state news agency reported on Thursday the soldier, identified by the court as Noah Harrington, would be detained pending trial for attempted kidnapping and murder. The soldier's arrest is likely to further complicate relations between the US and Russia, which have grown increasingly tense ever since the end of the Vietnam conflict."

"Great! The good news, Smoke is alive. The bad news for me is he cannot exonerate me," I said.

"Lloyd, you have a visitor," the zookeeper said.

Unlike civilian prisons, a prisoner in a military prison typically has limited access to mail, phone calls, and visitors. If it was my lawyer, Lt. JG Comeaux, the guard would have said so, and I would have been escorted to a room devoted solely for lawyer-defendant privacy. No, this visitor was someone else. *Lord, I hope it isn't my dad. I could not bear to see the disappointment on his face.*

As I was escorted to the room where prisoners meet their visitors, my mind tried to make a list of who would have cared enough to come see me. The list was bare. As the zookeeper opened the door to the visiting room, a rush of warm air draped my body. Immediately, I saw that thin mustache and remembered my first impression of Lt. Kiggans. *Damn, he does look like a porn star!* Seeing Lieutenant Kiggans and knowing he had to take leave in order to visit me was more than comforting. Other than my attorney, who was compelled to defend me, I felt as though I finally had someone on my side.

"Lieutenant, thanks for coming! Sir, I didn't do this. I didn't do anything they said I did. I love my country. I would never turn my back on her," I said.

"I believe you, Cal. That's why I am here. Listen, I'm told we have only 20 minutes. Tell me everything you know. I will hire a private investigator to get to the bottom of this. I do not trust NCIS. There are good investigators who work there, but I am afraid they are being guided not to gather all the facts and evidence to see where it may lead them; rather, they are being directed to find any evidence to solidify their case against you. Cal, don't worry. We will get you out of here. I promise."

The Lieutenant offered the first comforting words I had heard since my arrest. If anyone could get me out of this, Lt. Kiggans could.

After spending nearly a month in The Castle, things became a little more relaxed. Relaxed, in that I was allowed to move freely between my cell, the showers, and the common area where inmates in my pod spent their time when they were not at their work assignments. I finished my daily chores of waxing and buffing the passageway, so I went into the common room where some inmates were gathered around the television mounted to the wall.

"Hey, Benny, you're on the tube," some inmate yelled when I entered the common area. I felt like telling him to quit calling me Benny or I would knock out all his teeth so he couldn't yell anything, but I thought better of it. I had enough problems. I looked up at the television to see an attractive blonde news anchor talking about my case. There was a photo of me in the upper right-hand corner of the screen.

Petty Officer Calvin Lloyd was arrested in Piraeus, Greece, having been on a special assignment. He was immediately flown to the States where he is being held on espionage and murder charges.

In other Navy news, Congress has announced....

That was not the 15 minutes of fame for which I would have hoped. I walked back to my cell.

I had adjusted to prison life as well as could be expected. It was more my emotions I had to constantly keep in check. Depression, anxiety and, most of all, hopelessness, were all constantly lurking around every corner ready to assault my psyche. But they were not the only dangers lurking.

One afternoon I headed for the showers to bathe, something I normally did when there were few other inmates in there, for protection sake. I never turned my back from the entrance to the showers. I never would let my guard down. I was not in the showers long, when an inmate I did not recognize, entered. He was dressed and was not carrying a towel. That was my first clue I was in danger. The inmate pulled a shiv, an improvised knife, constructed from a simple toothbrush handle, filed to a sharp point.

I quickly grabbed my towel and threw it in his face and punched him as hard as I could in his stomach. Unfortunately, while throwing the punch, I slipped on the soapy bathroom floor, giving the assailant time to compose himself. He bent over and stabbed me in my side. Had I not turned my body away when he lurched for me, it would have been a fatal blow.

From out of nowhere, Bear appeared, grabbing the inmate by the collar of his prison jumpsuit, and threw him backwards. The man fell hard on his back against the floor. Bear then punched him twice in the face, and repeatedly bashed his head against the tiled floor.

The commotion brought several zookeepers into the bathroom. The inmate who tried to kill me was unconscious. They took me to the infirmary and took Bear to "The hole."

At the prison infirmary, I received nine stitches to close the wound in my side. On the bed next to me was the inmate who assaulted me. One would think I would have been segregated for my safety, but then again, I am not sure my safety was a high priority for the zookeepers. In their minds, I deserved the death sentence, but the high court had abolished capital punishment for espionage. Of course, if I somehow came to an untimely death at the hands of another inmate, justice would have been served. Thankfully, my assailant was securely strapped to the bed. His face was swollen and his eye black and blue from Bear's beating. He was conscious, just lying there, saying nothing.

"Why did you attack me?" I asked, expecting an answer that included he despised traitors.

"Someone paid me. I'll have an extra five thousand bucks when I get out of this shithole," the man said. "Nothing personal."

"Who? Who paid you?"

"Now that, I am sworn to secrecy. You should feel lucky your bunkmate saved you."

I did feel thankful Bear came to my defense. Believe me, it is not easy to fight naked. I am not sure I would have been able to defend myself had I been clothed, but it would have definitely leveled the playing field. It would be two weeks before I would be able to thank Bear. He was put in administrative segregation, or what the inmate population called "The Hole."

The hole is a 7-by-9-foot cement room, with a steel door that had a slot for receiving meals. The cell only had a cot, a thin mattress, a toilet and a sink. Showers were permitted only once a week. One was also allowed an hour outside each day as long as no other inmates were in the yard.

I was escorted back to my cell. The corpsman who stitched me up had not given me any pain meds, and as a result, every time I moved, my side screamed in pain.

I needed to find out who hired the inmate to kill me.

For weeks I was reluctant to leave my cell after what happened in the showers. Bear was still in The Hole, and I really did not have any other friends. The inmate who stabbed me was also in The Hole, which gave me a little comfort, but I was more than a little paranoid.

I felt like a boxer in the ring who, incidentally, would have been larger than my jail cell. I was up against the ropes being pummeled. Every time the imaginary referee separated us, I was hit with another overhead left. Emotionally, I was given a standing eight count, seconds away from a technical knockout. The problem with this boxing match was I was fighting a foe much stronger than I, and I had no idea how many rounds the match would go.

I had been told the NCIS would arrive on a particular day to do another interrogation, this time much more thoroughly. The first time I was interviewed, I told them everything that had happened. I had no idea what else I could add to the story.

When I was ushered into the interrogation room, I saw my lawyer, Mr. Comeaux. That gave me some solace. When the conversation began, I realized this was not an interrogation, but rather a conversation on my court martial. In many ways, court martial hearings are similar to civilian criminal hearings, but there are also many differences.

I learned I had a choice to have my case heard by either a jury, called a court member panel, or by only a judge. In either case, the military judge would be a commissioned officer of the Navy who is a member of the bar of a federal court. Mr. Comeaux and I agreed I would have a better chance with the panel. The panel would be composed of my peers including commissioned officers and enlisted persons. I was also told the panel may be composed of up to one third officers.

The last piece of information I received that afternoon was the most disheartening. Unlike civilian court cases, in a court martial case, a vote of only two-thirds is all that is required to find a service member guilty of an offense.

Any self-confidence I had before being arrested, had dissipated, like the last spot of snow on a sunny April day. My anger was replaced with something much more productive: *purpose*. I was humbled in every way imaginable, but my new-found meekness was far from weakness. I was determined to fight to be exonerated.

The next day Bear was escorted back to our cell. I'm not sure which of us was happier.

"Bear, I don't know how to thank you for protecting me. I owe you my life, but I am not sure how I can ever repay you," I said,

"You don't owe me. I would do it again. How is your side?" he asked.

"I got the stitches out a few days ago. It's still sore. I can't sleep on that side, but I'll be fine."

Changing the subject, Bear said, "I am being transferred to Leavenworth."

"When?" I said with disappointment.

"I don't know, but they are definitely shutting down this trash heap, permanently. You will be sent somewhere too," he said.

"Well, my attorney said since my case is high profile, it will most likely be held in D.C. Some politicians want to be involved. Just what I need, some holier-than-thou senator looking for an opportunity to showcase his lack of talent."

"Damn! You better hope it isn't televised," Bear said.

"Televised? That is all I need. Oh, and by the way, that piece of shit who stabbed me said he was paid to do it."

Bear leaned forward with intensity on his face. "It was a hit job? Someone does not want you to testify. You know something they do not want exposed. You have to watch your back, Lloyd. I would even consider telling the warden you want to be kept in the hole. It sucks, but you will be safe."

Bear was transferred to Leavenworth less than a week after he was released from the hole. When I asked if I would also be transferred, the sarcastic remark I received was they had a "special place" where I would be sent.

The next couple of days I was ultra-focused on my case. I requested, and had been given, a legal pad and a small pencil, which I used to jot down my notes. I wracked my brain to remember specific things everyone had said about the mission before we left the ship. I excluded no one, not even the steward who spent all the time in the galley except for when he brought us our meal in the wardroom. I wrote down statements made by the Captain, XO, Lt. Kiggans, Braun, everyone, no matter how insignificant they seemed. I was convinced something someone had said would reveal the traitor.

Within the Department of the Navy, the Naval Criminal Investigative Service is the civilian federal law enforcement agency uniquely responsible for investigating felony crime, preventing terrorism and protecting secrets for the Navy and Marine Corps. Their interest in my case was overwhelming. It was a once in a lifetime type of case that could be a boost to one's career. The case included sex, multiple murders, and espionage.

As I continued to write on my legal pad, I could not help but think how the military trains a kid from Cornstalk, Iowa, to be a killer, then sends him home after a handful of years and tells him to act like a normal citizen.

Man has an incurable desire to kill. It is almost as if, had there been no wars instigated by geographic territory, or a need for natural resources, man would create wars simply to kill to satisfy his addiction. As a child, I remember stepping on caterpillars and hearing them pop. I felt a sense of superiority and justification putting an end to the insect's life, knowing even then, if allowed to live, they would devour our garden pea plants and cherry tree (I lived for my stepmother's cherry pie). I killed to protect our natural resources. It was a sense of power scarce in a 6-year old's life. Playing God I got to decide if the caterpillar lived or died. Now I found myself the caterpillar.

CHAPTER TWENTY-SEVEN

O nly a few days passed when I was informed I was being transferred to Washington, D.C. Actually, to be accurate, I was sent to the Alexandria Detention Center located in Virginia, but since there were enough government offices there, it was an expanse of the capital.

The Alexandria jail housed high-profile defendants, including foreign and domestic terrorists, spies and traitors. Now, I became one of their illustrious guests. Among those incarcerated there was Mason Hughes, the FBI agent turned Soviet mole.

The Alexandria Detention Center in Virginia is a compound of low-slung brick buildings just off the Capital Beltway, and a few blocks from the federal courthouse, where I would eventually be tried. I hated being imprisoned at the same place where the real cowards were detained. I felt the same hatred towards these men that the inmates at Portsmouth felt for me. I had a better understanding of why I was looked upon as scum. These pathetic traitors turned their backs on their country for either monetary gain or for some warped political philosophy. As much as I despised being in Alexandria Detention Center, I did feel much safer at this facility.

To my disgust, some of the inmates convicted of espionage tried to befriend me, as if I qualified for their exclusive club. What seemed lost by the Navy, the U.S. government, the zookeepers, and inmates, was I am innocent! So much for the accused to be presumed innocent until his guilt is established by legal and competent evidence beyond a reasonable doubt.

Mr. Comeaux met with me the second day I arrived in Alexandria. He had another surprise for me. Apparently, I was summoned to appear before The United States Senate Select Committee on

Intelligence, (sometimes referred to as the Intelligence Committee or SSCI). The committee was created in 1976 and was comprised of 17 senators. The Committee's purpose was to oversee and provide continuous research of the intelligence activities and programs of the United States Government. They would provide Senate appropriate proposals for legislation and report to the Senate concerning such intelligence activities. My attorney wanted to prep me before my appearance before the committee.

All this before I even went on trial.

Mr. Comeaux spent hours with me explaining why the United States Senate Select Committee on Intelligence wanted to question me and prepared me for the carnival show. I questioned whether this was appropriate and even legal. His response was something to the effect that the Senate can basically do whatever it wants when it comes to counterintelligence. He assured me this was just a fact-finding session, but anything I say *could be used against me in my trial.*

Hypothetically, the primary reason they wanted me to appear before them was to determine how much damage to national security had been done, and how vulnerable our military and homeland are due to everything that happened in Ukraine. Mr. Comeaux told me I could explain the security breach without incriminating myself, and he would be at the interview and would instruct me not to answer a question if he found it to be compromising to my defense.

Mr. Comeaux bought me a suit to wear to the closed-door interview. First impressions are important, of course, but these Senators had previously met me through scuttlebutt and the press, and they had already formed their impressions.

Despair. That was my biggest enemy while in the Alexandria prison. Having been transferred from Portsmouth Naval Prison, my upcoming fate seemed to fast forward from the distant future to imminent. Like ships of Tarshish scattered by the east wind, so too my thoughts and hopes became weary of the voyage. I needed some encouragement, any encouragement, and it came from an unlikely source.

As I entered the common area in the prison, a television was on, broadcasting the news.

"Hey, Lloyd, they're talking about you," some inmate said.

Here, among true turncoats, I was not called Benny.

My photo was in a box at the top right of the screen. I only caught the tail end of the broadcast, but the reporter was explaining I would appear before a senate sub-committee to answer some questions about the intelligence brief. My photo was replaced with a picture of the Alexandria Detention Center where I am being held. I went back to my cell.

My mind wandered to an unanswerable philosophical question. *Can anyone truly know another person?* I doubt it. Does anyone *really, truly* know the person's inner thoughts? His fears? Regrets? Shame? Hidden secrets? I don't think so. One can be married to someone for 75 years, finish his sentences, know his favorite color, song, animal and food, but can one ever completely and honestly *know* someone? In the best relationships one can invite someone into his being, into his psyche. One can give him carte blanche and access to every room in his psychological home, every room but that little closet. The one with multiple locks. That one room guarded better than Area 51 in Nevada. That *special* room one doesn't even want to enter. That is both sad and scary.

I was played a fool by Paula. She placed a mortgage on my heart that I would be paying off for the remainder of my life. The interest was much too high. I wanted to hate her, but I could not. I wanted to forget her, but that was and still is impossible. Her betrayal cut deep within my soul. I was overwhelmed by a sense of loss. It is said when one loses a loved one, it will get easier over time. That's wrong. When one loses something of great value, what does he do? He looks for it until it's found, but when looking for something that can never be found, he spends the rest of his days on an endless, fruitless, disappointing journey.

Too many people live with the fallacy of true love, then hate because of something the person did. If that's the case, true love doesn't exist. Infidelity is one of the greatest betrayals. What's that old cliche? Hate the sin, love the sinner? Love *is* forever. One may despise something someone did. The heart may be splintered into a thousand pieces. The *want* to hate is real, but it is nearly impossible to do so. Sadly, the hurt remains a lifetime.

The next morning I dressed in the suit my attorney bought me. It was a bit long in the sleeves, but it was better than the utility uniform made of denim I had been wearing. I looked like a fine upstanding young man, but I doubted a new suit would change any of the senators' minds who already found me guilty without a trial. I was transported to the Hart Senate Office Building in a white van. Besides the driver, there were two United States Marine Corps Military Police escorting me. Two of the three marines were in the back of the van with me. *Like I had any plans of escaping.*

The van parked in front of the building and two of the marines grabbed me by my elbows, one on each side, as we walked to the entrance. The fetters on my ankles prevented me from taking anything but short steps. My hands were also cuffed. I was being treated like a terrorist. The Hart building had a more distinctly contemporary appearance than the buildings nearby, though it did display a marble façade in keeping with its surroundings. Inside the building, a 90-foot-high skylight brightened the atrium. The large Central Hearing Facility on the second floor was designed for high-interest events where the questioning would take place.

I would be lying if I said the experience did not unnerve me. I have always been good at play-acting, and this situation called for an Oscar winning performance. It wasn't that I needed to lie or play a role I had not lived out. It was more the need to engage in pretense to gain an advantage. The cards were stacked against me, but that was something with which I had a lot of experience. My entire life I had to take the harder road. I just did not want to be played by a bunch of senators who thought their junk did not stink. I would not be intimidated. Whether they wanted to believe me or not, I was innocent, and I had no reason to feel ashamed.

As my attorney and I entered the hearing room, I leaned over to Mr. Comeaux and asked, "Who are all those people sitting at the prosecutor's table?"

"The man in the officer's uniform is the prosecutor. I have worked with him before. He is assigned to JAG. The two men next to him are with the FBI. The FBI is the lead agency for investigating espionage and other intelligence activities. They are responsible for all counterintelligence investigations. Remember, I am here to make sure the questions are not incriminating. Be polite. Address them as sir, ma'am, or senator," Mr. Comeaux said.

Once we sat down, the hearing began.

"Good morning Mr. Lloyd," Senator Madelline Lilburne said.

"Good morning, Senators," I said, as I silently read the nameplates in front of each senator. My senator from Pennsylvania was not present.

"Today's hearing is simply an opportunity to determine what type of security breach occurred during a mission you were part of in March of this year. This is not a trial, however, anything you share with us today can be used at your upcoming trial. Do you understand that?"

"Yes, ma'am," I said.

"This committee is the Senate Select Committee on Intelligence," the Senator said. "We are charged with the oversight of the intelligence activities and programs of the United States Government. We submit to the Senate appropriate proposals for legislation and report to the Senate concerning such intelligence activities and programs."

In a fruitless attempt to deny the inevitable aging, Senator Lilburne had climbed into a costume well-suited for a Halloween party. She had had a boob job that made her breasts perfectly symmetrized (everyone knows no woman has two identical breasts, one is always a tad larger than the other, just like a man's testicles). Her face had been drawn tight by a facelift, causing her eyes to look more Asian than Caucasian. Her lips swelled from numerous injections, as if having been punched by a boxer's fist. Botox tried to hide the roadmap of wrinkles dispersed throughout her forehead and around her eyes, and her hair was bleached some bizarre color. The California senator looked like a human sideshow freak.

The senator continued her banter. "Petty Officer Lloyd, were you a part of a secret mission in Romania code named *The Dental Appointment?*"

"Yes," I responded, trying to keep as many of my answers brief as possible.

"When were you informed about the mission?" She asked.

"Well, truthfully, I never was fully informed about the details of the mission. I received information piecemeal. Originally, I was not to be on that mission. I had no prior knowledge of it. The original team consisted of one man who understood Ukrainian. That man, James Mayfield, was with the CIA. He was killed when a helicopter landing on our ship crashed. A piece of the prop flew off and struck him. The team was desperate for someone who could communicate in Ukrainian, and the team did not have the luxury of time to wait for Langley to send a replacement."

So much for keeping my answers short!

"Were you briefed on the mission before leaving the USS *Charles F. Adams?*" the Senator asked.

I should answer, "Asked and answered!" This better not turn into some redundant, repetitive barrage of questions!

"Again, only in part. To be honest, Senator, I received information a little at a time. I guess in accordance with the need-to-know basis," I said.

"Who did you share what you knew before leaving the ship?"

"No one."

"You made no phone calls or communicated even the smallest, insignificant detail about the mission with anyone?" she asked again.

"Asked and answered," Mr. Comeaux interjected.

Finally! Make sure you push back, Mr. Comeaux.

Another senator, Josh Padro, took his turn to ask some questions.

"Petty Officer, Lloyd, were you in a romantic relationship with a Soviet spy?"

Before I could answer, Mr. Comeaux said, "My client had no knowledge anyone with whom he had a relationship was a foreign agent."

"I want to answer that question," I told my attorney.

"I met Paula Delgado in Spain. Yes, we had a relationship, but I never shared any classified information with her and when I found out she was working for a foreign intelligence agency, I killed her."

This, apparently, was a revelation to all the senators as they turned to each other and talked in low voices. I had taken them by surprise.

"You killed her?" Senator Padro asked.

"Yes. I met her in Athens when I finally made it back from Ukraine. It was the day before the *Adams* was to pull into Piraeus, Greece. I caught her with a phrase peculiar to Ukrainian. That was a red flag that helped me realize she was not Spanish. When I pushed her on the subject, she admitted she was with the Russian Federal Security Service and the KGB, but for this unique mission, she was temporarily assigned with China's IPA. She pulled a gun on me and was forcing me to sign a letter stating I was the traitor on the *Adams* who fed them classified information about the mission. Mr. Houston, one of the CIA agents assigned to this mission, gave me an ink pen that was actually a gun capable of shooting one bullet. I picked up the pen as if I were going to sign the confession and shot Paula in the chest. I left her in the hotel room in Athens."

"Her name is not Paula Delgado, and you are correct, she was not from Spain. Your girlfriend's name is Nataliya Kravchenko. She is a Ukrainian spy working for the Soviets and apparently the Chinese, too. She played you like a Stradivarius," Mr. Padro said, leaning forward with a pompous demeanor meant to intimidate me.

"Senator," interrupted Mr. Comeaux. "I object to your sarcastic remark. This hearing is to be a fact-finding session, not an opportunity to demean my client."

"My apologies," the senator said.

After what I had been through, no silver spoon politician would ever be able to unnerve me. I looked through the senator as I do with anyone who attempts to manipulate or intimidate me, like the frog I dissected in 9th grade. Clearly, he was taken with himself. He had been accustomed to everyone bowing before him. If he thought I was going to roll over and let him step on my jugular, he was in for a surprise. The senator clearly was living in a delusional state. Having been in the senate for nearly five decades, he had been living a lie to the point he actually believed it himself. Like a wildly popular movie star loved for the character he portrays, he had been play-acting a part that gave him great power.

I find it more than interesting how politicians find killing people extremely easy when, from hundreds or thousands of miles away, they give an order or push a button. When one does not see the results of his actions, he becomes immune to the horrors of war. Only when he sees a flag-draped coffin being carried off a plane might he experience a reality check.

Another senator wanted in on the fun. Senator Meredith Reigner, another "lifer" who was in the senate for over 40 years, spoke.

"Petty Officer Lloyd, were you in love with Nataliya Kravchenko?"

There's the question I had expected. I had mulled for days how I would answer that question, but when it was finally asked, I became mute.

"Your Honor, would you please instruct the defendant to answer my question?" She asked.

"Petty Officer Lloyd, please answer the question," the judge instructed.

"Yes."

"So, is it safe to say since you loved Ms. Kravchenko, you would do anything for her?"

"No! That would be a false assumption. Nothing and no one could ever cause me to turn my back on my country. That is safe to say."

Moving on from that answer, the senator tossed me another. "Petty Officer Lloyd, did you kill anyone other than Ms. Kravchenko?"

"Yes. Chief Petty Officer Harrington was attacked by a Chinese agent while we were at the abandoned Olympic Training Facility. It was at the archery range. I found a bow and arrow and killed the assailant. I also killed a Romanian Securitate on a train when I was trying to make my way back to Piraeus to meet my ship," I explained.

"You expect us to believe you shot a man with a bow and arrow?" Senator Padro said with a sarcastic smile on his face.

"I don't expect you to believe anything I say, Senator." I said with a little attitude in my voice. "You know, Senator, I think John Fogerty was right."

"What do you mean by that?"

"I ain't no fortunate one," I answered.

"Would you like to explain that?" Senator Padro asked.

"You want an explanation?" I said, raising my voice a bit. "Let me ask you this, Senator. Have you ever served in the military?" The response was nothing but crickets, so I continued. "No, I didn't think so. Well, contrary to what you might think, the real world in which sailors and soldiers and airmen live is not a board game with little men one can slide from square to square. It is not a game of Stratego. I may not have a degree from an Ivy League School hanging on my wall, like you, Senator. I cannot quote from authors as you have. Instead, I rely on something much more valuable. Experience."

"You are out of line, sailor," the senator said.

Mr. Comeaux put his hand on my shoulder as a message for me to shut-up. But it was too late for that. What were they going to do to me, throw me in the brig?

"No, you are out of line, Senator. Regardless of the well-planned mission, regardless of one's orders, regardless of how you people who sit behind a desk think a mission should have gone, there's always something that amends the best laid plans. If one does not deviate from the plan, he is dead. Period! One has to alter plans in a millisecond. Believe it or not, senators, sometimes all a soldier can do is react, because there isn't time to sit and recalculate. He who hesitates has his brains splattered all over the guy next to him."

I was on a roll, so I continued.

"I got thrust into Mission Impossible, with no preparation. No one told me 'The plan,'" I said as I made quotation marks with my fingers. "I wasn't privy to *the who, what, and where.* I was not given the big picture. Hell, I didn't even have a torn corner of the picture. I was lied to about the entire thing. Oh, it's no big thing, I was told."

I saw Senator Reigner open her mouth to speak, but before she could, I continued my lecture.

"Our translator was accidently killed by the helicopter blade, and the team needed someone who could speak Ukrainian. Enter Petty Officer Calvin Lloyd. The whole thing would take only 36 hours, I was told. Easy Peasy. I was made to believe we were staying in Romania. Before I knew it we were in Ukraine. No one said I was going into the

Soviet Union! No one told me I would be dodging bullets. I wasn't even given a weapon, for cryin' out loud." Nope! Keep Lloyd ignorant, even though he will be laying his life on the line. How dare I ask any questions. Once I was served a fresh plate of bullshit, I should have asked, 'Sir, if this is no big deal, why are we leaving at sundown instead of the next morning?' They should have just said, 'shut up and do it, sailor.' But, no, let's keep jerking his chain."

"That is enough, Petty Officer," one of the senators said. I ignored him.

"I was told we did not want the press to know that Meiyang Fang was coming to the United States until he actually arrived in Washington. You know how the press is, senator, don't you? High level diplomat? High level, yeah! He was a scientist working in a bioweapons lab in China! The Chinese would have done anything to kill him. They wanted our extrication team eliminated, too. And they mostly succeeded."

"Are you through?" asked Senator Lilburne.

I assumed that was a rhetorical question, so I said nothing.

"What exactly happened to the other 5 men? There were four SEALs and two CIA agents on that mission with you. We know Chief Petty Officer was captured by the KGB and taken to Vladivostok."

"Petty Officer Deerstone, Petty Officer Brudzinski, LTJG Kovacs, Mr. Paxton, and Mr. Houston were all killed at the abandoned Olympic training location. They were killed in different ways, as if the enemy was trying to send some kind of message. You know what happened to Chief Petty Officer Harrington. He had gone back to our agent's safe house and was captured by the KGB. He, by the way, can prove I had nothing to do with the murder of my team."

"We will certainly question Mr. Harrington when he returns to the States," she said.

"Why don't you wait to hear from him before assuming I am guilty of something I did not do?" I asked.

Crickets.

"I believe that concludes our questions. Thank you for coming, Petty Officer," the senator said.

Like I had a choice.

CHAPTER TWENTY-EIGHT

I t was the first day of my trial. My attorney, Mr. Comeaux, received the list of witnesses for the prosecution which included, the XO from the *Adams,* LCDR Lynch, Petty Officer Robinson, and Lt. Kiggans. As soon as I saw Robinson's name on the paper, my blood ran hotter than lava. *He had something to do with this!* Mr. Kiggans was the only witness we had planned on calling to the stand, so the fact that the prosecution beat us to the punch did not matter. We were confident he would be more beneficial to our defense than the prosecution.

"Remember, Cal, the government has the burden of proving you, the defendant, committed the crimes with which you are charged. I will attack all of their weak arguments," Mr. Comeaux said, trying to reassure me.

While we were meeting in a side room of the courthouse before the trial was to begin, Mr. Comeaux received a note from the bailiff. He read the note, then looked at me astonished.

"Well, Cal, things just got a lot better for you. Noah Harrington is going to be released from the Soviets' custody within the next few days!" he said with a smile on his face.

"Excellent!" I screamed. "This case will be thrown out of court! I will be exonerated, and my name cleared!"

"Don't get too excited," Mr. Comeaux said. "There is still the charge of espionage. Chief Petty Officer Harrington can prove you did not kill any of your teammates, so the murder charges *will* be dropped, but the espionage charges likely will not. He will not be able to prove you did not send those encrypted messages from the ship, giving the Soviets and / or the Chinese advanced warning."

I felt a hard slap of reality across my face, like the first time one gazes into the mirror and realizes he looks *old*. I was hoping when the murder charges were dropped there would be less meat on the bone on the case against me. I was also hoping Smoke would arrive in the States soon. Very soon.

"Look," Mr. Comeaux said. "Let's hurdle one obstacle at a time. I will amend my witness list to include Mr. Harrington."

We entered the courtroom and sat at the table. I could almost smell the drool coming from those who tried me in the kangaroo court of their minds. I was the wounded prey; they, the predator. My heart was racing like a shooting star, but shooting stars fade away. I feared my hope would follow the same course.

The presiding judge spoke first.

"The defendant, Petty Officer Second Class Calvin Lloyd is charged with espionage and six counts of murder. Both NCIS and the CIA have been involved with this case as it involves counterintelligence. The Secretary of the Navy Instruction 3850.2E defines counterintelligence as 'information gathered and activities conducted to identify, deceive, exploit, disrupt, or protect against espionage, other intelligence activities, sabotage, assassinations conducted for or on behalf of foreign powers, organizations, persons, or their agents, or international terrorist organizations or activities.'"

"Is the prosecution and defense prepared to make opening statements?" the judge asked.

"Yes, your honor," said the prosecutor.

"Yes, your honor," Mr. Comeaux added.

The prosecutor stood and walked over to the jury.

"The prosecution will prove Petty Officer Lloyd and Petty Officer Ronald Womack worked concertedly to deceive the United States of America and work in conjunction with the Soviet Union and the People's Republic of China, for monetary gain. Although much of the evidence lies somewhere in Soviet Ukraine, we have been able to figure out the framework of the crimes committed. This is what we know," the prosecutor said.

They are going to drag Dakota's name through the mud? Let the poor man lie in peace!

"Petty Officer Lloyd allowed himself to be seduced by a KGB agent named Nataliya Kravchenko. We have many photos of the two of them together. She must have persuaded the defendant to give her some classified information, either verbally or as a document. Once Petty Officer Lloyd was compromised, she owned him. We are not sure how the Soviets or Chinese knew the defendant would end up on that mission, but clearly they knew."

How and where did they get photographs of Paula and me together? Leaning toward Mr. Comeaux, I whispered, "Find out who gave the prosecution these photographs. Whoever it is, he is part of this conspiracy. This may show us who the real traitor is."

Mr. Comeaux simply nodded.

"Petty Officer Lloyd convinced his Radioman friend, Petty Officer Ronald Womack, to join the espionage. Money must have changed hands. Womack communicated with the KGB through code. We have records of some encrypted messages sent from the *Adams*. They came from Radio Central, so it had to be someone with access to the transmitting equipment. At some point, Womack came to his senses and wanted to tell Naval authorities the KGB had penetrated our security wall, and the *Dental Appointment* mission was in grave danger. That is when Lloyd killed Womack."

"While in Ukraine, we believe Lloyd used the opportunity when his teammates were separated to kill each one-by-one. All except for Petty Officer Harrington, who the Soviets have behind bars and is accused of espionage."

The prosecutor took a seat, as my attorney stood and addressed the jury.

"The prosecution's so-called evidence is more than sketchy. It is non-existent. The prosecution just stated the Soviets and/or Chinese knew Petty Officer Lloyd would end up on that mission. If they did, it could not have been my client who told them. He had no access to Radio Central. In fact, he would have immediately stood out as being in a high security area where he had no reason to be. There are no witnesses who can recall ever seeing Petty Officer in that workspace," Mr. Comeaux said. "Mr. Womack is deceased, and there is no proof my client had anything to do with his demise. In fact, they were best friends."

"The prosecution alleges money had to have changed hands between Mr. Lloyd and Mr. Womack. Again, no evidence. Mr. Lloyd's bank records do not show any large or unusual deposits or withdrawals. Where is all the money Petty Officer Lloyd was supposed to have made for his illegal spying? Underneath his bunk mattress? Mr. Lloyd did not commit espionage, never gave any information to any foreign agent and as such, never received any compensation from them."

"The travesty here is not only that a patriotic sailor who volunteered on a dangerous mission is here on trial, but that NCIS, and the FBI have wasted valuable time and resources by not searching for the real traitor. Gentlemen, you must find Petty Officer Lloyd not guilty on all counts."

Just before Mr. Comeaux sat down, he asked the judge if he could approach the bench. Both he and the prosecutor walked up to the judge's desk to have a private conversation.

"Your honor, we added Chief Petty Officer Harrington's name to our witness list. As you know, his release from Soviet custody is imminent, but it will be a week or so before he will be able to testify for my client. I respectfully request a motion to stay. Mr. Harrington is crucial to our defense," Mr. Comeaux said.

"I see he is your only witness," the Judge said.

"Your honor, this is simply a tactic to delay this case further," the prosecutor argued. "It has already taken too long to get this case to trial. Any additional delay will make a mockery of the criminal justice system. The United States Navy, and the American people deserve justice to be served."

"Don't you think that is a little melodramatic, Mr. Shone?" The judge said. "I do not see the harm in delaying the trial for a week or two. It certainly would not tip the cradle of justice. If Mr. Harrington is the only witness for the defense, I think we should provide every opportunity for him to be available for the defense. Under the extraordinary circumstances that prevented Mr. Harrington from appearing here today, I am going to allow the stay."

Turning to my attorney, the judge added, "Mr. Comeaux, we will not wait for Mr. Harrington indefinitely."

The judge motioned for the attorneys to go back to their respective tables and then addressed the court. "This court is adjourned and will resume two weeks from today."

It was late afternoon when Mr. Comeaux and I got back to the prison. As we were going through security we noticed a group of guards fixated on a television. Mr. Comeaux and I stopped to see what was so interesting. On the television screen we saw Smoke being escorted onto an Air Force plane, confirming he would soon be back in the States.

"Breaking news! Chief Petty Officer Noah Harrington has just been released from a Soviet prison in Vladivostok. President Lashley agreed to exchange Harrington for two Soviet nationals. Boris Ivanov was convicted of espionage against the United States while he was working at the Russian embassy in Washington. Alexander Nikitin was working for a military contractor in Bangor, Washington, when he was convicted of photographing top secret submarine sonar systems at the time he was arrested."

"Yes!" I shouted loudly enough that the guards turned and looked at me. "This is huge! If Smoke gets released, he can explain I did not kill the five men from our mission and the traitor had to be someone else. He will tell them the traitor is someone still stationed aboard the *Adams*. Smoke will prove I am a scapegoat!"

Back at my cell, I tried my best not to get overly anxious about Smoke making it to my new court date, but after an entire week passed, I lost the battle. I was more than tense. I felt like I was in a canoe with no paddles, approaching an inevitable waterfall. I had been trying to paddle with my hands for months, but the current was moving me precariously close to going over the falls.

On the ninth day after the trial was postponed, and only five days before it was to resume, I received much needed solace.

"Lloyd, get up. You have a visitor," the zookeeper said.

Mr. Comeaux must have some good news!

When I entered the visitor's room I looked right past Mr. Comeaux and immediately saw my friend.

"Smoke! What the hell are you doing here? Damn, am I glad to see you! Listen, man, you know I didn't do this," I said

"I know you didn't. That is why I'm here. I would have arrived sooner, but I was interviewed for three consecutive days by NCIS, the FBI, and the CIA," Smoke said. "First of all, you were with me when our team got slaughtered, so the murder rap just vanished. There is also no way you could have been the one who screwed us. You weren't privy to the details of the mission till we got to Kiliia. No, it wasn't you, but it was someone on the *Charles F. Adams*. That I can promise you."

"What about someone at Langley?" Mr. Comeaux asked.

"No one knew the timing of your meeting with the agent in Ukraine. They knew of the helicopter crash that killed Mayfield, and that we had a replacement who could speak Ukrainian. Vegas and the Leopard asked your Captain to hold off informing Washington and to tell them the plan was still a go. They were not completely confident the entire mission might have to be aborted by the time we reached Kiliia."

"Now, don't be pissed at me, but I need to tell you something else," Smoke said. "Just about everyone thought there was a better than 50-50 chance you would be killed before you returned from that pub. We were going to give you exactly 100 minutes. If you did not come back, we were to return to the ship."

"And, if by some chance I was held up, and returned to our rendezvous point in 101 minutes, you would have left me for dead?" I asked.

"I'm sorry, Shroom, but that's just the way we work. We won't jeopardize six men's lives for the sake of one. If we have to abort, then that is what we will do. In such a mission, we must minimize our losses. You told me you enjoy playing cards on the ship. You know when to cut your losses. Look, I need you to think who on the ship could be the traitor. The truth is there is enough evidence to bury you.

A lot of it is fabricated. Someone created bullshit evidence. The only way we will get you out of this mess is to find the real Judas. I need you to rack your brain and make a list of everyone you think could have done this."

"What do you think I have been doing? I've had nothing but time to think of who it could be. This is what I do know. My friend Dakota, eh, Ron Womack, was a Radioman. He figured out who the traitor was, and he was killed for it. He told me before we reached Constanta that someone used the secret transmission equipment to transmit a cryptic message. Even stranger was the traitor did not use the standard symmetric key algorithm we normally use. The sender used something Dakota had never seen before," I said.

"So, no one knew about this but you, Womack, Lt. Kiggans, and whoever sent it? Any thoughts on who that might be?"

"Correct. Only the four of us. As far as my suspicions go, well, there's only a handful of people who had access to the details of the mission, and access to Radio Central. Every radioman, of course. Not every officer, however. Well, I should say, any commissioned officer is allowed to enter Radio Central, but only a few have a *reason* to go in there. Besides the CO and XO, there are a couple of department heads, like the Operations Officer, Lieutenant. Kiggans, the Weapons Officer, Lieutenant Commander Braxton. Then there are division officers with responsibilities giving them a legitimate reason for being in Radio Central, the communications officer, Lieutenant Junior Grade Czajkowski and the combat systems officer, Lieutenant Lavigne. There is no real reason for the engineering, supply or navigation officers to frequent Radio Central." I said. "Someone needs to take a closer look at Petty Officer Robinson. He is currently number one on my suspect list."

"What about this Czajkowski? That sounds Russian or Ukrainian," Mr. Comeaux asked. "Is he a possibility?"

"It's actually Polish," I said. "I don't know much about him. Hey, at this point I wouldn't rule out anyone."

"Well, I've been asked by your XO to report to the *Adams* on Saturday," Smoke said. He and a committee want to discuss your court martial before the hearing. I have already been interviewed by the prosecutor. I told him there is no way you could have been the turncoat, but I think he has an agenda. It seems as though he is more bent on crucifying you than doing the work needed to find out who is the real culprit. The scary part is this person is still out there collaborating with the enemy."

"Saturday? The trial begins on Monday!" I said.

"Not to worry. Nothing will keep me from this trial."

"Smoke, thank you."

"Thank me when I get you out of this fiasco. I feel partly to blame for getting you into this mess in the first place. Calvin, hang in there. I believe in you."

"Hey, you called me Calvin instead of Shroom."

"See you soon," he said, just as the guard entered the room.

"Time's up," the zookeeper announced.

CHAPTER TWENTY-NINE

As expected, all of the murder charges against me were dropped. It appeared as though the prosecuting team was deflated over Smoke's testimony, but I was in no position to get optimistic. They would just put that saved energy into convicting me of espionage. The bedrock of their case against me was Paula, or whatever her name was. My relationship with her was damning. Mr. Slone, the prosecutor, would certainly focus on that relationship.

There was not an open seat in the courtroom when we arrived. The only friendly faces I saw were Smoke and Lt. Kiggans. The prosecution wasted no time beginning their attack.

"Nataliya Kravchenko, known to the defendant as Paula Delgado, was actually an *illegal*, a foreign intelligence agent living on U.S. soil, operating undercover and unknown to American authorities. She was a *Swallow*, a female agent employed to seduce people for intelligence purposes. She lived in San Diego, the largest Navy base on the west coast, but she received orders to go to Roto, Spain, and initiate a relationship with Calvin Lloyd, to seduce him."

"Although trained by the KGB, she was temporarily assigned to China's Central Investigation Department. China wanted to retrieve Meiyang Fang, a bio weapons engineer who worked at The Wuhan Institute of Virology. Fang was trying to defect to the U.S. and the purpose of this mission was to get Fang out of Ukraine, onto the *USS Charles F. Adams*, and ultimately, to the United States"

Mr. Slone continued. "The Chinese did extensive research on Petty Officer Lloyd. They knew he was ambitious and had a desire to earn a lot of money. In high school he had a thriving landscape business in his home town and had a bank account totaling $1,334, not a small feat for a 17-year-old kid still in high school. They also knew he made homemade explosives and sold them to other kids, that is, until he was arrested. They knew his stepmother was from Ukraine and that he had a poor relationship with her."

"Lastly, they discovered a friend of his in Pennsylvania had been murdered. Another friend of Petty Officer Lloyd was accused of the death, and ultimately, the man hanged himself in his prison cell. A lot of baggage for a young man, and quite possibly a perfect candidate to be compromised and to groom as a Chinese or Soviet asset. Ms. Kravchenko used appealing ideology, ego, greed, and love to recruit Petty Officer Lloyd."

For three days, the prosecution continued to lay out the flimsy case they had against me which was in itself amazing since they had very little evidence. They had rested their case. Being a realist, I knew the case was not going well for me. I knew the only chance I had at being exonerated is if the actual traitor is exposed. Mr. Comeaux was doing the best he could with the limited amount of evidence he had, but at the same time, the prosecution had the same limited evidence. They had constructed their case on the scaffold of suspicion, rather than evidence.

The following day, Mr. Comeaux would begin my defense. We had discussed at length whether I should take the stand or not. We weighed the pros and cons, and in the end, Mr. Comeaux thought taking the stand might help my case. When Mr. Slone, the prosecutor, cross examined me, I was prepared.

"Petty Officer Lloyd, how did your team know where they were supposed to find Mr. Meiyang Fang?"

"I was told to meet our agent in a pub in Kiliia, Ukraine. They sent me because I was the only one in the group who could speak and understand Ukrainian. The agent told me we would find Mr. Fang at the abandoned Olympic Training facility," I said.

"So, was it only you and our agent who knew the rendezvous location was the Olympic site?" Mr. Slone asked.

"I guess so. I don't know who else he told, but someone else had to have known because we had company when we got there."

"Just a yes or no answer, please."

"It's not simply a yes or no question," I said.

"Your Honor?" Mr. Slone said, looking at the judge.

"Petty Officer Lloyd, please refrain from any editorial. Simply answer the questions asked," the judge said.

Mr. Slone walked closer to the jury and continued questioning me. "After you left the pub, our agent was killed. You were the last person to see him alive."

"Objection, your Honor. Is there a question here?" Mr. Comeaux asked.

"I will reword, your Honor. Petty Officer Lloyd, since you were the last person to see our agent alive, did you kill him?"

"I wasn't the last person to see him alive," I said.

"Who was?" Mr. Slone asked.

"Whoever killed him," I said.

Before the second day of the trial, Smoke joined my lawyer and me in a side room. Mr. Comeaux wanted to review the questions he would be asking him, and what cross examination questions the prosecution might ask.

"Where did you sleep last night," asked Mr. Comeaux.

"I did not want to waste money on a hotel room. You know, the Navy is never going to reimburse me. To them, this is not official business. I stayed at Bolling Air Force Base in Southeast D.C. It is located between the Potomac and Anacostia rivers off Interstate 295. Only problem was they did not have any vacant private rooms. I was stuck in an open barrack with a few dozen airmen," Smoke said.

"That stinks. You probably didn't get much sleep," continued Mr. Comeaux.

"Actually I did. I am used to crowded bedrooms," Smoke said with a laugh. "I am one of eleven kids. Growing up, I had to share a bedroom with three of my brothers."

"Eleven? God bless your mother," said Mr. Comeaux.

"Yeah, she used to call herself the old lady who lived in a shoe, who had so many children she didn't know what to do," he said, laughing again.

The look on my face made both Mr. Comeaux and Smoke wonder what I was thinking.

"What?" Smoke said, looking at me like he may have said something to upset me.

"Smoke, you are beautiful!" I said as I put his head in my two hands and kissed him on the forehead.

"What did I say? Weren't you ever read fairy tales as a kid?" Smoke asked.

"I was, but you just said the magic words! Two absolutely gorgeous words, *fairy tale*. You just solved the mystery of who the traitor is," I said with an excitement in my voice that made both of them look bewildered.

"Do explain," said Mr. Comeaux.

"We are not looking for a traitor. We are looking for *traitors!* Two to be exact. Husband and wife. Lt Kiggans and his wife Hua," I said.

"Kiggans?" Mr. Comeaux asked. "I thought you told me he was the one officer you could trust."

"I thought I could trust him. I feel like a fool. I was played by Paula, Lt. Kiggans and his wife. Hua, the lieutenant's wife, once told me a story of Five Chinese brothers. I will give you the Readers Digest version. One of the brothers was falsely accused of killing a boy. Each brother had a special ability, a gift. These gifts prevented the king from successfully executing the brothers."

"The first brother could swallow the sea. Salmon was found with his head hanging off the back of the chair. A fish had been wedged in his mouth. The second brother had an unbreakable iron neck. Lance's decapitated head was impaled on a spike. The third brother, with his special talent allowing him to stretch his legs all the way to the bottom of the ocean, could not be drowned. Leopard was lying prone on his back. His eyes were wide open, as was his mouth. His mouth was filled with water. He drowned. The fourth was immune to burning. We found the burnt corpse of Vegas. And the fifth brother, with his ability to hold his breath, survives overnight in an oven full of whipped cream. He could hold his breath forever. Tonto's body was found in an oven where he suffocated," I explained. "Think about it. This is exactly how each of the men on the mission was executed."

"You know, one of the people who interrogated me when I was in that Kiev prison was a Chinese woman who spoke excellent English," Smoke said. "She knew several highly confidential details about the U.S. Navy and our mission. I never met Kiggans' wife, so obviously, I did not recognize her," Smoke said.

"Did she have a mole on her forehead?" I asked.

"She did!" Smoke confirmed.

"Damn! It all makes sense now and I could kick myself. There was another clue I missed. I remembered Hua called the egg rolls nem rán, the North Vietnamese term for a spring roll, not chả giò, the South Vietnamese term. You may recall that Lance corrected me back in that barn when I called them nem rán! That should have been my first clue that Hua was involved with mainland China. I am so stupid!"

"You are far from Stupid, Cal. How could you have known?" Smoke said.

"I wonder how these spies get into the country," Mr. Comeaux thought aloud.

"Our border is very secure. Customs and Border Control make sure of that. In fact, Soviet and Chinese agents have tried to cross our borders and have been caught. As a result, now they enter legally through diplomatic channels, as secretaries, assistants, and personal security bodyguards," Smoke said.

"I am going to ask the prosecution, NCIS, and the FBI to meet me in the judge's chambers so I can give them this revelation of facts. Hopefully they will delay the trial till after they investigate Kiggans and his wife. I will also contact your CO and XO so they are aware Kiggans is the traitor," Mr. Comeaux said.

"Can we trust them?" Smoke asked.

"I think we have to," answered Mr. Comeaux.

The discussion in the judge's chambers was heated, but the judge agreed that in light of this new evidence, a delay was proper, at least until our findings could be proven or disproven. The FBI told Mr. Comeaux not to inform Captain Stansbury back at the *Adams*. They would handle that.

After the dust settled, XO Lynch filled me in on exactly how things went down. He said four FBI agents arrived at the *Adams* and met with Captain Stansbury and LCDR Lynch in the Captain's quarters, instead of the wardroom. They did not want any wandering ears to hear their discussion. After being briefed on the situation, the Captain ordered all hands on deck, where the crew was instructed to muster on the dock. As the sailors deboarded the ship, the XO stayed behind. When the last sailor walked off the ship, the XO went into Lt. Kiggans stateroom and began searching for any incriminating evidence.

In the rush to report to the fantail of the ship, LT Kiggans had taken a match and lit a small piece of paper, leaving it to burn in an ashtray. When the XO entered Kiggan's stateroom, he could smell the lingering smoke. In the ashtray, the XO found the half-burnt One-Time Pad, a virtually unbreakable crypto algorithm where text is combined with a random key and is used only once to encrypt a message. What makes it unbreakable is only the sender and receiver have the pad, or the key, needed to encrypt and decrypt the message. Someone would need access to the secure pad to read that specific message, as the same key will never be used again. Kiggans assumed the One-Time Pad would be destroyed when he hastily lit it and left his stateroom. The XO carefully placed the remnants of the One-Time Pad in an envelope and exited the stateroom to find the FBI agents.

Finding the agents and the Captain on the pier, Mr. Lynch showed the men what he had discovered.

"I think this is all you will need to arrest Mr. Kiggans," the XO said.

"Is this what I think it is?" asked the Captain.

"Yes. It is the One-Time Pad Kiggans must have used today to communicate with the Chinese."

"That makes me sick to my stomach," Captain Stansbury said. "What a betrayal."

"Gentlemen, why don't you give me five minutes alone with Kiggans. All you will need is a body bag to transport him to Washington," the XO said.

"We will take it from here," one of the agents said. "What you were able to find in his stateroom is exactly what we needed to convict him of treason. Kiggans will talk. We will make sure of it. We will tell him we will go easier on his wife if he cooperates. Trust me, we have creative ways to make him sing."

And sing, he did.

Lt. Kiggans was arrested on the pier and taken to the FBI field office in Jacksonville, Florida where he was questioned for several days. In an attempt to save his own hide, Kiggans began singing like Frank Sinatra, throwing his wife, Hua, under the bus. Kiggans gave the FBI names of Chinese spies planted in the United States, places they were targeting, and techniques he and his wife used to infiltrate sensitive areas and classified information. He also provided an extensive history of the various clandestine operations in which they participated over a span of 13 years. The information the FBI received from Kiggans was extensive and frightening.

During questioning, Lt. Kiggans first explained how he had been recruited by the Chinese. He was on special assignment to Saigon from the Secretary of Defense. A graduate of Annapolis, Kiggans was a Navy intelligence officer, assigned to South Vietnamese units. He gained the respect of the South Vietnamese as he learned to speak their language fluently and worked alongside them. It was not until he met

Hua, a North Vietnamese working for China's Central Investigation Department that Kiggans decided to work for the Chinese.

Nataliya Kravchenko was a KGB/SVR operative. The Soviets agreed to use her to help the Chinese. In return, the Soviets wanted information the Chinese had gleaned from their clandestine work on a new U.S. Air Force jet. A win-win for both countries. Due to her appearance (being Caucasian instead of Chinese), and the fact she was fluent in Ukrainian, English, Spanish, and Russian, Paula was selected as the perfect agent for the job. She easily assumed a new identity and ethnicity when she was sent to Spain to seduce me.

Hua was a mole, an agent of China's Central Investigation Department, sent to penetrate a specific intelligence agency by gaining employment at the Pentagon. Her real name is Ah Lam Xu. Ah Lam is a common Chinese name for a girl, meaning "peaceful." A true oxymoron. There was nothing peaceful about Ah Lam!

Ah Lam and Nataliya Kravchenko had known each other for several years, having worked on an undercover mission in London. After I, Paula (Nataliyaof), Lt. Kiggans and Hua (Ah Lam), met for lunch in Rome, Hua and Paula left for Beijing to be briefed on a biochemist who disappeared, and who they feared would seek asylum in America. The Biochemist, Meiyang Fang, had been working at The Wuhan Institute of Virology and had extensive knowledge of China's biological and chemical weapon program. The Chinese could not afford for the U.S. to find out the extent of the biological weapon program.

The Chinese received intelligence from one of their agents planted in Washington about America's plan to extract a biochemist, but they had no idea who it was. The biochemist's name was protected by the codename Cowbird.

When the plans of the mission had to be adjusted due to the death of Mayfield, the CIA agent who was killed in the helicopter accident, Kiggans had to communicate with the Chinese about the change of plans. It was risky for Kiggans to transmit the information through Radio Central, but he had no alternative. That transmission is what began Dakota's search for the traitor.

When Fang did not show up for work one day, the Chinese discovered the defector. Their objective was only to kill Fang, but when the CIA chose the *Adams* to launch their mission, they could not believe their luck. Kiggans was already a plant, so he was able to discover the location where the U.S. agent and I would meet, and he communicated that to the Chinese Central Investigation Department.

Dakota had spoken privately to Kiggans about his findings in Radio Central. He said only two people could have sent the encrypted message to the Chinese, Kiggans himself, or Radioman Third Class Robinson, and he assumed Kiggans never would commit such a treacherous thing. Dakota showed Kiggans the timing of the transmission and told him that if a search was made of everyone who had access to Radio Central on that day, and at that specific time, they would surely find the One-Time Key Pad the traitor used to transmit the message.

For Kiggans, Dakota was too close to exposing the lieutenant, so killing him was the only option. Kiggans went to Radio Central and told Dakota he found some critical information regarding the traitor and for Dakota to meet him on the fantail at midnight when he got off watch. That is when Kiggans stabbed Dakota with a marlin spike, tied a deck grinder to his waist using a Kevlar lifeline, and threw him overboard.

Hua was a psychopath who loves her job, murdering people. She had always been a lover of Chinese literature, and her eccentric nature demanded warped creativity in her killings. Hua was told to accompany two other Chinese assassins to Kiliia to thwart the efforts of the American mission to escort Fang to the *USS Charles F. Adams*. Hua orchestrated the killings of the extraction team. For Hua, the killings had to have a literary flare. It was her twisted sense of humor and also her undoing. In London she decided to kill a target by shoving a pocket watch down a diplomat's throat, causing him to choke to death, simply because London used the code name *Sundial*. Killing each team member of *The Dentist Appointment* mission by matching the murder with her favorite fairy tale, *The 5 Chinese Brothers*, was simply for her amusement, not to send some symbolic message to anyone, contrary to the CIA's assumption.

Hua was arrested at the Pentagon. When the authorities searched her desk, the FBI found more damning evidence of her intent to send classified documents to the Chinese. Against my wishes, instead of having her rot in prison, they asked her to become a double agent for the Americans. They thought she could be valuable as a spy who could pretend to be working against the United States, but who in fact would be working for them. I was outraged! I had many reasons to want to see her executed.

First of all, she killed, or had one of her assassins kill, three Navy SEALs and two CIA agents. Second, how could she ever be trusted to spy for the United States? Her entire life in America was one big lie. Her public persona was not based in reality. I guess that is the life of a spy. And lastly, if she were not executed, some president down the line could use her as a bargaining chip for an exchange of Americans held captive in Beijing, much like how Smoke was returned to the States. The thought of Hua ever returning to China to resume her work against the United States made me want to vomit.

I was not the only one wanting Hua and Kiggans executed. The debate scratched the scab of those still reeling from the Supreme Court Decision made just 5 years earlier. In 1972, The Supreme Court knocked down a series of capital punishment provisions, including the one for espionage. The last time anyone was executed in the U.S. for spying, was 1953, three years before I was born! Julius and Ethel Rosenberg were convicted of spying for the Soviet Union and were executed by electrocution at Sing Sing in Ossining, New York.

How I wished the debacle with Hua and Kiggans had taken place before 1971. Then the death penalty would be on the table. I understood the arguments against killing Hua. The fallout could almost be worse than the alternatives. My suggestion to the FBI, which I am sure fell on deaf ears, was to have her *disappear*. Wasn't the CIA good at that?

EPILOGUE

S hakespeare's, *All's Well That Ends Well*, is a wonderful premise for a play, but in real life, even when there is a happy ending, there can be scars that last forever.

I was released by the Alexandria Detention Center and given a plane ticket to Jacksonville, Florida, where I would take a taxi to Mayport Navy Base to join the *Adams*. To my delight, Mr. Comeaux and Smoke were waiting for me outside the prison.

"You both are a sight for sore eyes," I said.

"You must feel pretty good how things turned out," Mr. Comeaux said.

"I am happy the truth came out and I am no longer in that dungeon, but I am bitter. I'm trying to deal with that," I said.

Smoke put his arm around me as we walked toward Mr. Comeaux's car. "A wise old man once told me refusing to forgive someone is like drinking poison hoping someone else will die."

"Yeah, I know. Easier said than done."

"We are going to take you out for the biggest steak you have ever eaten," Mr. Comeaux said. "Then I will take you to the airport."

"I should be taking you two out," I said. "I really do appreciate everything you have done for me. How can I ever repay you guys?"

"A thank you will do," Smoke said.

"Thank you!" I said, giving each of them a bear hug.

I slept throughout the flight to Jacksonville. My fatigue was more emotional than physical. Taxis were lined up outside baggage claim. I got into one and told the driver to take me to Mayport Naval Shipyard. The driver was chatty, but when I gave him one-word answers only, he got the message I was in no mood for conversation.

The marine at the gate to the base asked where we were going. I opened my window and told him the cabbie was taking me to my ship, the *Charles F. Adams*. He instructed the cabbie to drop me off and come immediately back and leave the base.

My emotions were about as confused as I had been in my high school physics class. Of course, I was happy to have been released from prison, but putting everything behind me was challenging. I wondered how my shipmates would react. *Would the XO give me any flack?* The XO was the one who found the half-burnt One-Time Key Pad which incriminated Kiggans. I would think he would see the big picture and understand how I was falsely accused and what I had to go through. But then again, no one knew what I had gone through. They couldn't.

When the taxi pulled up to the ship, I saw the entire crew in dress whites manning the rails. They were standing "at ease" with their legs spread and their hands behind their backs. Inspections in dress uniforms did not occur very often. They happened only for a very special occasion. My guess was an admiral, or special dignitary, was visiting the ship. I walked up to the brow of the ship and asked for permission to come aboard, but instead of the Officer of the Day, who would normally man the quarterdeck, it was Captain Stansbury, and next to him stood the XO, LCDR Lynch.

"Permission granted," said the Captain with a broad smile as he returned my salute.

Then the Captain turned to the crew and said, "Crew of the *USS Charles F. Adams*, attention! Salute!"

The entire crew of the ship, all enlisted men and officers, saluted…*me!* I was dumbfounded, so much so I was fighting back my tears. If that wasn't enough, all 345 crewmembers lined up to shake my hand, the XO was first in line.

"I owe you an apology, Lloyd. You are a patriot and one helluva sailor!" the XO said.

"Thank you, Sir," I said.

The Captain was second in line to shake my hand. He also apologized, not that I felt he needed to. I believe he was apologizing for the way the government jumped on accusations and assumptions with the absence of any evidence. I am sure he could not have appreciated everything I had gone through, but the fact he cared meant a lot to me. Captain Stansbury was a good man. He invited me to eat dinner in the Stateroom that evening, but I declined. All I really wanted was to return to some sort of normalcy, whatever that was.

It took nearly an hour to shake each of my shipmate's hands, at which point, the Captain called the crew to muster on deck and called me to stand before him. A microphone and a small podium had been placed before him. He then opened a small box.

"Attention!" the Captain ordered.

I stood before the Captain in street clothes, the only man not in dress whites.

"Petty Officer Second Class Calvin Lloyd, by orders from the Secretary of the Navy, I have the privilege of awarding you the Navy Cross. This distinguished award is the United States Naval Service's second-highest military decoration awarded for Sailors and Marines who distinguish themselves for extraordinary heroism in combat with an armed enemy force. Your actions while participating in a secret mission in enemy territory reflects the highest standards of the United States Navy and your country. Well done, Sailor," the Captain said as he pinned the medal on my chest. With that, the sailors yelled "Hip hip hooray," and threw their covers into the air.

My, how the current had shifted.

ACKNOWLEDGEMENTS

I enjoyed my time in the Navy (for the most part). Those experiences helped shape the man I am today. The camaraderie, the thrill of being at sea, those dress white uniforms, and, of course, living with an oceanfront view—it doesn't get better than that! Trust me, sailors have more fun!

To all my Navy brothers and sisters, especially those who served aboard the Charlie Deuce (DDG-2), Semper Fortis! For all you civilians out there, that's "Always Courageous." And for those of us who served as enlisted sailors, perhaps our motto should be Semper Pingere—"Always Chipping and Painting."

A special thanks to my editor and friend, Rick Marsico. Your attention to detail and invaluable time, along with your patience and perspective made this book a much better read. Your encouragement throughout the process meant more to me than you will ever know.

Bayley Ramos, my daughter, has contributed to this book in numerous ways, including designing the cover and inserts for the book, to name a few. Thank you for being one of my biggest fans!

And, as always, to my wife, Carolyn. Thank you for always believing in me, even when I doubt myself. Your suggestions and insight, as well as the many hours you spent reading draft after draft, meant the world to me. Oh, and you may think my Navy days were the best five years of my life, but they weren't—I hadn't met you yet.

AUTHOR'S BIO

Making Waves is G. Bradley Davis's second novel, following his highly praised debut, Bellamy. With a life as adventurous as his fiction, Davis has worn many hats: Navy veteran, corporate CEO, ordained pastor, competitive archer, mountaineer, angler, scuba diver, devoted husband, father, grandfather, and author. His diverse experiences infuse his storytelling with authenticity and depth.

Davis holds degrees from Temple University (BA) and Bethel University (MATS). When not writing, he enjoys life on Marco Island, where you'll often find him playing senior softball, pickleball, golfing, fishing, singing, or crafting his next novel, *Sense-less*.

To learn more about G. Bradley Davis or to get in touch, please visit the author website: www.GBradleyDavis.com